the green sari

Marion Lindsey-Noble has worked as a translator/ interpreter and language teacher before embarking on a writing career.

She has published the R.F. Delderfield biography, *Butterfly Moments,* which had been short-listed for the annual prize of the Biographers' Club, London, and is a regular contributor of short stories and articles in popular magazines. *The Green Sari* is her first novel.

Also by Marion Lindsey-Noble:
The R.F. Delderfield biography, *Butterfly Moments*

marion lindsey-noble

the green sari

Cashmere Publishing

First published in Great Britain in 2010 by
Cashmere Publishing
Brompton Regis
TA22 9NW
Somerset

marion.lindseynoble@btinternet.com

A CIP catalogue record for this book is available
from the British Library

ISBN 978 0 9557932 1 9

Printed and bound in Great Britain by Booksprint

DEDICATION

To my husband
Who gave me the freedom to be myself
and the confidence to write this book
And, naturally,
To my beloved sons

ACKNOWLEDGEMENT

The quotations from the poems of Rabrindranath Tagore were taken from the 1977 edition of the *Collected Poems and Plays by Rabindranath Tagore*, published by Macmillan London Limited, with the kind permission of Professor Kumkum Bhattacharya, Director of the Publication Department, Visva Bharati University, Kolkata, India.

PART ONE

'Karin Auntie,' the short letter says, 'this is to inform you that uncle Raj is seriously ill in hospital. I thought you ought to know.

Best wishes
Priti
P.S. Still miss you.'

Chapter One

ര൪ൟ

A Message came from my youth of vanished days...
Rabindranath Tagore

Karin Khan's long, elegant fingers glide over the smooth silk of a green sari, tracing the contours of gold-thread embroideries in the shape of exotic flowers. She has been tossing and turning all night, her mind and emotions in turmoil. The message has upset the carefully crafted harmony of her solitary life. Karin sits wearily on the edge of her pine slatted bed, the sari on the white duvet next to her. An empty brown leather suitcase, lid open, lies at her feet on a cheap Indian rug which covers up the worn parquet flooring. After receiving the short letter, Karin is uncertain whether she has made the right decision to follow the plea hidden amongst the few words.

She has started packing, still unsure whether she should go at all. If she does, should she take the sari with her? After all, this trip is going to be quite different from the one she had made nearly forty years ago. Then she was young and excited, tall and slender, with blond hair which fell straight down to her shoulders and a fringe tracing the bows of her slightly darker eyebrows and emphasising the blueness of her sparkling eyes.

Karin smiles. There are now wrinkles around her much calmer eyes and the blond hair, pulled away from her face into a chignon, has turned grey. After a few attempts at dying it herself, she had given up fighting the inevitable. She would consider it extravagant to use the services of a professional hairdresser and prefers to let nature take its course.

Using make-up has gone the same way. It had felt like plaster on her face, as if she was hiding behind a rigid mask. Consequently and with determination, she had thrown away the bottles, tubes and tubs some time ago. Cleansing and nourishing her pale, flawless skin would have to do. The wash bag, she will pack this time, will be light. There will be no-one she either needs or wants to impress.

She hasn't lost her trim figure which is an occasional source of pleasure to her, maybe even cause for a little smugness. The daily yoga exercises which she has faithfully continued throughout the years have paid off. They give her poise and an upright posture without making her look haughty. Yoga to her is not just exercise. She uses it as a scaffold of discipline when the storms of life threaten to batter her. She clings fiercely to her early morning routine and does not allow anything to upset it. Yoga is a sedative for inner turmoil, sure to restore peace, a guarantee to prevent the inflexibility of age, recapturing the subtleness of earlier years. Time, she muses, has been kind to her and clinging on to yoga feels like a last link to the life she once had. She withdraws her hand from the silky cloth, gets up and walks the few steps to her pine wardrobe. She will decide about the sari later.

Karin chooses three cotton trousers, one with a gentle print in pastel colours, one plain white and the third in navy. She reaches for several hangers from the rail, one by one, and lets two white, short-sleeved blouses and three polo-shirts, which pick up on the colours of the trousers, glide onto the bed. Almost absent-mindedly, she folds them and puts them into the suitcase. She is relieved that most of her clothes fall into the category of 'time-less', so selection is uncomplicated and she is sure that the classic tailoring would not over-expose nor offend. She used to have many skirts in Indian prints, reaching down to her ankles, and frilly tops to go with them. She had discarded them a few years ago, convinced that she would never wear them again. They were bound to make her look like an ageing hippy.

There won't be any need for sensible, heavy shoes; comfortable sandals will be fine, which will save a lot of luggage space. Should she require anything, she will surely be able to buy from the local markets. She stuffs several changes of underwear together with two long summer nightdresses into a champagne coloured silk bag trimmed with lace, a present from her daughter. She pulls the drawstring and stashes it next to the wash bag in the suitcase.

For a brief moment, she considers jewellery.

She smiles again, remembering how her sisters-in-law, her *bhabis*, had regularly discussed, schemed, chosen and finally pestered their husbands for the purchase of another investment in precious stones. It was one of the few games women usually won with the argument that they were entitled to make themselves beautiful for their husbands. They could never understand that Karin had shown no great interest in jewellery, however beautiful, but they were mollified when she submitted herself with amusement to their efforts of wrapping her in finery and adorning her with gold earrings, necklaces and a rainbow of bangles covering her arms nearly up to her elbows.

'I will soon have ears like an elephant', she had complained jokingly, pointing to the rain of gold filigree, dripping from her newly pierced ear-lobes. It was greeted with tut-tutting by the exasperated *bhabis* who could not understand her reluctance to show herself to her best advantage.

The one piece of jewellery she had coveted, a silver chain with little bells to be attached round an ankle, was denied her.

'Only dancing girls wear those,' she was told firmly and that was the end of it.

Karin hasn't changed in her attitude to jewellery. Nowadays, she wears her grandmother's turquoise ring on the middle finger of her right hand, and only on special occasions and to rare invitations, she takes the simple pearl necklace that had been Raj's first present, out of its box and fastens it round her neck. She won't bother packing it. What is the point of jewellery in a country where the majority of people struggle to feed their children? She puts the necklace back in its box and closes the lid.

Apprehension sweeps over her and for a moment she begins to doubt again the wisdom of her decision to go on this journey. It was all such a long time ago. She looks down on her still half-empty case.

She remembers well the size of the luggage on her first visit, full of unsuitable clothes for the climate, either too warm or too skimpy. Shortly after her arrival she had decided that she would put them aside, dress like the local women and drape herself in five meters of cool, fine silk, much more comfortable under the baking sun. She had liked the cotton saris, too, but was told that they were for servants only.

Her eyes sweep lovingly over the green sari again, the colour of the Bangladeshi flag, the proud banner of this small, hopelessly over-populated country.

Warmth and sympathy had risen within her, when she had first glimpsed its sweep of lush green paddy fields, divided by a multitude of rivers, from the small window of a ten-seater aeroplane pointing towards Dhaka airport.

The memory brings back a faint thrill of excitement, which she had felt then, but cannot quite recapture now. It is muffled by fear that she might be foolish wanting to re-connect with the past.

Looking at her young self across the expanse of the intervening years, she cannot help but marvel at the changes that have taken place within her and dread the differences that have distanced her from a life that now seems strange, like an old silent movie reel stored at the back of a rarely opened cupboard. She had not expected to be contacted ever again, but it had occurred to her, particularly on special occasions like birthdays, that her ex-husband and she were both entering an age where one of them might become frail. Whenever such a thought occurred she briefly wondered whether the family would let her know. In her musings, she had never come to a conclusion what her feelings would be if they did. Would she be upset or relieved? Would she feel pangs of guilt or would she be unmoved? She had checked the entire range of emotions she might experience when the news of death would come, but shrugged it off as a fruitless exercise as she was quite convinced that she would not be told. She would be ignorant, carrying on as normal with her well regulated and calm life thousands of miles away, oblivious to the fact that the most brittle of links between them would be finally and irrevocably broken.

Yesterday someone has contacted her.

Karin takes only a few steps across to a worn pine desk in the corner by the window. She picks up a blue airmail letter and scrutinizes the exotic stamp on the envelope and her address in a vaguely familiar handwriting.

'After all these years, she still misses me...' Karin is both astonished and pleased.

Priti was the niece she had been closest to. Karin pictures the bubbly teenager whom she had helped more than once to circumvent social conventions.

'She must now be a middle aged woman, with a husband and a crowd of children.' she thinks affectionately.

'I wonder whether she still has this beautiful long black hair, which, twirled round her fingers for a few minutes, would stay in curls all day.'

The letter does not make any suggestion whether Karin should reply or store the information away without reacting to it. Too much time has passed for her to feel confident enough to know what is expected of her, what will be the right thing to do, what will be appropriate or inappropriate. She does not want to intrude into the family's grief, but – and there she surprises herself – she does not want them to think that she doesn't care. Maybe they don't even know that Priti has made contact, but – suspecting a plea between the lines – Karin does not want to disappoint her as if she has been brushed out of her western auntie's life entirely.

'In the end, I can only follow my instinct and my heart,' Karin decides after reading the letter for a third time. 'I'll think about it, mull it over, sleep on it', but instinct and heart immediately agree without hesitation that she must go.

The longer she takes for packing the less sure she becomes. She can still cancel the flight which she has ordered over the Internet. The confirmation and reference number came by return press of a button, bringing an unexpectedly rapid end to her dithering.

When she had first travelled it seemed so much more of an adventure.

Nowadays, it is a common and casual deviation from the routine of one's life to take a plane to the furthest parts of the globe.

The picture above her desk grabs her attention, one of the few decorations in her otherwise colourless room. The overall blueness jumps from the clean, white walls.

It is the simple print of a garden gate leading out onto a narrow stretch of beach, an azure blue sea and a cloudless sky. Karin loves this picture and can almost smell the sharp salty air. She has often thought that she would be suited to living on a remote island, free of human company. She can see herself standing by this gate looking out over the sea with solitude wrapped around her like a comfortable blanket. It is the vastness and power of the sea which fascinates her and the possibility of freedom from social obligations.

The picture is like a window which she sometimes allows herself to open for a few moments. It is certainly a more pleasant view than the one she looks at now through the bedroom's peeling sash-window. It reveals a row of uncared for Victorian houses opposite, which stand menacingly close, threatening to intrude into her ordered little world. Noises from the busy road billow up to her like smoke and interrupt her thoughts.

As she averts her gaze from the hectic bustle outside, it is captured by a neat pile of white sheets of paper and a green note book on her desk. It is the beginning of her dabbling in a memoir. Ideas and first drafts go into the green book which she types into her laptop once she is pleased with a version.

She can't remember when and why she had begun to write. It could have been boredom, something to fill the heavy, empty evenings since her son and daughter had left to embark on their own lives. Or when she had retired from twenty years of working for a bookseller who had decided to sell the shop.

Or was it when the only other person who had touched her life, after years of solitude, had unexpectedly left her?

Guy had been a kind, gentle and patient widower who had put no demands on her except for occasional companionship which suited her fine. Later, the possibility of a greater investment into their relationship had entered her thinking, but by then he had fallen ill and died. He had left a vacuum of unfinished dreams like half-drawn plans for a building that would now never be built. His picture appeared sometimes in her head, always smiling indulgently. She has no idea whether they would have been happy or successful in their relationship, but there was no point in speculating. She accepts that this chapter is closed, too.

Karin is content with the modest, but peaceful life of a single, retired woman. She appreciates its harmony, the lack of complications. It is a peace without glamour but exuding the promise of no uncomfortable surprises and no emotional roller-coasters.

The memoir she was going to write will have to wait now. She closes the lid of the laptop, disconnects the wires from the plug and zips it all into a protective black nylon case. She straightens the few pages in the already neat pile and puts them in the bottom drawer of her desk. She lays the green notebook on top, pushes the drawer shut and abandons it all to fate.

Chapter Two

༄ (ornament)

Oh Mother, the young Prince is to pass by our door...
Rabindranath Tagore

Karin was the ideal material for a Bengali wife.

Admittedly fate had placed her in the 1940s in a western society, but she had been an obedient child, a conscientious pupil, still a virgin at eighteen and the compliant centre of her mother's life and ambitions.

Her father was less involved in her day-to-day upbringing due to business commitments which took him away a lot. What he didn't provide in emotional support, her mother more than made up for.

Only much later did Karin realise that she had grown up in an emotional hot-house, tended like a rare and delicate plant, pampered forcefully into flowering.

She made only one attempt at escape which went spectacularly wrong: The Music Conservatorium many miles from home, she had chosen, was not as keen to accept her as she had hoped. In an urgent call, she promised her parents that she would return to the fold and follow unquestioningly their advice in the future.

That's when she met Raj.

She was on her way home from the shattering experience that she had failed her entrance examination when Raj first appeared in the shape of a black mop of windswept hair, hurrying along a blustery station platform, past her train window. He must have jumped onto the departing train throwing himself minutes later in the seat opposite her.

'Would you mind, if I sat here?' he asked quite unnecessarily as he was seated already.

He beamed a smile at her which sparkled in his dark brown eyes, revealed a row of the most perfect white teeth she had ever seen on anyone, and made his black moustache quiver a little.

'No, not at all,' she answered shyly under her breath, renewing a firm grip on the book in her lap and lowering her eyes, pretending to read.

She decided to ignore him, while he fussed taking off his smart trench coat, folding it neatly and putting it on one of the empty seats, before sitting down again. She desperately tried to concentrate on the story reading the opening paragraph for the third time without having taken anything in. Finally, she gave up, closed the book and looked out of the window. In the pane's reflection she could see that her fellow passenger observed her discreetly with a smile playing around his lips.

'What are you reading?' The man with the brown face and black moustache spoke with a heavy foreign accent.

'A Passage to India by E.M. Foster'. Karin volunteered.

He smiled again and the conversation faltered.

'Have you been on this train long?' he revived their polite exchange.

'No, only half an hour.'

'And where are you going?'

'Home', she said absentmindedly, not sure whether she should really be talking to this stranger.

His smile turned into a teasing grin: 'And where is home, if you don't mind me asking?'

'Stuttgart'.

'Oh, that's my destination as well!'

She was astonished how well he spoke German in spite of the accent. Karin's feeling of unease persisted and increased with every scrap of information she gave away.

She changed tactics, looked him in the face and returned his smile: 'Where do you come from?'

18

'Have a guess,' he teased.

'India?' was the first idea that sprang into her mind.

'Close. India is a big country and it used to be even bigger. I come from East Pakistan.'

It was not a country she had heard of much and she wasn't at all sure where it was in relation to India. He was eager to explain:

'Pakistan has two parts, West Pakistan and East Pakistan. They are separated by nearly a thousand miles. East Pakistan is basically squashed in between the Bay of Bengal and the Himalayas. In the North and East it borders onto Assam and Burma and to the West onto the Bengal part of India. Have you heard of Calcutta?'

She nodded and thought of Mother Teresa, starving children and squalor.

'My family came originally from Calcutta. It is India's largest city. Have you ever been to India?'

No, she had not been to India. In fact, she had not been to anywhere very much, but that was none of his business. She simply shook her head.

'Bengal is the home of artists,' he continued. 'We love music, poetry, art, crafts and, of course, films', he seemed quite passionate about this fact. 'Our films last hours and are full of tears and laughter,' he explained. 'Do you like films?'

'Yes, I do, but I don't go often.'

'Too busy studying?'

'Yes'. The conversation had turned to her again and she did not like it.

'Tell me more about East Pakistan,' she deflected his enquiries.

'It is a relatively young country. It was founded in 1947 with the partition of the Indian subcontinent into India, where the Hindus were in the majority, and the Muslim states of East and West Pakistan. Have you heard of Mahatma Ghandi?'

She nodded.

'And of Muhammad Ali Jinnah?'

'No,' she shook her head getting slightly bored with the unexpected history lesson.

He carried on regardless:

'Jinnah founded Pakistan and was its first governor-general. Ayub Khan is the Head of State now.'

She nodded politely; it was all a long way away.

'Are you here on holiday?' She couldn't think of anything else to ask.

'No, I am on Government business, or rather I have attended a course to improve my skills in exporting our products.'

'So you work for the government in Pakistan?'

'You could say that. I am in charge of exporting one of its main products – jute…'

'It's used for sacks and ropes,' he added to explain.

'How long will you stay in this country?'

'I have to fly home in a week's time.' He sighed. 'I shall be glad to see my family again, but it is so nice here… So comfortable.'

Karin sighed as well, but for a different reason: she was relieved; within a fortnight, he would be thousands of miles away. Strange idea! Why would she be relieved? He was just another passenger on the train. She was shaken out of that thought by an unexpected request:

'Can I see you again, while I am still here?'

She felt unsettled by his blatant boldness and uncomfortable with this unashamed flattery.

Whenever Karin looked in the mirror, she saw an undistinguished, thin face with dark shadows under huge blue eyes, a strange mixture of the two families' features. Her thin hair cut into a little girl's bob had the colour of limp straw, and left a high forehead exposed which she had, in her opinion, unfortunately, inherited from her father's side.

She was a skinny teenager who took a long time to develop any curves which worried her a little when she looked at girls of a similar age. Broaching the subject of looks with her mother one day, she was reminded that the family found her beautiful and that personality and goodness in a person were more important than transient beauty.

'I shall be very busy trying to find a university place – I just lost one,' she extricated herself quickly, adding: 'My parents would be very unhappy if I didn't get on with it.'

'What about just one evening?'

She was desperate not to be rude, but she panicked at the prospect of explaining such a change of plans to her parents, distressing them even further than they were already. She could just imagine their reaction if she had the courage to inform them nonchalantly that, instead of phoning furiously around for a university place, she would swan off to go sightseeing with a complete stranger, who looked not unlike Omar Shariff and was at least ten years older than her.

'I really can't,' she pleaded apologetically. 'But if you give me your home address I can write to you once everything is settled.'

'I understand,' he said hardly suppressing a friendly chuckle, took out a pen and a small pad from the inside pocket of his beautifully tailored jacket and scribbled several lines onto the page.

'I shall look forward to hearing from you,' he said handing the piece of paper to her.

'Don't lose it!' he teased her again.

'I might throw it away,' she thought fleetingly, but she folded it carefully and put it in her book.

'I shall let you read now,' he said, picking up the newspaper from the seat next to him, and they spent the rest of the journey in silence. After several more stops, he folded the newspaper diligently and offered it to her, but she shook her head.

'I think, we are nearly there,' he commented, checking the names on suburban station signs which flew past the window.

When he saw her struggling to retrieve her suitcase from the luggage rack, he helped her gallantly.

'Thank you,' she whispered while he stood so close to her that she could feel the sleeve of his arm brushing against her shoulder. Ready for the arrival, they sat down again opposite each other, waiting nervously for the train to stop.

'You will write to me, won't you?' It sounded neither like a plea nor a demand, more like a polite request of not much importance.

'I shall,' she promised unenthusiastically, assuming that he would forget her the moment she left the train.

He helped her through the various doors and let her disembark first. As she stood on the platform, about to lift her suitcase, he was beside her:

'Let me take that for you,' he said simply.

'It's not necessary,' she replied panic stricken, looking along the platform for her parents. She did not want to face them with this stranger by her side. She could see them at a fair distance and while rushing towards them, she tried to tell him that she would be fine carrying her own luggage. But he either did not hear or pretended not to understand.

They were now only a few feet away from her parents. Karin was surprised and delighted that they had not come alone. Aunt Hella was not only her mother's best friend but also Karin's beloved god-mother, a bachelor woman who was great fun to be with. Her presence should make this unusual situation easier.

The stranger stood there smiling at everyone and about to introduce himself, when Karin's father grabbed his daughter's suitcase out of his hand and send a furious look in his direction.

'Thank you for helping my daughter', he said curtly, almost rudely.

Karin cringed and said apologetically:

'That was very kind of you. Thank you and have a good flight home.'

The man's smile turned into a wistful shadow.

'Good-bye, and good luck with your studies.'

Before she could say any more, he had disappeared in the crowd, followed by her father's incensed glance.

Confused but relieved, Karin turned her full attention to her parents. Her mother looked terribly worried, while her god-mother could hardly suppress a naughty grin.

'Shall we go,' someone suggested, and Karin took gratefully her auntie's arm, which squeezed her reassuringly. They hung back a little.

'Who was he?' she enquired with glee.

'Just a passenger,' Karin explained. 'I really didn't want him to carry my suitcase, but…'

'There is no harm in that,' her aunt announced firmly, and added dreamily: 'Did you see his eyes? He had beautiful eyes, like… black velvet. 'What's his name?'

Karin had to admit that she didn't know. They had reached the exit and had caught up with her parents.

'Best not to mention him again,' suggested her aunt in a whisper, and Karin could not have agreed more.

❀ ❀ ❀

Finally installed at the local university of her parents' choosing, Karin carried on being a good girl, attending every class and lecture on her timetable, writing furiously essays and translations set by lecturers and reading every book on the course list.

She shared an attic flat with two other girls, who constantly grumbled that the landlady would not allow visitors to their digs. It suited Karin fine. On most days, she had the top floor to herself.

After the first term, Karin was welcomed home with open arms. It felt strange to leave behind months of independence, however studiously spent, to return as her parents' daughter, trying to pretend to still be the young girl that they knew.

Her submission made her mother smile with the recaptured happiness of being needed while Karin felt increasingly like an insect that had fallen into an open honey jar. Any struggle to free herself would have spoilt the holiday and upset her mother.

The next holiday however, did not go according to plan. No sooner had Karin put down her suitcase in the landing and shrugged off her coat, when her mother took an envelope out of her apron pocket and waved it in the air. It was blue with air mail stripes as borders and the stamps looked colourfully exotic.

'Are you expecting anything?' her mother asked in a distinctly disapproving tone..

'No,' Karin looked truthfully blank at this waving envelope.

'This arrived for you a week ago,' continued her mother. She clearly had her doubts as to how clueless her daughter really was.

'Who is it from?'

'Well, I haven't read it, but don't you know?' Her mother obviously sensed a secret.

'I have no idea,' Karin was a little irritated, but curious at the same time.

'It was stamped in East Pakistan.' Her mother watched her reaction.

A slight feeling of guilt rose in Karin as it dawned on her that this letter was a reply to her friendly greetings on a postcard.

'Have you written to that fellow from the train?'

Karin had completely forgotten about him, knowing that he was safely thousands of miles away, with not much prospect of returning to Europe or even turning up at her doorstep. Since she had not had a reply for three months, she had assumed that he had lost interest or given her a fake address.

The worried expression in her mother's face and the deep lines between her eyebrows made Karin shrug her shoulders, feigning little interest and assuring her that it was of no importance, reminding her that East Pakistan was at the other end of the world.

23

She returned to her room, without taking the letter, but it lay on her desk that evening. Before going to bed, Karin slit open the envelope hesitatingly, musing what it might contain. She had never received a letter from a man, never mind a thoroughly grown up man and a foreigner at that.

She slowly unfolded the two thin pages of airmail paper and began to read:

'Dear Karin,

'I was most surprised and gratified that you deemed it worthy your while to remember our chance meeting on the train and to write to me.'

Karin giggled.

'I have often remembered my pretty young co-passenger who shortened my journey time with such animated and interesting conversation. It was a delight and pleasure to talk to you and I felt sorry that I could not meet up with you during my last week. My heart ached thinking that I might never see or hear from you again.'

Karin put the letter in her lap. His flowery language amused and unsettled her at the same time. It sounded over the top, and Karin was not sure whether she should attribute this to his way of expression or whether it was insincere flattery.

She read on about his life in Dhaka, the capital of East Pakistan, his numerous sisters and brothers – seven in all – a little information about his job as a government official in charge of the Trade Department and more compliments aimed at Karin, her beauty, intelligence and pleasant manners. He ended with the hope that this would be the beginning of a long and happy correspondence.

It took Karin another day to hand the letter to her mother, who read it silently, neither with a frown nor a smile.

'Are you going to reply?' she asked at last, folding the pages and putting them carefully back into the envelope.

'I am not sure,' Karin was truly undecided. 'Not yet anyway. I see how I feel in a few weeks' time.'

Her mother nodded. 'Keep him at a distance,' she advised.

Once returned to university, Karin immersed herself in her studies and had quite forgotten about the letter, when her mother forwarded another one, in which her acquaintance wondered anxiously whether she had received his reply, whether she had changed her address or whether she had decided that she did not want to correspond after all.

The outpouring was a little overwhelming and overly dramatic. Karin decided to defuse the situation by writing to him a friendly, but stern letter reminding him that she was busy with her studies; that she would not mind staying in contact, but that she would not be able to write as frequently as he might expect her to do.

Their correspondence over the next year turned out to be erratic, depending on work schedules, unreliable postal services and fluctuating levels of interest, mainly on Karin's part. Raj's communications were often flattering, flowery, romantic and increasingly passionate.

The first familiarities had shocked her, and her first reaction was to discontinue their pen-friendship for a good few months; but then she had missed his news, funny descriptions about his huge and chaotic family, outings they all went on to exotic sounding locations and his grumbling comparisons of life in a third world country to the abundance and efficiency in Europe. He wrote about extreme heat, monsoon rains, rivers flooding, eighty million people, most of them poor, living in a small area the size of Wales, but somehow Raj and his family seemed to be untouched by any tragedy that seemed to engulf the rest of the nation rather frequently.

'Insh' Allah, my family has been spared', was an often repeated phrase, and Karin sighed with relief.

Karin had largely managed to put her mother's mind at rest. There had been a crisis a few months ago, when he had sent a portrait photograph of himself looking distinguished, handsome and well-groomed, with dark, soulful eyes staring longingly out of the picture. Her mother had seen this as an attempt to strengthen the relationship with her daughter, but Karin had reassured her that there was no way he could return, not for years anyway. Her mother knew better than to carry on with objections. It was wiser to resign oneself to waiting with vigilance and patience.

'She probably hopes that it will fizzle out,' thought Karin by herself and accepted that this might well be the outcome anyway. The news arrived like a bolt out of the blue:

'I have secured another Government grant to attend a course in Geneva, Switzerland, which will begin in September this year. This is lucky indeed and I can't wait to meet you!'

Raj had explained to her that he had to wait at least two years to qualify for another study grant or trip abroad. He needed permission from the Government to exchange *takas* into foreign currency which was hard to come by. Working in a Government agency, he was in a better position than most, but he had been doubtful that the same favour would be bestowed on him for a second time soon. In any case, Karin was not at all sure whether a reunion was what she really wanted. She replied more quickly than usual. She needed to arm herself with more details before informing her parents.

'Don't panic!' he wrote back teasingly. He sounded immensely pleased with himself that he had managed to surprise her and amused that he had put her in a spin.

The subject of his study course was not mentioned, obviously secondary to the excitement at seeing her again.

Karin wasn't sure whether to laugh or to cry, whether to be swept along by his enthusiasm or dread having to tell her parents that the huge distance between their two countries had ultimately not been the big barrier for a reunion that she had made it out to be. She had no choice but to accept the fact that he was going to come over and spend weeks or months close to her, which would make constant contact possible and available. She could not summon up any anger towards him because he had gone ahead and applied for the grant without telling or consulting her. As far as she could make out, he had gone through an enormous amount of trouble to achieve this, favoured by a great deal of luck.

The fleeting thought crossed her mind that it might be fate.

If she was honest, she was flattered by his attentions and compliments. Maybe he saw something in their friendship that she had not detected yet. After all, he was a good ten years older and possibly wiser than her. She had never asked him his age, thinking it might be construed as rudeness. She did so in her next letter.

'You are not going to bar me from entering the country because I am too old?' he wrote back jokingly. He was eleven years older than her, and it turned out that his birthday was on the same day as her father's.

26

Karin left the not inconsiderable task of informing her mother to the last moment of her summer holidays, when she walked arm in arm with her to the station to return to her student digs.

'Mum, Raj will be studying for a few months in Switzerland,' she summoned up the courage that had eluded her since having received the news herself.

'Will you be seeing him?' her mother asked suspiciously.

'I hope so,' Karin replied with an edge of defiance in her voice. The atmosphere between them cooled rapidly.

It was a much less affectionate parting than usual and Karin was glad when she could climb onto the train. She gave a quick wave to the stony face outside and busied herself to find a seat in the compartment.

Chapter Three

❦

At this time of my parting wish me good luck...
Rabrindranath Tagore

The phone rings. It is an unpleasant, shrill sound. Karin goes out into the narrow landing.

'Hallo', she says absent-mindedly.

'Hi, mum. I was just wondering whether I could come home for the weekend.'

Karin pictures the pretty, heart-shaped face of her daughter, Jasmine, often flushed happily from a busy working schedule and a hectic social life. Jasmine has thick black hair and an olive tan which grows darker the more it is exposed to the sun. Green, oval-shaped cat's eyes give her an appearance of mystery and cunning. She is only the third person in her father's family to have eyes other than brown. His two youngest siblings have the same eyes which the family attributed in all seriousness to genes stemming from Alexander the Great.

Jasmine is a solicitor in Manchester and usually too busy to visit her mother more than twice a year. Karin knows that she could make greater demands on her daughter's time, but she has acquired an aversion to emotional blackmail and would never dream of using it on her children. 'I much rather know they come and stay because they want to than out of obligation and a feeling of guilt,' she tells herself whenever missing them becomes too painful.

She didn't want her daughter to find out about her unexpected trip this way. Confusion and a slight feeling of guilt swirl around Karin's brain.

'Darling, I am so sorry, but I won't be there.'

Embarrassed silence. Finally, Karin explains:

'I am just packing. Abbu is seriously ill and I shall fly out tomorrow.'

'Tell me you are joking!' It has come as a shock.

'Are you going by yourself?' Karin hears anxiety in her daughter's voice.

There is no need to answer that. It is also pointless to ask Jasmine whether she wants to come along. There is no love lost between father and daughter; and it is too short notice anyway.

'How long are you going for?'

'I am not quite sure, but two weeks at the most.'

'That's a bit sudden!'

'I know. I'm shocked myself, but I feel I need to go,' she adds apologetically.

'Will someone pick you up at the other end?' says her daughter, practical as ever.

'I don't think so, but I shall stay at the Radisson Water Garden Hotel in Airport Road for the first couple of nights. I will be safe there and if necessary, I can always look for something cheaper once I have arrived.'

'I don't like the idea of you travelling all by yourself. You haven't been back there for years.'

'I know, I'll be careful, I promise,' she says, grateful for her daughter's concern.

'Ring me when you have arrived and let me have a contact number.'

'Of course,' Karin assures her, and then remembers that Jasmine has wanted to visit her unexpectedly. She feels bad that in her unusual state of excitement she has completely forgotten.

'Was there any particular reason why you wanted to see me this weekend?' she asks, 'because if you need me…'

'No, no, it will keep,' is the brusque reply. 'When is your flight?'

'Tomorrow afternoon at three.'

The conversation stalls.

'Take care then.'

'I shall,' she reassures her, 'and you must come and see me as soon as I am back.'

'Bye Mum.'

The receiver at the other end is replaced before Karin can whisper her guilty good-bye.

There is so much more she wants to explain to her daughter, that she knows how irrational this must seem, after all this time, after all the hurt. She has brought up her children to be independent, self-confident individuals, instilling a little caution in them when it comes to matters of the heart, so that they would not have to suffer like she had done. They both seem sensible in their relationships, treating the idea of the 'great love of my life' with a healthy dose of scepticism, shying away from commitment. They are both in their early thirties and there would be plenty of time for commitment at a later stage. Her past was, as far as they were concerned, a closed chapter, never to be opened again. Her decision to return would not even begin to make sense to them.

Karin feels a little sorrow that the relationship with her daughter is never one of easy closeness, but more like that of teacher and pupil in age-reversed roles. Karin thoroughly dislikes the disapproval and reprimand in Jasmine's voice, which seems to come so naturally to her.

Censuring herself, Karin wants to remain fair to both her children, but she has always found it easier to be with the boy, Ali. Whenever he rings, he is cheerful and entertaining. He is not particularly interested in details, but listens dutifully to her reports which she keeps short. He is a good-looking boy, very much like his father, but shorter, a little bit below average which does not seem to bother him. His entire face lights up when he smiles, revealing the same perfectly regular white teeth. His dark eyes, framed by long lashes, have his father's velvety quality. Only his hair is a lighter shade of brown and, to his sister's annoyance, his skin stays the same healthy shade of bronze at all times.

At the moment, he lives in New York, working as a teacher in an inner-city school. According to him, life is good. He has always been an idealist; he was never going to chase huge salaries. It was more important to him to be needed, to fill his days by doing things for others. This is how he conducts his life and Karin fully approves.

She half expects Jasmine to contact her brother in exasperation and ask him to talk Mother out of this hastily arranged trip. Should he ring, she would be able to deal with him and plead for his understanding. Barely half an hour has passed since Jasmine's call, when the phone rings again and Karin expects her son's voice. She is taken aback by how angry and panicky he sounds:

'Mum, is it true what Jasmine says…' He even forgets to greet her. They both wait, before he continues:

'That you are flying to Bangladesh tomorrow… on your own?' The last three words are emphasized by incredulity.

'Ali, please try to understand. Whatever happened, I must see him one last time.'

'Why?' This is not meant to be a question, but a reproach as if telling off a silly and stubborn child.

'Ali, please, I am a grown woman. If I want to speak to my ex-husband before he dies, try to understand.'

'He does not live in another city in England you can reach by train. You have to fly for half a day and you haven't been there for years. As you always say, it's such a different world.' He takes breath: 'I cannot believe that you are willing to put yourself in such danger, for what? He will probably not even want to see you. And I don't think the family even remembers you.'

'Well, somebody did,' Karin thinks, but doesn't say it.

He tries very hard to talk her out of her plans with a torrent of arguments and exasperation in his voice. Karin listens patiently. In a way, it is endearing that her son cares so much for her, but he must realise that she has to follow her heart.

'Ali, I do understand your concern and I am very touched. But as I said, I am a grown and free woman and I have to do this. I promise I shall be extremely cautious and circumspect and I shall come back as soon as possible.'

She can tell by his silence that he is offended. This must be the first time that she doesn't take up his advice, and he is hurt.

'Ali?'

'Yes,' he says crisply, maybe even a little hostile.

'Darling, please understand.'

'I can't. But you can do as you please, as you pointed out.'

'It's not like that, Ali.' She realises she is losing her battle for his compassion.

'It obviously is, but I am not happy and I don't agree.' He spits out a 'bye' which does not even consist of one syllable, as if he has picked up a fruit full of maggots and thrown it from him in disgust.

Karin puts the receiver down with sadness. She expected her children to be bemused or confused, but she had not expected to encounter their wrath. She has trouble directing her thoughts back to packing her suitcase. She sits back down on her bed with a heavy heart, the case still at her feet.

Her conscience is wrestling with the various scenarios and possibilities: She can simply give up and stay; she can go and ignore her children's concerns; she can forget about Priti's note altogether, pretend she never received it, and put her dying ex-husband out of her mind. All yesterday's battles of conscience that she thought she had put to rest once and for all, are revived and laboured through again.

At the end of her deliberations, her decision is the same as before: She will go. She knows that her heart rules over her head, but her head has given it a firm foundation − she has booked a safe hotel, she will be very careful, she will take every day as it comes and not get upset about anything. If nothing else, it will be an exotic trip back to her past for a very short period. She has taken all the precautions she can think of; she owes that much to herself and her children; but she is not going to cancel.

With renewed determination, she adds a thin, woollen cardigan in her favourite colour of powder blue for cooler evenings and places it with the items in her suitcase. Finally, she puts the green sari on top, smoothing it lovingly, before closing the suitcase lid, zipping it up and fastening the two belts with a click.

Karin lifts the small case and is satisfied that it will qualify as hand-luggage.

'It will save time at the airport,' she feels relief and is determined to approach the journey with businesslike briskness from there on. She will not be able to rely on anyone but herself. This time there won't be a huge reception committee of curious in-laws who would usher her through customs and passport control unchecked because well known families like theirs had privileges. She would have to take care of her things. She shudders at the memory how eagerly Bangladeshi taxi drivers used to compete for custom, wrenching the luggage out of her hands to secure a fare. She has no idea whether it is still like this. She will have to wait and see.

She picks up her passport and flight details from the pine desk and stores them in the outside pocket of the suitcase. There is no need for a handbag. One more night. She knows she won't be able to sleep, too many thoughts storming through her mind, memories flooding her exhausted doze.

When she finally gets up, she is ready to step back into the past.

Chapter Four

CB⌘SO

Thy sunbeam comes upon this earth of mine...
Rabrindranath Tagore

'Please send your letters to my university address only,' Karin wrote to Raj without explanation.

'Oh dear,' was his perceptive reply, 'you have not fallen out with your parents over me already.' He continued to console her, ending with the mischievous promise that he would practise his oriental charms on them.

She did not feel like joking and her mind was in a constant whirl. What a disaster! Raj had taken all this trouble to get another grant, only to visit her, as far a she knew, and she could not even offer him any accommodation. Her landlady had made it very clear from the beginning that no visitors were allowed in the rooms, particularly no male visitors, and certainly no boyfriends who might be tempted to stay over night.

Now, she could not even take Raj home to introduce him to her parents. How could she ever explain this to him? What were the reasons she could give? Was it that her parents were protective or unsociable or possessive or unnecessarily anxious? It could even be construed as prejudice towards a foreigner. Karin's heart sank when she thought of how Raj would perceive it.

Karin's dutiful, twice-weekly telephone calls home were received frostily. She spoke to her mother about her studies, the progress with her thesis, which neared completion, and university gossip, but Raj's visit was never discussed. It hurt Karin that she could not share her anxieties, fears and hopes in such an important matter with the one person who had always known everything about her. Their closeness had been cut in two by a wall of disapproval and hostility.

Karin's mood sank to an all time low, when her landlady refused categorically to let Raj spend a few nights in her house. Karin offered to pay a generous bed without breakfast rate; assured her that they would put a mattress down in the lounge for him to sleep on to observe moral proprieties, but none of this could sway her. She would not even have him visiting during daytime.

'You knew the rules when you rented the room,' she ended the conversation curtly, clearly enjoying her moment of power.

Karin went back to her room, dejected, as if someone had poured icy water over her. She did not have the heart to inform Raj of most recent developments and put his latest enthusiastic letter to the side of her desk.

'*Have you got cold feet?*' His next letter sounded worried. She had not replied to the one before. '*If it creates too much upheaval in your life, I won't come. Well, I am committed to go to Geneva now, and my heart will break knowing that you are so close but yet so far, but I do not want to be the cause of a rift between you and your parents.*'

Karin was suddenly gripped by fury. Her parents had no right to undermine this friendship. There was nothing wrong with it. She was a good person, and so was Raj. He was considerate and thoughtful, much more so than they were. If they thought that she might begin an affair with him, possibly run the risk of getting pregnant and endangering the rest of her studies, they were wrong. She was disappointed that they seemed to have little trust in her ability to handle a relationship without losing her head.

They also had no right to suspect Raj of any ulterior motives like wanting a European passport, as her mother had hinted. He did not need it; he lived the life of Riley in his country. Why would he want to move permanently to Europe? He was just a pen friend and wanted to see her.

She began her next letter to him with a lame excuse about her silence and reassured him emphatically that everything was well and that she could not wait to pick him up from the airport. She did, however, have to tell him that he could not stay in her digs and asked for his advice.

'I was so looking forward to staying among all those pretty girls,' he wrote back jokingly, 'but seriously, it would not be proper. I suggest you book me into a local B & B for the first few days before I shall have to travel on to Geneva. There accommodation will be provided for me and I hope to welcome you at weekends.'

Short, excited last minute arrangement notes were flying furiously between their two countries. Karin felt occasionally faint pangs of sadness and guilt that it was all happening behind her parents' back.

'It's their own silly fault,' she decided bitterly. 'Instead of being happy for me they try to spoil something that is harmless but means a lot to me.' Only a few days before Raj was due to arrive, Karin's landlady called her downstairs to her private telephone, which the girls were only allowed to use in emergencies.

'It's your father,' she announced ominously before guiding her through a dark corridor into a gloomy and cluttered sitting room and pointing to an old-fashioned black phone on the alcove window sill.'

Karin picked up the receiver.

'Hallo,' she said into the mouth piece.

'It's Dad,' he said quietly. 'Listen, I can't talk long. We don't want to annoy your landlady. I just wanted you to know that Mum and I have talked it over, and we would like to meet your friend from Pakistan. What's his name?'

'Raj', she whispered incredulously.

'Tell him to visit us any time, and if he does not know what to do at Christmas he can stay with us.'

'I don't know whether he celebrates Christmas, he is a Muslim.'

'Well, ask him. The invitation is open. He will be welcome.'

A lump in her throat hindered her to express her gratitude. Instead she swallowed hard to hold back tears of relief.

'Keep us informed,' he ended the conversation.

'I will,' she promised and added quickly 'Thank you, Dad,' before she heard the click of his receiver having been replaced. Their plans were changed completely. He would arrive at the airport nearest to her parents. She would pick him up from there and take him back to their flat; they would spend a few days with them before going their separate ways, Karin back to university and Raj on to Geneva.

Raj was a little apprehensive whether that was a good idea: 'Are you sure you want to present me to your parents, tired and dishevelled after a sixteen hour flight?' he quipped.

'They will be very kind to you,' she reassured him post haste. Now that everything was settled she could hardly wait to see him. She now did what she hadn't dared to do once in the last two years: She missed lectures and lessons, informing her tutors dutifully and arranging with a friend to take notes for her during her absence. Suddenly, everything was easy.

Having returned to Stuttgart, she did not stop at her parents', but took a tram straight away from the station to the airport. She rang them though to say that she had arrived.

'We shall see you in a little while for dinner,' said her mother, trepidation in her voice.

'Lovely!' Karin tried to sound confident and cheerful without conveying the exuberance she really felt, but promised:

'I shall ring before we leave the airport.'

Karin sat down opposite the big *Arrivals* board which indicated that Raj's plane was expected to be on time and would land in about half an hour. It would take approximately another thirty minutes for him to collect his luggage and to get through passport control. Every minute of waiting felt like hours; the fluttering in her stomach increased constantly and she felt glued to her seat.

'What have I done?' she thought. 'I am here to meet a complete stranger, and I am not even sure what I want from him or he from me.'

There was nothing she could do now. There was no way she could back out. She had fought for him to be accepted by her parents, she had told people at university and most of all, Raj expected her to be there and welcome him with open arms. Would he be as apprehensive as she was? It was a lot worse for him because he stepped into the unknown while she had the backing of her family and the familiarity of her surroundings.

'Pull yourself together,' she told herself, got up, walked over to the book shop and began to browse among the bestsellers.

'It will be wonderful; a great experience and at the end of it they would, at worst, part as friends and at best...' She did not allow herself to think along those lines any further.

'No dreams, no expectations!' that was the deal she had made with herself.

Suddenly, the plane had landed and baggage was announced to be 'In Hall'.

'Not long now,' Karin thought with a trembling heart. She positioned herself by the barrier where the automatic exit doors disgorged travellers.

'Will I recognise him from memory or his photograph?' she suddenly panicked. 'Or are we both going to stand in this big place, looking around, searching, but looking past each other?'

When he finally came out of the doors she had no doubt it was him. He was taller than most of his fellow passengers, olive skinned, like someone from the Mediterranean rather than the Indian subcontinent, dark, straight hair precisely cut, trimmed moustache, dressed in a beautifully tailored pinstriped suit and highly polished black leather shoes.

When he discovered her, a bright smile spread over his face, pleasure glinting in his eyes.

'I didn't make you wait too long?' he asked raising his eyebrows, but it was a rhetorical question. 'It is so good of you to pick me up.'

All she could do was beam at him, feeling terribly proud to be seen with him. Finally, he set down his designer travel bag and two sealed duty free plastic carriers, which seemed to be the only luggage he had brought with him. Still smiling and looking deep into her eyes, he gave her a gentle hug and a kiss on each cheek. She blushed and he laughed out loud.

'Let's go. I shall follow you where ever you will take me,' he said and added mischievously:

'For the next few days I shall be entirely in your fair hands!'

'I am afraid, my parents are expecting us for dinner,' she confessed meekly with more than a hint of regret in her voice.

'That will be just fine,' he replied consolingly. 'It's very kind of them to invite me.'

He picked up his bags with one hand, put his free arm around her shoulders and steered her to the huge glass door above which a sign said 'Exit' and 'Trains'.

Chapter Five

Cs℞

I am restless, I am athirst for far-away things...
Rabrindranath Tagore

Karin locks the door to her little flat with determination and lifts her small, battered suitcase. She has changed her mind about not taking a handbag. Zipped up, it would be a safer place for her travel documents. She slings it over the right shoulder, and climbs cautiously down the three flights of stairs, holding on occasionally to the metal banister, a small concession to her age. No point in being proud; should she stumble she can catch herself by tightening her grip. Having arrived at the bottom of the stairwell, she is lucky enough that the young woman, who lives in the flat above her, has just entered and holds the heavy oak door open.

'Going away?' her neighbour enquires curiously.

'Only for a short while,' answers Karin, looking past her at the scene outside beckoning her. She can't explain why she feels sheepish as if caught in an illicit act.

The woman expects her to elaborate, but Karin simply smiles and turns away. She can hear a faint 'have a good trip' through the narrowing gap of the closing door.

Enveloped by a sudden throng of people on the pavement and continuous waves of noise, Karin regrets having dismissed the idea of hiring a taxi.

She is not used to being profligate; she might treat herself to being chauffeured on her return journey. She straightens up and tightens the grip on the suitcase handle. The Underground stop isn't far; the few steps down the road will do her good.

However, she hasn't counted on the lunchtime rush-hour. Karin hates crowds and avoids meticulously bumping into people while fighting her way forwards. Some of the passers-by, however, don't seem to make any effort to avoid her, brushing the sleeves of her light coloured trench coat or interrupting the rhythmical swing of her case or dislodging her bag. One gangly youth knocks against her shoulder which nearly throws her off balance. He mumbles a breathless 'sorry' before hurrying away. Karin sighs with relief when she reaches the gates of the Underground station. A colourful crowd of people clusters around the entrance, pushing to be sucked into the black depths of tunnels like grains of salt falling through a funnel.

Karin aims for a counter to buy a ticket. She is afraid that she might not be able to figure out the procedure how to get a travel pass out of one of the many machines.

'Heathrow, single,' she says, puts the money in the carousel and receives the ticket in return.

'Thank you,' she whispers and, looking up, sees the wide flash of a broad smile in a very dark face framed by thick, black curls.

'You are welcome, Madam and …have a good journey.'

Karin nods gratefully and smiles back. There was a time when a trip like this would not have fazed her, now her heart beats fast and she has to gather all her will-power not to turn back and go home. Karin follows the signposts through corridors and down the escalators. When she arrives at the platform an electronic board tells her that her train will be next and should arrive in two minutes. No need to look for a bench. Most of them seem occupied anyway. A strong draft indicates movement in the tunnel; it is getting stronger until the train pops out of the darkness like a cork from a bottle of wine. Coming to a stop it clatters and rumbles busily as if it resents the interruption in its run.

Karin aims for the door nearest to her, joins an orderly queue and climbs into the already crowded compartment. Inside, she finds a corner just opposite the entrance where she can put her case on the floor and hold on to a rod. The doors shut automatically with a bang like a car crashing into a wall. Karin clinging onto her rod prepares to be shaken off balance by the train's starts and stops.

After a while, the compartment empties and Karin finds a seat. She is now in the company of travellers judging by their baggage. The hectic of the inner city has been replaced by an atmosphere of adventure. People smile at each other conspiratorially, all fellow travellers who leave the drudge and tedium of daily life behind.

The train screeches to a halt and Karin joins the throng of disembarking travellers, clutching again case, handbag and Underground ticket. She feels hot and wishes she had not chosen to wear a coat.

She walks along endless corridors among strangers. Most of them carry, pull or push luggage. Some rush past her, obviously in a hurry to either catch a flight or pick someone up.

Finally, Karin reaches the check-in desk, manages to hold on to her modest suitcase and is given a boarding card. She proceeds to the stern looking group of officers who take it very seriously to check passports and hand luggage. Fortunately, no embarrassing beeps sound and she is waved through to take possession of her things and to enter the departure lounge.

In spite of everything having gone well, Karin is a little flustered and sinks into the nearest empty seat. She checks the time; still over an hour before she will be called for boarding. She reads the message on a nearby monitor: Flight BA 6437 Dhaka – wait in lounge.

She can allow herself a little nap. Karin wakes up from her doze when 'Flight BA 6437 to Dhaka' is announced.

She grabs her bag and coat, which she had draped over the seat next to her, looks around to locate the sign directing her to the correct group of gates and aims for an arch at the far corner diagonally across the hall. She hurries, not sure how often the message has been repeated over the tannoy before it woke her up.

Rushing along the corridor, she begins to sweat. She notices with relief that at the end of the corridor, where she presumes her gate to be, there is a long queue of mainly Asian families.

The younger people are dressed in the western uniform of jeans and T-shirts, while most of the women wear saris.

Karin had always loved saris. She thought they made any woman look elegant. If well chosen, the colour could emphasize beautiful paleness or shiny tan. Saris could easily hide plumpness; in fact, it had always been bemoaned by her sister-in-laws that, even when wrapped in five meters of delicate silk, she was too skinny to look womanly.

The crowd of passengers is gripped by exuberance and anticipation. They chatter to each other noisily, some constantly checking their passports and boarding passes, others rummaging around their hand luggage or trying to appease querulous children.

Karin joins the end of the queue. Nobody takes any notice of her. Each family forms their own excited nucleus, edging forward every time passengers in front have been waved into the gate's lounge.

By the time Karin is admitted to the waiting area, all seats are taken. She leans against a wall. She begins to feel untidy and tired. A strain of hair keeps falling into her eyes and she has an inkling that the back of her white blouse has slipped out of the waistband of her skirt.

Karin is looking around for a toilet, in order to adjust her clothes, but it is too late: airline staff are speaking animatedly into walkie-talkies using the word 'okay' a lot, then inviting the crowd to surge forward for another document check before allowing everyone to board the aircraft.

Karin breathes a sigh of relief when she passes the well-groomed and smiling ground staff, walks down a few steps and ends up outdoors in the fresh air. Two gangways are leaning against the aircraft's doors. Seeing that most passengers aim for the back entrance, Karin heads slowly for the one in front. She enjoys the fresh wind after hours enclosed in underground trains and the airport building.

The cabin staff greets her with warm 'welcomes', which she reciprocates. One of them indicates vaguely that her seat is through the curtain in one of the first rows by the window. Karin is pleased that she does not have to fight her way through a crocodile of passengers who, still milling around in the aisle, are trying to cram their hand luggage into the over-head lockers.

She slides quietly past two empty seats into seat 'A', turning her back on the mixture of voices, clatter and engine noise. Before sitting down, she tucks her blouse into the skirt, strokes the unruly strain of hair back into place and stores her small suitcase and coat under the seat in front of her. There is nothing more to do than to look out through the small, oval window onto the tarmac and a few stationary planes. The sun has come out and bathes the scene in a warm, yellow light.

Only during the last minutes of boarding are the two seats next to her taken by a young Asian woman with a boy of about six.

'Do you mind if he sits in the middle?' asks the young mother courteously.

Karin smiles: 'Of course not,' she says. Her love for children is a little rusty but nonetheless existent. The little lad looks pleasant enough and could possibly even provide some amusement. Karin extends her smile to him, admiring secretly his large, dark brown eyes framed by long, curling black lashes. He reminds her of her own children at that age.

She stretches to sit upright and leans her head against the rest. She is ready for take-off, waiting with a mixture of curiosity and dread: her decision is irreversible; now there is no turning back.

Chapter Six

CBED

Give me the supreme courage of love…
Rabrindranath Tagore

'So tell us about your family'.

Karin's parents really made an effort to be polite and welcoming in their formal, stuffy sort of way.

They were all sitting around the oblong, well-polished oak refectory table on high-backed chairs with leather seats.

Raj put his fork and knife down and looked his hostess in the eye.

'I have three sisters and four brothers. They are all married and have children. The youngest sister and the oldest brother don't live in Dhaka. Mumtaz lives in Sylhet, the tea producing region and Khaled lives in Chittagong on the Bay of Bengal.' He paused and looked at Karin's father who was busy loading his fork with meat and peas.

'Actually, my younger brother Jamal lives in London at the moment, with his wife and young daughter. He is studying to be a doctor.'

'Will you visit him while you are in Europe?' Her mother showed polite interest.

'I would like to but I shall have to see whether it will be possible.'

'Tell us about your parents', he was encouraged.

'My father,' Raj continued focusing his attention on Karin's mother, 'lives with my eldest sister and her family in the old part of Dhaka, but he takes it in turns to stay with the other children'.

'And your mother?'

'She died in 1947,' Raj answered, 'during the birth of her ninth child.'

Karin's mother tried to suppress a gasp, but did not quite succeed. 'How sad,' she finally said, so that she could not be misunderstood. To have nine children seemed to her irresponsible, but it was none of her business.

Everyone was suddenly most interested in what was left on their plates and cutlery was clattering busily.

'Well, in 1947, Pakistan was born,' Raj continued after a while changing the topic, 'and my family moved from Calcutta to Dhaka in East Pakistan.'

'Good gracious, with so many children?' burst out Karin's mother.

Raj wanted them to understand.

'There has always been unrest between the Muslims and the Hindus in India. Many people were killed. After years of negotiating, the Islamic state of Pakistan was founded to separate them. Two million Muslims streamed north. My family moved from Calcutta to the eastern part of the new country re-named East Pakistan; others moved north-west to the new West Pakistan. The two Pakistans are separated by 2,000 miles of Indian territory between them.'

Karin and her parents were intrigued. They had never heard any of this.

Raj had suddenly a twinkle in his eyes: 'To be honest, I think our father only moved to get rid of his liquor store in Calcutta. Alcohol is forbidden to Muslims except for medicinal purposes, and to sell to foreigners. He had always felt guilty about doing so.'

Karin's parents' eyes widened in astonishment until they realised that he was joking; the atmosphere lightened, but only slightly.

Karin was still ruminating on the family's history: 'So your father travelled with eight children hundreds of miles to a new country when his wife had just died,' the pained expression on her face reflected the horrific picture she painted in her mind.

'Yes, that's about it. It was very brave of him.'

Karin's father shook his head in admiration.

'How did he cope?'

'As soon as they arrived, he married off the oldest daughter and placed two of the younger siblings with her. She was just fourteen years old. Soon afterwards my eldest brother married and took me and my brother Babul in. Abbu found husbands for the other girls as soon as they were old enough.'

Nobody dared to ask what age that would have been, but considering that the oldest girl was fourteen on her wedding day, the same kind of age would presumably apply to the other daughters. Karin could see the disdain in her mother's face while her father was inscrutable. They obviously found the business of arranged marriage, particularly at such a young age, distasteful.

Raj saw it as well.

'My father really had not much choice. He had to go to work, to build up a business again. Apart from that, those were the traditions of Muslim society,' he tried to explain.

'Is it still like that?'

'Mainly in the villages. Girls are not married off that young any more, but most marriages are still arranged by the parents.'

When no one said anything he added cheerfully: 'Luckily, all my sisters and brothers are happily married. It worked out well for them.'

Silence preceded her mother's next question. She had kept the most important enquiry to last and had clearly turned it several times around in her mind, so as to formulate it least offensively:

'And you? Are you married?'

Raj laughed out loud: 'No, good God, no! My family tried hard over the years to match-make, but I managed to resist. I am enjoying life. There is still plenty of time for the right girl to come along.'

Karin's mother nearly choked on her piece of chicken.

'Would you like...' she offered hastily some more food.

'No, thank you. That was delicious!'

'Are you certain?' Karin could see that her mother was unsure of how to handle her guest. She obviously tried not to appear patronising.

49

'No, really. I have eaten my fill.' Karin giggled at the expression and hoped that his old-fashioned courtesy would charm her parents.

Her father took him to his study, while the women cleared away and washed up in the kitchen.

'He is very nice,' said her mother cautiously. Karin simply nodded. It was not a good idea to be over-enthusiastic at this point. It was assumed that Raj was tired from the long journey and a bed was made up in the spare room.

Standing in the landing outside the bedrooms, they said awkwardly 'good night', while her parents hovered behind the sitting room door.

'I am so hungry,' he whispered to her astonishment.

'Why didn't you eat more at dinner? Mum offered you more,' she stated.

'I didn't want to give the impression that I am a glutton. In our culture it is immodest to ask for seconds.'

'So even if you are still hungry you say "no"?' she asked incredulously.

'Well, the host insists that you eat more and pushes food on your plate.'

'You don't need to do that here. Say yes, when you want some more. It's a compliment.'

'Okay. Lesson number one!'

'Wait here,' she turned round to dive into her room and reappeared within seconds holding triumphantly a packet of chocolate biscuits.

'Here,' she sniggered conspiratorially. 'That should keep the wolf from the door.'

'You are very sweet,' he replied tenderly, taking the biscuits gingerly out of her hand without touching her.

Her mother rustled ostentatiously behind the door, before opening it.

'I think we better go to bed,' he whispered. 'Sleep well and sweet dreams!'

'You, too,' she replied happily

'I am sure I shall sleep well, but I'll miss…' He stopped himself, just before her mother appeared in the door. Karin was left to guess what he was going to miss.

'See you all tomorrow morning. Good night.' he said formally to mother and daughter before disappearing into the guest room.

He had three days at his disposal, which they filled with sightseeing, shopping and chatting. One evening, her god-mother came for dinner; she was far too curious about her god-child's dark, handsome beau to let this opportunity pass. They had a lovely evening, full of laughter and fun.

'You certainly have my approval,' she whispered into Karin's ear while pretending to kiss her good-bye. 'He is even more handsome than I remember …and so chivalrous'. Karin rolled her eyes in mock despair about her aunt's flippant attitude, but heartily agreed.

The last evening before his departure for Geneva was spent making plans to see each other again. They compared calendars and timetables and decided that they should give themselves a couple of weeks to settle back into their studies; they would meet up at the end of the month.

'By then, I shall be familiar with Geneva and can show you round.' Raj concluded sensibly. He obviously assumed that she would visit him.

If it had been for them, they would not have minded getting together every weekend, but they both realised that it would look unseemly and upset her parents. Karin desperately wanted to keep them on their side.

Karin's father had left for a business trip, when she and her mother took Raj to the station. In fact, Karin had brought her own little suitcase with her to board another train soon after his departure.

For the first time in her life, duty and studies had been pushed to the back of her mind. She did not feel guilty about it and wished she could abandon them altogether in favour of travelling with Raj.

She swallowed hard, smiled bravely and knew that it was out of the question.

The days back at university were tedious, and Karin was glad that she had finished her thesis and only needed to oversee and edit its typescript. Karin was restless and her thoughts scattered between the need to study and the desire to be with Raj. He wrote almost daily, usually picture postcards, in an attempt to lure her to Geneva a little earlier, but Karin was determined to keep her promise to her parents. The weeks passed quickly and the weekend of her visit approached. She bought the train ticket with a trembling heart. Now she was like the other girls at university she knew: she would visit her boyfriend at the weekend.

Her mother rang on Friday afternoon, just as Karin was packing her duffle bag.

'When is your train?

'At four.'

'Do remain circumspect,' her mother pleaded.

'Of course,' she replied half-heartedly

'Remember, he will lose respect if you throw yourself at him.'

'Mother!' she exclaimed..

'He is a grown man,' her mother kept on.

'You don't show much trust in me and the way you brought me up.'

'I just wanted to be sure you remember.'

'I do remember, Mother,' she said, exasperation in her voice.

'I hope so,' her mother conceded, and added reluctantly: 'Have a good time and give him our regards.'

※　※　※

However, once Karin had left her room and had shut the door to her digs behind her, she forgot all about her parents. She was overjoyed at the prospect of seeing Raj again, at travelling, seeing a new town, even a new country, and most of all, she was looking forward to his company. She had missed him more than she had admitted to herself. Something about him made her feel comfortable, light-headed and cheerful. He understood her, treated her with respect and something told her that she could trust him with her life. If this was love, she would not struggle against it.

She was told that she had to change trains in Zürich, which she knew was in the German speaking part of Switzerland. However, she would not have enough time to go sightseeing. She didn't mind. The sooner she hurtled towards Raj the better. He had sounded beside himself with joy at the prospect of her visit when they had spoken to finalise arrangements.

'I shall pick you up from Gare Cornavin,' he promised eagerly. She avoided asking him where she would stay, even where he was accommodated.

She gave up reading the newspaper which she had bought and marvelled instead at the stunning views from the train window. Well-known names on boards flitted past – Bern, Lausanne, Montreux – and then the train swished along another lake, Lac Leman, Lake Geneva.

The sun was shining, as she arrived and she carried her blue woollen coat with the velvet collar over her arm. She rather liked to show off her favourite paisley patterned dress with puff sleeves and a wide swinging skirt.

She had hardly climbed out of the carriage, coat over one arm and duffle bag in the other hand, when she was lifted off the platform and swung around.

'I thought you might be at the front of the train,' Raj laughed, breathlessly and obviously delighted that he had guessed correctly. He put her down on the platform and planted a hearty kiss on each cheek. Then he took her bag, put the other arm around her shoulders, as he had done at the airport, and led her out into the city of Geneva. 'I suggest, we first go to my apartment, so you can freshen up, and then I shall take you out for dinner,' he declared proudly.

They took a bus for around twenty minutes which transported them through busy streets in the centre of town to a much quieter area. All the way, they chatted – about her journey, his course, her studies and his most recent pieces of news from home. Nothing much had occurred, although one of his nieces, Nisha, had had a baby girl.'

'Don't look so horrified,' Raj said cheerfully. 'The whole family will be delighted and helping her. Every young mother employs an *ayah*, a nursemaid-cum-nanny.'

Karin waited for him to continue when she heard him mutter: 'Next time it will be a boy. She is still young.'

A strange comment, Karin thought, but she let it pass.

They didn't have to walk more than 500 yards from the bus stop before they reached a solid brick town house, five storeys tall. Raj unlocked the heavy oak entrance door and they slipped into a high-ceilinged landing with Roman mosaic flooring and carved wooden banisters. These were certainly no student digs.

53

'I live on the top floor. We better take the lift.' Raj pressed already the button which lit up green.

'I don't mind walking up the stairs,' she suggested, but he looked deep into her eyes and said with mock-seriousness: 'I am an old man, remember. I'll die of a heart attack if I walk up five flights of stairs.'

She gave him a playful punch in his chest and protested: 'I do not go out with old men.'

'Oh, have I blown my chances already?' he teased her, faking despair.

'Funny you should say that.'

He unlocked the door to his flat, bowed and motioned her to enter first. It was a small, but perfectly equipped one bedroom city apartment with stylish modern furniture in the minimalist fashion. He showed her around with pride, the lounge with a dining table by the window, the Japanese style bedroom with only a low bed and a wardrobe of the most beautiful reddish wood in it, and the kitchen.

Finally, he said: 'The bathroom is here on the left – in case you want to freshen up.'

'In a minute,' she answered and stepped towards a French door which led out onto a tiny balcony. It revealed the most fabulous view over the city.

'I was lucky to get this,' he said, standing behind her. 'The family of a friend of mine own it and use it whenever they come to Europe.'

'You still haven't told me what you want to eat,' he persisted.

'I really don't mind. I am not fussy,' she assured him. 'You choose!'

'Have you ever eaten Indian food?'

'No.'

'Do you think you might enjoy eating foreign food?'

'Raj, I am a linguist, remember?' she said with indignation. 'I like everything foreign.'

She put her palm in front of her mouth in embarrassment. Raj laughed. 'I know,' he said, his eyes twinkling with mischief.

'Alright then, Indian it is.'

She had an idea that it would be something with rice, other than that she was prepared to be surprised.

A little later they took the bus back into town to the Grottes district, famed for its ethnic restaurants. They entered one which was advertised on the outside with bold twinkling lights as The Taj Mahal. It was like stepping into a different world. Indian waiters standing in line welcomed them. Gentle music, played on a string instrument, which she did not recognise, pervaded the air. The walls were covered in sumptuous red and gold paper, the floor was tiled with blue, green, brown and white mosaics and the tables were arranged in niches, which resembled the lavish sedan chairs she had seen in fairy tale books as a child.

The waiters fussed over them immediately as they chose a table. They pulled the chairs out for them to sit down, unfolded large white napkins and put them on their laps. Then they rushed to bring bowls of water with a slice of lemon. Karin watched as Raj dipped his fingers into the water and then dried his hands on another serviette. Tentatively, she followed his example. This was new and exciting.

'Why are we washing our hands?' she whispered across the table.

'Because I shall teach you to eat with your fingers,' he replied confidently.

Her eyes widened, but she was up for it.

A great number of oval dishes arrived and were put on heating trays in the middle of the table. She admired the rich colours of the food and inhaled the unusual smells.

Raj encouraged her to take rice and then a spoonful from each of the serving plates.

'The yellow one is called chicken korma. It is quite mild,' he explained. 'This is lamb curry; there is beef curry which might be a bit hot. You probably know all of the vegetables, except for okra, Lady's fingers. And these are chutneys in the little bowls.'

He showed her how to form little rice balls with his finger tips which he dipped into sauce or chutney adding meat or vegetable. Finally, the thumb pushed everything into the mouth. It looked so easy when he did it. Soon she had made a terrible mess of the beautiful white, starched table cloth and her entire right hand was covered in delicious gravy, dripping back onto her plate. When she tried to take her left hand to help, Raj shook his head: 'We don't ever use the left hand when we are eating,' he said.

Her 'why' got stuck in her throat, when he shook his head: 'You don't want to know just now.'

She noticed that the waiters were crowding at a distance from their table, watching her efforts with amusement. Karin could see the pride in Raj's eyes.

'You can use fork and knife if you feel awkward,' he offered, but it was a matter of honour to her that she would not give up.

She loved the *korma* best, as he had predicted, and she was intrigued by the sticky texture of *okra*. Every mouthful was an explosion of spicy tastes and sensations.

They ended the meal with another bowl of lemon water in which they washed off most of the grease, followed by cloths wrapped in plastic. Karin observed how Raj opened his little parcel, buried his face in the sweet smelling towel and then wiped his hands on it. When she did the same, she could have drowned in the softness and refreshing scent of these unfamiliar, oriental spices.

'Now you must have a sweet,' Raj said when they were clean again, and ordered *roshgullas*. He watched her attentively as she tucked into the soft round balls of curd scented with rosewater.

She beamed at him – they were wonderful.

'I won't be able to eat anything for the rest of the weekend,' she sighed with pleasure, leaning back in her chair.

'Excellent!' he said and was clearly pleased with her.

'Do you ever cook?' she enquired.

'No, my sisters do on special occasions, but usually, we employ a cook.'

She nodded, unfamiliar with the concept of having servants and Raj did not elaborate.

'So tell me, what shall we do tomorrow?' They spent the rest of the meal planning the programme for the following day.

They strolled back to his flat arm in arm, laughing and joking. If she had felt apprehensive about where she would sleep, it had been unnecessary. He insisted to bed down on the black leather settee in the sitting room, while vacating his bed for her. She disappeared in the bathroom to have another shower and to brush her teeth, but she crossed the lounge fully clothed again. Before she could slip into the bedroom he grabbed her by the waist and planted a gentle kiss on her forehead.

'Good night, Karin. It's so nice to have you here!' She disentangled herself slowly, not to offend him.

'Good night Raj. Thank you for a lovely evening.'

'Sweet dreams...' she heard him say while shutting the door. The rest was muffled and sounded like: '...of me.'

※ ※ ※

He was already folding away his bedclothes, when she woke up and appeared tussle-haired in the door.

'Good morning,' he greeted her, bright and cheerfully. 'And how did my princess sleep?'

'Very well, thank you, Sir,' she answered coquettishly.

'Breakfast is coming up,' he announced.

'Can I help you?' she offered, but he insisted that she should get ready in the bathroom instead.

They had a continental breakfast of café au lait, croissants, baguette and butter, before striding out into town. They aimed for the Old Town on the tallest hill in the heart of the city to visit Saint Peter's Cathedral. Karin was not a little astonished that her Muslim friend had chosen a Christian church to start with their sightseeing.

They climbed up the winding stone steps to the North Tower and enjoyed the most breathtaking view over the houses, the lake and the river Rhône.

'I love it up here,' he said simply. 'It is peaceful compared to the bustle of the inner city.' Back in the streets, they strolled across the Old Town's cobblestones, across the Bourg-de-Four Square and past the 15th century Town Hall. They admired the Maison Tavel, the oldest house in Geneva, and rummaged through second hand bookstores.

Next they headed for the lake, the Lac Leman where they collapsed in the chairs of a little bistro on the promenade close to the famous fountain called Jet d'Eau.

After lunch, they decided on a two hour cruise on the lake. It would be relaxing. She was glad to have brought her coat, because, in spite of the autumn sunshine, the air was crisp, and the fresh wind blew her hair constantly off her face. They sat on deck, arms wrapped around each other for warmth and comfort, soaking up the scenery of lake and mountains.

Once back on the promenade, Raj insisted to buy her truffles in one of the famous chocolate shops, before they hopped across another river called L' Arve, using one of the many bridges to the

Bohemian part of town called Carouge. They just caught some of the local artisans still at work in their studios before they realised that they were peckish again and had dinner in an artsy little restaurants.

When they re-emerged it was dark and music seeped from behind most doors.

'Shall we go to a jazz club?' he asked

'It's not for us, is it?' she said and laughed when she saw relief crossing his face.

They also realised that they were tired after having done such a lot in one day.

'I can't face another bus ride,' Raj said and hailed a passing taxi. They fell exhaustedly into the plush seats. Raj put his arm around her shoulders and pressed her gently towards his chest.

'I look forward to a bit of peace and quiet,' he sighed. Karin simply smiled, happy to follow any suggestion.

* * *

'I shall cook dinner for us tonight,' she declared at the breakfast table.

'You don't have to,' he protested.

'I would very much like to,' she insisted and added: 'it will be nice to eat at home.'

He looked pleased.

'I am not a great cook,' she warned, 'but I won't poison you.'

'Whatever you cook will be delicious,' he flattered while she briskly pointed out that in that case, they had to go food shopping.

Back in the flat, Karin made a simple meal of spaghetti Bolognese with lots of parmesan cheese and a crispy salad. To round it off, she had bought some eggs, sugar, Marsala wine which she now beat with a hand whisk into fluffy *zabaglione*.

Raj tucked into the meal hungrily and made satisfied noises, looking at the chef approvingly. After the first spoon of the dessert, he hesitated for a moment, but carried on eating.

'Is something wrong with it?' Karin asked anxiously.

'There is alcohol in it, isn't there? Muslims are not allowed alcohol.'

'Not even in cooking?' She watched as he scraped out the last spoonful.

58

'There are exceptions,' he continued without answering her question, 'for example, for medicinal purposes or if one travels and it would be rude to refuse one's hostess.' Embarrassment and disappointment left her face, when she saw him smirking cheekily:

'By the way, it was delicious!'

They both loved the atmosphere of sharing their first meal in privacy. Raj helped her to wash up and put away. They then settled side by side sinking into the soft cushions of the settee. She nestled into the crook of his shoulder and sighed with contentment. After a while, he showed her photographs of his family. He mentioned a name every time he pointed to a face, but she found it difficult to remember who was who. When she tried to repeat the names, her tongue tripped over the unfamiliar combinations of letters. He finally gave her a little test and thought it was hilarious when she got completely muddled and mispronounced names hopelessly.

They had a glass of red wine, which surprised her, but to her it was another sign how westernised he was.

'Allah is great, ever-loving, all-knowing and much more tolerant than some of his followers make him out to be,' he simply said, seeing her enquiring look.

'Is everyone in your family so open-minded?'

'Most of them. One of my cousins is married to an Italian lady. They live half of the year in Rome and the other half in Dhaka. There was never a big drama about it. He went to university there and the family half expected him to return with a foreign wife. They are very happy....'

He paused to look at her, but whatever he had meant to ask her, he kept to himself. Instead he continued: 'Most of my sisters and brothers have travelled many times to Europe and America. One works for a British company and travels to conferences in London twice a year.'

Every time Raj talked about his relatives, the gulf between their two countries and societies narrowed, the cultural gap closing gradually. It crossed her mind that he might hope that she would ask him to join her in bed on their last night together, but she did not feel ready. She felt bound by the promise to her mother, ignorant of how to prevent a pregnancy and fearful of losing his respect.

He held her close and kissed her gently on the lips, stroked her hair, but no sooner had she whispered 'I am sorry,' he let her go and said reassuringly: 'You have nothing to be sorry about.'

❧ ❧ ❧

It was self-understood that he would repay the visit during the next bank holiday weekend which was only weeks away. They decided that Karin would organise bed & breakfast accommodation for him close to her student digs and that they might go on a day-trip across the border to France to get away from the student crowds.

As it happened, the B & B was not needed. Someone in Karin's Spanish class was desperately looking for a tenant to take over his flat while he was on his year abroad in Argentina. It worked out excellently: Kurt would come back just when Karin would have finished her exams. As he was considered to be the university's lothario, visiting rules to his flat were well established and pleasingly lax. The landlord, a busy local farmer, lived miles away and did not bother much about the place, as long as no-one got involved with the police or burnt the house down

'You might as well leave at the end of the month,' Karin's old landlady sniffed, when she handed in her notice. The end of the month was in a fortnight, just in time for Raj to help her with moving. He was delighted when he heard the news.

Karin's heart lifted. She seemed to glide on clouds these days; lessons and homework seemed easy.

Karin reported back to her mother regularly via the telephone. Lately, an unspoken question stood between them, and Karin knew, that her mother wanted to know how far her relationship with Raj had blossomed. As Karin needed advice anyway, she picked up courage and came straight out with it:

'Mum, how do I avoid getting pregnant... if it happens?'she added quickly.

There was a brief silence at the other end, but, to her credit, Karin's mother answered matter-of-factly as if a mathematical problem had been submitted to her.

'Go to your GP and ask him to prescribe the Pill.' When Raj arrived two weeks later, Karin was well prepared in all respects. They had great fun moving her few belongings, which consisted mainly of dictionaries and novels, to her new flat. The old landlady stood at first in the door, hands on hips, barring the

60

entrance, but when Raj turned up with a bunch of flowers and a box of Swiss chocolates, she turned all giggly and professed to make a rare exception, letting him in the house to help carrying Karin's boxes.

'Silly woman,' muttered Karin, while she was still gathering the last of her belongings. 'She doesn't deserve those lovely chocolates.'

Raj had just come up the stairs again: 'Ah, I see, it's not a matter of principle, it's the chocolates,' he laughed. 'You will be pleased to hear that I have brought a box for you, too.' She had hired a taxi to take them to her new address, only a few roads away. When they had managed to lug everything into her new home, he pulled out a bottle of champagne from his suitcase and announced:

'I can stay till next weekend... if that's alright with you.' She threw her arms around him and kissed him on the mouth.

'I shall have to write an essay, but I can do that while you attend lectures.'

'Oh, I can skip a few,' she said carelessly.

'No, we are not going to ruin your chances to pass your examinations next spring. You have worked so hard, you might as well see it through. Just imagine, once you have your degree, you will be free like a bird. You will be able to work anywhere in the world.'

She was astounded by the passion in his voice and nodded in agreement. He was absolutely right. Her parents would be pleased to hear him speak like that. There was definitely an advantage to having a more mature boyfriend: He would remain sensible when her youthful enthusiasm was about to carry her away.

They had the most wonderful weekend. When alone, their companionship was easy-going, loving and fun. She was terribly proud to be seen with him and to introduce him to some of her fellow students. She was suddenly not so keen anymore to go on a day trip, but rather wanted to enjoy the comfort and privacy of their little world. There was a whimsical pop-song the radio station kept repeating: *The monkey's forgot you, the zebra's forgot you and so did the kangaroo, but me and the elephant will never forget you!*

They found it endearing as it seemed to reflect exactly their sentiment of everlasting love.

It was equally easy to become lovers, accompanied by lots of caresses and giggles. She wasn't quite sure whether he had de-flowered her – she had always imagined that it would involve floods of spilt blood. She could hardly detect any on the bed sheet. All she remembered was a short, piercing pain, which had hardly surfaced in her general ecstasy.

🌸 🌸 🌸

Soon, the autumn term came to an end. Christmas loomed, but Karin felt too uncertain to broach the subject until Raj told her that he intended to use his holidays to visit his younger brother in England. As she already knew, Jamal was studying medicine. Karin had extended an invitation on behalf of her parents, but Raj had set his heart on spending some time with his brother, Nasma, his sister-in-law and their baby daughter Kitty.

She was torn between disappointment which turned into anger and not a little embarrassment at having to explain to her parents, that Raj's brother seemed more important to him at Christmas than she was. Whenever she turned these thoughts over in her mind, she ended up feeling unkind and narrow-minded.

'If you want to be with a man from a far away country,' she scolded herself, 'from such a different background, you must expect that in some matters he will think and act differently. You will have to learn to make compromises.'

Her parents took his decision calmly with a non-committal nod of the head. They did not seem to be half as disappointed as she was.

As it happened, he had bought flight tickets from the airport nearest to her parents, so that he could spend the first two days of his holiday with them. They organised a pre-Christmas dinner and exchanged small presents. Karin gave him silver cufflinks engraved with his initials. Her parents had bought him a silk tie in a surprisingly daring red, which he loved and put on immediately. Raj had chosen a beautiful crystal bowl for her mother and a bottle of vintage Scotch for her father.

Finally he took a flat square box wrapped in fine white tissue paper from his jacket pocket and gave it to Karin. He watched how she un-wrapped it carefully, marvelled at the little red box with foreign lettering and fingered the lock with trembling hands.

He savoured the delighted look on her face, when the lid snapped open and she found a pearl necklace. He put it around her neck and fastened it at the back. The warm glow of the pearls suited her pale skin. He was satisfied that he, or rather his sisters, had chosen the right present.

They had one term left after Christmas, three months, twelve weekends, to enjoy the illusion that they were a couple and had a future together. Karin couldn't bear to think of what would happen afterwards.

They carried on visiting each other during weekends. Towards the end of spring term, their cheerfulness became stilted and frantic, their happiness tainted by insecurity about their future and simple heartache. They desperately told each other that Raj's departure would not be the end of their relationship and that they should enjoy the present time left to them. As the weeks passed, their hearts became increasingly heavy. Karin tried hard not to think about the imminent separation when she was with Raj for fear of bursting into tears in front of him. Raj remained demonstratively loving, putting his arms around her whenever he saw shadows cross her face.

They agreed that he would spend the two weeks before and after Easter with her and her parents, but then he had to return home. His visa was running out. However much he wanted to prolong his stay, it wasn't possible.

They spent the Easter holidays shopping for his family back home. Raj became visibly excited when he spoke their names, and described their likes and dislikes, but he dithered, buying any presents, weighing up the pros and cons of suitability. Finally, he put Karin in charge of the task of choosing presents for his sisters and nieces. She felt honoured and took her task seriously. She picked pretty, feminine things, within the budget he had set and considering the weight restrictions for air travel. Raj bought some additional cosmetics written on a shopping list by his sisters. Karin was astonished that they seemed to know their way around brands better than she did. 'Just as well, I did not bring much luggage for myself,' he laughed when they both had to sit on two bulging suitcases, one of them new, to close the lids. They kept sitting there for a little while longer.

'I am so sorry that I have to leave you!' he said suddenly.

She tried to smile while he looked very serious, stood up, reached into his trouser pocket and took out a tiny box, square and dark blue with a rim of gold pearl-droplets. She took the box and turned it in her hand. This time, she found the name of a Stuttgart jeweller.

'This is for you to remember me by,' he said uncertainly. 'It is my thank you and expresses my hopes for the future.'

It was an engagement ring, white gold with a sparkling diamond in a filigree setting.

She remembered him staring at it in the shop window during their shopping spree for his family. She had dragged him away and had jokingly dismissed the idea of ever getting married.

'What do you say?' His voice was choked with emotion, hope and anxiety.

He was asking her to marry him. She was speechless. She had not expected to put their relationship on such a serious footing before his departure.

The question crossed her mind, what her parents would have to say about this. They would probably point out that it was foolish considering his imminent departure. They would warn her that relationships tended not to survive endless months of separation and with no prospect of a reunion.

They would also point out that she had important examinations coming up and that she needed all her concentration for her studies. After that, she knew, they expected her to find a good job to start on the first rung of a promising career. This to them was the natural progression, the path they had brought up their daughter to follow.

Karin considered the different backgrounds, but brushed the thought aside: It had not mattered so far; in fact it had made their relationship interesting and exciting. They had both risen above the conventions of their societies, treasuring the best of each of them.

If in the back of her mind, she felt obstacles were looming, she did not take much notice. Love would overcome them; they would face any problems together, as a couple. She had always imagined that she would feel blissful happiness on her wedding day; most young girls dreamt of it. Now that she was on the brink of becoming a wife, she knew that such happiness could not be guaranteed whatever the circumstances.

He now knelt in front of Karin, took the ring out of its box and put it on her finger.

'Will you marry me?' he said.

'Yes,' she whispered immediately. He stood up, pulled her to him and kissed her passionately.

Her mother stood in the door. They hadn't heard the knock.

'We just got engaged,' Karin explained breathlessly. Her mother's gaze rested on Raj, reflecting shock, disappointment and resignation.

'You had better tell your father tonight,' she said stiffly, but kissed each of them on the cheeks to congratulate. When her father returned home, he was informed by his wife in a shower of whispers and Raj was led into the study. Karin waited with a trembling heart, but could not imagine that her father would refuse his blessing. What would become of them if her parents disapproved and discouraged Raj? Or if they suggested postponing the engagement to a later date, maybe after 'they had proved that their union could survive anything?'

She needn't have worried. The two men emerged together smiling and equals: her father had handed over the responsibility for her happiness to his prospective son-in-law. Karin could not believe her luck. A bottle of vintage champagne was opened to celebrate, making them forget for a couple of happy hours that Raj had to catch an early flight.

His departure happened in a whirl of activity, hugs, suppressed tears and hysterical laughter, when his suitcases were weighed.

'You have half of a department store in there,' Karin teased him, but her cheerfulness was forced and her heart felt like lead.

'Too many women in my family,' he tried to parry, but the joke fell flat.

Final hugs and promises were exchanged. Her parents stepped back to give them the illusion of privacy. They readied themselves to take back a confused and distraught daughter.

'You concentrate on your exams now,' they heard him urge Karin.

'I shall,' she choked.

'Just imagine how thrilled my family will be when I tell them that I am engaged to be married.' He tried hard to cheer her up. 'They will go crazy! They have tried for so many years to marry me off,' he chuckled at the thought of his surprise announcement.'

Karin only nodded unhappily. She wished she could be there, with him.

He pulled her close again and whispered in her ear: 'I shall do my very best to come back soon.'

Karin's parents reminded them that it was time to say good-bye. Raj gave a respectful embrace to his future mother-in-law and shook hands with her husband.

'Look after yourself, and come back soon,' the father said and clapped him on the shoulder in a gesture of friendship.

'I shall, *Insh' Allah!*'

Another hug and kiss for Karin and a desperate: 'I love you, princess!' Then he tore himself away and rushed towards passport control. He turned round one last time to wave and then disappeared in the crowd.

It was as if the light had gone out in Karin's world.

Chapter Seven

CR&RO

Yet my heart is sweet
With the memory of the first fresh jasmines

Rabrindranath Tagore

The plane with Karin on board is up in the air.

'We must be flying over the Mediterranean by now,' she thinks and remembers the first time she had ever flown this route stopping over at Cairo airport. Hundreds of men in white robes and turbans had been milling around, billowing over chairs or squatting on the floor, some even lying down on the cool tiles to sleep, a sea of white sails on a still evening.

To Karin's astonishment there had been no women and she can still recall the overwhelming feeling of intimidating authority, mass male presence and some clearly hostile looks in her direction. In spite of the reassuring presence of her husband, she couldn't get back quick enough to the plane to continue her journey.

The air hostess offers a dinner of chicken curry with rice and cauliflower on a tray, supplemented by bread, cheese, butter, biscuits and chocolate to cater for all tastes. The oriental fruit salad in a little cup looks refreshing and the promised cup of coffee afterwards will revive her spirits.

Karin gives the chocolate bar to her little neighbour, who grabs it quickly before she can change her mind. She laughs out loud, but his mother is embarrassed:

'You do not snatch, Omar!' she scolds the little man. 'What do you say?'

His big, brown eyes turn to Karin and rest on her still smiling face.

'Thank you,' he says obediently. Only then is his mother satisfied and leans back in her seat.

'You are very welcome,' Karin reassures him and begins to eat.

Once the trays have been collected, a general hubbub of activity begins; passengers get up to stretch their legs, to use the toilets, to reorganise their seating arrangements or to rummage around in the overhead lockers. Finally, everyone calms down, including the most restless of children, and people prepare to snuggle into their seats, trying to snatch a little sleep knowing that hours of darkness are ahead of them.

The coffee is keeping Karin wide awake. She leans her head against the window's blind, which she has pulled down. Behind her, silence has descended and even the cabin crew have retired.

Karin makes herself comfortable in her seat and dozes off eventually.

A low hum of engine noises and chattering pulls her gradually back to reality. She does not know whether she has slept for hours or only a little while. She registers, looking at her watch, that it must be very early morning at home, but cannot work out what the time is in the country several miles below her.

The babies among the passengers are beginning to wake up one by one, some gurgling happily, others querulous, while the toddlers and older children are chatting animatedly with their unwilling parents whose voices still sound overwrought with sleepiness.

Karin would like to go to the toilet, but the little boy next to her, is fast asleep and his mother in the aisle seat, too.

'I'll wait until they wake up', she decides, lifts the blind a little but drops it again when she can only see stationary darkness. If she did not hear the engines roar, she would not know that the plane was moving. She leans back in her chair and closes her eyes again.

The next time, she is awoken by bustling next to her. She must have fallen soundly asleep again; she hadn't heard the young mother and her son leaving their seats. They are now coming back and about to sit down again.

'Could you, please let me out?' Karin smiles, and mother and son retreat a little to let her pass.

'You slept very well,' the young woman remarks.

'Yes, I think we all did,' replies Karin warmly. 'I'll be back in a minute.'

When everyone is settled again, it is nearly breakfast time. Newspapers in several languages are distributed. Families are tidying themselves up, rubbing the sleepiness from their eyes and signs of a restless sleep from their clothes. There is constant low-level activity and the humming of voices.

Uncharacteristically, Karin involves the young woman in a chat:

'Are you visiting family in Bangladesh?'

She sees a hint of sadness clouding the young mother's eyes.

'Yes, we have family in Sylhet. We haven't seen them for two years.'

'Where do you live?'

'In Manchester. My husband is a doctor, and I have applied at a teacher training college.'

'Good for you,' exclaims Karin a little more enthusiastically than she intended.

'It will be quite hard; I shall be very busy,' continues the Bengali woman, now in full flow, glad to unburden her niggling thoughts to a sympathetic listener.

'The thing is, Omar will have to stay with his auntie in Sylhet while I am studying. I really couldn't look after him properly and do the course.'

Karin can see the young woman's burning question in her face: Am I doing the right thing?

'That is very sensible,' Karin hopes that she sounds convincing.

'Do you think so?' follows the anxious reply. 'My husband does, and he is very supportive, I am very lucky!' she adds hastily.

'Yes, you are,' Karin thinks by herself, 'luckier than I have been.'

'It is eminently sensible. Omar will have a wonderful, long holiday being spoilt by his aunty. Your course will be over before you know it. You could not concentrate properly with him being there all the time.'

'That's what we thought, but it's hard to give your child away.'

'It will be just for a few months. In my experience, children are resilient. As long as they know they are loved, nothing much harms them.'

Karin feels uncomfortable how easily she blurts out personal opinions to a complete stranger. She had felt similar embarrassment a lifetime ago when her sisters'-in-law had tried to turn her into a talkative girlie gossiper.

They themselves did not lack in self-confidence, but were only confident in spheres, society and tradition allowed them to be. To them western women seemed to have limitless freedom, making their own decisions in all aspects of their lives, the men totally powerless to keep them in check. This topic never ceased to fascinate them and they discussed the pros and cons among themselves ad infinitum, changing the conversation as soon as a man entered the room.

'I am Serena,' says the woman suddenly, 'it's good to talk to you. I keep turning it over and over in my mind. I feel so guilty.'

'It won't be forever,' Karin consoles her. 'Once you have your teaching degree, you can choose a job that fits in with having a child. And you will have all the holidays together.'

Serena nibbles at her lower lip, deep in thoughts. Her face lights up:

'That's true, I hadn't thought that far,' she whispers and adds a grateful 'Thank you.'

'Mummy, will you read me a story!' Omar's querulous request becomes insistent.

'I had better,' smiles Serena at Karin, digging already in a big travel bag by her feet

She pulls out a large picture book, opens the first page, and soon the two of them are engrossed in its fictional world.

Karin looks at her watch again. 'Not long to go', she thinks and feels a flutter in her stomach, the type of flutter that makes her feel twenty-three years old again. She is suddenly looking forward to this adventure whatever the outcome.

Chapter Eight

CʒʒʒʒʒʒʒʒO

It is the pang of separation…
It is the sorrow of separation
That gazes all night from star to star…
                                    Rabrindranath Tagore

Karin sat at the rickety, improvised plywood desk in her rented student room, interrupting her exam preparations for yet another letter to Raj, frowning over what to write in response to the more worrying aspects of his news.

Weeks had passed and all they had left from their dream were letters. Raj wrote every few days, sometimes even daily. With time, he became more passionate, calling her 'Princess of my World' and declaring over and over again, that he could not live much longer without her.

At first, she was flattered and soon sucked into the frenzy of the struggle to keep their young love alive, fresh and burning. Sometimes, he did not write like the older participant in the relationship, but rather like an impatient, lovelorn teenager. Then she had to reply with a sensible letter and had to calm him down, reassuring him that she was not about to give up on their plans of a reunion.

Since their separation, Karin had thrown herself dutifully into her studies, smothering her private longing with an enormous

71

revision program, occasionally interrupting her self-discipline by allowing herself to pour her feelings into yet another letter to her fiancé.

She had no choice but to study hard, to make sure that she would pass the examinations this year. She wanted to be free should she need to follow him. She heard her parent's warning ringing in her ears, that there would be no wedding if she left university without a degree.

Karin thanked her lucky stars that she had had the foresight, common sense and stamina to finish her thesis almost a year before it was due. It had already been typed up and lodged with the university librarian who would organise its binding

Karin sighed loudly. The house was silent; everyone who shared it with her had gone out. She unfolded the thin airmail pages of Raj's latest letter. The rectangular pale blue envelopes with their red and blue striped edges had become a lifeline, a symbol for their tenacity and an affirmation that they were not about to forget about each other. Two applications for a work and stay permit had already been rejected, not honouring the hours Raj had spent filling in forms and queuing up outside the German Consulate in Dhaka. The latter was a particular feat, according to his report, as the offices were only open twice weekly for two hours each time, allocating little time for the ever existing queues of impatient applicants. There was only one thing to do: to turn up long before the opening time and join whoever had had the same idea.

What Raj found most irksome was the fact, that his family could have fixed any amount of problems in their own country due to connections in almost every part of government, but they were powerless when it came to the world outside.

The first time, the papers had been sent off for approval in Germany, Raj and Karin had been so hopeful; in fact, they felt that the luck of the sincere would be on their side, but it wasn't to be. The application was swiftly rejected and returned to the Embassy like a well-launched boomerang. Raj had tried to ring Karin at her student flat from his office, but the telephone connection had broken down and he had to resort to explaining the details in yet another letter. They were both stunned and disbelieving, and decided unanimously that the best way forward was to remain persistent.

By the time the second request for residency had been rejected, their hearts were hardened and ready for the blow.

They had agreed that they would make as many attempts as needed to achieve their goal. The carefully filled in forms would be sent off for a third time, hope clinging to them like a drowning man to a buoy. Although Karin's youthful optimism and confidence were shaken, she refused to speculate on the outcome. A nervous knot in the pit of her stomach became a daily feature, like a burdensome companion whose presence she couldn't shake off.

Sometimes she allowed herself a small dose of self-pity. The only reward she truly wanted was denied her; just when she was supposed to race joyfully towards the end of her time at university, the end of all the efforts of the last three years, when a degree was in imminent reach, her private life had erred into a cul-de-sac and her future brought to an abrupt halt. Sometimes she thought that she did not even care about the degree any more, if she could not have the love of her life. What would she do, if Raj would never be granted to live with her in Germany: if he wasn't allowed to take up paid work? She would not mind being the bread winner if circumstances demanded it, but would he, having been brought up in the old-fashioned tradition, accept such a role reversal? And what else would he do – unpaid or charity work? It sounded unpalatable and undignified and she could, in her mind's eye, see him shaking his head in sadness.

There was one other solution: She could go to East Pakistan. However, there was one big obstacle – she wouldn't be welcome there until they were husband and wife.

Her parents were adamant that they would not allow her to be so foolish, that there would be no way that they could attend a wedding in East Pakistan. Marriage of their only daughter to a Muslim in their own country was fraud enough; they were not going to let her out of their sight to disappear to - what felt to them- the other side of the world. They would arrange the wedding as they had always intended to do, in their own country, the bride in a white dress being led up the aisle in a Christian church by her father.

'If you go to East Pakistan, we won't be able to help you if things go wrong,' they pleaded with panic in their voices.

Karin was past caring, but their plea opened a little chink of reason and gratitude into her armour of hopeless passion. She realised that they were looking out for her, and that was good to know. Surely, Raj would understand and appreciate it, too. Karin put a piece of cardboard from her cornflakes packet underneath the wobbly table leg to steady it. She read Raj's last letter again, which had arrived this morning.

'Princess of my Heart!'

He began most letters like that, adding more endearments as the writing progressed. Sometimes she feared that their relationship was becoming unreal, that they were clinging to an unattainable dream; that both their efforts might be futile in the end however much they railed against the injustice of it; and that maybe a union over such a distance wasn't meant to be.

She scolded herself when thoughts like these flitted across her mind.

'We have to remain positive,' Raj had chivvied her more than once, *'we shall win in the end'.* Often it did not feel like it.

On her desk, above Raj's letter, lay a book, opened at the page of a poem she had learnt at school. Leafing through her poetry collection, she had found it again and re-read it almost every day. Now she understood its meaning far better; it had become her consolation:

Mit zwei Worten – 'With two words' by Conrad Ferdinand Meyer.

It described the hopeless journey of a Saracen princess to find her beloved, the pilgrim Gilbert Becket, who had been imprisoned by her father and whom she had helped to escape. No warnings deterred her and she set out to find him knowing only two words, London and his name. She never wavered in her search until she was finally led to him and the poem concluded that *'Liebe wandert mit zwei Worten glaeubig ueber Meer und Land* – love travels with only two words trustingly over oceans and continents.

Karin took the Saracen's single-mindedness and faith to heart and resolved to follow her example. The poem inspired her whenever her spirits flagged and drove her on to explore new avenues which might lead to success. She would be a modern Saracen. Karin stared at the still blank sheet of airmail paper in front of her. She nibbled at the top of her pen, frown-lines between her brows deepening. She did not like the sound of what was happening in East Pakistan.

She knew that Pakistan had been founded in 1947 to separate the Hindus and the Muslims of India, who were constantly at each other's throat, and that the resulting states of East and

West Pakistan were supposed to be one country, in spite of being separated by two thousand miles and totally different languages, Urdu in the West and Bengali in the East.

Recently, Raj had indicated that there was unrest in his part of the country, that the Bengalis of East Pakistan were dissatisfied with their rulers in Karachi. They felt that all the profits from their jute and rice exports were being invested in building the new capital Islamabad in the western part, rather than being ploughed back into the country of origin. The Bengalis were tired of living in one of the poorest countries in the world where nothing ever improved, to be exploited economically like a colony, and to be ignored when it came to investments.

The rumblings of discontent had now become audible; the momentum towards a fight for independence grew. The Bengalis had not much to lose and thought it worth a try.

The students were the first to organise protests against the Pakistani rulers. Trying to hold back tears of fear and frustration, the letters swam in front of Karin's eyes and she could hardly summon up enough concentration to read:

> 'Princess of my Heart!' Raj wrote, 'I have sent off my third application to join you in Germany, but to tell you the truth, our political situation is deteriorating. If things carry on the way they do now, we shall sooner or later be at war with Pakistan, which means, that I might not be able to leave the country at all.'

A cold hand squeezed Karin's heart as if the ice-age had arrived.

'I shall go to him,' was her first impulse, but deep down she knew that, while it would have been against the Muslim customs to join Raj without being married to him, she certainly couldn't go there in war times. Her parents simply wouldn't let her throw herself into such a dangerous situation. If she still went ahead, they would never forgive her, never mind the heartache she would cause them. She was sure that they would try everything to stop her. Her anxious thoughts were interrupted by the intense ringing of the telephone.

Her mother called, who had heard some disturbing news about East Pakistan on the radio. Karin played down its importance and assured her that she had first hand information and that everything else was an exaggeration by the press.

Karin was surprised how easily it came to her to act and deceive, but thought it better not to communicate her sinking spirits and to protect her parents from worse news just a little longer.

Karin forced herself to reply to Raj's letter in a cheery and optimistic tone, reassuring him that she would wait for him whatever happened, hoping that she didn't sound frivolous.

She tried to discuss the political developments with some friends in her class, longing to hear some uninvolved, independent voices apart from her own, which kept going round and round in her head. However, they knew very little about East Pakistan, one of the smallest and poorest countries in the world. It was not a gap-year destination, and no-one had heard of an imminent independence war. She had to wait a week for the next instalment from Raj:

> 'The rumblings are getting stronger,' he wrote. 'We had elections, but the Pakistan National Assembly won't convene to install Sheikh Mujibur Rahman, as Prime Minister although he has been elected as our leader.'

Karin had never been much interested in politics and found it trying to be indirectly involved and dependent on the politics of a nation. Who ever was supposed to take up his position, what ever needed to be done, she didn't really care, she just wanted them to hurry up and finish the business, so that calm could be restored and Raj's third application could be processed as quickly as possible.

She began to read daily newspapers eagerly, scanning them mainly for news from East Pakistan. Indira Ghandi, the Prime Minister of India, seemed to take a keen interest in what the President of Pakistan, Yahya Khan did or didn't do. She voiced her dismay that Yahya Khan was dragging his feet and deliberately hindered the process of installing the leader of the winning Chattra League in East Pakistan, Sheikh Mujib, in his rightful place. The Pakistani Government had good reason: Sheikh Mujib had been very vocal in favour of an independent Bangladesh – land of the Bengalis. West Pakistani officials tried everything to avoid such a development, treating their brothers and sisters in the East like naughty children who needed punishment rather than more freedom.

More than two months after the elections, the Bengali regiments in the Pakistan Army mutinied and regrouped.

'They are training young Bengalis as guerrillas, called the Mukti Bahinis,' reported Raj dejectedly.

If she hadn't been personally involved, Karin would have thought: 'Good for them,' but this was not the news to clear the way for their reunion.

'The Mukti Bahinis with their red caps are everywhere,' he wrote, *'sneaking around the streets, houses and crouching in bushes. Even our neighbours' sons have joined. No one breathes a word when they re-appear not to endanger their safety. There are terrible rumours going round what will happen to them if they are caught by the military. University students are constantly on protest marches or sit-ins and normal lessons have been suspended.'*

By March 1971, Raj's letters began to arrive only sporadically. Karin was sure that he had continued to write, but that the political upheaval in his country was now affecting normal life and public services.

One very thick envelope got through. Raj had put all the latest information on ten sheets of thin airmail paper:

'Mita, my soul-mate, princess of my heart, if you have read the following report before don't think I have gone senile. I keep writing to you but fear that none of my letters will reach you. On peril that I might duplicate or even triplicate my news, this is the momentary situation:

Last Tuesday, the university students protested again, shouting their slogan of JOY BANGLA! , when the Pakistan Army under Tikka Khan, whom the students have now re-named THE BUTCHER OF BENGAL, came along the Phulbaria railtrack, bulldozed the slums of cardboard and tin shacks on either side, proceeded through Shakaripotti, a Hindu part of town, and fired indiscriminately into houses, while their megaphones were screaming 'Take Down The Bengali Flags!'

Karin took a deep breath before reading on:

'Sheikh Mujibur Rahman, our elected leader, has been arrested and flown to West Pakistan.

Our Major Zia has immediately declared independence on behalf of Mujib and as the provisional commander-in-chief of the Bangladesh Liberation Army.'

Raj left the worst news to the end:

'The rampage of the Pakistan Army ended at the University. They bombed the dormitories, the canteen and the Teacher-Student-Centre and many lives were lost.'

Karin was stunned. The indescribably dreadful had happened. Their fight for a visa had turned into a fight to survive occupation and war.

'Life has become complicated, my princess,' Raj continued, *'We are under curfew for most of the day and night; it is only lifted between two and six p.m., announced by shrill sirens. How I hate them! Even then we don't really feel safe to go out. Most businesses have stopped trading. New Market, where we used to do our shopping, has closed, and where ever we go there are check-points. Anyone, whom the soldiers suspect of having anything to do with the rebels, whether proven or not, can be arrested and imprisoned in the dark dungeons of the police stations.*

We have heard horror stories of torture. Completely innocent people have literally disappeared. Most of our neighbours, particularly the Hindus, have left Dhaka to return to their villages, where they expect to be safer. I hope for their sake that the rumours of a Pakistani Army trail of burnt out villages aren't true.'

Karin stood up from her desk, numb with shock and fear. Her legs were hardly supporting her and her knees were weak and trembling.

'I hate it,' Raj continued, *'when the army jeeps and tanks lumber through our streets megaphones blaring 'PAKISTAN ZINDABAD', followed usually by the latest warning or threat. They know fully well, how hated they are and that no right-thinking Bengali feels any allegiance to these occupiers.'*

Karin needed to enlist help and support. This was becoming too big for her to bear on her own. She decided on the spur of the moment to buy a train ticket and to use the May Bank Holiday to visit her parents in order to discuss strategies.

❧ ❧ ❧

'You see what a dangerous and volatile country this is.' Her mother overlooked entirely that, far from being glad that she was far removed from any such danger, Karin was worried out of her mind for Raj and his family.

Her father took a more understanding and practical attitude, sensing that she had come for advice rather than a lecture:

'I wonder whether my uncle in the Home Office could help...,' he suggested, throwing a yet imaginary life-line to Karin.

She had rarely heard of this uncle and she wasn't sure how and whether he could help, but it didn't matter now. Any path was better than just standing still, paralysed with terror and doing nothing. Karin decided to spend the rest of the week at home in order to find a way to contact this man, who ever he was, and beg him to save her future and her happiness. Two days later, Karin had an unexpected call from the local police station:

'Fraeulein Bach?'

'Yes, speaking...'

'Here is Sergeant Schmidt from Stuttgart Central Police Station.'

Karin held her breath and said nothing.

'We have here an application...' So Raj's third attempt had been sent off just before the political situation had worsened. '... an application for residency and work permits of a certain Mr. Khan?' The officer was fishing for a remark from her side. When none was forthcoming he asked, slightly more exasperated: 'Do you know such a person?'

'Yes,' she replied stiffly and thought by herself, 'and so should you from all the previous applications which you refused,' but she kept quiet. However, remembering that she might jeopardize the sergeant's good-will, she added in a more conciliatory voice: 'He is my fiancé'.

She heard him mutter under his breath: 'Is he now...' She chose to ignore this cutting remark and the disapproval in his voice.

'Well, just before I send it back to our Embassy in.... Where is it again?...' he seemed to rifle through a pile of documents, 'ah, there it is… Mr. Khan has applied from East Pakistan. So, before I send the answer back, I wanted you to know, because you were mentioned as the guarantor.'

Karin hated his rambling style, never finishing a thought or sentence properly. He still kept her in suspense about the most important part of his message: whether they were going to grant the permits.

'Yes?' Karin urged him on, her heart beating faster by the second like a car parking sensor approaching a wall.

'I am sorry to…' Karin heard the officious voice droning on while her world collapsed and her hopes were dashed once again. She did not listen to a word of the meaningless explanations and justifications. Through the fog of unhappiness, she could only hear him babbling on like a turned down radio in another room.

Suddenly, there was silence. 'Are you still there?' he asked concerned to be rid of this task which was becoming increasingly unpleasant.

'This is the third application to be turned down,' she tried to plead with his conscience. 'His country is in turmoil; he needs to get out.'

'I am sorry, rules are rules; the decision is irrevocable,' back into his official stride he seemed to enjoy rubbing salt into her wound.

'What am I to do?' she wailed more to herself than to this horrible man at the other end of the phone.

'There are only two possibilities, if you ask me,' he volunteered eagerly: 'you either forget him or, if you want somebody from the jungle, you have to join him there.'

Karin was so shocked by this unwelcome advice that she dropped the receiver, which dragged the entire telephone to the floor and cut the connection off.

She bent down to pick it up, placed the receiver on top and put it on the small hall table where it belonged. She then stumbled the few steps to the sitting room in a trance, threw herself into the nearest armchair and cried.

Her father found her there an hour later, tears still streaming down her face, sobs strangling her breaths. She did not need to say much; her father gathered without words what had happened.

'I tell you what,' said the man of action he liked to be, 'I shall ring uncle Konrad right now.' Karin had been lucky in her search for Konrad's whereabouts during the previous days. He had steadily climbed up the ministerial ladder and was well enough known to make it easy to find out how to contact him.

Her father got up and went to the telephone on the landing. She heard the clicks and rattles of the dialling wheel and then a hushed, brief conversation, of which she could not distinguish the words.

'He wants to see you tomorrow morning at ten in his office in the Federal Parliament Building,' her father proclaimed triumphantly. Karin's reaction was immediate: She sprang up, threw her arms around her father's neck and pressed her still wet cheeks against his face.

'Hold on, hold on,' he laughed. 'I didn't say that he would do it; he can't promise anything,' but when he saw a shadow cross her face, he quickly added: 'but he will try.' The next morning, she was up early and left the house well in time for her appointment. She felt as if she was going into battle; she needed to win this war against bureaucracy, nonsensical rules, prejudice and politics. Their future depended on it

'I have seen you last when you were that high,' uncle Konrad, every inch the distinguished minister, smiled kindly and held his hand at the height of a three year old. Then he motioned her to sit down opposite his vast mahogany desk on a lusciously upholstered armchair.

He listened attentively to her story, which she tried to keep free of accusations and criticism. He made notes on a yellow legal pad, nodded from time to time, asked an occasional question and smiled encouragingly at her answers.

They were interrupted by a phone call, which he kept brief, and then he brought their meeting to a close. He stood up, came round the desk and shook her hand warmly.

'I shall look into it and do my best,' he said in his deep, sonorous voice, but already in a businesslike manner, eager to be getting on with his next task: 'You will hear from me soon. Will you be at your parents' house for the next few days?'

'Yes, for as long as it takes,' she assured him gratefully and turned to go with a little more spring in her step than she had come in with less than half an hour ago. It felt good to have a mighty ally.

She had hardly set foot in her parents' place, when the telephone rang and she was called to it.

81

'Here is Konrad,' he said, obviously in great haste, 'I can't talk long, but I want you to go this afternoon to the Central Police Station. Give them two hours to organise the paperwork. The visa and work permit will be waiting there. Good luck, Karin, and let me know when you get married!'

She had only seconds to express her gratitude and immense feeling of relief and joy, before he hung up with a 'you are very welcome. And give my regards to your parents.'

Shortly afterwards, a policeman rang to say that Karin could pick up the visa at 3 p.m., that they would fax copies of the papers to the Embassy in Dhaka immediately and that she might wish to send various copies, too, in order to make sure that at least one got through to its destination. Karin was hovering outside the police station's door long before three o'clock and went in on the dot.

'Sergeant Schmidt?' So that's what he looked like, tall, athletic, squashed into a uniform which seemed a little tight, bully-ish with a miserable expression on his face.

'He does not enjoy his job,' she concluded.

'Yes?' he looked at her raising his eyebrows until he realised who she was. Karin hoped that he would remember how rude he had been to her that same morning and would squirm inside. But his arrogant demeanour indicated that he had probably seen nothing shameful in his comments.

'I have come to pick up the visa and work permit for my fiancé, Mr. Khan,' she said in a determined voice, looking straight at him. She would have liked to add that she didn't have to go to the jungle after all, but she bit her tongue. There was nothing to be gained from being sarcastic.

'Fine,' he said curtly avoiding sheepishly having to look at her again. 'I don't know why the boss suddenly changed his mind,' he muttered, waving wads of papers undecidedly in the air.

'Never mind,' Karin chose a conciliatory tone to hurry him along to hand them over. The sergeant suddenly lost his taste for verbal fencing and, as if bored, he put the papers on the counter, turned and disappeared behind a door.

Karin grabbed them as if fire was threatening to burn them and ran out of the building. The telephone lines in East Pakistan had been out of order for weeks, so she went to the nearest post office and sent telegrams to Raj's home, his office and the Embassy:

'Visa granted. Papers in post. Prepare to leave. Mita.'

It had become quite natural for her to adopt and sign in the Bengali name he had given her inadvertently as a term of endearment – Mita, my soulmate, my love.

Elated and impatient, she waited for days for any reaction to her good news, but none came.

Instead, she received a letter delayed by three weeks, describing the incarceration everyone had to suffer daily. At least, Raj's family lived in nice houses and the servants could smuggle themselves out to buy whatever food was available. It wasn't a matter what was needed any more, but of what people had managed to salvage, had grown in their gardens or had stored away which they were now offering on the black market.

Appetites had diminished and communal mealtimes, usually such jolly gatherings of young and old relatives and friends, had become silent, sad affairs. The country was hoping for Sheik Mujibur's return and guidance, but war on his behalf was much more likely.

Reading this belated letter, Karin felt as if time had stood still and events of past weeks were repeating themselves, while things her end had moved on. What she was waiting for never came, the news that Raj had received the visa and that he was on his way out of the country, out of danger to join her. The waiting seemed endless and cruel. Every night she went to bed in the hope that the new day would bring the message; she dragged herself through the day, revising half-heartedly for her final examinations, always listening out for the telephone to ring or a postman to knock with a telegram. In the evenings she packed her books away, down-hearted, but having done her duty. She usually watched a little television with her parents to give them company, and when they went to bed she crept silently into hers, trying to hold back the tears. She was exhausted, physically and mentally.

Before falling asleep, she forced herself to think positively of the tomorrow, avoiding strenuously to entertain guesses what harm Raj could have come to, preventing him to reply. She became quite adept at convincing and consoling herself that their reunion was only a matter of time, and she usually fell immediately into a deep, heavy sleep, feeling pinned down as if an elephant had sat on her chest all night.

Helplessly, she watched the pictures on news programmes of pre-war chaos in Bangladesh to which the world had suddenly woken up. Karin hoped fervently that Raj would be well enough placed to protect himself and to find a way out.

She was proven right. Finally, one morning the telegram was delivered:

'Arrive Saturday 8.45 p.m. from Karachi. Raj.'

Saturday was today. Karin was totally confused by elation and non-comprehension; the sudden resolution of her worries seemed unreal. Her parents took the news stoically, emitting signs of relief that the strain their daughter had been under was lifted. After all, their priority had never changed: They still wanted her to do well in her imminent examinations.

It was the second time that Karin waited for Raj at Stuttgart airport. This time, she was less curious and excited, but tired and impatient after months of worrying and fighting. When she saw him come through the automatic doors, she could not belief the visual change in him. He looked dishevelled; his usually glossy, black hair was greasy and had resisted a hurried tidy-up. He had dark shadows under his sunken eyes and he carried one medium sized, battered suitcase, as if he had only come for a weekend visit.

They couldn't speak, choked by emotion; they stood there clinging to each other as if encircled by sharks.

Happiness was the wrong feeling for the occasion. He hugged her lifelessly as if clinging limply to a wet rock, prepared to be swept away again any moment. She took his face between her hands and looked into his sad eyes.

'My brother in the Pakistan Army helped me to get out, but I was arrested in Karachi because no one could understand my German visa,' he whispered. It was laughable but neither of them felt like laughing.

She realised that he had gone through many more privations than she had. No wonder he looked haunted and ill.

'How long did they keep you?'

'Three days,' his voice was clipped with bitterness.

'But...', Karin felt that what he was about to say was what was really breaking his heart.

'War has been declared and I had to leave my entire family behind. I have no idea whether I shall ever see them again.'

He put his head on her shoulder and wept almost silently.

Chapter Nine

 C380

Yet my heart is sweet
With the memory of the first fresh jasmines
Rabrindranath Tagore

'How long will you be staying?' Karin enquires glad to chat away the boredom and discomfort of a long plane journey.

'Only two weeks; I have to get back for enrolment,' Serena sighs, gathering her belongings in the efficient way of a Western working parent used to multi-tasking.

'Omar, make sure you do not leave anything behind,' she admonishes the little lad.

Karin scribbles something onto a thin, white paper serviette, a left-over from breakfast.

'Here is my London telephone number,' she says kindly to Serena. 'Call me when you get back!'

Karin has really taken to this young Bengali woman who is in the unenviable situation of being torn between the traditional role as a mother and wife and that of a career girl. If Serena were married in Bangladesh, the problem would not arise. The path of a Bengali wife is well trodden and does not allow for diversions like career or hobbies. Serena is not likely to find sympathy with the relatives for her need to study and improve herself beyond the role of wife and mother; they will, however, be delighted to look after the little one.

How well Karin understands the dilemma! After all these years, she can still recall the boredom that had engulfed her and the wave of panic sweeping over her, when she wasn't allowed to do anything about it, panic that life would pass her by.

'I'll give you a ring,' Serena promises. She folds the serviette several times and stuffs it into a flat leather purse embossed with green and gold squares.

'She looks so vulnerable', thinks Karin, 'too delicate to carry such a heavy responsibility on her thin shoulders,' but then she remembers that she had been in a far worse situation and had coped.

'Have a lovely holiday,' she says.

She can just hear: 'You too,' before the young mother and her little boy slot into the orderly queue in the aisle. Karin can see the young woman bend down to Omar to say something, before both of them give her a last wave. Her heart warms and she waves back happily. Seconds later, they have disappeared in the crowd.

Karin leans back in her seat and looks through the small oval window onto the grey runway. The sky is overcast and does not give an indication of the temperature outside.

'Are you alright?' One of the air hostesses smiles down on her.

'Oh, I am sorry,' stutters Karin in embarrassment and tries to gathers up her three things all at once, dropping her handbag on the floor in the process.

'That's absolutely fine. You take your time'. Her voice is reassuring, but Karin knows that the crew is tired and keen to head for a hotel bed or home.

'I won't slip into my coat,' she decides. 'It is probably boiling hot outside'. She drapes it between the handles of her handbag, grabs her little suitcase and gets up. Passing the aircrew on the way out, she gives her thanks and steps out into the dull summer's day at Zia International Airport, Dhaka.

The heat hits her like a squall of steam and she finds it hard to breath.

'Slowly… count to eight… in… out…. in… out,' as years of yoga have taught her. The heat is all-enveloping, inescapable and stifling and the noise from crowds of people milling around assaults her ears with brute force. Everyone is busy with something that seems most important. It reminds her of returning to school after a peaceful summer break and hearing the avalanche of hundreds of fellow pupils' voices excitedly comparing notes.

She climbs down the steps of the gangway, holding on to the handrail. She is the last to leave the plane. Karin can see the low, flat-roofed airport building. It doesn't seem to have changed much. The white paint is flaky as can be expected after the monsoon season. She remembers that residences had to be painted every year to keep their fresh and clean look of opulence.

It is a short distance to walk across the tarmac and she makes her way from the gangway to the entrance of the building in a few minutes. It feels like wading through a sauna.

The heat does not diminish when she steps inside the airport building, in spite of the whirr of air-conditioning and ceiling fans. The air is thick with the breath and sweat of passengers, their families, who have come to pick them up, airport officials, and people trying to make a meagre living out of the comparatively wealthy travellers passing through. However, there seems to be more space between bodies than in the past when half the population seemed to have gathered in this one hall.

To her surprise there are no beggars.

'These are new, too,' she thinks as she notices huge signs directing her to 'baggage' and 'passport control'. There are two luggage carousels which are separated by a transparent glass wall from the luggage handlers. Karin can't help smiling. She is impressed by the two conveyor belts for passengers' luggage. Somehow, she doubts that they are wide enough for big suitcases, but they will do for hers.

'I bet the rate of theft has gone down at the airport with all these precautions,' she thinks.

Her family had always been disparaging about the blatant dishonesty of staff who would steal whenever an opportunity arose. When she was part of them, it had been a bone of contention and Karin's remark about the tremendous gulf between the rich and the poor, which made stealing often an act of necessity, had been received with stony silence.

She feels awkward and fears she might stand out by being dressed in western clothes, however modest. The women around her wear mostly saris or shalwaar kameeze.

'Please come this way, Madam.' A young airport official, as handsome as if he had just stepped out of a Bollywood movie, with thick black hair, soulful eyes and a neatly trimmed moustache, waves her out of the disorderly queue with the most ravishing smile.

Karin scolds herself for even noticing, but follows him on a shortcut route to his immigration desk.

He scrutinises Karin's passport at great length. He then asks her politely but sternly to open the small suitcase she has retrieved. He hardly touches what she has packed, but stares at the inside of the case in bafflement.

'Have you no other luggage?' he asks with the fiercely rolled 'r' and clipped vowels of the Bengali accent. She seems to be the only traveller who doesn't produce huge bags full of – she guesses – presents for the relatives.

She shakes her head.

He studies her face but shies away from looking into her eyes. They both remain silent, and Karin is uncertain what will happen next. She looks around, over the heads of her fellow passengers. She can't see Serena with her little boy. Dhaka has swallowed them up already.

At last, the immigration officer closes Karin's suitcase, hands it to her, nods and indicates with an impatient wave of the hand that she should proceed. She smiles gratefully, but he is already busy with the next person.

His voice suddenly booms behind her, fast and precise like fire from a machine gun. Karin can see from the corner of her eyes that the victim is a Bengali man with two huge, bulging pieces of luggage. The official, joined by two more nosey and self-important colleagues, pounces on him with a battery of questions.

Karin is a little stunned how this charming young man can change into a ferocious bully within seconds, but she catches a warning look from him. She has no intention of getting involved, and scuttles quickly away, following the sign to the exit. The automatic doors open and she steps out into Dhaka life.

☙ ☙ ☙

Karin's senses are assaulted as they have not been assaulted for nearly forty years. She feels as if she will be sucked into a nation, a country, a life without being able to resist. She is engulfed by a crowd of people which stretches as far as the eye can see. Many seem to wait for relatives or friends to be spewed out from the automatic airport doors.

No sooner has Karin appeared in the open door, when men, most of them shorter than her, thin, wiry figures, run towards her, gesticulating wildly, to tout for her fare. She tucks her suitcase between her feet on the ground and tries to assess the situation. One particularly eager chap tries to get hold of the handle, assuring her in broken English, that his taxi was the best of all and that he would take her anywhere she wanted to go, however far.

'Anywhere in world, Madam,' he stutters excitedly, giggling about his own exaggeration.

Karin shakes her head and waves him away. It is safer to ask an airport official to choose a chauffeur, she remembers. Before she heads back into the building she marvels at the colourful, chaotic scene.

There are three distinct crowds:

The well dressed who seem to wait for relatives and consist of men in formal suits or western leisure wear; they are joined by women in their best saris, neatly arranged at the waist, gathered a little to the left, so that the folds of the precious material sway and open with every step like a fan; in their midst are old men in white Punjabi pyjamas, skull caps and sleeveless, black Nehru overcoats; girls still young enough to dress in *salwaar kameezes*, baggy trouser suits in striking colours and with most delicate embroideries on the tops which reach down to their thighs; and finally, little boys in jeans and T-shirts, running around, being bored by it all. There is an atmosphere of jollity, laughter and expectation until they recognise the guests they have been waiting for. Then they storm towards them like a big jellyfish to absorb them lovingly into their circle.

The second group consists of men in scuffed trousers and shirts; they are the chauffeurs of baby-taxis or company cars. There are some rickshaw wallahs wearing cotton *lungis*, cloths in square pattern prints which are wound and knotted around their waists, reaching down over their knees. Most of them wear a white shirt over the *lungi* to give them a more professional appearance. They are descending eagerly upon the visitors like a swarm of bees around a flowering bush. Their day's profit depends on their efforts; thousands compete against each other.

Karin can see a few bicycle rickshaws, but far fewer than she remembers. Most rickshaw wallahs seem to have prospered enough to be owners of baby taxis. The three- wheeled motor scooters look cheerful boasting lovingly painted side panels and roofs, depicting popular movie scenes or religious symbols.

The third group, the poorest in the crowd, wear crumbled cotton saris or tattered *lungis* without tops: they are the beggars, who furtively stretch out their hands, mumbling a few words to encourage the tourist to part with coins, before they are being moved on by impatient airport officials.

It is a clash of the new and the old; the new system trying to establish discipline and an air of western progress and modernity, while the sheer numbers of the old threatens to overwhelm most good intentions.

Karin spots a little girl, about eight years old, in a blue dress which looks odd and alien on her. It is too big, stained and clearly from a past fashion era in Europe or America, something that was distributed by a charitable organisation. The little girl stands in the middle of the crowd, all by herself, motionless. She stares at the hubbub around her, bewildered and overawed, with big dark eyes in a tiny brown face. One of her little hands is stretched out in a beggar's gesture, but it hangs in the air as if it had forgotten its purpose..

Karin steps towards her and pushes a bank note into the little palm. To her surprise, the fingers snap closed over it with the speed of a carnivorous plant.

Karin hates to give money – she has always preferred to pay for clothes or food instead to be sure her gift was useful – but at the moment she has nothing else to offer. The girl's huge eyes light up and her whole face bursts into a smile: This will probably feed her family for a week It makes Karin's heart sing as it hasn't done in a long time.

A man in uniform approaches and Karin quickly puts her hand over the girl's palm.

'Go quickly,' she says.

She doesn't know whether the girl understands English, but her urgent tone seems to convey the message. Another burst of happiness spreads over the girl's face before she disappears among the bodies and legs. 'Mrs. Khan?'

Karin straightens up in alarm and faces the man who now stands in front of her.

'The Radisson Water Garden Hotel sends me. I am your chauffeur.'

The surprise must show in Karin's face because he adds in

faultless English: 'We always pick up our guests to guarantee their safe transfer.'

'That's very kind,' Karin mumbles and feels relieved to be given an escape route to calmer surroundings. He leads her to the new airport car park and a shiny, black limousine. He holds the door open to the back seat and she sinks gratefully into the luxurious upholstery.

It takes less than ten minutes to swish along the wide Airport Road. From the sheltered, air-conditioned interior of the limousine, she looks out onto the traffic and the struggling masses of people on and beside the road. She is now too tired to feel anything for them and is looking forward to a cooling shower, a few refreshments, maybe a little nap and a dutiful call to her daughter to say that she has arrived safely.

'

Chapter Ten

CRXO

That I want thee, only thee –
Let my heart repeat without end
Rabrindranath Tagore

It came as no surprise that Karin had passed her degree course in record time. There were no official celebrations to go back to and the degree certificate was sent through the post in a strengthened and padded brown envelope. Deep down she was pleased, but her mind was on other things.

Her father insisted on one evening without wedding talk in order to salvage some importance for her achievement. He uncorked several bottles of champagne which even Raj could not resist. The four of them spent a merry evening like on an oasis of light-heartedness, before – as they knew they would – the hectic wedding preparations would take over again.

Years later, she wasn't sure whether she had coaxed Raj into a hasty marriage. He seemed to trot along resignedly and to agree to everything she and her parents suggested. Even when she asked for his opinion, which she often did, he did not seem to care much one way or another. She attributed this lacklustre absentmindedness to his worry for what was happening in his country and concerns for his family.

She justified to herself the briskness in driving on proceedings with the argument that he was old enough to stop her if marriage wasn't what he wanted.

It was clear that nobody from his family could make the journey to the wedding, but he assured her that once peace had descended again, he would take her home and that his family would organise unimaginably lavish celebrations for the new couple. It would not be soon, by the sounds of the radio and television news, so she pushed those plans to the back of her mind.

Karin was immensely surprised that the protestant vicar had no objections to marry them in a Christian church.

'Raj, are you sure you won't mind us getting married in a Christian church?' she enquired, a little doubtful that everything should work out so smoothly.

'No, our religions are fundamentally similar. Jesus is a prophet to us, while to you he is the son of God. We respect that and it's not an obstacle.'

She sighed with relief.

'When we visit your family, we shall marry again, according to your customs,' she promised, Her eagerness to show that she had preserved her sense of fairness, was rewarded: Raj laughed out loud, a rare event since his return. The wedding celebrations began on a Friday, when they went to the Registry Office in the Town Hall. However, first of all, they had to say a big 'thank you'.

'This is my fiancé, Raj Khan,' she introduced him to the man who had come to their rescue. Her eyes shining with happiness, she found uncle Konrad even more impressive than on her first visit. He smiled broadly from one to the other, revelling in their togetherness and his good deed.

'Well, your husband in an hour's time,' he shook their hands warmly in congratulation.

He thoughtfully enquired after the welfare of Raj's family, expressing regret for the political situation, but moving back swiftly to the imminent joyous event of their marriage vows.

'We shall go for lunch afterwards. Would you care to join us?'

'That's very kind of you, but I shall be on my way to the airport in less than an hour. So thank you for your invitation and for taking time to come and see me on such an important day.'

They said their good-byes and he sent them off with many good wishes.

They rejoined her parents and Karin's god-mother, who would act as best woman, while her father had agreed to be best man to his new son-in-law who had no one from his side of the family there. Raj bravely kept assuring everyone that his relatives were thinking of them, secretly doubting whether they had actually received the news of his wedding date.

The official ceremony went ahead good-naturedly and with a lot of grinning and nudging from her aunt.

When they were legally husband and wife, everyone present kissed them, and her aunt whispered in her ear:

'If you hadn't married him, I would have.'

'Auntie!' Karin exclaimed in mock-horror and added in a fit of giggles:

'Too late! He is mine!'

They had booked lunch in a renowned restaurant nearby, and the rest of the afternoon was taken up with last minute preparations for the white wedding in a Rococo castle on the following day. In the morning, they were expecting a very special guest.

'I feel so sad that none of your relatives can come to our wedding,' Karin had said one evening shortly before their big day.

'Well, I haven't heard from my brother Jamal who is studying in London, which means he can't afford the fare,' Raj replied wistfully. He saw a sudden impish gleam in her eyes and knew that she was hatching a plan. He got up and rang his brother as she asked him to do.

'He will try to come himself, but it will have to be by train, and he can't bring his wife and little daughter,' was the outcome.

Raj had hardly finished speaking when she blurted out her next idea:

'Let him come by train, but it would be so much nicer if he could have his wife and baby here as well...'

'They really can't afford it; he is still a student and Nasma is only working part-time in a nursery.'

'We can,' she brushed his argument away. 'We shall book them on a flight, so that they arrive in the morning of the wedding. We just have to send someone to collect them from the airport.'

'I don't think his wife can take leave at such short notice,' he warned.

'She can fly home on Sunday if she wishes. Just imagine, it would be so much fun.'

Karin was in full flow. Nothing would stop her.

They rang Raj's sister-in-law, Nasma, in London who happily agreed to the sudden change of plan and promised to keep it a secret. The flight tickets were easily arranged over the telephone and sent by telex to London, while Karin's father volunteered to do the taxi service.

There was no way that Raj and his bride could be in separate houses before their wedding day, as would have been the custom in his country, so her parent's flat was overflowing and the hairdresser had to do her job in a chaos of clothes, shoes, cosmetics, presents, cards and flowers.

Brother Jamal appeared suddenly at the door, dishevelled and tired after a fourteen hour train journey. They plied him with strong, sugary tea and sandwiches and then left him to slump in an arm chair, while they buzzed around him.

Karin's father had slipped away quietly but wasn't missed. An hour later they heard footsteps on the stairs, chattering voices and a key turning in the lock.

Jamal woke up from his doze, when the high-pitched voice of a little girl made everyone turn. Kitty, a little confident three year old with her thick black hair bunched at the sides of her sweet round face and dark eyes blazing with excitement, strode through the door.

'Daddy, Daddy!' she shouted happily, throwing herself into his lap before he had a chance to get up. Nasma, her mother, followed in, smiling with pride, indulgence and pleasure at the surprise she saw on her husband's face. Karin embraced her new relatives with warmth and gratitude for agreeing to represent at least a part of Raj's family.

'I have bees in my veil,' Karin whispered to Raj while they were kneeling in front of the altar and the vicar had turned his back.

Raj looked at her incredulously and then they both had to suppress a giggle.

'You have to wait till we are outside,' he whispered back, 'we don't want the vicar to be stung,' which set them both off again.

Striding along the central aisle, she had felt regal in her white Marie-Antoinette Empire style dress with short puff-sleeves, tear drop embroideries and a white long lace train trailing behind her on the floor. But now she longed for the ceremony to be over and to be declared husband and wife. The bees buzzing around her head didn't help. There was no kissing the bride in a German chapel but after sliding their wedding rings over each other's ring fingers the service came to a close. The eighty odd guests, seated in the pews, got up and smiled at the young couple as they passed on their way out to the sonorous sounds of an ancient organ.

After many months of struggle, it felt for the first time that everyone was on their side, that the bad times were over and that from now on life could only get better. It was an extremely hot summer's afternoon and the stifling air hit them as they came out of the cool chapel to the cheers of family and friends.

No sooner had they reached the portals when Raj lifted her lace veil and after much gentle shaking and coaxing, he managed to release the bees from their confinement and Karin from considerable anxiety. Well-wishers streaming out of the chapel and gathering around the happy couple to congratulate were at first intrigued, but the consternation turned quickly into general hilarity when everyone realised why Raj tried to dismantle his bride's headdress.

People had been very kind but as Karin looked around, she saw only friends of her parents, none of her own. 'How odd,' she thought; growing up as a single child, she had obviously been too sheltered to form any lasting friendships of her own. She couldn't wait to join Raj's big family and maybe have one of her own. The celebrations continued with pomp and luxury. The young couple's meal was served on gold platters and seemed to go on for hours. This was followed by a short break for everyone to freshen up and rest before the evening's dancing began. Karin and Raj had chosen a waltz to dance to in front of their gathered guests and did well considering that she had to teach him ballroom dancing from scratch in her parent's flat and within a few weeks. After their first round of waltzing alone on the dance floor, several other couples joined them and Raj relaxed considerably, swinging her around less energetically than when all eyes had been on them.

They couldn't remember much afterwards, but fell into bed, both exhausted and elated as if they had climbed a huge mountain and had reached the top. There was no question of making love; they fell asleep instantaneously, arms slung around each other, never to let go again.

Through the mist of her busy new life after the wedding, Karin took not much notice of developments in East Pakistan and its fight for independence. She enjoyed the responsibility of her new job as an interpreter in a multi-national company; furnished their spacious new apartment, which her father had organised through an architect friend of his, and settled down to married life. Apart from being the bread-winner, she had taken over single-handedly the running of their finances, the household and Raj's career plans.

He was short-listed for two positions in well-known companies, he deemed worthy of his education and expertise, but he wasn't chosen and ended up taking a less glamorous job close to home. The small company importing fruit and vegetables were delighted when they secured his services.

Karin realised that Raj battled against inner demons telling him that he was under-selling himself; the unsatisfactory career prospects did not exude the permanence she had hoped for. However much she consoled him pointing out that this lowly beginning would surely not be for long, Raj plodded listlessly from one working day to another. At home he immersed himself into writing letters to his relatives and searching for news in newspapers and television.

His letters didn't elicit replies, but sometimes an out-of-context snippet found its way across the thousands of miles, assuring him that the family were surviving intact, Insh'Allah.

The political wrangles between the two parts of Pakistan turned into an international headache. India and Russia signed a treaty and supported the rebels of the Independence movement. Pakistan failed to secure international assistance; even the United Nations ignored their appeal. Finally, after nine months, Pakistan lost its hold over its Bengali brothers and sisters. The guerrilla war was won by the Mukti Bahini rebels with the help of India.

Raj and Karin were unaware, when it happened, but during late afternoon of the 16th December 1971, the phone rang at Karin's parents flat.

They quickly re-directed the callers to the young couple's new number. Ten minutes later, Raj received the crackly news that the war was over, that his country was now officially independent and called Bangladesh, that Sheikh Mujibur Rahman had been released and installed as first Prime Minister of the new state and most of all, that everyone in his family had survived the war in good health.

The only drop of bitterness in the family's fortune was that Rashid, their brother in the Pakistan army, was now a prisoner of war. No-one knew for how long. Raj felt particularly sad knowing that Rashid had pulled many strings to get him out of the country moments before the outbreak of war.

Raj's excited voice and the high pitched, near hysterical sounds coming through the receiver told Karin, how overjoyed everyone was, notwithstanding the worry about Rashid's fate. When Raj hung up, tears were streaming down his face.

Their life resumed and Raj was writing even more letters home than before, knowing that they would reach their destination.

Karin enjoyed her new job, but however much pecuniary reward and professional recognition it brought, she could not ignore that Raj had become restless. It was not discontent alone with his mediocre job; it was more a matter of wanting to be back with his people, sharing in the celebrations of their new status in the world and about wanting to be part of the country's reconstruction.

Karin averted an immediate decision by suggesting he invite some members of his family for a reunion. His eldest sister Hasina and her husband Ahmed took up the offer immediately and stayed for a month in the following spring. This, she was told, was a great honour because, according to Islamic law, Karin and Raj were not yet married, but it was acknowledged and accepted that in the eyes of European law they were husband and wife. It was a relatively sunny spring but a lot of woolly garments had to be bought and the central heating had to be switched to higher temperatures so that the visitors would not catch a chill. Their roomy flat looked suddenly crowded.

Raj perked up and seemed so much happier chatting the evenings away after elaborate meals which his sister had cooked 'with her own fair hand'. At home, Karin was told, Hasina rarely cooked because she had the services of a professional chef who wouldn't even let her in the kitchen.

Outings with the guests were complicated because the saris were not suitable for the chilly outdoors. They had to be supplemented by thick cardigans, pullovers and coats; the flimsy sandals were replaced by sturdier shoes and bare legs and feet clad in nylon tights, to which the saris clung.

It was nice for Karin to come home at night to a cooked meal, but she hardly dared look at the curry splattered cooker, wall tiles and kitchen floor. Obviously, her sister-in-law was a great cook, but was not used to a small kitchen nor to cleaning up as she went along.

Usually Karin ended up attacking the stack of dirty pots and dishes alone in her kitchen, too exhausted to protest or ask for help. When she once mentioned it to Raj in their bedroom, he reproached her:

'They are not your servants. It is an honour that she cooks; you can't expect her to do the washing up as well.'

And that was that. Karin was too tired to argue, maybe on the lines that it would be nice if h e could offer some help, but she knew that he was busy enjoying their company. She felt ungrateful and, to atone, asked her sister-in-law to teach her Bengali recipes at the weekends.

Privacy was non-existent, but nobody seemed to miss or desire it like she did. Snatched moments of intimacy with her husband; an occasional hour of quiet reading or listening to a radio play; or just going for a solitary walk – there was no time for any of this; her longing was drowned in companionable chatter.

Karin's suggestions of visits to historical and cultural places were tolerated but ticked off on an invisible list of 'must see' points after a hurried inspection and everyone's photograph being taken in front of it. No-one showed any genuine interest.

The only activity her visitors seemed to throw themselves into whole-heartedly was shopping. Karin was absolutely astonished how well-informed they were about brand names of all sorts of things from cosmetics to electrical equipment. Karin had never been an avid shopper and found it excruciatingly boring to scour the shops up and down the malls only to end up buying from the first place they had visited hours beforehand. However, her visitors relished rummaging through items on offer at a snail's pace, and Karin had to muster every ounce of patience not to leave them there and head for home.

The visit had clearly revived Raj's spirit. It was, therefore, decided that two more should follow, one by his brother Khaled and his wife Farah and the second by his youngest and most favourite sister Mumtaz. They all left children behind in Bangladesh, but they knew that the extended family and a large support group of servants would look after them well. Mumtaz, however, brought her youngest daughter Suriya with her and, unaccustomed to look after the child herself, she struggled and left a lot of the childcare to Karin who had taken some days off work. Karin felt often schizophrenic: power dressing in the mornings for work, only to change into a cotton sari when she got home, slaving over a hot stove for hours over recipes she had only just learnt. Thankfully, these visitors did not insist on cooking and messing up her kitchen. During the day, Karin was the efficient, highly paid western career woman while turning into a Bengali housewife in the evenings making every effort to please her husband and his guests. She became worryingly thin, felt permanently exhausted and edged towards readiness for a change.

When Mumtaz and Suriya had left, Karin took stock. Raj had never really settled. Admittedly he praised the comforts and amenities of western life, shops full of goods, food in plenty, well-organised and well-functioning public transport, health service, easy access to travel and the lack of natural disasters, but his heart was elsewhere, he never stopped hankering after his homeland, his old life and his family.

When she once asked him whether he didn't consider her to be his family now, he looked at her in a hurt, puzzled way and replied that she had married into his family and was therefore part of their lives. Her heart, it was obviously expected, should belong to Bangladesh, too. The last visitor during their first year of marriage was a young girl of seventeen, the eldest daughter of Lakshmi, Raj's middle sister.

Priti was strikingly beautiful in a womanly way beyond her age. Her skin shimmered like cocoa-coloured satin, her large brown eyes blazed with youthful exuberance and sheer joy of adventure, and her long mane of thick black hair cascaded down her back and framed her round face with defiant curls. Her dazzling smile revealed rows of perfectly straight, white teeth and a dimple on either side of her mouth completed the impression of cheekiness whenever she laughed. Priti was a delight to have around, cheerful, a little flirtatious, a little disrespectful to her upbringing, knowing that her western auntie would remain discreet; discreet about things she was up to during her stay; innocent things like promenading provocatively up and down the main shopping street in her most glamorous saris, enjoying the attention she attracted and the ripples of curiosity and chatter she created. She would come home after such an outing and tell her auntie, excitedly and laughing happily, all about it.

Nothing of this could, of course, be relayed to uncle Raj who would have felt compelled to tell her off as the guardian of his niece's virtue. He would not have understood the innocent pleasures the young girl derived. Niece and auntie, not too distant in age from one another, kept quiet about what would have upset him unnecessarily. Karin did not feel guilty; she had Priti's promise that she would always tell her the truth and that she would be most careful with new acquaintances.

Karin only followed her once at a safe distance, to supervise an invitation to an ice cream by a lanky young student. They sat on an outside terrace of a café in the middle of town chatting animatedly. After a little more than an hour, Priti got up like a good girl, leaving the young man totally confused by her dazzling smile, but without proffering any points of further contact with him. Priti met her auntie at a safe distance, slipped her arm through Karin's and proceeded to tell her breathlessly about this harmless date:

'He was nice,' she said grinning sheepishly, but she was obviously not impressed enough to repeat the experience.

Priti would have loved to stay longer in Germany, but her family recalled her. College was beckoning – she was to study Bengali literature; very suitable for a young woman who was going to get married anyway; nothing that would lead to the desire of an all consuming career. As this was the fate of most Bengali girls, she accepted it, simply shrugging her shoulders and hoping that her parents would choose a good husband for her..

'I shall see you soon in Bangladesh, auntie,' Priti said when they took her back to the airport. Karin wasn't quite sure whether her niece knew more than she did.

PART TWO

Part Two

Chapter Eleven

*I thought I would write love's words
in their own colour...*
Rabrindranath Tagore

Karin's parents were appalled when their daughter first suggested that the young couple might move to Bangladesh. They fought tooth and nail with water-tight and very plausible arguments: 'Once you are in that country, we won't be able to help you if things go wrong,' her father pointed out more than once with genuine anguish in his voice.

'Raj will be looking after me. Why do you think it should go wrong? What exactly?' she retorted hotly, hating herself for rejecting their caring concern.

'We thought we had made it clear that we wanted you here,' her mother added coldly.

'Raj is not happy in his job and he misses his family.'

'So will you... we hope. You will give up more, than he ever did coming here,' her mother sounded embittered and sarcastic.

'Why did you both fight so much for his visa and work permit if he wanted to go back all along?' Her father's arguments hit her where it hurt. She had asked herself the same question.

'It just hasn't turned out as well as he had hoped,' she replied lamely.

'He hasn't given it much time. He should know better. He is old enough and he has been to this country before.'

There was nothing more Karin could add in reply.

'Just don't convert to Islam, keep your passport with you at all times and take your marriage contract with you; at least it will guarantee you the protection of the German Embassy and a free flight home. I shall keep a copy here, just in case.'

Karin hated the businesslike and pragmatic approach displayed by her father in looking at relationships and what was to her an exciting new life. She was grateful that he worried and maybe he was right in some points, but her relationship with Raj was built on love, trust and respect for each other. It might have looked foolish to some outsiders that her life was leading her away from German society and conventions, but in a way, she was glad about that. Competitiveness and materialism had never been her thing; she had never understood why it was so important to consider what other people might think.

Raj was her husband, admittedly enigmatic at times which had to be expected considering he came from a completely different culture. She had come to love the unconventional, the exoticism and the courage it gave her to be different. It appealed to her romantic, idealistic and – a hitherto undiscovered – adventurous nature. If she was ruthlessly honest, moving away would give her the opportunity to forge a life for herself without interference and guidance, however well-meant. As she had never formed close friendships, there was nobody else she would miss apart from her parents. She felt a pull of guilt on her heartstrings but not enough to drop her plans. She had to put a stop to such thinking. Raj had not hesitated to leave his family behind in a war-torn country when it mattered to be at her side. Her inner strength and conviction grew daily that her destiny was at her husband's side and that he had a right to her undivided loyalty.

After much discussion and thought, they began preparations. She resigned her job and devoted herself to sorting and packing. There was no help forthcoming from her parents and no more visits to her flat. Whenever she knocked on their door, they were disgruntled and distinctly distant. At one stage, they had an unfortunate Foreign Office statistic ready for her, listing how many marriages between Germans and foreigners ended in divorce. Karin took it, folded it and stuffed it wordlessly in her coat pocket. It would go in the bin at home.

Karin packed several suitcases with her belongings, her favourite books, photographs of her parents, a family album and an address book with contact numbers. She wasn't too bothered about clothes; she assumed that most of her time in Bangladesh she would – like all the other women and quite happily – wear the traditional *sari* or a *salwaar kameez*.

Her parents said a grim-faced good-bye and forced themselves to wave them off at the airport, but she knew she had hurt them. Never in their lives had they been rejected by their beloved and compliant daughter, and they had not expected that she ever would. She could see the torture in their faces, the regret that they had supported this alliance and not come on stronger when ties could be still cut and emotions nipped in the bud.

'You must come and see us soon,' Karin pleaded, but she knew that to them they were empty words which only deserved an empty stare in return.

Karin and Raj flew first to London. During their short transfer time, they met at Heathrow airport with his brother Jamal who had been at their wedding. Nasma, his wife, had to be at work and sent her apologies; little Kitty had been deposited at nursery. The brothers exchanged news interspersed with banter and laughter until the flight was called. Nobody had noticed that Karin had gone very quiet.

The sixteen hour flight to Delhi was to be interrupted several times. The first stop was Cairo. On arrival, they were ushered off the plane into an airport lounge which seemed to be flooded with a sea of men in white, sail-like robes and dome-shaped turbans. As far as she could make out there were no women. Karin attracted a number of disapproving glances but did not think that her sensible travel outfit of navy gabardine trousers and a short-sleeved white blouse could in any way be offensive.

Admittedly, she had not covered her head and her hair was short. Since her wedding, she had let her hair grow but had it trimmed just before their journey. Her longish bob fell just below her ears, framing her excited young face.

She had no idea whether there would be hairdressers in Bangladesh at all. She might end up like her sisters-in-law who twisted their long hair, when in the way or not freshly washed, into a *beni*, a bun or chignon.

'These men surely can't resent me – I am a European woman,' she thought, but she was glad when the passengers were herded back to the aeroplane. She had felt intimidated by the mass of men with no other woman in sight.

They settled quickly down for another couple of hours on a flight where she seemed to be the only fair-skinned person. She smiled a lot when people mustered her with curiosity as she walked past their seats on her way to the loo. Most of the women smiled back, while the fathers, husbands or brothers looked strenuously away. There were also a lot of children of all ages, their mothers trying desperately to curb their exuberance which seemed to spill over from the confined spaces of their rows. Some children looked hopefully at Karin as a possible new playmate but she shook her head and hurried back to her seat.

The next stop was even briefer than the one in Cairo which was a blessing. At first she couldn't find Doha on the map provided with the airline magazine until Raj pointed out the island in the Persian Gulf. It turned out to be a wind-swept desert. The passengers were asked to remain on the plane while it was refuelled; blankets were distributed from overhead lockers because the temperature had dropped considerably. Karin leant forward to have a view through the small window. It was a strange, eerie night scene on the airport's tarmac, men servicing the plane in white turbans and robes, billowing like balloons as if preparing to take off themselves. Sparse lighting from the building at a fair distance and a few lanterns being carried by airport staff hardly managed to illuminate the area where the plane had stopped; sand seemed to be everywhere. In the dim light it could have been snow, but according to Raj, Doha consisted mainly of sandy desert. Meanwhile the plane had filled up with more passengers and every seat was taken. Raj explained to her that many Bengalis sought employment with the oil companies in the Gulf States in order to improve family finances. It was supposed to be hard work, often bordering on exploitation, but still, it was better than no job at home.

As the plane took off again and they unbuckled the seatbelts, Karin leant her head on Raj's shoulder. They hadn't had much time for intimacy recently due to their hectic preparations. Leaving all she had ever known behind and feeling excited but a little uncertain about her future, she was in need of reassurance. But was he really ever so slightly pulling away from her or did she imagine it?

'Not in public', he whispered with a side nod to the young fellow passenger next to him.

She looked at Raj, who was now staring ahead, from the side, at his handsome face, his still immaculate suit in spite of hours of travelling. The only concession he had made was the slight loosening of his tie, which gave him a rakish appearance.

When she finally caught his eye, she spoke what was on her mind:

'Do you think your family will like me?' She wanted to add 'and will I like them, and shall we be happy there?' but it seemed to insult their spirit of adventure and anticipation, so she didn't.

'Of course, they will!' He padded her hand like a father reassuring his child. 'You know already some of my siblings and you got on well.'

She agreed meekly. That was on her home patch, but how would they treat her when she would be the outsider, the guest, the newcomer? How would she fit in?

'Are we going to rent a flat?' Karin asked innocently. Raj laughed in amusement.

'No, we don't need to do that. We shall live with Lakshmi, my middle sister, in Dhaka for the time being. She will be offended if we don't move in with her. She is the only one who hasn't seen you yet... at least for some time,' he added quickly when he saw Karin's horrified face. '

He had never told her, even when she had asked before. She was told not to worry about such details; in his country he would be in charge and he wouldn't let her down..

'Lakshmi has got a huge house and about ten servants,' but he could see that Karin was not impressed. She obviously had not expected to share her new home with anyone but him.

Their conversation began to falter. She suddenly realised that nothing of that sort had been discussed with her; decisions seemed to have been made without consulting or even involving her. When her anger had subsided, she laid her head determinedly on his shoulder; he didn't have the courage to rile her further by insisting on etiquette again. He sat there stiffly while she dozed off. It was a blessing that his neighbour had also fallen asleep and was beyond sending critical looks.

When Karin climbed down the gangway of the aeroplane at Delhi airport, three things hit her with such force that she nearly fainted: The heat which was like a wall of steam, the sea of faces and bodies milling around in dense clusters so that not one piece of ground could be seen, and the noise which engulfed them and seemed to swallow up any effort to communicate.

Raj proceeded briskly to a counter. She was glad he knew his way round and she watched him with pride as he negotiated forcefully with airline staff. He had left her and their luggage standing near the main entrance of the airport building. After a while she became aware that she had attracted a group of skinny Indian men, gathering around her. Some were dressed in trousers and tucked-in shirts, others had a chequered *lungi* cloth wrapped around their waist over which fell a shirt to their hips. They shouted excitedly all at once either in their own language – she assumed it was Hindi – or in broken English at her whilst pointing at various vehicles standing outside the main gate. They were obviously competing to get her fare and it sounded more and more like a quarrel to her.

'Oh, I am so glad you came,' she gasped when Raj returned, 'I couldn't have held out much longer'.

He was just in time to bellow at two of the men, who were wrestling with each other for possession of the suitcases which they dropped immediately like hot potatoes. Raj's sharp intervention had the rest of them scurry away, too. Karin was mightily relieved having feared that these strangers would run off with her luggage while she would not have been able to leave her post.

'I'm sorry, I shouldn't have left you here, battling by yourself,' Raj apologised and explained that he had been trying to sort out their onward flights.

'I thought we had through-tickets.' She didn't quite understand the problem.

'My relatives booked and paid for the tickets in *Takas* to save foreign currency. Karin still didn't understand his reasoning but decided to trust his judgement.

'So why did it take you so long to get them?'

'I still haven't got them. The chap who deals with them has gone for lunch.'

'He must have known that our plane has landed. Why didn't he wait for us?'

'This is India,' Raj hissed and shook his head in disgust.

'Couldn't his colleagues let us have them?' she persisted.

'They don't know where he keeps them.'

'What?' Karin suddenly remembered her brother-in-laws advice he had given just before their departure from Heathrow: 'Forget everything you have grown up with. Don't ever compare. Just enjoy it the way it is.'

Inefficiency was obviously one of the things one had to bear; but she decided that she shouldn't generalise just yet. In a way, it was funny.

'So what are we going to do?' she asked smiling at him reassuringly. She didn't want to aggravate his embarrassment.

'They suggested we go to a hotel nearby, so we can freshen up. They recommended one and promised that they will ring us as soon as they have located the tickets.'

'Are we going to be on time for the connecting flight?' She just wanted to be in the picture.

Raj cringed and had to admit that he didn't know.

'No point in getting upset,' Karin thought and grabbed her suitcase while Raj went back to the desk to organise an official taxi driver.

The ground staff called over a shy looking man who had hovered modestly in a corner near their desk. He was now put in charge of the travellers and their luggage. He led his passengers through the main exit doors, nearly dragged to the ground with the weight of the suitcases.

No sooner had they stepped outside when they were speared by the angry looks of the other drivers, whom Raj had shushed away. Head bowed, their chauffeur rushed the couple to his old Ambassador car, stowed their luggage in the boot, held the doors open for them to sit in the back seats and then glided noiselessly into the driver's seat. The air in the car was stuffy, but the windows, he explained, couldn't be opened. Instead, the door on Raj's side didn't shut properly and they could see light coming through the gap formed by bent metal halfway down the door frame. As the driver revved the engine into action, the door began to rattle rhythmically.

'You better hold on to that.' Karin laughed, but Raj was not amused.

'If the door swings open when we turn a corner,' she mused, 'Raj will be flung out'. It was surreal.

111

'I thought the hotel was nearby,' Karin enquired, after checking her watch. They were now driving around for more than half an hour, and she could have sworn that she had seen some of Delhi's landmarks twice already.

There ensued a heated discussion between Raj and the driver, and within minutes they were deposited by a very disgruntled chauffeur outside the hotel lobby.

Another argument developed about the price of the taxi ride. Raj had been advised by the airport staff how much the journey would cost. The price demanded was three times as much, and the driver defended his stance hotly. Raj got more and more flustered but was not going to give in, offering a bundle of notes which were rejected.

The palaver was swiftly ended by one of the impressive looking doormen of the hotel stepping in and sending the driver off with an even smaller amount and a flea in his ear. Even Raj was relieved at the outcome and thanked the doorman profusely. It irked him that he was considered as much of a helpless foreigner as his wife.

Karin simply watched, listened and marvelled at this new world. She marvelled at the doorman's uniform, a startling red, knee-long jacket, held in at the waist by a white belt; the cuffs of the sleeves and the Nehru collar of the jacket braided with gold thread, setting off sparkling brass buttons down the front; white trousers peeping out from underneath at the knees only to disappear into highly polished black boots; and the red turban decorated on the side by a white fan of cloth.

Karin was impressed by the dignity and authority with which he had handled the situation.

They had hardly had a shower and thrown themselves on the pristine white beds for a snooze, when reception put a call through from the airport. The tickets had been found and the passengers were advised to hurry back; there was a slim chance that they might catch their onward flight to Calcutta.

This time, the hotel lent them a driver and a car and the entire journey took less than ten minutes. By the time they had made their way back to the desk, explained who they were and the tickets had been proudly proffered, it was announced that the Calcutta flight had indeed been on time and was just about to take off – without them. There would be, however another flight in two hours time, the last of the day.

112

Resignation set in while they waited on hard airport benches; they were glad to leave Delhi when they were called to the boarding gate.

'We could have seen the Taj Mahal, if we had known,' Karin said matter-of-factly.

'It's quite far out. We couldn't have made it in a few hours,' Raj contradicted. 'We can always do it later,' he promised.

She smiled at him: 'We have a whole lifetime ahead to see it; it won't run away,' she agreed to his relief. Too many things had gone wrong today; he did not want to add another bad first impression.

There was more in store. By the time they arrived in Calcutta, night fell and they had missed the connecting flight to Dhaka.

Raj was getting distraught when he realised that there was no hotel nearby. The airport officials strongly advised him against taking a taxi into the city after night fall, adding examples of gruesome attacks on foreign travellers. There was nothing else for it than to accept the four chairs which had been brought out from safe storage behind an iron gate and which were offered to the young couple. It was still better than sleeping on the floor as many Indian fellow travellers seemed to be doing. Raj and Karin were the lucky ones and earned envious glances.

Shortly afterwards, they were joined by a middle-aged German lady, who, she told them, was visiting her daughter who was married in Assam. The mother was an ice-cream seller in Hamburg during the summer time and spent the winters in India with her daughter and son-in-law. Now she wondered whether the small plane which used to fly her every year across Bangladesh to this north-eastern part of India was still in operation. The airport staff promised to make enquiries.

Raj and Karin gave up one of their chairs for her to sit on, and all three shared the fourth chair to rest their feet. Karin was amazed when she realised that she had indeed nodded off and had slept soundly in this awkward position for at least a couple of hours. Raj must have kept guard; he looked dreadfully tired.

There was a flight to Dhaka first thing at day break which they intended to catch. Raj retrieved their luggage, which had taken the place of the chairs in the lock-up behind the iron gates. They were now unlocked with great gravitas and emphasis on the impenetrable security arrangements in place for passengers and their possessions. Raj came grudgingly forth with the expected *bakhshish.*

The German lady seemed happy having found that her onward transport was still available and had been arranged for her.

While Raj was busy with the luggage, Karin went to the ladies loo, a cavern-like suite of two rooms, one with sinks and the other with cubicles. Strangely, four generations of women seemed to have made it their home. No sooner had she entered when they all sprang into action, including the woman who must have been the great-grandmother. They began busily wiping a grey, plastic toilet seat in one of the cubicles while another ushered her toward it as if she was leading her to a throne. For a moment, the four of them stood crammed around the toilet, everyone looking at her encouragingly.

'I am surely not expected to pee with spectators around me,' Karin thought in a state of confusion.

Finally, the women got the hint and great-grandmother, who had slumped onto her rickety chair again, gave a sharp command which had the desired effect. Everyone scuttled out of the cubicle, giggling, and Karin couldn't get rid of the feeling that they were right outside, ears flapping to the business going on behind the locked door.

There was another reason why Karin had gone to the ladies. She wanted to surprise Raj and the family and was now battling to drape the five metres of a pink chiffon sari around her as Priti, her niece, had taught her.

When Karin left the cubicle, the women went silent in amazement. Karin was pleased about their reaction to her transformation. They clapped their hands in delight and started pulling at the sari here and there, to get it absolutely right. Karin applied make-up, which they examined suspiciously. When they realised that it was quite different to the shade of their own skin, they lost interest.

She was glad that she had a pocket mirror to hand as there was none to be seen on any of the walls. The younger women and the little girls wanted to have a look at themselves and shrieked with pleasure and delighted embarrassment when their faces stared or laughed back at them.

They showed also great interest in her lipstick and Karin, after having applied it to her own mouth, painted everyone's lips with the creamy red substance. Again, they looked reverently into the pocket mirror, marvelling at themselves. Finally, Karin sprayed everyone with Chanel No.5 to excited squeals whenever the

114

bottle hissed and a spray of scented droplets hung in the air before landing on their forearms and necks.

Karin turned round one last time and saw two of them sniffing each other while the rest huddled over the lipstick she had left with them. Smiling, she slipped quietly out of the door.

Chapter Twelve

❦

It was only the other day
That I came to your earth…
Rabrindranath Tagore

'I have a message for you, Mrs. Khan'.

To Karin's surprise, the well-groomed male receptionist hands her not only her room key but also an envelope with the hotel's logo on it.

'That's nice, thank you.'

Karin concludes that it is from her daughter. Jasmine. She must have looked up the telephone number of the hotel on the internet. Karin finds modern technology confusing, but on this occasion; she is grateful, feeling not quite so alone, thousands of miles from her usual surroundings.

No doubt, the message will repeat warnings to be careful, circumspect and to call home if she feels threatened in any way. Jasmine with her sharp mind is the personification of the independent, self-confident, successful and fearless woman of her time. Nothing and nobody intimidates her, least of all men. It is reassuring to know that such a daughter is looking out for her.

'I shall ring her a little later,' Karin decides, thanks the receptionist and turns away, still clutching the unopened envelope.

For a moment it strikes her as strange that still in this day and age, there is not one female receptionist in the hotel lobby.

'Is this a coincidence or are women still prevented from holding down a job of that kind?' she wonders.

Karin is too tired to think more deeply about anything.

Her little case has been taken care of by a hotel boy striding proudly across the hall, looking splendid in his white uniform with gold epaulettes. He walks swiftly ahead, first to the lift, then on the third floor along a thickly carpeted corridor, occasionally checking that his charge is following. Finally, he unlocks noiselessly a door to a luxurious room which is flooded with light and exotic scent. The air conditioning is gently whirring in unison with the brass ceiling fans, which turn slowly and elegantly like old-fashioned carousels.

The crisp white bedclothes are strewn with *shaplas*, water lilies, the national flower of Bangladesh. Otherwise, the room looks like a typical five-star accommodation anywhere in the world, sumptuous and comfortable. Karin has never had the privilege of such luxury and is determined to enjoy every minute of her stay. Her first inclination is to unpack and have a shower, but then she remembers the message. She sinks onto the pristine white bed, brushing a few of the water lilies into a heap, slides her digit finger underneath the envelope's flap and slits the edge in three jerks. She takes out a thin sheet of paper and unfolds it. Karin begins to frown as she reads the first few words. This is not a message from Jasmine. It doesn't make sense because no one else knows that she has arrived.

'Welcome,' it reads, 'I knew you would come. Please ring me tomorrow on 0765 43698; it's my personal mobile, so no-one will find out that you are here. I look so much forward to seeing you again.'

The message stops. The receptionist forgot to mention who left it.

Karin dials zero on her room telephone for reception.

'Room 160.'

'At your service, Madam,' is the smooth, efficient reply.

'You handed me a message. Do you know who left it?'

'I am sorry, Madam. It must have been put in your pigeon hole before I began my shift,' he burred in perfect English rolling his 'r's enthusiastically.

'Would anyone else know? There is no name,' she explains her persistence.

'I shall ask my colleagues and ring you back, Madam,' he promises.

Only a few minutes pass before her phone rings:

'Ahmed from the reception, Madam.'

'Yes?' she waits in suspense, but is disappointed.

'I am sorry, Madam, my colleague who took your message won't be on duty before day after tomorrow.'

Too late. Karin has been asked to ring sooner. She will just have to pick up the courage, dial the given number and find out who is on the other end. Karin has a slight inkling that it might be Priti, but she can't be certain.

It is a pleasant thought that she has a whole day in hand to relax, to soak in the now unfamiliar atmosphere and to go exploring.

She gathers the water lilies, empties the fruit bowl of mangoes, lychees and grapes, which stands on the writing table near the window, fills it with water and lets the lilies float.

On her way to the bathroom, she passes a vase and buries her nose in the heavy scent of frangipani blooms

Refreshed by a lukewarm shower, just as she likes it, she wraps herself in the fluffy, white towelling robe, the hotel has provided and pads across the marble floor on bare feet to switch off the air conditioning and ceiling fans. She has always disliked artificially produced cold air; in the past, it had given her a cold or a sore throat. She had preferred to bear the heat like any ordinary Bengali. If they could, so could she.

Karin lies down on the crisp white bed, underneath the dome of gathered mosquito netting. 'No mosquito would dare to blemish the sumptuous cleanliness of this room,' she chuckles to herself. The next minute she is asleep. When Karin awakes she can see darkness outside the window. She has not drawn the ample, light green curtains and can hear traffic noises in the distance, hooting of car horns, ringing of rickshaw bells and shouting of sellers offering their goods. She dismisses the idea of leaving the hotel in search of a restaurant. Bangladesh might have made great strides into the twenty-first century technologically, but she doubts that it has become acceptable for a woman to walk about the streets after night fall. It would be asking for trouble.

Karin rings room service and orders a simple meal of rice, dhal and vegetable curry. She doesn't have to wait long and when she begins to eat, she suddenly realises how terribly hungry she is. It tastes wonderful; she enjoys every mouthful of authentic, gently spiced, un-anglicised Bengali food. When she finally puts the fork, knife and spoon on the empty plate, she feels satisfied, at peace with the world and drowsy.

'It's too late to do anything. I might as well have a good night's sleep,' she decides.

Her head has hardly touched the pillow when she falls into a deep black hole of exhausted sleep.

The sky is electric blue and the sun is already blazing, when Karin opens her eyes. She feels wonderfully refreshed and raring to go, a feeling she has not experienced for many years. She fights her way out of the mosquito net cloud around her bed, patters over the cool marble floor into the bathroom and takes another shower. She loves the little bottles of perfumed shampoos and creams routinely provided by classy hotels. She selects the mango shower gel, the papaya shampoo and the coconut body lotion.

'I'll smell like a fruit salad,' she smiles to herself. It won't matter; she won't meet up with anyone; no one will get close enough to notice. More importantly, the lovely scents make her feel relaxed and in tune with her surroundings.

She dresses in her white cotton trousers, a white, short-sleeved blouse and her favourite powder-blue cardigan. She twists her hair into a chignon, fastens it with a few hairpins and slips into her sensible sandals.

'Ready!' she thinks, pleased with her appearance in the bathroom mirror.

From her room, she heads for the lift down to the lobby, from where she is directed to a vast dining room. Only a few tables are occupied. Sheepishly, she looks at the clock: it is already nine. Business residents must have left over an hour ago to disperse to their various places of work.

She is glad to notice that she has plenty of places to choose from. She has never been an early bird nor greatly sociable in the mornings. Even now in her holiday mood, she does not feel like making small talk with strangers.

She chooses a table near the French windows which look out onto the garden and swimming pool. A great number of hotel staff, dressed in snow-white uniforms with gold braids, larger versions of the boy from the previous evening, walk swiftly among the sunbathers catering busily for every whim of their guests without appearing to be in a hurry.

'In my outfit I could be one of them,' quips Karin to herself.

No sooner does she give an indication of where she will sit, three waiters glide towards her, two taking up a position a little distance away, while the third, obviously the more senior of them, pulls out a chair for her.

'Good morning, Madam. I am Karim, your head waiter, at your service.' The other two nod and smile.

She has hardly sat down, when one of the juniors places a large, white, starched napkin in her lap and the other puts a jug of fresh, cold water on her table, before handing her a leather-bound menu card.

She is a little embarrassed about this royal treatment and afraid that her embarrassment might show, but they take no notice. The two juniors are given whispered instructions in Bengali and remain posted within her earshot, hands clasped behind their backs, while the headwaiter walks away to check on other tables.

Karin begins to work her way through the long list of meals on offer and soon gives up. She lifts her eyes and is startled by the sudden appearance of the waiter right next to her.

'Madam?'

'What is your name?' Karin can not deal with someone nameless.

'Ahmed, Madam,' he replies with dignity.

Karin is slightly amused at the popularity of that name.

'Ahmed, I wonder whether I may have a prawn cutlet for breakfast…? I don't think it is on the menu,' she adds apologetically.

Ahmed's mouth opens to a very white-toothed and delighted grin. Not many foreigners know about prawn cutlets; it is more of a meal one cooks at home.

'Of course, Madam,' he says eagerly, 'it is a pleasure. I shall tell chef immediately.' He rushes off to fulfil her wish.

Soon afterwards, she tucks into the most delicious, crunchy, breaded, flattened crevettes which she dips into thin yoghurt spiced with fresh coriander, mint and cardamom, alternating with a hot, luminously red chilli sauce. She leaves most of the fluffy basmati rice dome on her plate, but eats the mixed salad leaves with gusto. This is followed by a hot cup of tea and a brown, round *roshgulla*, another favourite from the past. She is delighted to taste again the honeyed sweet after so many years.

'It takes the spiciness away,' explains the head waiter helpfully, a discreet shadow of approval playing around his lips. He knows that this guest is not the usual tourist, one who wants to visit a third world country without compromising her western creature comforts. He senses a genuine interest in his homeland.

She doesn't need to reply but only returns a conspiratorial smile.

'Ahmed,' she says eventually, leaning back with satisfaction, 'I would like to go a little sightseeing today. Could you recommend a driver?'

Ahmed calls over the headwaiter who rushes to her table.

'You need a driver, Mrs. Khan? I shall tell reception. He will be here in ten minutes.'

'Marvellous,' she says and adds a quick 'thank you.' The most wonderful day stretches ahead of her: sightseeing in Dhaka as she has never done before; she is free to follow her whims, instincts, interests and moods. Bengali wives used to be chaperoned at all times; they never went out by themselves, taking charge. This time, she won't have to conform.

Pictures flicker across her mind of being dragged along on impulsively arranged journeys – either no one had bothered to tell her or she had not understood – squashed on backseats in cars, wedged in between sisters-in-law, eager to reach their destination, to visit other relatives a day-ride away. Karin used to crane her neck to look out of the car window past the heads and arms of her companions, seeing paddy fields, palm trees and the occasional village huts. On the rare occasion that she had been given notice, she had read up about any temple, shrine or Mosque they were likely to pass before the start of the journey; she had always been eager to learn and to soak up some local culture but she had often been disappointed. Realising too late that they had long driven past anything worth seeing and long before she could make her relatives understand that she had actually wanted to stop for a visit..

'That is far behind. We can't turn round,' was the usual reaction. 'The relatives at the other end expect us,' was the decisive argument, 'and we don't know what the roads ahead will be like.' Nothing seemed to be worth stopping. Today will be different: she will be free from someone else's planning, free from family expectations and pressure. Today she is a western tourist and will explore.

'This is Farook, my brother. He will take good care of you, Mrs. Khan.'

Karim, the headwaiter, introduces a younger version of himself, a little shorter, with darker skin, the beginnings of a moustache, but the same large, dark, blazing eyes.

Farook's black trousers are well laundered and pressed, but shiny and thin in places with wear and washing. His clean, white shirt is not tucked in, but is hanging loosely from his slight shoulders and over his thin waist.

He seems shy, respectful and awestruck in view of the responsibility of looking after a western *Memsahib* for a whole day.

'You can trust him,' adds Karim anxiously when both his brother and Karin remain silent.

Finally, Karin utters a business-like 'okay' and smiles encouragingly at the driver.

His task fulfilled, Karim turns to attend to his duties.

'Let's have a cup of tea in the dining room while we work out where we are going,' Karin suggests to Farook, but he looks pleadingly at the disappearing back of his brother and shakes his head.

Karin understands immediately that the hotel management would take a dim view if a lowly driver used their facilities and mingled with hotel guests, though he might have been invited. Karin had always hated this great divide between 'them and us', the wealthy and the poor, the tourists and the servants, the employers exploiting employees, between members of her family and the household staff, including the indispensable and very talented cook.

In secret, Karin scolds herself for not remembering and to have put Farook in this embarrassing situation.

'Forget I said that,' she says brightly trying to put him at ease. 'Let's go to your car.'

She points vaguely at a few vehicles parked outside the vast glass doors: 'We can discuss my plan there.' She has to wait a few minutes before Farook brings his car round to the front entrance. She steps through the hotel's automatic glass doors, which glide noiselessly like ice-skaters to open and shut. The late morning heat hits her with a vengeance and wraps itself round her body like a stifling quilt. Farook leads her to an old Ambassador, which, she notices with relief, has all four of its doors in place and the blue body work is highly polished. Blue is Karin's favourite colour and she takes this as a good omen.

'I am sorry,' says Farook with a much stronger accent in his English than his brother. 'I not have air conditioning'.

He rushes around the car before her as if afraid that she might change her mind. He holds open the passenger door in a more subservient manner than Karin likes.

'That's fine by me,' she reassures him. 'Air-conditioning makes me ill.'

He nods solemnly: 'We can open window.'

'Yes, we can do that,' Karin agrees and climbs into the car. The leather seats are of a lighter blue, a little hard to sit on, but not as hot and sticky as she expected them to be.

'He must have parked the car in the shade' she thinks and is pleased that she won't be driving around in a limousine which to her mind would be completely inappropriate in a third world country. She likes the simplicity of an old banger lovingly restored and cared for, the pride and joy of its owner, who has worked hard to afford it. The lack of comfort will be superseded by her feelings of nostalgia. It will keep her from slumping and force her to remain alert.

After taking out a few leaflets, she arranges her handbag close to her feet.

'Now, where shall we go first,' she muses without expecting an answer.

She frowns with concentration, studying intently the small, colourfully illustrated tourist map of Dhaka which the receptionist had given to her on her arrival. After a few minutes, during which Farook observes the traffic with interest and waits patiently for her to make up her mind, she decides to begin with a tour of the mosques. She remembers the names of the most famous ones: The Seven Domed Mosque dating back to the seventeenth century, the Baitul Mukarram-National Mosque, the three-hundred year old Star Mosque, the Chawkbazar Mosque and the Huseni Dalan Mosque. Farook mumbles discreetly with approval.

'We go?' he asks and drives off as soon as he sees Karin nodding.

They move out of the orderly, calm, sand-coloured gravel-snake leading away from the hotel and join the throng of Dhaka's morning traffic, a cacophony of horns, hooting, rickshaw bells, old engines spluttering and newer ones roaring. Karin notices that here, too, are far fewer bicycle rickshaws on the road, which used to be propelled by pure leg-strength of their skinny drivers. Many rickshaw *wallahs* seem to have graduated to tricycle-rickshaws or baby-taxis, three-wheeled motorised scooters. Some of them are even holding a mobile phone to their ear, steering their vehicles with one hand.

Karin is pleased to see that, in spite of the obvious technological improvements, the colourful artistic pictures on the rickshaw hoods and back-flaps have been preserved. She studies the paintings with interest to see who the darlings of the film world were at the moment.

'Are the rickshaw painters still across the Burigonga?' she asks Farook, which he confirms.

There had always been a community of rickshaw artists on the other side of the river − an entire village busy with painting the continuously changing screen-goddesses and hunky, romantic film heroes onto the back panels of the city's rickshaws. The lane near the hotel is elegantly wide and lined by palm trees. As they approach the city centre, the road soon clogs up with all kinds of vehicles; cars of all shapes, sizes and in various states of repair; rickshaws weaving in and out between them; overloaded lorries; an occasional ox-cart plodding on regardless of the modern traffic, followed by a screaming person trying to keep up with it; and rickety old buses, brimful with passengers.

Karin remembers times, just after the Independence War, when there were few buses; once their insides had been filled to capacity, people had hauled themselves and their luggage onto the roof to secure a passage; or they would hang out of door-less entrances during their journey, clinging on to a handle for dear life.

The buses still look over-crowded, creaking under the load, but at least no one seems to be in danger of falling off or out.

There is no thinking of driving anywhere fast. People might want to and many hoot their intention, but traffic is slow and in some place stagnant.

Karin winds down the window. A mixture of damp heat, petrol and exhaust fumes mingle with the smells of cooking and garbage from the roadside, where people live under tent-like shelters made of torn fabrics or corrugated iron sheets balancing on four stilts. Thousands of people walk, squat or do business there. The noise through the open car window is indescribable, an assault on the ears. It looks like utter mayhem, but for the people of Dhaka, this is daily life. Finally, they arrive at their first destination, the Star Mosque. Karin knows that she won't be able to go inside.

The entrance to the women's prayer room is where it has always been: at the back of the building, well tucked away, where figures in black *burqas* glide in like mysterious shadows. She won't even be able to go there without being invited and accompanied by a Muslim woman.

She recalls, with a little shudder, the first time she had come across the full force of Muslim men's fury. On her way to a market, she had been accompanied by her seventeen year old, favourite nephew who had desperately tried to deter her from getting out of the car, never mind approaching the mosque. Taking no heed, she had climbed the most beautiful marble steps embracing the entrance to the holy building. She had been dressed in a sari, had covered her head respectfully with her *achol* and was going to leave her sandals outside. None of this had impressed the men coming out of the mosque and down the steps towards her. *Jumma*, the Friday prayer, had just finished. The first men, heading the crowd, had hardly reached her when they started shouting, what sounded like abuse, gesticulating wildly. She had felt a pull at her elbow; her nephew was only one step behind her, begging her to leave.

'What do they say?' she had asked him over the din, completely taken aback by the fierceness of the men's hostility. 'Why are they so angry?'

'Auntie, they say: Don't you know where the women's entrance is?' Her nephew had felt obviously guilty that he had brought her here at all.

'But I don't want to pray; I only want to see the Mosque, …like people visit our cathedrals back home,' she had protested.

By then, the men had come threateningly close, still shouting and gesticulating, until she became afraid they would hurtle both of them down the steps.

'Please, come with me,' her nephew had pleaded. She had felt furious, but powerless.

'I won't hurry for them,' she had thought defiantly, turned and walked provocatively slowly downwards, the crowd following three paces behind her. She had dared to look over her shoulder once and had been shocked by the blazing eyes of fervent believers.

'No reasoning with them,' she had thought and had shaken her head in anger.

They had both been upset, Karin and her nephew, and had abandoned their shopping mission. She had tried to lighten the boy's conscience with the assurance that none of this had been his fault; in fact, she had joked that he couldn't possibly have disobeyed his auntie's wishes. It hadn't worked as well as she had hoped, and it had taken several weeks until he had agreed to be her chaperone once more.

Of course, they had never told anyone, guessing that the family would have been horrified at their foolishness and audacity. Now, many years later, she knows better than to leave the protection of the car, preferring to admire the brilliant white buildings and their golden, star-spangled domes from the outside. The deep azure blue sky forms a dramatic background to the round roofs gleaming in the blazing sunlight.

Farook drives on and they pass the Lalbagh Fort, as she had done so many times before, on her way to the bazaars. She had forgotten that, according to the leaflet, it had been built in the 17th century by the son of a Mughal emperor, and had been the scene of a bloody battle against the British.

'It is museum,' Farook interrupts her thoughts. Last time she had seen it, it had appeared empty and ready to disintegrate. Now it looks restored and cared for.

'I should really visit the Bangabandhu Memorial Museum,' she thinks while reading in her brochure about it: It used to be the residence of the father of the nation, Sheikh Mujibur Rahman, and now houses a collection of his personal effects and photographs of his life.

Karin feels that her own story is intrinsically linked with the country's first president, who ruled when she first came to live here. It had been an anxious time. The labour pains of the 1971 Independence War and Mujib's reign, cut short by his assassination, is not something she wants to remember just yet while she is lulled in the pleasurable contentment of a tourist.

No point in confusing Farook either, who is eagerly heading for the next mosque. She might get a chance to see the museum later.

An hour and two more mosques later, Karin suggests that they visit a park. She needs to stretch her legs.

'Baldha Garden or Mirpur Botanical Garden?' enquires Farook.

'Mirpur? Isn't that a zoo?'

'Botanical Garden is next to zoo,' he confirms.

'Baldha Garden is a bit touristy,' Karin muses, but then she is not fond of seeing caged animals either.

She suddenly remembers another park, where she had often been deposited by her nieces and nephews, who, instead of going officially shopping with her, used their understanding, liberal western auntie as an alibi while meeting secretly with the young man or woman they were supposed to marry shortly afterwards.

Karin had been a willing instrument in helping to ease the anxiety of the young people a little before they embarked on an arranged marriage. She found it hard to resist their pleas and trusted them when they promised that they would just talk with their future husband or wife somewhere in the quiet corner of a Chinese restaurant. To Karin it was self-understood that the young couples should get to know each other. The custom, insisting that there should be no unsupervised contact between the bride and the groom before the wedding didn't make any sense to her at all. She found it downright cruel. Karin could never reconcile herself to the idea that parents should choose a partner for their children, however much the adults extolled the virtues of preliminary selection of future sons and daughters-in-law by the level-headed and experienced elders.

Officially, however, she had to tow the line. She had taken the diplomatic way out when asked about her opinion, but had determinedly undermined the system by helping the young people to flaunt the rules.

'Farook.'

'Yes, *Memsahib*,' the driver answers eagerly.

'Is there still a park near the Sheraton Hotel?'

'You meaning Ramna Green, *Memsahib*?'

'Yes, that's it, Farook, Ramna Green.' She lets the words tickle her tongue like sherbet. 'Let's go there.'

He only nods, turns the car niftily around and drives off in the opposite direction.

He parks discreetly a few steps away from the entrance, helps her to get out and gestures that he will stay with it. He will not take a risk.

Karin opens the black, low, rod-iron gate and begins to amble along the gravel paths, which are flanked by the most luscious blooms. She recognises *rojonigondhas*, *bokul*, *champa* and hibiscus; she sniffs at the half-closed head of a yellow rose and the ever present jasmine. Karin takes a seat on a bench under a magnolia tree and breathes in deeply, peace and pleasure flooding through her soul. For a while, she watches people strolling past, mainly young people, probably students, small groups of chattering girls in *saris* or *shalwar kameezes* carrying books, young families, toddlers holding the hand of a parent or older children, skipping, running before being told off. There is not a lot of sound. People speak in hushed voices, as if not to disturb the peace of this little piece of nature in the middle of a bustling city. Nothing has changed much; maybe the paths are cleaner and the plants more regimented in their abundance, but nothing more. Finally, Karin gets up and strolls back to Farook and the car. 'That was nice,' she sighs contentedly, but Farook is already holding open the car door and takes no notice.

'Where now?' he asks.

'We need to eat something,' Karin is indeed feeling peckish. 'Take me to New Market, Farook,' she decides.

New Market is immediately like an old friend. The wooden shops don't seem to have changed much. The more well-to-do owners have managed to afford shop-windows and sometimes even a door, but most of them offer their merchandise on a wooden stall which only has a back wall and a roof, exposing everything on display to the elements.

Karin walks slowly along the crowded, dusty paths between the rows of stalls, enveloped by hot, damp air, to the shouts and noises of bustling market life. The market seems too small for the thousands of shoppers and shop-keepers, bursting nearly at the seams but never quite. She is surrounded by people whose skin is darkened by their outside jobs, some sizing her up discreetly as a potential customer, others more persistent trying to lure or nearly drag her into their establishments with a rapid flow of words and encouraging gestures. Her Bengali is not good any more and she can't keep up and understand what they say. However, she smiles when she hears a familiar word and remembers its meaning.

Bare-chested children are milling around, begging or selling one thing or another. Only the lower parts of their bodies are dressed, often in rag-like skirts or ill-fitting shorts. Few of them wear shoes. They are cheerful and some a little too forceful in their attempt to generate pity and extract money from the shoppers.

There used to be hundreds of them, some with baskets full of second-hand knitwear, slightly inappropriate donations from somewhere overseas, snapped up by the most cunning of urchins. Karin had used to buy entire baskets full of pullovers, cardigans, body-warmers, scarves, woolly hats and gloves, often with a hole or a rip and had distributed them for free among the beggars' children. Their delighted grins had never ceased to touch her heart. It wasn't much to keep these poor children warm on chilly winter nights but certainly better than nothing.

This had been another thing that had surprised her, how cold nights could be even in a country where the high day time temperatures were often unbearable.

New Market works its magic again. The wares on the stalls are colourful and varied: bales of cloths and fabrics, saris draped seductively over faceless mannequins, shoes on their boxes, household items gleaming with newness, shiny brass plates, vases and jugs offered as suitable wedding presents. The market ends finally with the fruit, flower and vegetable section, colourful like a rainbow.

The middle of the market is still formed by a cluster of tea-rooms and open-air street restaurants from which emanate the most mouth-watering smells of spices, meat and vegetable curries and sweets. She sits down on a rickety chair at a small, round, but heavily polished metal table and orders tea. She can see the kettle in which the water is boiled, an important lesson to be learnt to avoid food poisoning. She won't have milk, but a cardamom pod and a spoonful of sugar; *chini* she says with glee and the waiter smiles back in recognition. She sits there for a while, watching hundreds of people go past.

She used to bring her children to little places like this when they were thirsty, hungry and bored with the adults' shopping. They had usually chosen a place where they could sit inside, out of the burning sun, but no sooner had they entered when children with dirty faces, matted hair and in rags, which hardly covered them, had gathered outside and had gawped at the fortunate, foreign children with their neat hair-cuts and their trendy and freshly-laundered trousers and T-Shirts. To the horror of her family, Karin had bought bags of biscuits every time for the waifs outside. As she had opened the door, she had felt the throng of the little bodies which were almost pushed through the crack by the ever growing, shoving crowd behind

'You can't start this sort of thing,' her family had complained bitterly. 'There are millions of them,' but she had carried on regardless.

Now there seem to be fewer children. Several uniformed policemen, strutting about with great dignity and authority might be the reason. No sooner does one come round a corner when all the children scatter with giggles or shrieks of alarm.

Refreshed, Karin gathers up her handbag – she left the cardigan in the car – and walks over to the nearest shoe shop. She has to pass a sari shop first and admires the beautifully printed or embroidered chiffons, damasks, satins and silks. Her hand glides over a heavy, red wedding sari with the most intricate gold stitching, but when the owner approaches to serve her, she shakes her head apologetically and walks away.

She is not sure whether she will get a chance to wear the one sari which she has brought with her; it is her favourite one, the colour of the Bangladeshi flag and the contours of the *shapla*. She has kept it as a last link between her past and her present, East and West, a remnant, ready, should a concession be needed. She saunters on and buys *chappals*, typical, locally made sandals consisting of a sole and two leather strings held onto between toes. She chooses elaborately decorated ones, with multicoloured and sparkling beads. The exotic, joyful scene has rubbed off on her and she wants to join in.

Pleased with her purchase, she can't resist another tea-shop which offers her beloved *roshgullas*, stored in large, lidded stoneware jugs. The shop-keeper fishes them out of their container, drains off the syrupy juice and wraps the ball-shaped sweets into a paper bag. Then he swaddles the package with a clean kitchen towel and binds it at the top with a piece of jute. Karin hopes she won't leave a trail of sugary *roshgulla* juice behind her while walking hurriedly back to the car. Farook waits at the entrance to the Market where he had deposited her. Laughingly, she offers him a roshgulla which he accepts hesitantly. Like children, they suck on the soft, milky balls and lick the juice before it can run down to their wrists.

The heat has become unbearable and Karin misses her London straw hat; however, she realises that if she wore one, the sweat would simply trickle down her neck.

It is time to release her loyal and patient driver from his duties. She pops another *roshgulla* into her mouth, scrunches up the paper bag, wraps the towel round it and thrusts the little parcel into Farook's hands.

'For your children,' she says and suddenly realises that she doesn't know anything about him.

'You do have children?' she enquires quickly and is relieved when he says that he is the father of a boy and a girl.

'My children love *roshgullas*. Thank you very much,' he says modestly but beaming. Karin suspects that he can't treat his family to sweets very often.

While they make their way back to the hotel, she chatters on: 'Do you live near the hotel?'

'Oh no, too expensive. We live in old town, next to Burigonga river.'

'That's Sadarghat, isn't it? I used to live there for a while,' she blurts out and immediately regrets it.

Farook is not likely to live in a house with thirty rooms. In her mind she can still picture the verandas which wrapped themselves round the building on every floor. On the west side, they had jutted out into the empty space above the river and had made Karin think of flying carpets

'You live in Dhaka?' Farook asks in astonishment and forgetting his reserve.

'Yes, for a little while,' she answers uneasily, 'a very long time ago.'

'But tell me about your family,' she changes the topic and, for the rest of the journey, Farook chatters happily in his broken English about the two children he is so proud of, how well they are doing at school; he doesn't divulge much about his wife, only that her name is Mumtaz, 'like in story of Shajahan, who built Taj Mahal for wife'. Karin has heard the story many times, but it never ceases to affect her, the devotion of a man to one woman, a love tearing him apart when she had died.

Farook's parents seem to live with him. It is generally the

132

custom that brides move in with their in-laws, so that the men rarely need to leave the home of their childhood. The car arrives back at the Radisson Water Garden Hotel. Karin pays Farook a sum which seems very modest for an entire day's work. She gives him a generous tip and a quick glance at his face tells her that it is more than he expected. A moment later, he lowers his eyes again in subservience.

'You need car tomorrow?' he mumbles shyly.

'Yes, I do. Maybe only for a short while, but it would be nice if you could be available. I shall tell your brother at breakfast.'

She can't be sure what tomorrow will bring.

He runs around the car to open her door, *salaams*, and wishes her a 'good night'. He is so obviously pleased with the day and watches her until she has safely entered the hotel. He is surprised when she turns around and waves at him; his hand twitches, but he can't be seen to wave at a *Memsahib*, so he replies with the biggest and most grateful smile he can muster, before climbing in his seat and driving home.

The coolness of the hotel lobby is a relief after the relentless heat of the afternoon.

Back in her room, Karin showers, enquires over the phone about dinner times and rests on the bed. She knows that there is something she has to do tonight. She leafs for a while through brochures, reads the English paper which room service has put on her bed and stretches out. Finally, she picks up courage, lifts the receiver again and asks the operator to put her through to the number on the piece of paper.

133

Chapter Thirteen

☙❧

Ah, these jasmines,
        These white jasmines!
                Rabrindranath Tagore

As soon as Karin climbed down the gangway of the ten-seater plane, the fairy tale began.

The heat hit her like a wall of steam in a sauna, but the morning sunlight was lying golden on the world around her, giving it a welcoming glow. She was glad that she had changed into a sari. It felt light, appropriate and provided gentle breezes when she moved.

They hadn't talked to anyone on the plane; Raj had guessed that their fellow passengers were mainly Russian aid workers or embassy staff, which Karin found a little disconcerting.

'Their presence has to do with the recent Independence War and reparation aid,' he explained.

'Knowing politics, it's more a matter of a super-power getting her claws into a poor, defenceless country and increasing her influence,' she thought sarcastically.

Subsequently, there were no 'good-byes' and 'have a nice stay' to be said to anyone.

Karin spotted a little group of people which had gathered at the bottom of the steps. At first, she took them for airport staff, but other figures rushed across the tarmac to join the group and Karin suddenly realised that this was her reception committee, her new family.

No sooner had she reached the last step when flower garlands were thrown over her head in a game of quoits. She suppressed a giggle at the thought and converted it quickly into a broad smile. The heavy scent of the jasmine and lotus blooms made her dizzy as if she had been doused with the content of a whole bottle of perfume. Everybody seemed to be talking at the same time, some only to Raj with friendly side-glances directed at her; others were talking in English like machine guns to her, but she could not distinguish from amongst this cacophony who had said or asked what. She could only nod and smile a lot.

Raj was slapped on the back by several male relatives while his sisters, sisters-in-law and nieces beamed at him and angled for his hands. The younger people fell down onto their knees and paid *salaam* at his feet. Karin had seen this respectful greeting of an elder before. They touched his shoes with their hands, their heads hovering above his feet; for all she could make out, it looked as if they were kissing them, until Raj picked whoever it was up by the shoulders, indicating that there was no need for that.

'I should think so,' Karin thought with the practical mind of a westerner, 'just imagine the dirt of the entire journey clinging to their lips.'

Karin was surrounded by a sea of new faces, all bright with excitement, warm with welcome and encouragement. The smaller children, who had willingly bowed before Raj, were hiding behind their mothers' skirts, overcome with shyness, when they were introduced to their new auntie and asked to pay *salaam* to her as well. They did so hurriedly, as if someone might snatch them from the spot. Karin had no idea what to do; so she smiled at them and padded their heads. Their duty done, the children quickly turned and disappeared behind their mothers' backs again to the laughter of the adults. Only occasionally could Karin see them peep out with their saucer-like, shiny eyes.

'Auntie!' A familiar voice broke through the crowd and Priti's lovely face appeared. It was wonderful to see someone she knew. Then she discovered Hasina and Mumtaz who had visited her in Germany, and the feeling of having arrived on a different planet vanished.

They had stood there for ages when they were, politely and with profuse apologies, ushered on by maintenance staff. The group which had grown to nearly fifty, began to roll at snails pace towards the airport building like a big beach ball prodded by a toddler.

They snowballed through the wide open doors of the terminal, where they were met by an even bigger crowd. The hall seemed to be packed to full capacity and everyone shouted at the top of their voices, demanding priority and attention.

One of Raj's brothers gesticulated wildly, discussing something hotly with an airport official who had dared to stop their progress. Karin dipped into her handbag fishing for her passport, but Priti, still next to her, shook her head:

'It won't be necessary,' she said.

Finally, the official made a telephone call and a few moments later, an important looking man in a dazzling uniform came out of the backroom. Instead of telling Raj's brother off, he came from behind the desk and embraced him heartily. He then bellowed a command at the young chap behind him, who had only tried to do his duty. Karin felt sorry for him because she saw that he was quivering and that his face had gone a darker shade of brown with embarrassment.

'What happened?' she whispered to Priti. Raj, engulfed by relatives, was too far away to hear her question.

'He called Nadeem *chacha*. He is the head of the airport,' she explained in a tone which conveyed that they always expected preferential treatment.

'So who is going to stamp my passport and visa, proving that I have entered?'

'He'll pick it up tonight and get it done tomorrow.'

Karin didn't quite understand: 'Why can't they do it now?'

'Because it is far too crowded and there is no need for us to stand in a queue for hours.'

Karin, unused to such unfair advantage, realised that since her arrival she had been pushed to the top of a social ladder. Unease would not let her enjoy that she was whisked through the building within minutes while hundreds of people behind them had to follow the usual lengthy, sweaty and nerve-wrecking route of entry.

They found themselves outside in the blazing sunshine. Karin looked with wonder at the azure, cloudless sky and a canopy of palm trees spreading their green leaves like ribbons from their crowns, too high up to provide shade.

The family dispersed, still chattering animatedly, into smaller clusters and climbed into various cars.

Karin and Raj were left with Lakshmi, her husband, whose name she remembered was Amir, and Priti. Amir gave an order and one *taka* to a little beggar boy who rushed off to summon their driver. It was a Bentley which glided towards them, one of those older models which were built for grandeur rather than speed. It stopped soundlessly next to where they waited. The driver got out, rushed round and busied himself with accommodating the luggage and the flower garlands in the ample boot. Then he held the doors open in turn to let his master, mistress, their daughter and their guests take a seat. Priti's two sisters had chosen to accept a lift from other relatives.

From their lofty and plush seats inside the Bentley, the mayhem on Dhaka's roads appeared through the wide glass panes like a chaotic theatre production. Karin asked for the window to be opened a little in spite of air-conditioning on the inside. She wanted not only to see but to hear and smell.

A wave of sounds assaulted her through the opened gap – shrill horns; deep bellowing like foghorns; blaring horns; impatient staccato horns; long, imperious, get-out-of-the-way-I-am-important horns; powerless rickshaw bells; or ridiculously small squeaky baby-taxi horns whose sounds were drowned immediately by all the others.

Karin could not see where any traffic rules applied. Everyone pushed forward in spurts, once the log-jam had disentangled. Carts, bicycle rickshaws, three-wheeler baby-taxis, over-loaded and colourfully decorated trucks, a few private cars and pedestrians all seemed to share the same road and were weaving around each other. There were no markings, not even a central divide, indicating a separation of traffic directions; liberal sprinklings of potholes were a constant threat to vehicle axles. There were no pavements on either side and people walked at their own peril.

'How dreadful,' Raj said, and 'shut the window' to the driver.

Karin wondered why he had been surprised by the hullabaloo. After all, he had grown up here.

Their driver did not hoot once. He remained calm and confident in a situation where most westerners would have panicked.

Raj had just said that they were nearly at home, when they were held up by a huge lorry which had obviously failed to negotiate one of the potholes and had now a broken axle. Boxes of goods had fallen off and were scattered on the road. A great number of people – many more than could have been involved in the accident – was surrounding the unfortunate vehicle, shouting and gesticulating, while the driver desperately tried to stop urchins and beggars to hurry off with his cargo. The hooting concert was deafening and Karin half expected someone to be run over, while the rest of the traffic tried to sneak around the scene of disaster.

The inside of the Bentley felt like an oasis in the middle of a tropical storm. It edged its way slowly but with authority around the scene and carried on until it came to a silent and gentle halt outside an enormous white house towering above them. There was no front garden and the garage doors bordered onto the busy road. Several men sprang into action at the sight of the car and opened them wide. The Bentley glided through and stopped.

A door was flung open by a servant and Karin stepped into a family home which continued the calm, distinguished atmosphere that the Bentley had provided, a world away from the chaos outside.

Ceiling fans whirred discreetly in every room to cool the air; the marble floors were refreshing to the feet; the furniture, more ornamental than practical sparsely lining the walls, was made of dark wood. Rattan settees with plump cushions stood along the walls. Nobody flopped down the way people in the West might throw themselves onto their sofas. Everyone took a seat, daintily perching on the edge.

Lakshmi had begun giving orders to her servants to bring refreshments. Karin sank gratefully into the deep cushions. She caught a glimpse of something moving and watched with fascination lizard-like creatures clinging lazily to the edge where the walls met the ceiling.

'Gheckos,' Priti explained, who had followed her glance.

They hung there, immobile like small porcelain ornaments displayed far too high, until something buzzed past. With one lightening-fast strike the prey was snapped up before the gecko reverted to complete inertia.

As they sat there, the rest of the family, who had been at the airport, trundled in as well. Chairs had to be brought from other rooms and the children sat on colourful, plumped up floor cushions. Everyone was happily chattering away, mainly to Raj, who was in his element. Sometimes they switched from Bengali to English to include her in the conversation, nodding encouragingly for her to make a comment. Karin was quite happy just to watch and listen. She loved the sound of the Bengali language; it was melodious and gently flowing; less staccato than Arabic which demanded rolled 'Rs' like chainsaws.

Jet-lag and fatigue following the excitement of the journey and arrival were catching up with her. The heat, in spite of being ruffled constantly by fans, contributed to her sleepiness from which she only surfaced when someone shook her gently by the shoulders.

'Have a cup of tea, auntie,' Priti said, 'then you must go and have a rest!'

The tea tasted different, not unpleasantly, but unexpectedly so. Some sort of spice had been added. They asked whether she wanted it white, but she declined. It was certainly refreshing. She nibbled listlessly at a crumbly biscuit which was salty and studded with another spice she couldn't define.

'*Nimki*,' they said urging her to take more.

Soon tiredness took over again and Karin was gently shunted off. Accompanied by her hostess, her niece and the two other daughters of the house, Sultana and Royeya, she was led to her new bedroom. Her luggage had already miraculously appeared and had been stacked neatly in a corner. The room was large and dimmed by curtains hiding a wooden patio door. A ceiling fan whipped the hot air into waves of little breezes which made Karin shiver whenever one hit her bare arms.

The girls fussed with the bed, making sure that the mosquito net was tucked in securely on all sides. When reassured that all was fine, they pushed her towards the bed:

'You sleep now,' they insisted.

A servant girl, hovering by the door, was ordered to bring *pani* and returned with a carafe of water and a glass which was put on a sturdy bedside table. Then they shushed each other out of the room and left Karin by herself. She was certainly tired enough for a nap, but before she lay down she wanted to see what was behind that curtain. It was firmly fixed in place and did not slide to one side on its pole. Karin simply lifted it from the right, folding it in her hand, and slipped through before it fell back rigidly into place.

She found herself on a balcony which stretched along the entire floor. It was empty bar a servant's child occasionally flitting across it in the distance, appearing from one doorway and disappearing in another. Karin couldn't hear any voices in spite of knowing that the family were still gathered in the sitting room. She loved the unconditioned, unstirred heat on her skin and the unusual clanging, clattering and hooting coming from below.

As she leant over the balustrade, she realised that the balcony overhung the waters of a wide river. Raj had mentioned that they would at first live in a house overlooking the Buriganga. The waters were crowded with cargo boats, ships and passenger ferries, each jostling noisily for space. People on the shores bathed, did their laundry or pursued a trade. No-one noticed her up there on the balcony. The water's surface sparkled as if diamanté had been sprinkled upon it, and the air smelled faintly salty and fishy, mingling with wafts of cooking oil and petrol from the boats.

At home in Germany when Karin had looked out of the window, she had seen orderly queues of cars, cyclists and motorbikes, pedestrians hurrying along pavements and, on the opposite side, other multi-storeyed houses.

This scene was so different, a wide river under a blazing sun, river noises and smells, and time stretching endlessly.

Karin tore herself away lazily and settled down to her first nap behind mosquito curtains. The servant girl, short and slight, wrapped in a cotton sari of washed-out, undistinguishable colours, was still hovering by the door. She was probably not even a teenager yet but had already the burden of a working woman edged on her face. She now glided towards the bed and tucked the fourth side of the mosquito net firmly under the thin mattress. While doing so, she smiled shyly without looking directly into her new mistress's face, as if waiting for further instructions. When none came forth, she tip-toed out of the room. Seconds later, Karin was submerged in deep sleep.

❀ ❀ ❀

'A cup of *cha*?' Priti stood at the end of the bed, carrying the refreshment already. Karin sat up, pulled the mosquito net aside and sipped the sweet tea.

'Tell me, what is in it?'

'Cardamom seeds – we add it to almost everything,' she laughed.

'Grandfather has arrived,' Priti informed her. That would be Raj's father, Karin's father-in-law. It was a bit daunting to be presented to him so soon. Priti helped her auntie to re-arrange her sari and smooth it back into shape.

When they both emerged into the drawing room – there did not seem to be any internal doors in the house, only curtains – Karin saw Raj sitting on a saddleback cushion at the feet of a skinny old man in white cotton trousers, a white Nehru shirt hanging over them, a black sleeveless jacket, a black pill-box hat on his head and a long, white beard cascading down to his chest. Old-fashioned round glasses sat on the tip of his nose and his jowls drooped from his cheeks like those of a bloodhound. Raj beamed up at his father with great reverence. No sooner did the old man see Karin, when he heaved himself up from his deep armchair. His small eyes the colour of hazel nuts inspected her with curiosity as if trying to find an answer in her face.

'Abbu, this is my wife Karin,' Raj introduced her and hissed at her: 'Pay your *salaam*'.

Karin had seen it often enough to know how to bend down waving her hands three times from her lips over her father-in-law's feet, only touching them slightly. She was interrupted by one hand on the crown of her head as if receiving a blessing and another pulling her upwards. It was a sign that she had shown enough respect and that she should stand up.

'You don't need to do that. You are my daughter-in-law from the West. Welcome!' he said kindly in perfect English, laced with a heavy Bengali accent. His eyes reflected a warm smile and she knew instinctively that they would get on well. The family, who had dispersed, returned for the evening meal, a huge affair, a never ending stream of dishes on plates, in bowls and on trays. There were curries of chicken, lamb, prawns, fish, vegetables, potatoes, lentils; she lost count but, being curious, had a little of everything which pleased her father-in-law enormously. Everyone ate with their right hand, astonishingly only leaving signs of curry sauce on the tip of their fingers. Abbu had insisted that she should sit next to him. When Lakshmi ladled out curried fish pieces, the old man began to take charge of Karin's plate. She watched him as he mashed

142

the fish with his fingers to extract bones and shaped the flakes together with rice into balls, lining the rim of her plate with them like a bead necklace.

'I don't want you to choke on a fishbone,' he explained. Karin was speechless but secretly touched by his extraordinary and slightly peculiar thoughtfulness.

Karin, the single child, loved the mayhem around and across the table; the members of her new family were good-humoured, chatting, laughing and teasing each other. The servants rushed in and out of the dining room with ever more dishes and drinks, until they all groaned and professed that they could eat no more. A lazy, contented silence descended upon the room and slowly, one by one, the relatives departed to their own homes somewhere in Dhaka. Only Raj's eldest brother, Khaled, who had come all the way from Chittagong with his wife Farah, their three daughters and one son stayed on with Lakshmi's family. It seemed to be self-understood and a reason for great happiness to accommodate any number of visitors.

Back in their bedroom, Karin had Raj to herself for the first time since their arrival. He was elated and in such good spirits that he hugged her several times spontaneously, before they realised that the huge, dark eyes of the little servant girl were watching them. She was crouched in a dim corner of the room, fanning the smoke from an earthen ware pot into the room.

'To keep the mosquitoes at bay,' Raj explained, but then shooed the little girl out with an authoritative: '*cholo, cholo!*'.

'I hope you were nice to her,' Karin muttered.

'Of course,' he replied shrugging his shoulders.

'They like you,' she heard him proudly say, before she fell asleep in his arms.

After the first few days of adjustment and settling in, Karin fell into a lazy routine of ambling through the daylight hours.

She and Raj usually got up after the children of the house had left for school or college and the men had gone to work in Government offices or to their own businesses. No-one was ever in a hurry, and nothing seemed to be expected of the young couple. Household chores were done by servants who flitted around the house like friendly, unobtrusive ghosts.

'I don't have to lift the proverbial finger,' she wrote to her parents. 'I feel as if I am on a long, luxurious holiday and I love it!'

A lot of the time, she spent in the company of her female relatives while Raj went off without her to attend to manly business. What this consisted off, he rarely said, and she assumed that he was catching up on old friendships and contacts who might help him to resume his career.

Her weekly program was a round of visits from relatives or to relatives' houses, proud introductions of the western *bhabi* to friends, dining out in Chinese restaurants – 'Bengali food is much better cooked by our chef at home,' she was told – shopping in markets and posh tourist shops in the wide expanse of Elephant Road, followed by visits to *kulfi* and baby-ice cream parlours. Karin's favourite one was called 'Banana Split' and she collapsed with laughter when on their first attempt, the waiter had to rush out to buy bananas.

On another occasion, she had a complete culture shock when they entered the Hotel Intercontinental, to sample their Knickerbocker Glories, and several foreign women crossed the lobby in bikinis to go swimming in the hotel's outdoor pool. The culture clash seemed to affect her more than her gaggle of sisters-in-law, who hid their broad grins behind the *achols* of their saris. Occasionally, the men joined them at the restaurants and Karin thought it funny that Raj's brother Babul used to sit at the far end of the table, away from his father, until he whispered to her that Abbu didn't know that his second eldest was a chain smoker, and that he would like to keep it secret.

The English cricketers came to Dhaka to play the newly formed Bangladeshi team in the hurriedly tidied up stadium. Karin was so excited, but she soon realised that only men and boys were allowed to go. Karin tried to pester Raj to make an exception – she was after all a special case – but he was too embarrassed to plead for her in front of his brothers that he didn't even try.

A regular weekly event was their visit to the cinema. New films came out daily; they often filtered through to Bangladeshi screens from Bollywood in India. Many were in Hindi but could be understood by their Bengali audience. Karin's family tended to hire the entire balcony to accommodate everyone. People with cheap tickets stood below like the groundlings in Shakespearean theatres. The films excelled in length and pathos accompanied by shouts and whistling from the excitable spectators. Happiness

144

and tragedy were whipped up in equal measure to a frenzied conclusion. Love scenes were taboo and only hinted at through smouldering looks, pouts and dancing. Tragedy was often enormously exaggerated and more than once did Karin set her nieces and nephews off giggling with her practical comments.

In one story, the hero had lost his eye-sight and his long-lost friend, tears streaming down his face with compassion, offered to donate both his eyes. Karin caused a spasm of hilarity when she mumbled suggestively that 'one would do'.

There was a similar effect when she exclaimed 'You silly girl,' after a particularly naïve heroine fell for the all too obvious tricks of the cad in the film.

Soon after Karin and Raj had arrived, the family arranged a repeat of their marriage vows, not exactly the grand affair which Islamic weddings usually turn into. The fact that they had been married legally for over a year and the absence of her parents shortened proceedings considerably. But still, a whole day's celebration was planned for them.

Karin was still in bed, when her nieces fell over her like a swarm of bees, dragged her to Priti's room, sat her in front of a dressing table and began an elaborate session of making her up. They took great pride and pleasure to put layer upon layer of foundation and tinting creams on her skin, eye shadows, kohl to frame her eyes, henna for her hands, and a white creamy substance with which they dotted the contours of her face in intricate patterns. Then they dressed her in a red and gold chiffon sari, covered her head with an equally red veil, hung a gold *bindi* from her pulled back hair onto her forehead and covered every inch of bare skin with gold necklaces and bangles. After a heated discussion, they decided that a *nakphool*, a nose ring, looked ridiculous on her little nose

'I look like a red Christmas tree,' Karin thought to herself, but felt strangely moved by the diligence they employed as they would for any other bride.

Finding herself in this exotic role, she suddenly realised the momentous step she had taken to move to this far distant land and acknowledged with gratitude the tolerance and warmth Raj's family was prepared to extend to a stranger like her.

At last, the girls were satisfied and pushed her towards the sitting room, where the official registrar from the local Mosque was waiting. He was dressed in white pyjama trousers, a cotton shirt with a Nehru collar and a chequered cloth on his head. He seemed bemused by the unconventional request and circumstances, but proceeded to do his duty, which meant to register the couple's details with the stub of a pencil in a large, ruled book. It took him a long time to cope with the foreign names and Karin wasn't quite sure whether his mutterings were blessings, prayers or something else. Finally he asked the couple to put their signatures under his notes.

'I hope I am not signing my life away,' Karin just managed to stop herself from blurting out.. This was not the cinema, and even there her comments were not always welcome.

Tea and holy sweets were served after the ceremony and the *mufti* felt most important being the centre of respectful attention in such a distinguished house. It completely erased from his mind how peculiar this wedding between the foreigner and her Bengali husband was in which he had been asked to play his part.

Karin's make-up was lovingly refreshed, before the party moved to the northern part of Dhaka, called Dhanmondi, where Babul had erected a marquis in his garden and had invited a surprisingly large crowd of relatives, friends and neighbours.

Even Rashid, who had only recently been freed from Pakistan's war prison, put in an appearance. He looked drawn, ill at ease and rather shaken, still preferring, according to his wife's whispered explanations, solitude.

Again, tables creaked with food and Karin and Raj shook hands like royalty, accepting gifts and congratulations all afternoon. Occasionally they mingled with guests to simply stretch their legs, but for most of the time, they were expected to sit or stand on the same spot so that the happy couple could be introduced to the intrigued guests.

It was a strenuous but happy day and Karin thanked her brother-in-law profusely for the effort he had put in to give their union a formal base, acceptable to Bengali society.

With two weddings behind her, Karin felt well and truly married.

※ ※ ※

Raj was still no nearer a permanent job. He seemed to dabble, helping out in the various family businesses and nobody seemed

146

to mind. Whenever asked he said that he was really waiting for a job to become available at his old ministry. Karin, who had always been in charge of finances while they still lived in Germany, had now no idea what they were living on, whether they were kept by Lakshmi and her family or whether Raj had savings or regular income she knew nothing about. In any case, he would just laugh when she broached the subject and would say something like: 'Don't you worry your pretty little head about such things!'

If she persisted during one of their few private moments, he would wave the subject away with his hand as if swatting a fly. She had learnt to know better than to pursue it, because a deep frown line would appear on the bridge of his nose and the light atmosphere would turn heavy with anger and disapproval, if she did. Three months after their Bengali wedding celebrations she had news for him: 'I'm pregnant,' she blurted out and was surprised how he blushed and grinned shyly.

Word spread like wild fire in the family and from then on, she could hardly save herself from being pampered and bombarded with well-meant advice. The women took over completely as if pleased to have been provided with an important task. The disappointment in their faces was unbearable when she mentioned that she might be flying back to Germany for the birth of her first child.

Chapter Fourteen

☙☙

When the two sisters go to fetch water...
Rabrindranath Tagore

'Hallohhh?'

Karin recognises the coquettish voice of her favourite niece immediately. Priti has always been the most spirited and enthusiastic of them all. To Karin's relief it doesn't sound as if she has changed much.

'Priti, it's Karin,' adding as a reminder 'Mita auntie.' She hasn't used that name for years and it feels strange now.

Karin can hear a gasp at the other end, rustling and a hurried: 'Hold on a moment.' After a while of children shouting and laughing in the background and whooshing noises, indicating that the telephone has been carried to another room, Priti's cheerful voice re-appears.

'Auntie, I knew you would come. Thank you.'

Karin thinks that her niece has more faith in her than she did herself a couple of days ago.

'How are you?'

'Healthy and happy with a tribe of children and grand-children as is expected of a Bengali wife.' It isn't a complaint, just a statement accompanied by laughter.

Although it is perfectly natural for a fifty-odd year old woman to be a grand-mother, Karin gulps at the thought that her niece has pipped her to the post.

'Do you think we can meet up?' Karin suddenly feels the urgent need to see her, face to face, to re-connect with their past relationship, but she is not sure how much welcome she can expect.

'How long will you stay?' Priti hasn't answered her question.

'A week or so... I am retired, so no one is waiting for me,' Karin adds to explain.

The children's voices in the background come nearer again and seem to indicate a fight breaking out.

'It's difficult to talk at the moment,' Priti says, sounding beleaguered.

'Would you like to meet me in my hotel?' It is unlikely that they will be spotted there, should Priti feel the need to keep her auntie's visit a secret.

'No, I tell you what, auntie. Do you remember Ramna Green?'

'Of course, I do! You left me there often enough,' they both start to laugh.

'It was worth it though,' Priti's smug repartee is quick.

'Good,' replies her aunt, pleased to hear that this arranged marriage has obviously worked out well.

'Let's meet tomorrow at five in the park on the bench closest to the main entrance,' Karin suggests decisively.

'Do you still remember the Green that well?' Priti is astonished.

'No, I have been there today.'

'Oh auntie, you old romantic!'

The noise from children playing comes now directly from beneath the telephone.

'Is five o'clock tomorrow okay?' Karin urges.

'I think I can manage that. If not I shall leave a message in your hotel.'

'Will we recognise each other?' Priti wonders, but her aunt puts a stop to it with a determined: 'Of course!'

There follows a silence which Karin puts down to an unexplained awkwardness, and she is afraid that Priti is getting cold feet about their meeting. Her heart lifts when she hears:

'I can't wait to see you again, Mita auntie!'

A wave of unifying excitement and naughtiness sweeps over the two women and Karin confirms:

'Yes, it will be lovely.'

At the last moment, she picks up courage: 'Priti, how is he?'

'Not good.'

The shrieks are getting louder than Priti's voice and their conversation is suddenly cut off.

The phone call has been short and had an air of secrecy about it, although Priti must have expected her aunt to ring in response to the message left at the hotel. Karin waits a few minutes whether she will ring back. She doesn't, and Karin has to be content that she has extracted a meeting time and place. Considering Priti's slightly furtive tone, she concludes that the rest of the family have no idea that Raj's ex-wife is in Dhaka and that they might disapprove of her resurgence.

'This leaves tomorrow morning and most of the afternoon free to go on another nostalgic trip,' Karin muses with pleasure and rings the reception to send a message to Farook, the driver.

Chapter Fifteen

ৎ৪ৡ

When I thought I would mould you
An image from my life for men to worship
I brought my dust and desires and
all my coloured delusions and dreams...
Rabrindranath Tagore

The first six months of married life as a Bangladeshi wife were spent in gentle idleness. It was the common lifestyle around her. Raj was with her most of the time; only sometimes did he have to go out, she presumed, in pursuit of a job. He was a little unwilling to explain, but he reassured her that it wasn't important that she knew every little detail.

The heat was unrelenting and sapped everyone's energy. There wasn't much to do anyway. She was not allowed to go out without a male chaperone, but then she would not have known where to go and how to get there. For amusement, while Raj was away, she often joined the women, supervised discreetly by one male member of the family.

Now that she was pregnant this gentle, relaxing lifestyle turned into complete inertia. Her *bhabis* fussed no end around her as if she were the first and only woman ever to be expecting a baby. Whenever she busied herself with her own preparation, she was pressed into deep cushions, more were stuffed into her back and plates of rich and creamy curries or sweetmeats were put in front of her. The curries were now mild and made with coconut milk; rice puddings were lusciously sweet and made with thick cream. After a lot of pleading from Karin, they added fresh vegetables and fruit to her diet. Her every wish was their command except for a little personal freedom which they themselves did not seem to need. Sometimes, Karin managed to snatch a few moments to nose around the house on her own. No sooner had she entered and marvelled at the ultra modern western kitchen on the first floor boasting the latest cookery gadgets when Abdul the chef of the house appeared to find out whether there was something she required.

'Can I fry an egg on the cooker?' It sounded banal but at that moment it seemed really important to her; whether it was to reassert her independence or simple boredom, she wasn't sure. Abdul nodded rigorously, took a frying pan from one of the teak cupboards and rushed off to get butter and eggs from where ever the larder was. What had not occurred to him was that Karin had actually wanted to fry the egg herself, not because she was particularly hungry, but because she wanted to do something for herself, however small.

She was politely but determinedly reminded that she was the mistress. Abdul indicated to her to sit at the dining room table next door, his way to shove her out of his domain. By the time the beautifully fried egg and toasted soldiers, made of *paratas*, arrived she had gone off the idea, but emptied the plate dutifully not to offend the cook.

She told Priti about this incident in the evening and received a sympathetic hearing – after all Priti could appreciate what a busy life Karin had led before coming to Bangladesh – but was informed that it was offensive to the servants if their masters did their jobs; it might even be misunderstood that they thought them dispensable.

Another time, Karin climbed the steps up to the roof top. No one had ever bothered to show her what was up there. In spite of the scorching heat, the roof terrace was fanned by a light river breeze. The view to the river on one side was obscured by large bed sheets being hung up to dry. Reed sleeping mats were rolled up, held together by string and leant against the parapets near the doors of cubby holes the size of small coal bunkers. Three earthen mounds rose from the ground, like mole hills, with two or three holes on the sides to feed the fire with wood, while the tops were flattened and carved out to accommodate the shape of cooking pots.

The air was thick with moist heat, wood smoke, exhaust fumes rising from the road on one side and rancid saltiness from the river on the other. Fat, black crows dropped out of the sky with vulgar screeches to scavenge for any morsels that had fallen onto the concrete floor, before taking off heavily like overloaded aeroplanes.

On the neighbouring flat roofs, Karin saw two monkeys fiercely fighting over something. One tried to snatch it from the other until a young girl in a cotton sari shushed them away by banging a wooden spoon against a tin pot, creating an awful din. The monkeys fled at great speed, clambering over roof tops, jumping from one house to another, shrieking excitedly or making threatening rasping noises. They swung effortlessly from one place to another and ran light-footedly across the balconies trying to steal whatever was edible and unguarded.

It didn't take long before Karin was discovered by a horrified older maid servant, the mother of Ranoo, the little girl assigned to be her personal servant. Ranoo's mother put the *achol* of her orange cotton sari over her head and gestured to the intruder that this was no place for her to be.

'It's lovely and peaceful up here…' Karin ignored the woman's panic. 'I shall bring my camera and take a photograph. The view is breathtaking!'

Thousands of roof tops stretched before her, looking much whiter than they probably were in reality. The gold dome of a mosque glinted in the fierce sunlight and the cluttering and clanging from the river on one side and the log-jammed traffic on the other were reduced to a faint hum, hardly audible, like the gentle buzzing of foraging bees.

Ranoo's mother stood half respectfully, half frightened in the far corner where she had positioned herself and from where she watched Karin's every move. She seemed enormously relieved when this new, crazy, foreign *memsahib* wandered towards the stairs leading down into the house, without anyone having discovered the two of them. Somehow the poor woman seemed to feel responsible for this misdeed.

'Thank you – *onek dhonobad.*' The servant did an impatient *acha* sideways nod, which Karin had learnt meant something like 'okay'.

'What's your name?' She earned an uncomprehending stare.

'*Aponar nam ki?*' Karin was extremely impressed with herself. It was the first time that she genuinely needed to use the few snippets of Bengali she had learnt so far.

'Ayesha', The servant mumbled unwillingly..

'*Nam bhalo!*' Karin assured her that it was a good name, but Ayesha wasn't having any of it. She withdrew even further to the wall and kept stubbornly quiet. Karin got the message and, pressing her palms together in the Indian 'namaste' style, she took her leave. She hoped this slightly misplaced gesture wouldn't offend, but did not look back to see the reaction. She could well imagine Ayesha's sigh of relief.

Karin did go up with her camera at the same time on the following day and was relieved to find the roof top deserted. No one to watch her with reproachful stares!

Soon afterwards, however, the masters picked up gossip from whispering servants and Karin was instructed by her slightly uneasy husband that it was improper to intrude in the servants' quarters and that such visits had to stop.

'Raj, it's lovely up there,' she argued. 'You should come with me. One can see the whole city, and the air is not as stifling as down here,' she pleaded but to no avail.

'You will bring shame on the family, visiting servants in their part of the house,' he clucked his tongue and shook his head in disapproval. He was determined to stamp out any such nonsense.

With a heavy heart and not completely convinced that he was at least a little bit wrong, she complied. She began to feel like a pet bird whose wings were being clipped more every day.

Her father-in-law called her into his room the following afternoon. He was probably going to tell her off as well. Hesitantly, she approached.

'Would you like to read to me? My eyes aren't good any more,' his smile radiated warmth and reassurance.

For lack of anything else to do, she made the reading session a regular daily feature. Her father-in-law was so easy to please. Sometimes she read to him from the English version of the Koran, which he kept always at hand, or a poem from an old volume of *Rabindranath Tagore*, or a little historical novel by John Gloak called *Artorius Rex* which an old friend, fellow enthusiast of history and lecturer at Dhaka university, had once given him as a present long ago. The story and chaotic picture of the British Isles after four centuries of Roman occupation seemed to puzzle him, but it appealed to his eagerness for self-improvement and gathering of knowledge.

Karin and her father-in-law spent hours reading and chatting, and she gleaned many a hidden pearl of wisdom.

In return, she helped him to put on his socks and shoes; saw to it that he had tea and his favourite biscuits and followed up orders he had given to the servants.

One afternoon, as she entered his quarters, a totally unexpected scene shocked her to the core: The old man was hitting a servant with the leather sole of his pointy slipper; the boy was cowering against the wall and protecting his head with his arms,. When the old man noticed that his daughter-in-law was standing in the door, he stopped and the boy took the chance to scuttle away.

'I have not one clean handkerchief,' the old man complained like a sulking child, obviously hoping that Karin would take his side.

Instead she shook her head and said: 'Abbu, that wasn't very nice!'. He saw the shock in her face at having caught him being unkind and cruel.

'I told him yesterday that I was running low. They are supposed to do the laundry every day,' he muttered unrepentantly.

Karin just looked at him, trying to keep disapproval from her expression. She did not want to antagonise him.

'Wait a moment, Abbu.' She rushed to Raj's wardrobe and returned triumphantly with two of his handkerchiefs, which he rarely used anyway.

'You can keep those,' she told him, placatingly.

Problem solved, she suggested reading some Tagore, to calm down both of them.

'I am in the mood for a bit of poetry,' she said, already leafing through the tome's pages.

While she lived the life of a Bengali wife she kept in constant contact with her parents. The once-monthly telephone call was usually not so successful because of interruptions, crackles or distortions on the line. Therefore, she made it into a habit to write a kind of diary for them which she posted at the end of each week. It was another thing to do to fill the ample stretch of empty time. Her mother's replies were at first sporadic and cool in their wording, but as the months passed, she relented and answered them with ever increasing warmth and concern.

At first, Karin had found it disconcerting that letters from her parents would reach her opened and the pages creased as if someone had read them already. When she complained to Raj, she found out that whoever received mail from the postman would feel entitled to open it, never mind to whom it was addressed. Raj did not sympathise with his wife's protest, pointing out that no one except the two of them spoke German and would therefore have any idea what her parents had written. That was not the point Karin had wanted to make, but it explained why her nieces had come rushing in with opened envelopes and had stood there waiting for any news Karin was bound to impart: Any letter addressed to auntie was exciting and definitely of interest to the whole family.

Once the word was out that Karin was expecting their first grand-child, her mother and father urged her to return for the birth. It was a difficult decision to make and Karin found herself in a dilemma. So far, Karin had had two experiences of medical care in Dhaka.

The first time, she had tagged along when Lakshmi, Raj and a young nephew had to take Abbu for a blood test. The patient had insisted that she come along. After a short drive, they had entered a pretty garden where a queue of nearly a hundred people waited patiently in the relentless sun. The surgery was housed in a bungalow at the far end amidst a clump of trees. As they joined the queue resignedly and had just decided to lead Abbu back to the car for the wait, a young man distributed numbers on what looked like lottery tickets. Confused as the old man already was, he lost his temper, slapped the number ticket out of the boy's hand and yelled: 'Don't you know who I am? Our family does not wait in queues!'

With this, he reared to his full height and walked with surprisingly energetic steps, supported by his walking stick, towards the surgery building. The waiting crowd watched in fascination. Nobody stopped him. He reached the entrance and marched straight in, his startled family scuttling breathlessly after him. When they had finally caught up, two nurses were already trying to calm the old man. Negotiations began and a compromise was reached: In consideration of his age, they would make an exception this once and see him within half an hour; however, they insisted, he would have to comply with the rules on any further visits. Triumphantly, Abbu waited on a hastily provided chair, erect and regal as if he had wrestled his throne from the clutches of an usurper.

'I won't ever come here again!' Karin heard him mutter into his white beard.

'Why does your father think that he has privileges?' Karin asked Raj as they reached home.

'My grandfather used to sit on a golden throne at official functions, and he used to own half the country,' Raj said haughtily, putting his naive young wife in her place.

The second visit was to a female doctor, a far distant relative, who was a gynaecologist. Karin had been urged that she should make more use of the jewellery she had been given for her wedding, in particular of the several pairs of gold earrings.

When Lakshmi decided shortly afterwards to have her nose pierced to break up the expanse of it with a ruby, it was considered a good opportunity to drag Karin along and to pierce her ears.

The surgery was in what looked like a small private clinic. The white furniture, the beds and surgical instruments were gleaming with cleanliness and air-conditioning created a fresh and comfortable atmosphere.

Lakshmi groaned theatrically as the doctor drilled through the wing of her nose; she promptly developed a fever in the afternoon. Karin tolerated the piercing of her ear lobes silently, which earned her the praise of the doctor who did not think much of her Bengali patients screaming the house down when giving birth.

'Western women are much more stoical and accepting when it comes to pain,' she said, to which Karin only nodded half-heartedly, never having witnessed anyone giving birth in either country and being unable to compare.

She regretted soon afterwards having agreed to the procedure because she found it irksome to comb her hair without getting entangled in the filigree ear rings. She had frightful visions of ripping her lobes. She often joked that soon she would look like an elephant, with ears down to her shoulders. Her relatives thought this a very funny notion, but also a very silly one. Beauty was worth suffering for!

159

In all honesty, Karin trusted the doctors she had grown up with, more than the ones in her new country who were so clearly deprived of modern equipment and had to battle constantly to achieve some degree of hygiene. However, she had to take other considerations into account, and she decided to give herself a bit more time before making up her mind where to give birth.

Everyone was happy that she had postponed a decision, hoping that the longer she left it the less likely she was to leave the country.

They found quickly something else to occupy their minds and began to plan excitedly a trip to their youngest sister Mumtaz in Sylhet.

Chapter Sixteen

ೞ೩

*Days were drawing out
As the winter ended...*
Rabrindranath Tagore

Later in the evening, Karin is sitting in cross legged posture on her crisp white bed and, having arranged the daily fresh *shaplas* in a semi-circle around her, she is toying with the idea of undertaking a substantial journey. She has one and a half days to visit one of the many places she had always longed but had never been given the opportunity to see. The family, of which she had become an integral part, had usually rushed to their next destination – invariably other relatives.

Karin draws up a list of the possibilities on the hotel's headed notepaper. The first name she writes down is *Sunderban*, the mangrove forest to the south, home to the Bengal tiger, spotted deer, crocodiles, wild boar, monkeys and an abundance of exotic birds; and she remembers wistfully having heard excited tales about river cruises, to which she was never taken.

Next she writes *Sylhet*, in the north-east, with its tea gardens on the hills and its much frequented shrines; she has been there once visiting relatives.

This is followed by *Rajshahi*, north-west of Dhaka, where the thinnest of silk saris are woven beside the river Padma which is so wide that one can barely see the other shore.

Chittagong is added, the brave and beautiful city on the Bay of Bengal, portal to magical places further south. She had seen some of the town when they had visited Khaled and his wife Farah.

The list grows: *Cox's Bazaar*, the longest beach of golden sand in the world, framed in the background by the lush green, forested foothills of the Himalayas and tilting into the deep blue sea where tiny fertile islands glitter far out in the Gulf of Bengal.

Karin remembers having been taken to *Rangamati*, where Muslim Bangladesh meets the Buddist Mogh tribe from neighbouring Myanmar, then called Burma. She had marvelled at the flooded valleys forming the huge man-made Kaptai Lake and the ease with which Islam, Buddism, Hinduism and Animism lived respectfully side by side.

One and a half days is not enough for any of these places. Moreover, she may have become braver, but she will not take risks travelling cross country with someone she hardly knows, however modest and subservient. For a brief moment, her children's warnings and her promise to them to be careful beams into her conscience.

She finally decides to visit one of the oldest capitals of Bengal, Sonargaon, only twenty miles from Dhaka – a sensible compromise.

Hardly wanting to admit to it, there is another reason why she chooses to aim south. Karin and Raj used to have a plot in the area with a modest house. It was meant to be their country retreat, their private haven, where she had tried to create a flower garden, but it was a failure. She had been miserably beaten by the summers' heat and had finally kept her efforts to tame the fierce wildness of the place to a minimum. She grew to be content with the naturally established banana, mango and date trees, and had learnt to enjoy her views of the surrounding rectangular, lime-coloured paddy fields, framed by raised mud banks the width of a footprint. She had learnt to love the flat landscape and had adjusted to the annual event of the monsoon, when the land submerged itself in its rivers and re-appeared a few weeks later as if by magic.

There had been jute fields nearby, and it had often been relayed to her how important jute was for the country's export revenues. However, she had cursed it when remnants from its harvest had got wedged in their car's undercarriage, and it had taken hours to pull, slice and tear the tough strands away.

She had had such hopes to finally create a little paradise for herself and her little family in Sonargaon, but after a few visits Raj had been bored by countryside and declared that he much rather spent his time in Dhaka close to all the family.

Karin doesn't think that she will find any traces of her country home from almost forty years ago, where she had sought but had never found privacy.

Early in the morning, Farook stands to attention and ready for service. Karin has barely time to have breakfast. She knows he is absolutely right to insist on an early departure while the ascending sun is still gathering heat which it will beam down mercilessly by midday.

They muddle their way patiently through Dhaka's morning traffic and settle comfortably in for a pleasant ride south once the city is left behind. The road is straight and in various stages of disrepair. However, improvements have been taken in hand and groups of stone-cutters sit at the edge of the road under big, black umbrellas over their heads like hovering ravens. To Karin, the work appears brutal, hammering rocks until they crumble into gravel under an unrelenting, merciless sun, but the workers sit by their heaps busily clanking away, proud to have a job and such a prestigious one at that.

'Sonargaon was seat of Deva Dynasty until thirteenth century and subsidiary capital of Sultanate of Bengal,' Farook informs her. She admires his knowledge of history.

A narrow road, just enough space for two rickshaws to pass each other, leads into the heart of the old town of Sonargaon, now called Painam Nagar. It is lined by two dozen or more dilapidated mansions, which are occupied and jealously defended by tenants or squatters. A long time ago, they were owned by wealthy Hindu *shakha* (shell) and gold jewellery merchants, but they had fled at the time of the Partition in 1947.

The old splendour is faded and wan like an aged diva's beauty. Most of the buildings are more or less in a state of ruin because their inhabitants can't afford repairs. The liveliness of children running in and out of these buildings and hawkishly watchful old women in white widows' saris on their rickety verandas are strangely incongruous, combining discordant echoes of the past and the present.

163

Farook drives along Market Road, over the steep hump of the old bridge. Karin wants to have a closer look at the crumbling façades. They decide to park further along the road where tin-shed shops and thatched mud-huts take over from the magnificent mansions. Karin and Farook are surprised when, a few hundred yards on, the road merges into a muddy path, unsuitable for anything more than walking or cycling.

Local boys are competing to be given the task of guarding the car and are disappointed when Farook tells them that he will do the job himself. Karin's surprised look makes him realise that he can not possibly leave his foreign, female charge to walk on her own, unprotected by male chivalry through the town. He chooses the oldest and most serious looking boy from the ragged cluster, who immediately takes on an air of great importance, shushing everyone else away. Karin can hardly bear the mass of disheartened faces. Her gaze follows wistfully the lean, young bodies as they slunk off, dressed in outsized *lungis*, which they have stuffed in great bulges round their waists to adjust the length; the youngest ones wear shorts flapping around their thin brown legs and reaching below their knees; their tops vary from short sleeved men's shirts in dark colours or white T-shirts with western motives yellowed from frequent washing; to sport's tricots advertising western football clubs whom the wearer will never see play.

Strolling back up the road to the mansions, Karin and Farook come across a strange pair, grandfather and grandson, who invite them to a guided tour through one of the biggest houses in the neighbourhood. Graceful iron railings merge into a grand, wrought iron gate. The visitors are led through it and enter a large overgrown garden where pillars and ornate, low bamboo fences demarcate once manicured lawns, rose gardens and a *pukoor* or pond area, which used to serve as a household reservoir. They are then ushered into the house. The old walls are covered in dust and cobwebs, which swing from pillars and decorative niches. Broken furniture, bamboo sticks and some corrugated tin sheets litter the uneven floor where the brown soil bulges from underneath mosaic tiles..

Karin lingers a long time in the *naach ghar*, the ball room, and imagines the splendid parties held there in grander times, attended by ladies in richly embroidered saris and men in pristine Indian or, later, stylish western suits or uniforms.

She strolls dreamily out into an open-air court yard, tiled with a black and white floor mosaic. The diamond shaped pattern must have been the height of fashion and luxury in those ancient days. As she turns to go, she looks back and marvels at the old-fashioned glamour which has draped itself over the place like a layer of golden gauze.

Karin gives her thanks to the pair of unlikely guides and puts a few coins into their tentatively raised palms. She is rewarded with a toothless grin by the weather beaten old man and a serious, mustering stare from the big, brown eyes of the little boy who clings to his grandfather's *lungi*.

A little further on, there is a tiny green space with one tree. Farook explains that it is a *krishnachura*, a flame-of-the-forest tree. Karin spreads out a handkerchief to sit on and rests in the shade under the fiery canopy, while Farook stands respectfully at a distance, keeping an eye on her.

She doesn't allow herself to nap for long. Together they walk towards what tourists call 'the old Sonargaon proper'. They pass women in brightly coloured saris with babies in their arms. Some have wet hair, sleeked back to dry in the sun.

The villas behind them have balconies crumbling into gardens; or broken staircases which never reach the ground; some have lost their upper floors leaving walls and pane-less windows open to the elements. They discover makeshift workshops squashed between the grand ruins and a bizarre electric wire jungle trailing down from many directions to bunch up in one archaic meter.

Karin notices the same group of teenagers, who had gathered earlier round the car, following them languidly ready to grasp any situation which would need their assistance.

She is tempted to follow the white-painted board directing her to the 'Sonargaon Art Gallery' and studio of the locally renowned artist Aminul Islam. The mild-mannered and frail looking artist is present and leads her through a series of dark and dank, sparsely furnished rooms whose walls are covered in paintings and drawings of local scenes and scenery. She feels obliged to buy something and chooses three small canvasses, one for each of her children and one for herself. Mr. Islam seems overwhelmed by this sale and thanks her profusely.

Kathrine chooses the smallest of the boys to carry her parcel of paintings. Imbued with his new status, he almost runs next to her to keep up.

As she leaves the studio, the teenage boys are gathering around her, offering their services as tourist guides more forcefully, promising more delights if she would only follow them. The unwilling Farook can hardly keep up translating their sometimes contradictory commentaries and shakes his head disapprovingly that she bothers to listen to them at all.

They first lead her to another ruined building which has been taken over by lush vines winding themselves around pillars and crawling out of every crack, while sturdy trees pry the foundations and brickwork apart. She is told that this used to be the *Naach Ghar*, the Sonargaon dance hall. It looks fragile and unsafe and Karin resists the enthusiastic offer of the boys to go inside.

She is sceptical when she is led down a muddy side road, but she knows that Farook is following and watching everyone like a hawk. The path is flanked by fields of paddy stalks, bowing heavy with rice grains under the afternoon sun. The air is full of country smells mingling mud, dung, dust and the heavy scent of husk. They reach a statue of the elephant god Ganesh and the first of two Hindu temples. Farook stays uneasily at a distance. It being early afternoon, the temple is closed but, they are told, it will be open for prayer later.

As they trample back in single file on the same path, the boys chatter and laugh having discharged their duty and in anticipation of a reward. Once they reach the main street, they fall back and shout their 'thank you' for Karin's generous tip, and, for lack of further knowledge of English, they add: '*aabar ashben*', which Farook translates as 'come again'. The little boy having exchanged the parcel of paintings for a few coins turns round and waves.

When they reach the car, the driver releases its guardian from his duty, whose face lights up when he gets paid handsomely on Karin's request. Farook climbs in the driver's seat with a barely audible sigh of exasperation. Karin smiles impishly, knowing that he won't dare to tell her off. It is late afternoon. Both of them feel clammy, thirsty and dusty. When they finally – after several miss-directions – find Karin's old country retreat, it is disappointing: From the car window she can see hordes of strangers swarming all over it, and her lovely garden and house are in a sorry state. She knows she shouldn't have come and asks Farook to head back to Dhaka.

Chapter Seventeen

☙❧

The tame bird was in a cage...
Rabrindranath Tagore

Karin's sisters-in-law reckoned that once she had given birth, she would not want to travel for quite a few months; so the sooner they went the better.

The planning of the trip escalated enormously. They decided to combine visits to two different branches of the family: one in Sylhet, the other in Chittagong. The first leg of the journey would amount to over three hundred miles followed by Sylhet to Chittagong, a stretch of over four hundred miles. Endless discussions went on, whether the journey would be too much for pregnant Karin. Finally, the female relative, who was a trained gynaecologist, was consulted and enlisted after she offered to come along at least for the first part of the trip..

Karin, in the comfortable middle stage of pregnancy, was infected with their excitement. It would be a change to her predictable and monotonous daily routine. The pleasure of being pampered and served on hand, foot and finger was slowly wearing off and she ached to be busy and occupied.

Once the route and date had been set, the shopping expeditions became frantic. The luggage mountain grew by the day and looked as if the entire family was going to emigrate. Everyone laughed hysterically when Karin added a pathetically small suitcase, holding the things she thought she might need. It was so much easier to pack in a warm climate. A couple of saris neatly folded did not take up much space, plus the blouses and petticoats to go with the saris, one cardigan and an extra blanket for the cooler nights sufficed. Travelling in Europe, one had to expect rising or dropping temperatures within short spaces of time but in Bangladesh a huge wardrobe was unnecessary. No one had to sit on Karin's suitcase to shut it.

'I have got everything in there I need,' she assured her *bhabis* and nieces, but they decided that she couldn't have and therefore packed additional items for her. In the end, they filled the boots of three cars: One was going to be driven by Rakesh, the family's driver, while the other two would be steered by the two eldest nephews, Hasin and Pran.

Three weeks after the idea had first been conceived, the convoy set off, pushing its way north and eastwards through the congested roads of Dhaka. They drove through areas of the town Karin had never seen before and she became suddenly aware, how much damage from the Independence War still remained. She could detect hardly any attempts being made at repairing or rebuilding. The population too poor to do so, had substituted their dwellings with tent-like shacks in front of ruins. Why the new Government didn't come to their rescue was beyond Karin's comprehension.

The first time Karin had been confronted with the consequences of the Independence War, was when Lakshmi took her to visit her neighbours opposite. Karin had been surprised that anybody actually lived in the ruin; she had imagined that it had been left to dilapidate, unsafe to live in and destined to rot. She had wondered about the architecture and stone carvings still visible on some outside walls.

'It must have been a grand house,' she had thought, 'but quite different to the other houses in the road.' With its scultpures of heads and ornamental garlands it made an altogether more mystical impression in spite of its sorry state. When Karin mentioned the house opposite, Lakshmi promised to introduce her to the owner.

One day, a rickshaw was hired to cross the dusty, chaotic road.

'Why don't we walk across?' Karin was nonplussed.

'You can't imagine how dirty our saris will become if we do that,' Lakshmi dismissed the idea.

They climbed on board the rickshaw and got off again a few seconds later on the other side. There they found themselves outside an enormous wooden door. Lakshmi made a terrible racket banging on it and for a moment, Karin was worried that the panels might fall off their hinges.

'Safda *bhabi*,' Lakshmi shouted, 'it's me, Lakshmi, your neighbour.'

A little girl opened one side of the door to a slit and scrutinized the visitors suspiciously. Someone shouted something at the back of the house and the girl signalled silently to the visitors that they should enter.

The house, once a mansion, was a ruin on the inside, too. Only four walls encircled the yard of the once grand entrance hall, pointing erect towards the sky at different heights. There was no roof above to give protection from rain. Weeds were growing between the floor tiles, lifting some of them to form an uneven surface. Vines had started to wriggle through the brickwork, their tendrils threatening advance. Above, open to the sky, were only a few blackened beam stumps which hung precariously in the air like an abruptly halted flight path.

As they approached the back of the house, Karin noticed that there were a couple of rooms which were blessed with a remaining ceiling. An elderly, wrinkled lady in a purple sari with faded embroideries appeared in a vaulted opening, holding a piece of brocade, hung as a curtain, to one side. Greetings were formal, but warm. Karin understood that apologies were expressed for the reduced circumstances of the hostess, but they were courteously ushered into the room behind the brocade and soon served with hot tea and biscuits. To Karin's astonishment, the room had been furnished as if it was still part of a lavish mansion. The family had obviously been trying desperately to hang on to some of its dignity.

As Karin looked around, she admired the sumptuous sofas in rich reds and blues; beautiful marquetry tables crouching low in the middle of an oriental rug and a series of little altars in old and newly developed corner niches where candles illuminated

169

statues of Hindu gods. They were decorated with miniature flower garlands and threw shadows of their many arms, legs and heads eerily over peeling paint and ruined walls.

The conversation had halted as tea had been served with great decorum. Biscuits were offered, again with many apologies and comparisons to the highly praised box of sweets the visitors had brought. Karin felt as if she was suspended in a surreal world of make-belief, a scene taking place on the only island salvaged from the ravages of war.

'Life is so hard for them,' Lakshmi had explained once they had left and hired another rickshaw to cross the road homewards. 'Safda lost her husband when their house was set alight. He had a heart attack and died in the flames trying to save a servant girl. Now Safda lives alone with her daughter, who isn't quite right in the head since all that happened. She kept the little servant girl.... but she won't accept any charity.'

'Why would anyone want to burn their house down?' a horrified Karin had asked.

'They are Hindus and in war, age-old enmities emerge, however deep one thought they had been buried. ...They were such good neighbours and such a cheerful family,' Lakshmi said, 'now look at them!'

'Why didn't they stay in India after Partition?'

Lakshmi shrugged her shoulders: 'Business opportunities, I suspect; but I don't know really... It's such a shame.'

'Yes,' thought Karin, 'people usually get on with each other; it's the politicians and the fanatics who ruin everyone else's lives.'

🪷 🪷 🪷

Now the convoy at the start of its journey, had to negotiate a multitude of potholes, leftovers from the invasion of the Pakistani Army, worsened by monsoon rains.

As they left the city behind, paddy fields, left and right of the road, fresh, lush green and healthy, struggled against a picture of destroyed roads, villages and shrines. Most of them had been left to disintegrate forming heaps of rubble no-one had the strength to remove or to re-build.

They occasionally passed farmers' dwellings which had escaped unscathed, straw huts huddling together on the only bit of even, raised surface in the watery landscape. They stopped at one of

170

them. Karin thought, it was to ask for directions. Three short, thin men with leathery brown skin approached the strangers, but stayed at a safe distance, waiting for the travellers to talk first. Karin guessed that the white-bearded man was the grand-father while next to him stood his middle-aged son and teenage grandson. They were all bare-chested and wore faded *lungis* wound around their waists.

Serious words were exchanged between the two parties and Karin picked up the word *cha*. The farmer shouted a few words to the back of his compound. A young woman, standing half hidden by the curtain of her entrance, put quickly the *achol* of her sari over her head, grabbed the hand of a toddler and disappeared inside. A few minutes later, she came back, calling to her husband to help with the trays full of tea cups and glasses. The teenage boy was made to carry the heavy tin kettle.

Thus the travelling party was served with tea and a few stale, sandy biscuits. Considering the stare of the teenager at the biscuits, these might have been the only ones the family had, reserved as a special treat. While pouring tea, the farmer's family kept apologising that they could not entertain them more lavishly and they were adamant that they would not accept Lakshmi's offer of a few bank notes.

'Guests are a gift of Allah,' Priti translated, 'we are honoured by your visit.'

As the cars drove away, the passengers saw in the back mirrors, that the men, now joined by their shy women folk, waved. They would talk about this event, the visit of noble ladies in beautifully embroidered saris and city men in shirts and trousers, for months to come.

Soon the travellers encountered a big problem: The vast number of rivers they needed to cross to get to Sylhet. During the Independence War, the country's ally, India, had deemed it wise – like a patronising uncle who knew best – to blow up most bridges stretching as life-lines across the country's waterways. The official explanation had been that it would stop the Pakistani army to advance. It was doubtful that this had been justified, but now, two years after ceasefire, the bridges had still not been

171

restored. As the travellers approached their first river, stumps of the old bridge stuck into the air on either side. It looked dangerous and risky to attempt a crossing.

Karin sensed that their driver had not been prepared to show his more acrobatic driving skills. He had to consider that every seat in the car was taken by a member of the family whose lives had been entrusted to him. In the end, Lakshmi, the organiser of the trip, bribed him to at least attempt the river crossing on two hollowed-out tree trunks by absolving him from all blame should anything go wrong. The trunks were pushed into position at the width of the car wheels like wooden railway tracks. This was accompanied by a lot of shouting, gesticulating and heated discussions among villagers, boats' people and whoever else stood at the river's edge.

After many assurances, the tourists took their hearts and courage into their hands, supressed fear, prayed loudly to Allah and piled back into the cars.

Slowly, the first vehicle edged closer to the water and made tentatively contact with the tree trunk rails. Nothing moved, swung or shifted which gave the driver more confidence in the loud and wild encouragements from the people outside, who were holding on to the sides of the vehicle, as if the panels might come off otherwise. Once the tyres gripped the wood, the car rolled, in first gear, gently away and out above the expanse of the water. Everyone, including Karin held their breath and closed their eyes as the villagers let go, staying behind, applauding, more in hope than certainty. The car glided in slow-motion across the river like a high-wire acrobat, suspended in mid-air, defying catastrophe and common sense.

They reached the soggy shore at the other end where the tyres carved deep marks into the muddy earth and then clawed their way up the gentle incline onto firmer soil.

Everyone stormed out of the car, as if escaping from a watery grave. They looked back in astonishment to where they had come from, waving with relief, signalling to the cars left behind that all was well. Everyone on the other side waved back with wild delight. Particularly the locals, who had suddenly had doubts whether it had been a wise decision to endanger such a noble family, were relieved, and their children jumped up and down and threw both their arms into the air in triumph.

This first successful crossing gave the rest of the convoy

courage and the other two cars followed without hesitation, speedier and with strengthened confidence.

Having safely reached the other side, camping tables were erected and a picnic improvised, to dispel any lingering anxiety. Tempers calmed and the fraught atmosphere was replaced by a renewed sense of adventure, by the belief that the worst of the journey was over and by the joyful expectation that they would soon be reunited with their relatives.

It was evening when they finally arrived in the city, three hundred miles from Dhaka. Having been involved in the drama of the river crossings, they hadn't stopped at any of the shrines Karin had pointed to in her travel guide. It was a large book about the Indian subcontinent, in which Bangladesh owned only five pages and Sylhet appeared only in four short paragraphs. She was determined to visit whatever there was of historical and cultural significance; however, every time she brought up a name, she was assured that it hadn't been really worth stopping for and that they had gone long past it anyway. Furthermore, they had aimed to reach the safety of Sylhet town before nightfall which sounded reasonable.

The welcome was enthusiastic, emotional and noisy. The entire neighbourhood seemed to have turned up to ogle the visitors and many eyes were resting on the foreign woman in a sari whose face seemed deathly pale as if she were near fainting from the stresses of travelling.

Mumtaz, Raj's eldest sister, and her husband Tahir's home was a solid brick house on the outskirts of Sylhet and had just enough rooms to accommodate themselves and their three children. Although she was not shown the rest of the house, Karin had the distinct feeling that she and Raj were installed in their hosts' best room while everyone else seemed to huddle together somewhere along the dark corridor in the back of the house.

'We can't allow that they give up their marital bed for us,' she protested to Raj, but he accepted their generosity with ease, as if it was his due.

'Remember,' he reminded her, 'guests are a gift from Allah,' but she couldn't help feeling a twinge of guilt.

173

When she mentioned her doubt to Priti, the girl only shrugged her shoulders and told her to enjoy a decent bed after the rigours of the journey.

'Mumtaz told me that they bought a new mattress especially for you,' which made Karin feel even more uncomfortable.

When she heard Mumtaz pass by in the corridor, she rushed out and whispered: 'I really want you to sleep in your own bed! I can sleep anywhere, if necessary on a mat.'

The reply was laughter and a warm hug:

'You have travelled all this way to see us, *bhabi*. The least I can do is to make sure that you have a good-night's sleep…' and smiling cheekily, she added: 'We must look after this little one. We want him to be big and strong.'

Karin was taken aback at the certainty with which most of her relatives expected her to produce a son; it did not seem to occur to anyone that she might have a girl; somehow girls didn't seem worth mentioning.

While lying on the newly mattressed bed to rest, Karin read a little more in the travel guide:

Sylhet is the land of shrines, natural hills, tropical forests, teagardens and *haors*.

'What's a *haor*?' she asked Raj who was dozing beside her.

'A sort of natural dip,' he mumbled, unwilling to have his sleep disturbed any further.

'Where?' she persisted.

'In the landscape,' he muttered impatiently, 'do let me sleep.'

She read on: 'The *haors* are green in winter but turn into turbulent lakes in the rainy season (April to October). They provide sanctuary to thousands of migratory birds who have flown across the Himalayas to these wetlands particular to Sylhet to avoid the harsh winter temperatures of Siberia.'

Karin had indeed noticed a massif change in landscape on the last leg of their journey in spite of dusk descending. The flat land, always at sea level, had suddenly risen, first to moderate mounds and then to verdant hills. She had spied gaps in the wild vegetation where people had planted pineapples, chillies and tea on the slopes.

'They must be the forerunners of the Himalayas,' Karin thought.

The map in the guide book showed how the hills spilled over from Assam in India, across Bangladesh's north, ran along the entire eastern border and fizzled out further south before falling into the Bay of Bengal.

'Sylhet Town,' she read on, 'has a population of eight million people. It lies in the valley formed by the rivers Surma and Kushiara, fed by innumerable streams from the Himalayas. Sylhet city is popular with tourists, mainly for the Shrine of Hajrat Shahjalal who died more than six hundred years ago. Legend has it that the great saint travelled with a band of thirty-six disciples from Delhi to preach Islam. He defeated the local chieftain Raja Gour Gobinda, a non-believer, and established Islam in Sylhet.'

'I would love to see the shrine,' Karin said aloud, but Raj only grunted subconsciously.

By the time he woke up, she knew all about the splendid surroundings, the wonderful panorama of Jaflong; the most picturesque tourist spot on the Mari river surrounded by hills and tea gardens; the impressive boulders having been swept down from the majestic Himalayas; the Madhabkunda waterfall across the Indian border; the tea gardens of Srimongal, Sripur and Tamobil and the Wawacherra rain forest which promised the tourist a glimpse of gibbons, bee-eater owls, parrots, leopards, pythons and the rare chloroform tree. Karin learnt about the colourful tribes famous for their dances rooted in mythology and their cane and bamboo handicrafts.

'So much to see', she thought and looked forward to some sightseeing in the coming days.

Someone called from behind the curtain, separating the master bedroom from the rest of the house.

'They expect us for dinner,' Raj stretched comfortably and smiled in anticipation.

Priti appeared to make sure her auntie's sari was faultlessly wrapped and folded, and to adorn her with some of her own gold jewellery and a rainbow of glass bangles. The meal could not have been more lavish in this modest house. Tables had been arranged in rows, some of them completely different from others, probably borrowed from neighbours for the occasion. Once everyone had been seated on a collection of wooden and cane chairs, they could have been attending a banquet in a

175

castle and everyone forgot the sandy coloured walls crowding in behind them. A considerable number of servant children, each holding a plate or bowl full of food lined up to await their turn to add to the feast at the table: polao, chicken, lamb, fish, peppers, tomatoes, spinach, okra, dhal – the entire range of Bengali cuisine was represented, everything cooked somewhere in the dungeons of the house.

'Where is Mumtaz?' asked Karin.

'She is supervising in the kitchen and adding final touches.'

The din and chatter flattened and greedy silence was only interrupted by sounds of munching and chewing. When the first voracious appetites were satisfied, voices rose again intermingled by laughter and conversations across the tables.

Time and time again, someone put another spoon of food on Karin's plate until they believed that she would pop if she ate another bite.

At last Mumtaz appeared in the door, flushed and proudly accepting the cheers and praise heaped upon her for the delicious meal. The men jumped up in unison, each offering her a chair, but she lifted a stool from a corner and moved it close to the table next to her husband Tahir.

When the last of the diners leant back, sighing with pleasure and indicating that they could eat no more, everyone was ushered into the sitting room onto cushioned low cane settees. Karin looked back on the bustle unfolding in the dining room. Children and servants were crawling all over the remnants of the feast like a colony of worker ants to clear the tables, now a picture of destruction.

The settees in the next room had been arranged in a half-moon shape so that the concrete floor between the door and the audience was free like a stage. Karin was not sure what to expect and was afraid that she might fall asleep, squashed between Priti and Lakshmi, before anything happened. Raj was sitting on a rattan arm chair amidst his male relatives.

The hushed activities that had gone on outside the curtained door for some time – occasionally showing up the contours of a body pushed into the fabric – turned into frenzy when someone banged a drum and someone else lifted the curtain. Little figures appeared, some others still flitting to and fro in the background. A group of young girls and boys spilled into the room, taking their positions in front of the audience. They were dressed in resplendent garments, the girls in sparkling miniature saris, the boys in gold-coloured vests and pump-trousers. A group of musicians had crammed itself into the corner nearest to the door. A hush fell over the room, the *tabla* drums beat a gentle rhythm joined by the whining melody of the harmonium, sounding like a table version of a church organ. After the introduction, the fluttering trills of a flute completed the village band.

Karin sat up and felt immediately drawn into a world of fairy tales and myths. The young dancers began to move to the music with their arms twisting and turning; their feet stamping to the rhythm making the bells, tied around their ankles, tinkle; the movements of their eyes, eyebrows and lips expressing the emotion of the moment. The music rose and fell, weaving itself like a red thread through the dancers' story.

'It's a *Manipuri* folk dance... It's a sad love story, but it has a happy ending,' whispered Priti, before she was shushed into silence.

The dancers' faces gleamed with make-up and sweat as the story progressed; the *tabla* setting the pace sounded like frantic under-water bubbles while the harmonium's and flute's tunes told the story in notes, a story of love won, lost and won again.

Karin was enraptured; time and fatigue forgotten, she was enveloped by the unusual music, the graceful movements, the portrayal of age-old emotions and the warmth exuded by the closeness of the family and the exertion of the dancers.

While general fascination had cast its spell, the doorway cluttered up soundlessly with village children. They had not been invited but took advantage of the moment when the hosts' and guests' attention was diverted by the performance. Their little bodies, bare-chested and clad in shorts or loin-cloths, stumbled unaware into the room, pushed by the throng of the curious crowd behind them. They looked in wonderment and rapture at the miracle unfolding in front of their eyes.

When the music ended and the two lovers stood in simulated embrace, the audience remained silent for a few moments not to break the spell. Suddenly someone applauded and everyone joined in wildly and noisily among shouts of 'bravo' and 'well done'.

The girl dancer shyly extricated herself from her partner, bowed deeply and rushed to the door, pushing past the village children who became now conscious that their intrusion might be discovered and result in recriminations. When no one seemed to notice them in the general exhilaration they joined in the clapping and cheering with gusto.

Big smiles of pride illuminated the faces all around and the young artists were asked back time and time again to bow and accept the audience's appreciation.

Exhaustion slowly overcame the spectators and the uninvited guests by the door were shushed away. The happy group, having lost all fear, scrambled through the entrance in high spirits, laughing and exchanging reports of what they had just witnessed.

The hosts finally got up and Lakshmi said something to the dancers.

'What did she say?' enquired Karin.

'She sent them to the kitchen for dinner.'

'Won't they get paid?'

'Good Lord, no; they will be so happy and proud to eat a decent meal, things they usually don't get, in the house of a distinguished family. They will be the talk of the town for months to come.'

Karin felt a little sorry but it was not up to her to criticise. Everyone got up. Furniture was moved back with the help of the servants and people drifted off to their bedrooms.

🪷 🪷 🪷

They stayed four days, mainly chatting, eating and sleeping. It was deemed prudent for Karin's condition, and they had so much news to catch up on. They were just happy to be together. No one relished the thought of the next, even longer leg of their journey, and so conveniently they put it out of their minds.

Karin attempted to bring up names of places worth seeing. At first they were acknowledged with weak, indulgent smiles and nods, but never acted upon, until on the last day, they relented.

'You won't be able to see the Shrine anyway,' said Raj in exasperation, 'it's only for men.'

'Strange,' she thought, 'it was mentioned in her guide as a tourist attraction. She did not pursue the idea because her husband could get into a funny mood if she was argumentative while relatives were within earshot; and they were within earshot nearly every minute of the day. Karin tried to understand that it was important to his male pride to be seen to be in charge and in control of her. She had experienced that he was most proud of her when she showed obedience without prompting; he would smile approving at her, happy to show their agreement and unison to the outside world.

However, this time he gave in: 'We don't want you to think that we are not interested in culture,' he quipped ironically, and Laksmi's driver was ordered to take them sightseeing around Sylhet town. On the way into town, Karin caught a glimpse of the gate to the Shrine of Hajrat Shahjalal with a short queue of visitors spilling out into the road. She couldn't see whether there were any women among them.

To the delight of the girls, they spent the afternoon going round the bazaar. Karin would have preferred a gentle stroll in a park with Raj, but he had taken to walking ten steps in front of her rather than beside her – walking hand in hand in public was severely frowned upon and possibly illegal.

'We shall visit the tea gardens before we leave the area,' Raj tried to placate his increasingly sullen wife. 'They are beautiful and peaceful places, just the way you like it,' he added quickly ignoring her doubtful frown.

They eventually left Mumtaz and her family amidst tears, embraces and theatrical waving, as if they could pull them back on a long elastic band the harder they waved.

※ ※ ※

The three cars, leaving Sylhet town behind, meandered up and down hill through wild vegetation interrupted by pineapple, chilli, lemon and tea plantations. A few thatched huts or low houses with corrugated iron roofs lined the winding roads. The travellers met not a single car and saw only one man walking towards them, carrying a long arching bamboo stick much wider than his shoulders, nearly blocking the entire width of the road. Karin, sitting in the car again between Lakshmi and Priti, counted ten jute baskets the size of litter bins which were jutting out horizontally, their handles having been tied to the stick. The man had to turn sideways, carefully like in slow motion to let the car pass.

'He'll take those to the market to sell,' explained Priti.

'How far is that?'

'No idea. We didn't come across a village. Maybe he goes to Sylhet town.' She grinned.

'Surely not,' thought Karin; 'we have been driving for nearly an hour.'

Suddenly the road climbed steeply between terraces of man-high green bushes until they reached a plateau at the top. There was no gate and they drove along the gravelled drive which was surrounded by guest bungalows, impeccably manicured striped lawns and cottage garden style flower borders, until they reached a colonial-style mansion. Karin absolutely loved it.

※ ※ ※

The three cars had arrived in the early afternoon like a desert caravan at an oasis and were welcomed by a friendly young Bengali who introduced himself as 'Nurul, the manager'. They were immediately ushered to tables on the veranda of the main building and given the most delicious tea accompanied by crumbly biscuits and a box of *halwa*. The male servants – there were a great number of them, all beautifully dressed in white suits – glided unobtrusively around the guests, making sure that everyone had absolutely everything they needed and wanted.

'Mr. Thadani will be with you shortly,' the manager announced and encouraged them to look at and wander around the beautiful gardens.

It was a light and cheerful, elegant and gracious atmosphere which ruled up here. People walked with light steps and smiled as if on permanent holiday. The sun shone without glare, a light breeze deflecting the burning strength of its rays.

They had idled for a while, when Karin observed a man of almost western appearance approaching their group across the lawn. He was tall, trim in an athletic sort of way, wearing riding breeches, a white shirt, top-button loosened, and swinging a riding jacket and helmet from his left hand. His smile brightened his slightly tanned face while he shook everyone's hand in welcome.

'I am George Thadani,' he introduced himself. Karin's heart leapt a little as she watched him brush back his black locks, which had flopped into his forehead. He seemed perfectly at ease to represent the best of east and west within his personality.

180

'I am sorry I am late,' which sounded as if he wasn't sorry at all, 'my horse needed some exercise.'

First he shook the men's hands, then looked around the group of women who gazed up at him in shy adoration, some less veiled than others. His eyes came to rest on Karin:

'Are you a visitor to our glorious country?' he asked in the clipped voice of an English public school boy.

Before Karin could answer, Raj looked at her with steely eyes and answered without a smile on her behalf: 'May I introduce my wife?'

George and Karin shook hands formally.

'Enchanté,' he mumbled, bending over her hand to kiss it with an amused grin.

Karin sensing trouble, quickly pulled her hand away, positioned herself next to her husband and lowered her eyes to the ground. The brief moment of embarrassment passed, as George turned, called out to the servants and announced that he would have a quick shower and then take the guests for a tour round his tea gardens.

Sure enough, fifteen minutes later, he re-appeared, his still wet locks glistening in the sun. They wandered through terraces of tall, green, shiny bushes. Access to some of the rows was barred where tall, brown-skinned women in *saris*, their *achols* wrapped around their waists, pulled the top leaves off the plants which came nearly up to their shoulders. They carried huge jute baskets strapped to their backs, the type that Karin had seen the man on the road take to market. Into these they threw the picked leaves with speed and dexterity. Hard at work, the women were cheerful and confident of their status. As the visitors got closer, Karin saw that some of them had slanted eyes and looked very much like the country's neighbours in Burma. They stopped for a moment to smile at the guests and one young girl even waved.

'They are a happy bunch,' George said. 'They live in their own village at the bottom of the hill. They belong to the Garo tribe. Very hard-working, very reliable!'

The view from the tea terraces was beautiful over neighbouring hills, wildly overgrown or cultivated in orderly rows. A little further in the distance, the wetlands, the *haors*, began. Karin could make out little clouds of what looked like flies, but which were probably exotic birds.

The *bhabis* began to flag due to sandals totally unsuitable for a country walk and George diplomatically took everyone back to the house, professing that urgent business was awaiting him.

Servants had meanwhile prepared a lavish picnic on the lawn and everyone fell upon it with a healthy appetite. Towards the end, George came back and seated himself next to Karin on the rug. She would have loved to ask him questions, to talk about his life at the tea gardens, his childhood and school years, which she was convinced he must have spent abroad. In the end, she didn't; she felt tongue-tied and uncomfortable with Raj's suspicious eyes upon her, threatening and clawing at any initiative.

George asked her a few questions which she replied to in monosyllables.

'Whatever must he make of me,' she thought and sighed with relief and a little disappointment, when he got up and declared with a charming and apologetic smile that he had to leave them.

'You are all very welcome to stay over night in the guest houses,' he said, and as it was too late to travel on, they decided to accept his offer and have an early start in the morning.

Chapter Eighteen

⌘

Whence do you bring this disquiet, my love?...
Rabrindranath Tagore

'Hi, Mum,' Karin's son stands up from the plush hotel armchair, grinning a little sheepishly.

'Ali!' Karin has crossed the lobby deep in thoughts and is torn out of them by this unexpected turn of events. Astonishingly, she does not feel immediately joyful, but is overcome by irritation that her son has come to check up on her and that her freedom will be curtailed from now on.

She looks again at his beaming smile, at this handsome young man, a little unsure of his welcome, in his casual but carefully chosen clothes, the long curled eyelashes giving his big eyes a dreamy look, the thick, brown hair flopping into his forehead. She remembers well why she had fallen for his father.

'Come here!' She loves his big bear hugs and he laughs with relief.

'What are you doing here?' All feelings of pique have evaporated and warm love and pride for her boy fill her heart.

'You don't need to check up on your mother,' she adds teasingly.

'I was due some holidays anyway,' he replies, in a non-committal way, 'and I thought I'd join you.'

'You cheeky chap. You could have said something; I would have picked you up from the airport.'

'I wasn't sure whether I could organise it at such short notice, and I wanted it to be a surprise.'

'You succeeded,' she confirms. 'Are you staying here?' She points vaguely to the hotel reception.

'Yes, room number 155 on the same floor as you,' he laughs again with a tinge of embarrassment about his deception..

Karin is overcome by a, for her, most unusual, long forgotten pleasure of being looked after and cared for by a man. Since the end of her marriage many years ago, she had become completely independent and self-reliant.

This visit has already broken down some of her inner barriers and emotional scaffolding; it has replaced isolation with newly discovered sociability, as if she was gradually slipping into somebody else's skin. What brought this on? Is it re-living the memories or the prospect of putting a festering past to rest? She has no idea and she is in no mood to think about it.

Karin slips her arm into the crook of Ali's elbow and drags him to the lift.

'I have been out all day. I need to freshen up' she says.

'So I see,' he says, teasing her.

It is nice that he is neither judgemental nor disapproving, as her daughter might have been in her anxiety over mother's safety.

'They serve wonderful meals here,' she suggests. 'We can have dinner in the garden.'

'And you can tell me all about what you have been up to so far.'

❧ ❧ ❧

As they step out into the hotel garden, the evening air is heavy with the scent of bougainvillea, hydrangeas, ixora, jasmine and hibiscus. Hedges of flaming-red poinsettia crowns frame the garden borders in the distance, and the large leaves of the banana trees vault above them like green canapés, blocking a bright blue evening sky.

Karin and Ali are tempted by the long menu and finally settle for lamb curry with tomatoes, fried okra with onions, buttery *parathas*, curry of sweet *hilsha*, a big-boned river fish, *polao*, fine rice with raisins and almonds, and the food of the poor, *dhal*, cooked with onions and a mixture of exotic spices. Karin ends the meal with her beloved *roshgullas* while Ali chooses *kulfi*, thick ice cream flavoured with rose water.

In between mouthfuls, she opens up to him as she has never done before, about her dithering whether to undertake the journey, her pros and cons, and her sudden impulsive decision to follow her instinct; about the flight and her acquaintance with Serena and little Omar on the plane, about the message awaiting her at the hotel, her trips with Farook, and finally her telephone conversation with Priti.

'I better let her know that you will be joining us,' she says.

'No, Mum, you see her first. I'll join you later. It will be easier, just the two of you. You have so much to catch up on.'

Karin nods. He is a thoughtful boy, and he knows women better than his father ever did. Lucky the girl who will marry him! She doesn't know much about his private life; she has always resisted prying, and imagines that she will be informed about the one relationship which will be the important one.

They take the lift to their floor and he kisses his mother on the forehead.

'Sweet dreams,' he says gently and gives her a squeeze.

'You are a good boy,' she replies fondly and tweaks his cheek affectionately.

'Mum!' he exclaims in mock outrage.

Tweaking cheeks, as is done by Bengali elders to young children, has become a family joke. Her children have always hated it, but have suffered in silence, never picking up the courage to tell their uncles and aunts.

Ali laughs and watches her as she unlocks the door and disappears behind it, before he turns in himself.

In the morning, Farook stands in the lobby, ready for service. Karin introduces her son and explains that his visit is as much of a surprise to her as to him. Farook looks a little uncertain about what is expected of him now.

'We shall decide on a programme for this morning over breakfast,' Karin ends the speculation breezily and prods Ali towards the dining room. He is astonished by his mother's new-found self-confidence and initiative.

'I always wanted to visit the Bangabandhu memorial museum. It's in Dhanmondi, not far from the park where you are going to meet Priti,' Ali suggests.

'It used to be Sheikh Mujibur Rahman's residence and shows his personal effects and photographs.' she replies, nibbling at a prawn.

Karin is not keen to be reminded of the destruction and chaos she had found when she had come to the country for the first time just after the Independence War. Hasina's husband Ahmed had grown up in Tungipara in Gopalganj, the same village as the countries first President. He knew Mujib well. At one stage, she had made Ahmed feel so guilty about his enormous wealth and had teased him about his friendship with the President, that he went to the Palace with a cheque for the poor. Goodness knows where that ended up, but it had been a small victory for her.

It had never been a secret that, however honest and trustworthy the leader of the Awami League Party might have been, corruption was rife among officials. She had always been of the opinion that, for as long as the Bangladeshis, particularly the upper echelon of that society, did not change their attitude towards the poor of their country, no amount of donations from the affluent West would change anything. 'I have an idea. I would much rather go on a river tour. Afterwards, Farook can drop me off at the park and take you to Bangabandhu Bhaban. You can join us when you have finished. I am sure, Priti and I will have enough to talk about to fill the time.'

It is settled and Farook is informed. While they are finishing their breakfast; he makes enquiries about river boat trips and the opening times of the Dhanmondi museum.

As they return from their leisurely boat trip up and down the Burigonga, Farook is waiting faithfully and a little nervously just outside the toll-gate. They are glad to get away from the burning sun and throng of thousands of people trying to buy or sell produce and materials by the riverside. Karin and Ali hop in the car to retrace their journey back to Dhanmondi. It is nearly three o'clock as they arrive at the gate to the park.

'Take care.' Ali says. 'I'll join you in about an hour.'

'Where? By the gate?'

'No, don't worry. As long as you stay in the park, I'll find you.'

'Auntie!'

Karin would have recognised this exuberant chuckle anywhere. It bursts into her reverie just when she is about to determine which of the bushes around her bench wins the competition of sending out the strongest scent.

She stands up, gives this middle-aged woman in front of her a gentle hug, holds her by the elbows and scrutises her from top to toe. So this is what the cheeky teenager, who had practised her feminine wiles on the good burgers of Stuttgart, had turned into: Priti still has a flair for looking glamorous; her figure is even fuller than Karin remembers but the bright red chiffon sari with orange and yellow embroidery sets off her smooth brown skin perfectly and makes her look elegant. She has wound her hair at the back of the neck into a *beni*, which is held in place by a glittering clip in the shape of a lotus flower.

'Let me look at you again,' Karin says and laughs when Priti gives a coquettish twirl.

'You look just like your mother used to look,' she concludes. The next moment, she puts her hand in front of her mouth, stifling a giggle:

'Oh thank you, Auntie!'

'You are pretty as ever,' Karin reassures her.

'How is your mother?' Karin asks.

'Getting older, still moaning about her ailments, but she is alright really.'

'Good. Does she know I am here?'

'I haven't said anything, but I think she suspects something's up.'

This is obviously still the Bengali way: Problems or conflicts are being ignored and brushed under the carpet in the hope that they will solve themselves. Any direct discussion will be avoided for as long as possible.

'I am sure she would like to see you,' Priti adds lamely, 'if only out of curiosity.'

'And how are you doing?' Karin changes the subject and enquires warmly.

'You remember, I married Ansar?'

'Of course, I do. Is he still in the army?'

'Yes he is a Major now,' Priti replies proudly.

'Is he treating you well?'

'Yes, auntie, he is. He is a true gentleman.'

'I am so pleased. So it was worth, my covering up your trysts.'

Priti nods with shining eyes. 'I have three children, two boys and one girl.'

'What are their names?'

'Miriam, Pran and Hameed. Miriam is married and has two little ones, Pran only got married recently and Hameed swears that he will remain a bachelor.'

'None of mine are married,' Karin volunteers wistfully. 'Jasmine is a career girl; she is a solicitor, and Ali lives in New York and works with disadvantaged children. He is here, by the way.'

'In Dhaka?'

'Yes, he will come to the park in an hour.'

'How lovely that you brought him along!'

'No, I didn't. He suddenly turned up at the hotel.'

'What a sweet boy!'

'Yes he is.'

Silence descends between the two women until Karin picks up the courage and asks:

'How is your uncle?'

They both know that she means Raj.

'Not well at all.'

'What's wrong?'

'He had another heart attack, his third. The doctors think he might not make it this time.'

'Do you think he would want to see me?'

'I think so. While he was unconscious he kept muttering your name.'

'Did he now…' Karin nibbles at her lower lip, not sure what to make of this unexpected statement. Somehow she had thought that Priti had taken it upon herself to summon her, without anyone else actually wishing her to be there. Throughout her journey, she had prepared herself to be content with paying her last respects from the safe distance of the hotel. Now she realises that she is unprepared for an emotional reunion and that she had rather hoped she would be able to avoid it.

Karin certainly had not expected that she would still be in his thoughts. Now she scolds herself for being naïve and for lacking in foresight.

As if extricating themselves from quicksand, they change the subject.

'Tell me about the rest of the family.'

And so they chatter on, like in old times, about marriages, babies and one tragic death, about ailments and various states of health of the older folks.

'It's funny,' Karin thinks, 'I belong to the old folks now.'

As if she is reading her thoughts, Priti asks: 'How old are you now, auntie?'

'Sixty.'

'You are not!' Priti's surprise seems genuine.

'Well, you are a grandmother…'

'Yes, and uncle is over seventy, so you must be right…'

'Of course, I am right,' Karin laughs, 'we do have birth certificates to prove it.'

'Uncle hasn't.'

'Yes, he had one when we were married.'

Priti chuckles: 'That was forged. Granddad lost all their papers during the partition when they were moving from Calcutta to Dhaka in 1947.'

Karin shakes her head in disbelief. Not even the efficient German civil servants had questioned the document.

They pause, their conversation grinding to a halt, filling the space between them with sudden awkwardness. They look around as if to appreciate the colourful blooms on the shrubbery. One question remains.

'Oh there is Ali!' They are glad for the distraction as he ambles along the path towards them. The park is now almost empty, people going home for dinner. He kisses both women on the cheeks and throws himself on the bench beside them.

'Did you enjoy the museum?'

'Yes, interesting. Shame he was murdered.'

'Yes, Mujib was a good man, idealistic, but he didn't have much of a plan what to do once the country had gained independence.'

189

Ali is more interested in meeting Priti than talking about his museum visit.

'I remember you as a little boy; you kept pulling my hair,' she beams.

'I must have been admiring it.' Priti blushes.

'Let's go back to the hotel and have tea,' he suggests. 'I could murder a cup'.

All three of them link arms, strolling along the now deserted path back to Farook and the car. As they part after two hours at the hotel, Priti whispers in Karin's ear: 'I shall tell my mother tonight. If anybody can speak to uncle it's her. And I'll give Ali a ring tomorrow; he has given me his mobile number.'

With this promise she strides regally out of the hotel, the *achol* of her sari floating behind her.

Priti rings neither the following day nor the day after. Karin's heart begins to sink and she can't help feeling that she has imagined their meeting in the park.

'Don't be silly, mother,' Ali scolds her. 'They are probably working on Abbu.'

She hasn't heard him speak about his father in this warm tone for a long time. She feels a little foolish and cannot explain to herself why she is suddenly longing to see Raj, but her hope is fading with every hour that passes silently. Maybe he doesn't want to see her. If he refuses there is nothing she can do to change his mind; it is his prerogative to keep her away, and the same applies to his family. If they decide to keep her at arms length and to ignore her presence in Dhaka, she will have to leave, her subconscious desire to put ghosts to rest, to smooth things over, to re-connect if only for a moment, unfulfilled. On examining her motives closer, she realises that she wants to tie up loose ends; she wants to convey to him that there are no hard feelings; that they should forgive each other; that this time they should part as friends or at least feel mutual respect for each other. Theoretically, it sounds achievable and desirable, but maybe only to her. She has no idea how embittered, resentful or indifferent Raj has grown in the long intervening years; he may well wish to leave the past buried and forgotten. After two days

190

without a message, Karin is torn between willing the phone to ring and hoping it will remain silent. She feels embarrassed at having put Priti in such a difficult situation. She has no doubt that her niece will do the best she can, but the family will observe conventions, traditions and protect their honour, which she had refused to consider as a priority all those years ago.

There is also Raj's delicate state of health to consider and the doctors or the family may decide that her visit will upset his mental and physical stability even further. 'I have confirmed my return flight for the day after tomorrow,' she takes the initiative and tells her son.

He doesn't reply but gives her a knowing squeeze.

Chapter Nineteen

☙❧

Child, how happy you are sitting in the dust
Playing with a broken twig all morning…
                                    Rabrindranath Tagore

As they left the tea gardens the following morning, they saw the same group of tall, slender women, now their *achols* covering their hair and some carrying their jute baskets on their heads, stroll towards them, laughing and giggling and, in recognition, waving at them. They were ready for another working day while the travellers braced themselves for a day stuck in the car.

They followed the winding roads upwards and downwards through the Tripura hills south of Sylhet. It was an unsettlingly remote area; Karin did not dare to think about what would happen if they needed help. On the other hand, it was unspoilt, wild countryside and the views from atop were breathtaking: In the ravines wild ixora, pineapple and hibiscus bushes, elephant grass and bamboo were competing with coconut palms, mango, guava and plane trees

The sun was bearing down on the travellers and the air in the cars became stuffy in spite of all four windows being kept open. Karin looked out for animals or birds, but they seemed to have fled the midday heat. There was no human habitation to be seen anywhere.

Karin, like the other passengers, was jolted rhythmically into sleepiness and finally she dozed off.

She awoke when the car stopped and they had reached the end of their first stage, a Government Guest House which they had booked.

Exhausted from the heat and sitting in a crammed position for hours, they fell onto the freshly made beds and slept for the rest of the afternoon. The family met up for dinner which was provided by the wife of the caretaker and their small daughter who seemed hardly old enough to carry the hot tiffin pots. The guests fell hungrily upon the simple meal of rice, *dhal* and *murgi* curry, followed by *misti dhohi*, a kind of sweetened yoghurt and *firni*, rice flour cooked in milk. After the meal, they chatted drowsily for a while and drifted one by one back to their bedrooms.

* * *

Karin was torn out of a deep sleep by a cacophony of sounds. It was early morning and the birds and animals were going noisily about their business before they would be paralysed by the day's heat again.

Through the window she saw clouds of birds in the sky and on the ground pecking away. A bowl stood in the yard. The little girl which she had seen the night before rushed out of what Karin presumed was the kitchen, and shushed away half a dozen crows which were fighting over the bowl.

Raj was still asleep, so Karin quickly slung a sari around her without taking too much care and tiptoed out into the fresh morning. She sniffed the air but the scents were still muted from the morning mists and dew.

The little girl noticed her immediately and made moves to rush indoors again, but Karin gestured that she should stay. Shyly, they smiled at each other and took a seat on the front step to the kitchen. Karin could now see that the bowl contained lentils, soaking in water. A kind of language lesson developed and the little girl entered quickly into the spirit.

'Bird,' Karin pointed to the huge one with wings like black umbrellas.

'*Pakhi*,' replied the little girl.

Karin pointed to another bird which looked like a cross of a magpie and a robin and pulled a quizzical face. The little girl understood and said cheerfully:

'*Doel*.'

Another very pretty bird was called *minah* and they even saw a cluster of parrots on a lychee tree. Karin pointed to herself and said her name and the little girl followed her example immediately; her hand resting on her chest she said proudly: 'Nayantara'.

In the distance, Karin could hear the chirping of the *tiktikis* (grasshoppers) and crickets, joined occasionally by the shrieks of monkey and parrot families. It was paradise, and Karin and Nayantara savoured its freshness, peace and beauty in silence.

Raj came out of their bungalow, rubbing sleep from his eyes and breaking the spell: 'Come in,' he said sternly. 'There are mosquitoes and snakes everywhere. You don't want to be bitten. The next hospital is miles away.'

She smiled apologetically to Nayantara, who herself got up and turned to disappear in the kitchen.

* * *

The hills softened and panned out the more the convoy drove south and the closer they came to Chittagong. The passengers' weary mood lifted and was replaced by anticipation to see their brother Khaled, his wife Farah and their children Ayesha, Jaya, Asha and their precious son Shamsur.

Their home turned out to be an impressive mansion on a hill rising up in the middle of town. The grounds around it were enormous and reminded Karin of the private section of the tea gardens. Again, there was a stripy English cricket lawn, framed by orderly borders holding in a riot of flowers, age-old trees bearing limes, bananas, mango, guava, and even a banyan tree with a gnarled trunk the size of a giant's thigh.. Karin was shown around a tennis court, a carp pond, a rose garden and a croquet lawn; it was gracious living indeed.

The visitors were each allocated a separate bedroom suite and sent to freshen- up. A little later everyone gathered on the veranda to begin with their exchanges of news and gossip. Little Shamsur was overjoyed about the sudden choice of uncles, aunts and cousins who took it in turns to play with him. It was wonderful to let the children roam free in the safety of such a big garden and under the watchful eyes of the *ayahs* and servants who smiled indulgently at their high spirits and exuberance.

It gave the adults the rest they needed and an opportunity to talk without interruptions.

On day three, after doing nothing but rest, eat and chat, they decided to explore the city and headed straight for Goldsmith's Alley and Reasuddin Bazaar. Karin sighed. While driving, several temples, museums and Kadam Mubarak Mosque were pointed out to her, but none was obviously worth a visit.

'Maybe tomorrow,' thought Karin, ever hopeful.

The outing was declared a great success while the women spread out their new jewellery and saris before their husbands, who pretended to be shocked by their wives' profligacy, but who were secretly resigned and proud of their good taste.

Karin made a big effort to look appreciative, interested and enthusiastic, bearing her boredom with courteous stoicism.

'You don't like shopping?' Khaled, the host and brother-in-law had sidled up to her.

'I don't mind it,' she said lamely.

'What did you buy?' She hadn't bought anything, because the ankle bracelet with dancers' bells had been rejected as inappropriate again. Instead, her sisters-in-law had insisted on a silver snake-like ring which, she had to admit, fitted perfectly on her middle finger. This she showed to Khaled. It did not seem to impress him.

'Tell you what, would you like to see my school tomorrow?'

Karin's face lit up: Oh yes, please!' she exclaimed, but quickly put a hand over her mouth as everyone looked curiously up from their purchases.

'It's the school holidays, but the caretaker will let us in.'

'Shall I tell the others?'

'No-one else will be interested; I have bored everyone to tears with my school.' And so it was that she and Khaled set off the next morning, while the rest of the family had promised to meet them later at Chittagong's harbour.

From the outside the school was an austere bungalow-style building next to a busy street.

'We have four hundred pupils from the age of eleven to sixteen.' Karin could not imagine where they were all accommodated.

'We have classes of up to fifty pupils... Let's go in.'

He knocked on the big wooden door which was soon opened

196

by an elderly man from whose trouser belt hung a huge bunch of keys. From the back of the narrow corridor came noises of buckets cluttering and mops swishing around the stone floors.

Khaled opened the first door on the right and they entered a classroom which looked bare save for rows of well used desks and benches, held together by iron struts, and a black board, wiped clean, standing on wooden legs. One wall boasted a shelf which contained one set of school books. The room was clean but in a dull sort of way like a clean swept cellar.

'This is for the lucky ones,' Khaled sighed.

'How do you mean?' asked Karin in astonishment.

'Our pupils are lucky because their parents are able to pay for their schooling.'

'And what happens to the ones who can't pay? Do they go somewhere else?'

'No. They don't go to school at all.'

Khaled's compassion and social conscience were palpable.

'Won't the government pay towards their education?'

'No. The government will say that they can't afford to pay for millions of children, that there aren't enough schools or teachers. That it is impossible for children in rural areas to get to a school… They will always find an excuse.'

'And what about aid money from Europe, America and the United Nations?'

Khaled simply shrugged his shoulders. 'Corruption seems to be the curse of poor countries.'

'But that's terrible. If aid never reaches the poor where does the money go?'

'Into the pockets of officials, I guess.'

'So, unless the government and the wealthy of your country change their attitude nothing will ever change; the poor will stay poor and the rich get richer?'

'That's it!'

'So, correct me if I am wrong: there is actually no point of donating any money to a country like Bangladesh unless one takes it there personally and hands it over to whoever needs it most.'

'That's the ideal, but, of course, it never happens.'

'Why doesn't our family do anything to help?'

'I do.'

197

'No, I mean, build schools where children don't have to pay. Come to think of it, they own so many buildings in Dhaka, they could easily spare some of them and convert them into schools.'

Khaled looked wistfully at the floor and shuffled with his feet.

'Well, you have to start somewhere.' Karin persisted, already planning how to channel her idealistic ideas into practical execution. Maybe this is what she was meant to do with her life. Maybe this was the reason why fate had brought her here.

'How much do you earn?' Khaled nearly choked when she asked directly as no-one else in Bangladesh would dare 'Not enough... None of us do.'

By the sounds of it, it wasn't Khaled's salary paying for their mansion, gardens and fine living. His compassion was, it seemed, defended and supported by his wife but only just tolerated by their families.

'They think I am a crackpot,' he laughed, 'but who cares, as long as they let me get on with what's important to me!'

Karin smiled at him full of admiration.

'Don't say anything to the family,' Khaled begged her. 'They will think I influenced you with my socialist ideas.'

'I shall have to be diplomatic,' she thought, biting her lip. 'If I keep at them, chipping away at their indifference, their resistance will surely crumble with time.' How she would make these ideas palatable to her husband, she had no idea. He surely would be proud of her?

They had a look at more classrooms, the even barer staff room; only the headmaster's office displayed some sort of style with a polished oak desk and a swivel leather arm chair.

They thanked the care taker and left the building.

'Where is the playground?' asked Karin.

'Round the back.'

It was a postage-stamp-sized concrete slab just as wide as the building. Dustbins were lined up along the outside walls. There were no playing facilities like a little goal, basket ball or a tennis net, and there was no green of trees or grass to be seen anywhere.

'How do five hundred children play in that?' Karin shuddered at the thought.

'Many of them stay indoors; it's often too hot outside anyway.'

Karin could only shake her head in disbelief. 'This is a good school, you said?'

'Yes,' answered Khaled, 'our exam results are superb.'

They had promised to meet up with the rest of the family in the afternoon. Farah wanted to show Karin her father's business.

The girls were again in high spirits because they had been back to Goldsmith's Alley and another bazaar. They sat on plush sofas in the lobby of the office block. In the nearby corner was a heap of swish shopping bags from bespoke tailors and jewellers.. When the driver joined them, he was ordered to take the purchases back to the car and guard them.

'Had a good time at the school?' Karin was asked, but nobody was genuinely interested in her answer.

'Faizal will show you round.' Faizal was the office manager.

'We won't come,' said Farah.

Karin was taken through the various well air-conditioned departments of the shipping company and proudly shown the view of the harbour from a veranda looking out to sea.

'These are our cargo ships,' Faizal pointed importantly to a fleet of five which nearly filled the port. One was being loaded with huge containers; another had an army of workers carrying beams of wood from the ship to a warehouse next to the office building. A tall crane was in the process of lifting cement sacks off a third, while the last two ships seemed to have maintenance work done, hundreds of people swarming over them with tools, brushes, paint pots, brooms, cloths and ladders.

Karin smiled pleasantly to the long list of statistics proudly divulged by Faizal; she thought it polite to ask a few questions to feign interest, which set him off into further enthusiastic ramblings about the company's capacity for exports and imports, the variety of products transported, impressive profit figures and future expansion plans.

She felt quite exhausted when she was delivered back to the family, sitting in the lobby sipping tea from dainty cups and nibbling on crumbly biscuits and sticky *ladoos*.

'What a day – what contrasts!' Karin thought. It all seemed rather surreal.

They said their *khoda hafez* and *onek dhonnobads* and left behind a mess of dirty crockery and biscuit crumbs for someone else to clear up.

'Let's go to the sea front,' Farah suggested. They drove along the curving bay until the road led down to a stretch of pristine beach. Everyone tumbled out of the car like impatient children or unruly dogs. The girls took their sandals off and swung them from their wrists. Their feet sank into the brilliant white sand and grains were pressed between their toes like dry semolina. The sand was warm but not too hot to walk barefoot on it.

Karin was curious whether any of the men or women would go swimming. None of the other visitors seemed to be in the water and no one had sat down for sunbathing or a picnic.

'Are we going into the water?' Karin enquired.

'Of course, it's lovely and refreshing,' Farah assured her.

It turned out that the way Bengali women go 'swimming' is to walk to the sea's edge, to let shallow waves lap over their feet and to shriek with delight at the sudden coldness of the water. Karin walked a little further in, bunching and hoisting the bottom of her sari up to her knees. She would have loved to throw herself into the ocean and feel free like a fish, but she was called back by worried cries of her relatives.

'You'll catch your death. Then what will happen to the baby!' they scolded her.

'Our brother will kill us!' declared Lakshmi theatrically throwing her arms into the air. Karin had no choice but to apologise and blame it on erratic hormones causing her to be absentminded and foolish.

They sat for a while in the sand drinking coca cola, which had warmed up in the boot of the car and tasted nothing like the real thing; they also demolishing another box of *ladoos* they had bought from the market. Farah provided entertainment by impersonating film stars and re-enacting entire dramatic scenes from recently seen movies to which the assembled audience contributed with great hilarity. Somehow she ended up impersonating family members whom Karin vaguely recognised. Everyone laughed so much until Lakshmi had a coughing fit and had to be vigorously thumped on the back

200

Karin, having tugged her sari back down to her feet, stretched out on the sand, closed her eyes and felt the sea breeze fanning over her face. She had just fallen asleep when she heard everyone packing up. As she got up she shook off the sand grains which had stuck to the wet bottom of her sari, wistfully and with a little regret. How she longed to have just half an hour here without anyone else around, just enjoying the natural and mighty beauty of the place in silence!

She suppressed a sigh and followed everyone else back to the car. Looking behind, she marvelled at the glowing red lantern of the sun falling into the dark Bay of Bengal with the speed and grace of an Olympic diving champion.

'Did you know that children whose parents can't pay school fees, don't go to school at all?' she said to Raj in the evening as they were getting ready for bed.

'Of course,' it wasn't news to him, but he only shrugged his shoulders.

'When you compare that to Europe where some children have to be forced to go to school. They don't know how lucky they are,' she persisted.

'There are millions of them; the government can't possibly pay for them all,' he argued lamely.

'But they are the country's future. It should be in the government's interest to educate as many youngsters as possible.'

'So who is then growing rice or jute; no one who is educated will want to be a farmer or a servant or a *tiffin* or rickshaw *wallah.*'

'But at least, everybody should be able to read and write,' Karin defended her opinion hotly.

It suddenly dawned on her that it was not in the interest of the upper echelon of Bangladeshi society to loose their privileges and their servants to compulsory education.

'Many parents need their children to go out begging, do menial work or run errands to contribute to the family's budget. They have neither time nor money to go to school, however sad that might sound to you.'

'It doesn't seem fair. Privileged families like yours could and should do something about it, set an example' she was in full flow now, 'it would be so easy to set up a sch...'

With a furious look, he interrupted her:

'Karin, you are not in Europe; this is Bangladesh, one of the poorest countries in the world. You can't compare the two!'

'To set up a school in one of the many houses you own,' she carried on regardless, her voice getting shrill with indignation.

'Don't you get funny ideas!' he shot her a warning glance.

'You educate the masses and you won't have equality but a revolution on your hands!' he shouted furiously, climbed into bed, turned his back to her and switched out the light.

She was seething with anger at his lack of compassion, the brusqueness with which he had silenced her argument and his unwillingness to see her point. It took her a long time to calm herself enough to be able to fall asleep.

Chapter Twenty

ॐ

The song that I came to sing remains unsung...
                                        Rabrindranath Tagore

It is nearly lunchtime. Karin packs her few belongings with a heavy heart and increasing disappointment into her battered suitcase. Her movements fizzle out with reluctance. She cannot understand why the chirpy welcome has turned into stony silence. Why would Priti have written to her in the first place if she hadn't wanted her to come? Had her niece become frightened of her own courage?

Tomorrow, Karin will leave Dhaka for the last time. She knows that she will never return; there is no reason to come back, particularly if her presence and departure now remain ignored by the people she came to see.

'I wonder how Raj is doing,' she muses. 'Maybe he is much better... or much worse?' occurs to her suddenly. 'Maybe everyone is rallying around his bed? Maybe he has decided that he doesn't want to see her after all? Or maybe the family or the doctors have decided that it would upset him to much if she turned up?' She sighs. She will never know now.

There is a knock on the door. It is Ali. He frowns when he sees the opened and half packed suitcase and her miserable face.

'Aren't you a bit premature?' he asks matter-of-factly.

'He seems to worry more about my disappointment than about the reasons for Priti's lack of communication,' she realises and a great wave of affection wells up in her.

'I might as well pack now. I hate doing things in a rush,' she says listlessly, tears shimmering in her eyes and thickening her voice. A grey gloom billows in the room like hill fog.

Suddenly the hotel telephone shrills and both jump. For a moment there is confusion who should receive the call. Ali gestures that she should do so. She takes the few steps to the bedside table and lifts the receiver gingerly as if it would break any moment:

'Hallo, hallo…' Her whisper is so soft that the receptionist nearly gives up.

'Room 160', she says quickly with a firmer voice.

'Mrs. Khan?'

'Yes, speaking.'

'There is a call for you. Would you like me to put it through?'

'Yes, please… and thank you.'

'You are welcome, Madam,' is the courteous reply, before she hears a click and Priti's breathless voice:

'I am so sorry, auntie. It was mayhem. Uncle had another turn for the worse, but he is more stable now and he does want to see you.'

'I am leaving tomorrow,' Karin throws in meekly.

'You can't! Postpone it…! Hold on… give me your flight and reference number. I shall tell Nadeem *chacha*. He will sort it out.'

Karin fails to suppress a smile thinking of the advantages of nepotism.

'You can't do that,' Karin protests, more in disbelief than with conviction.

'Yes, we still can, however much you disapprove,' Priti laughs.

'I'll pick you up this afternoon. Shall we say four o'clock?'

'Wonderful. Thank you, Priti.'

'Oh auntie. I always wanted to do this, get you and uncle together again. I am so pleased you came… By the way, the family want to see you as well and are expecting you tomorrow; the whole clan will gather in mum's house,' she giggles naughtily, 'They are only nosey!'

'You are *prio tomo*, Priti,' Karin says fondly.

'I know,' her niece laughs. She is in her element. Karin can feel her beaming smile through the telephone. 'I must go,' Priti adds hastily 'see you at four!' And she is gone.

Ali's face has brightened with relief. She goes up to him and gives him a big and affectionate hug.

'Let's have lunch and then do something nice till four.'

They decide to behave like tourists for the afternoon and scour the shops in Elephant Road. Karin remembers it as one of the most modern parts of Dhaka even in the seventies. It hasn't changed much: a wide avenue bordered by rare, pristine pavements fleeced of beggars and street dwellers and leading along a row of classy shops. The windows display brass ornaments, jewellery, oriental clothes adapted for the use and taste of western tourists and souvenirs of all shapes and sizes.

'What shall I take for your father?' she says suddenly.

Ali shrugs. 'Do you need to take anything? I don't think he will want clutter around his bed.'

'You are right,' she agrees, but eventually chooses a little brass elephant as big as her palm. It is a cheerful little statue, holding his trunk triumphantly in the air; all that is missing is the exuberant trumpeting sound.

Ali is puzzled by her choice and she tells him the joke she and his father used to share: It had begun during their courtship with a soppy little song they had heard on the radio. Afterwards they could only remember the refrain: *Me and the Elephant Will Never Forget You.* When she had wanted to buy the record she could remember neither the title nor the singer and sort of described the contents of the lyrics to the salesman. A week later, he had rung to say that his search had been successful and that if she wanted it she had to buy a Val Doonican album. The joke had sprung from the opening of his call, when he had introduced himself with the words: 'Are you the lady with the elephant?' Raj had found it terribly funny and for a while called her 'my lady with the elephant'.

Would he remember now?

There are beautiful shawls on display.

'Let me buy one for you… As a souvenir,' Ali insists and they

205

rummage together through piles of the loveliest fabrics. After a lot of dithering they choose a creation of night-sky-blue silk embroidered with tiny silver stars and comets shooting across.

'Don't put it in a bag. I shall wear it immediately,' she tells the shopkeeper, who has kept discreetly and respectfully at the back of the store. The shawl wraps around her neck like a breeze and she plants a quick kiss of gratitude on her son's cheek. He rewards her with a half-embarrassed, half-delighted chuckle.

'Let me invite you to an ice-cream,' she proposes and they soon find a small parlour called Banana Split. Karin is amazed that it is still there. She bursts out laughing and tells Ali the story from all these years ago, when, on her first visit, the proprietor, surprised by the sudden demand, had to rush out to buy bananas from the nearby market.

Today there is no such hiccup. Karin orders mango *kulfi* for both of them, which they savour in the cooled air of the room. They are the only customers apart from a young couple trying to remain incognito at the table in the gloom of the back.

'I think, we better go now,' Ali suggests. 'It will give us time to freshen up before Priti picks us up.' They hire a wildly patterned baby taxi which takes them back to the Radisson Watergarden Hotel.

❀ ❀ ❀

Ten to four they meet in the lobby, sitting down on rattan sofas with sumptuous, bright red cushions, waiting for Priti to arrive. They chat sporadically about returning to their respective lives.

'Is there any romance in your life?' she asks cautiously, but uncharacteristically direct.

Ali answers with a surprised grin before revealing hesitantly that indeed, there was someone.

'Martha is a secondary school teacher in a run-down area of New York. We met on a course. We are actually both a bit tired of western inner city kids and are thinking of joining a charity to work with children. We wouldn't mind Bangladesh.'

Karin is stunned and lets this bombshell of goodness and idealism shower down on her like warm rain.

'He is fulfilling the dream I always had,' she thinks but simply says:

'That's my boy! Tell Martha, that I can't wait to meet her!'

'If it works out, we shall probably interrupt our journey in London before transferring to our new jobs. I might show her a bit of England before travelling on.'

'Wonderful!' Karin is overwhelmed. 'I shall look forward to that!'

He turns round casually to check whether Priti has arrived.

'There she is,' he exclaims, a little impatiently. Karin wonders whether he is pleased to escape more revelations or whether he is nervous on her behalf.

'Let's get going,' Priti has reached them and gives both of them a hug.

Chapter Twenty-One

༼ঙ৪ঔ༽

The bird of the morning sings...
Rabrindranath Tagore

Farah and Khaled had one more surprise in store for them – a trip to Rangamati.

'What is it?' Karin asked, a little despondent. Her pregnancy was now well advanced and long car journeys had become exhausting. She longed for her own bed in Dhaka.

'Wait and see!' Raj smiled mysteriously and obviously excited at the prospect.

To take account of her condition and shadows of tiredness appearing under her eyes, the family decided to spread the hundred mile round-journey over two days. It could be done as a day trip, but they were insistent to take it slowly on her behalf.

The convoy set off from the city in the early morning coolness so that they would reach the more moderate climate of the Hill Tracts before the burning noon sun. They passed several tribal villages and stopped at stalls to buy refreshments and local crafts. At one time, they all climbed out of the cars to stretch their legs and to admire one of the many waterfalls of the area and the thick vegetation of the hills.

They arrived at the Parjatan holiday complex in the afternoon, where they had booked rooms for one night.

'We shall have a very relaxing day tomorrow,' Farah assured Karin and put her arm around her shoulders. 'Nothing but leisure and peace!'

And she was right: They spent most of the following day leaning back in a boat which took them sightseeing around Kaptai Lake, one of the biggest man-made reservoirs in the world, surrounded by lush and wild vegetation on hills circling the water. It was strange to think that they were floating above the ruins of old Rangamati town, which had been submerged when the Karnaphuli dam was built for a hydro-electric power project nearby.

The tourist guide told them more about the various local tribes, who were Buddhists, Hindus, Christians or even Animists, each speaking their own dialect.

'Their rites, rituals and village life,' he assured his listeners, 'were unaffected by religion and have remained primitive.' Nobody else seemed to raise an eyebrow and Karin stifled an incredulous giggle.

'Like what?' she asked Farah who sat next to her in the boat, 'cannibalism?'

Her sister-in-law burst into laughter and soon a Chinese-whispers chain had everyone chuckling.

The next piece of news re-enforced the hilarity when the guide announced, that the tribal families were matriarchal and that the women-folk were considerably more hard-working than the males.

'What's new?' whispered Karin and everyone fell about laughing until their bellies ached and the boat began to rock.

Their guide, a serious young man, who was obviously proud of his job, was baffled. They left him, thanking him profusely and apologetically but sniggering again as soon as they had turned their backs.

The tourists only had to cross a picturesque wooden hanging bridge to reach their hotel. This was the only walking they did all day.

Even the most ardent of tourists amongst the family realised that travelling had lost its lustre after several weeks on the road. It was therefore decided that, after one more day of rest at Farah and Khaled's house, they would set off on the quickest way back to the capital.

❀   ❀   ❀

They drove through miles of flat landscape, paddy fields crisscrossed by rivers, their edges often dotted with houses on stilts. The convoy stopped at a roadside stall to take advantage of a villager's catch of *hilsha* fish. It was considered a delicacy and not easy to come by in the daily Saderghat market in Dhaka.

'It's a river fish. Its flesh is very sweet and it has big bones which you can remove easily,' they explained, as they bought the entire basketful to the delight of the fisherman and the dishevelled children crowding around him.

❀   ❀   ❀

There were no more stops before Dhaka and, if the truth be known, everyone was rather glad to be going home.

Karin longed to concentrate on the one thing that occupied her mind: the arrival of her baby. Maybe she would even succeed in getting Raj more involved, so they could finally begin to form their own little family unit. Maybe Raj might even agree to move them into a house of their own.

Chapter Twenty-Two

CᏀᏏᎧ

You in your timeless watch,
Listen to my approaching steps!…
Rabrindranath Tagore

The car weaves its way through the Dhaka afternoon traffic until it stops outside the sparkling white building of the new Dhaka Central Hospital. Priti seems to know her way round and is greeted by several people in nursing or doctors' uniforms. Karin and Ali have trouble keeping up with her as she sweeps through the crowded and noisy corridors. Finally, they reach a part of the building which is quieter and where staff are unobtrusive. Karin guesses that this is a private wing; she should have expected no less. The visitors stop outside an immaculately painted white door, but before Priti knocks, she turns round and smiles:

'Auntie, I managed to postpone your flight by two days.' Then she knocks three times rhythmically, as if tapping a secret code, and enters without waiting for an answer from inside.

To Karin's astonishment, the room is empty except for the patient. She had secretly steeled herself to meet half the family around Raj's bed. She is more nervous than she expected to be; her heart is thumping in her throat and leaves her voiceless. She lingers by the door, unaware that she is smoothing her creaseless navy trousers and tugging on the collar of her sleeveless white blouse. Raj is sitting upright in bed, his face obscured by the shadows of the blinds, filtering the afternoon sun. Only the white of the bed covers shimmers like the surface of water. Priti kisses her uncle on both cheeks and hands over a little basket of fresh fruit.

'Come on, auntie!' she urges. Ali steps closer to the bed and embraces his father gently.

'I am glad you could come,' Raj says with an unsteady voice, trying to clear its hoarseness several times. He looks frail, his beautiful wide shoulders, into which the young Karin had so loved to nestle her head, have shrunk to a skeletal frame and his arms have become thin like the wires of a marionette puppet. His eyes are protruding from deep hollows and ringed by dark blue shadows.

Karin is still rooted to the same spot.

'Come on then! Let me see you,' Raj says half-jokingly, half-impatiently and his haunted face lights up.

'He still manages to patronise me,' she thinks for a moment, but then she obeys and makes three steps into the room.

She feels awkward, conspicuous and under scrutiny like she had done as a young girl. They haven't seen each other for a long time. They have both aged; they have lived separate lives.

'For heaven's sake,' she chides herself, picks up all the self-confidence she can muster and steps closer. Priti and Ali make space for her by the bed.

'You haven't changed much,' Raj exclaims, genuinely surprised.

Priti looks curious and expectant, when Ali indicates that they should leave the two alone.

'Is there a canteen?' he asks, 'I could do with a cup of coffee.'

A reluctant Priti is ushered out by her cousin.

Before Raj can say more, Karin takes a seat on the edge of the stiff, wooden chair next to his bed.

There is no point in asking him how he is; it is for all to see that he is very ill and struggling to remain focused.

'How have you been?' he mumbles sadly.

'Okay, with the normal ups and downs of life, but nothing dramatic,' she stammers.

'Same here.' His tired eyes scour her face as if looking for something.

'Were you happier without me?' She realises that all those years ago he had truly believed that she couldn't live without him.

'More peaceful,' she answers firmly. She is slowly gaining control.

He nods.

'You had a good career?' It was more of a statement than a question.

'Yes, nothing spectacular,' she confirms with a sad smile. 'It was hard at times considering I also had two children to bring up.'

She can feel the words 'I told you so' standing in the room, but they remain unspoken.

'Did you get married again?'

He knows she didn't. Ali would have told him.

He is shaken by a violent attack of breathlessness. Sympathy wells up in her and she finds it hard to remember how much heartache this man has caused her. He presses an oxygen mask to his face and falls back into his pillow, exhausted by the effort.

When the attack subsides he continues: 'I didn't get married again either,' he whispers, tearing her out of her thoughts.

'Yes, but you lived with her,' she thinks with bitterness. How this was accepted in a Muslim society is beyond her understanding. It was probably brushed under the carpet, hidden or explained away.

She doesn't want to bring on another attack, so she remains quiet.

'I never had an affair with her,' he whispers.

'Don't. It's not important anymore.' She shakes her head as if trying to get rid of unpleasant thoughts.

'It's important to me that you believe me!' he insists stubbornly and adds, 'at least, not after we were married!'

She nibbles on her lower lip and is unsure whether to reply at all.

'You were never on my side once we were in Bangladesh,' she counters finally with as little hostility as she can manage and to her surprise he agrees:

'I know; for that I am sorry!'

'I wanted a deep, passionate and thoughtful relationship, both sharing each other's cultures and doing our bit for the poor of your country. Instead we bickered and fought like cat and dog and wasted our energies on making each other miserable.'

She takes a deep breath:

'We have wasted a whole mountain of opportunities.' Both lower their heads.

She realises that this is what she has come for, to explain to him what she as a young woman had expected from their marriage, had dreamt of to do with her, with their lives, and why she had been disappointed to such an extent that she had thrown it all away.

'When I met you, not only was I smitten and flattered; it was like an exotic dream, like a fairy tale… I had always wanted to escape the materialistic and competitive western society… Until I met you, I was aimlessly idealistic. With you I saw an opportunity, not only to have a marriage out of the ordinary, but also, with the wealth and standing of your family, to be in a position to make a difference where it counted.'

It feels like the most important speech of her life.

Staring down at the tensely clasped hands in her lap, she feels Raj's gaze on her. She looks up and nearly bursts into tears, meeting his eyes.

'I know, Mita.' His words flutter like the wings of a bird. 'I didn't know then. I was too involved with my own pride, just carrying on the way I had always lived, adored by my relatives, convinced of my own importance. I never made the leap in putting you and the children first, to consider you as my family. You made it too easy for me to forget that you were not a Bengali girl.'

'I knew that in your culture, the new wife is expected to adjust to life with the in-laws,' she continues. 'I did so whole heartedly, but you made no concession to the way I had been brought up.'

'I know. I should have been proud of you, an efficient, intelligent, caring European wife… be supportive when you wanted to do some good.'

'You could have simply made an effort out of love for me, if you had thought about it.'

The tidal wave of sorrow slowly subsides.

'I understood that not long after you left,' he says miserably.

They are both silent. 'There is no more to say,' she thinks and it provides a kind of closure. It is time to change the subject.

'The children are doing well.'

'Yes,' his face brightens immediately, 'not that I can take much credit for that… How is Jasmine?'

'Oh, she is doing fine. She is her own woman; very independent and very successful,' and Karin thinks 'a bit too much for my liking,' but doesn't say it out of loyalty to her daughter.

'Ali has inherited your idealism,' Raj smiles now broadly.

'I know,' Karin admits shyly. 'He has just told me this morning that he and his girl friend are planning to leave New York and to work for a charity, possibly here.'

'Aha,' exclaims Raj triumphantly, pushing himself up on his fists to his full seated height, 'he has finally found a woman!'

Karin smiles indulgently; the children are an unexpected bond after all those years of separation.

'There they are…' Priti and Ali come in, the young man hanging back a little, pulled unwillingly along by the woman, who can hardly hide her curiosity and looks expectantly from her uncle to her aunt.

'When will you fly back?' Raj asks to re-start the conversation.

'Day after tomorrow,' Karin replies as if this was the sort of inconsequential chat they had indulged in.

'Will I see you again before your departure?' There is resignation in his voice.

'Of course, I shall come back tomorrow.'

'Oh!' exclaims Priti looking crestfallen. 'I can't come. I have promised mother to help with cooking.'

'That's alright. I am sure Ali and I can find our way back here.' Karin reassures her, but they all know that this is not Priti's true concern. Karin sidles up to her disappointed niece and whispers into her ear: 'And I shall tell you all about it afterwards; promise!'

Priti is easily mollified.

'Stop! No secrets, ladies!' Raj teases them. He looks now terribly tired. They quickly wish him a good-night and go to the door. Before leaving, Karin turns round once more.

'I shall dream of you!' His tired eyes are lit by a cheeky gleam as the old, flirty Raj makes a brief appearance.

'Sleep well,' she says before closing the door.

Chapter Twenty-Three

⚭

If thou speakest not
I will fill my heart with thy silence and endure it…
Rabrindranath Tagore

'No, Karin, I won't let you fly to Germany in your state!' Raj was incandescent with rage that she even considered such a move. 'I know it would be nice,' he tried to sound conciliatory, 'but I won't let you endanger my son. Ask your parents to come over here.'

'You know, they are elderly and not adventurous enough to undertake such a journey.' Karin sounded terribly miserable. 'I know they won't come; they have never been outside their country.'

'That's their choice,' Raj was not in the mood to be sympathetic.

'I am their only daughter!'

Karin stood her ground. She could not give up. It was bad enough that her parents never saw her; that there were no plans in the foreseeable future for her and Raj to visit them. The least she could do was fight for their right to be at her side at such a momentous event in her life, the birth of their first grand-child. Raj wouldn't want to be at the birth, he had already said so.

'Karin, don't be silly. You can take the baby to your parents once he is a little older.'

It always disconcerted her when he did not entertain the notion at all that the baby could be a girl.

'But I promised them to give birth at home,' she wailed in distress. There weren't many more weeks left before the airlines would refuse her to travel.

They could hear the tropical rain, drops as big as marbles, clatter outside onto the veranda. A cold wind blew the curtains savagely into the room as if imitating the couple's mood.

'This is your home now,' Raj said firmly... 'and what about me?' he continued sounding hurt..

At this point, she got completely confused. She had always been under the impression that he would accompany her to Germany.

Suddenly, she remembered that in one of their letters her parents had come up with a valid argument and she was going to use it now:

'Hospitals in Germany are so much sa...', but Raj interrupted her before she could finish:

'We have a gynaecologist in the family, as you well know. You couldn't be in better hands!'

'Raj, please! They will be so disappointed,' she was now whispering tearfully.

'No!' Raj remained adamant and indicated with the sweep of his hand that he considered the matter settled once and for all.

'Come here; let me give you a hug.' It was no consolation. Tears streaming down her face, overwhelmed by disappointment and frustration, Karin accepted his embrace reluctantly.

❧ ❧ ❧

She gave birth in the small, private hospital of the same doctor who had pierced her ear-lopes. She had to admit that the surroundings were pleasant and the service first class. She could see the flowering trees and shrubs in the garden of the clinic greeting her through the window. Her little honey-coloured son slept in a wicker cot on gleaming white sheets, sucking an imaginary nipple with his tiny lips and framing his crumpled little face with two sprout-sized fists. She was so relieved that he was healthy and feeding well and that there had been no complications during the birth.

From the first sight of him, she had been overcome with tenderness and love, the unbreakable bond and fierce protectiveness of a mother emerging from deep within. Raj had not been present at the birth. He had declined the offer with the excuse that he couldn't bear to see her suffer.

'Strange logic,' Karin thought for a brief moment, but the doctor's look told her to let him go; he would just be in the way.

'You are a natural,' the gynacologist had declared.

They put little Ali into her arms and for most of the day-light hours she cradled the little trussed-up bundle, clutched him to her breast to still his hunger and only agreed to let him go when the nurses insisted that they should both get some sleep..

The following day, the stream of visitors past her bed began, everyone cooing into the cradle amongst cries of delight at the baby's beauty. Karin couldn't wait for them to go and to have him to herself again. Even when Raj finally turned up with an unimaginative bunch of flowers, planting a cautious kiss on her forehead, she could not hide her impatience to get rid of him. She still resented that her parents couldn't share these moments, but even those feelings were buried by the urgency to cradle her baby. It was suggested that she stay another few days in the clinic, but Karin chose to go home when Ali was three days old.

He was a delightful child, easy with his smiles, which conjured cute dimples on his hamster cheeks. Whenever someone spoke to him, he kicked his little bow legs and waved his tiny plump arms in the air in recognition and excitement.

Karin had to fight to have any private time with him against sisters-in-law, nieces and the hired *ayah*, who suddenly appeared to be in charge of the baby. They kept pushing the young mother into her bedroom insisting that she take a rest. Karin did not want to rest, she wanted to be busy doing things for her son. She absolutely refused to allow the wet-nurse to breast feed him which earned her stern looks and angry shrugs of shoulders. She knew they meant well and tried to save her from stress and exertion. They didn't understand that she craved stress and exertion, that she wanted to be involved and have sleepless nights for the sake of her son. She managed to insist that everyone leave the room before she began breast feeding him. Peace and solitude around her, she found it easy to settle him for a good feed while she stroked his little forehead, wrinkled with the effort of sucking. It gave her time to marvel at his tiny button nose and the long, black lashes curving over his closed eyes. After a while, his sucks would slow down, requiring more effort until they stopped altogether, soon replaced by a satisfied sigh and deep breaths indicating that he had fallen asleep. She cupped him tenderly over her shoulder until he burped, and then put him gently on the bed beside her. Propped up on one elbow, she stroked the feathery, black lock from his forehead and let him hold her index finger in his sleep. She treasured those private moments of mother and son and defended them against intruders. They were moments of pure bliss and happiness.

Raj was besotted with his son, in an intense sort of way. Whenever he came home, he would rush to the nursery, look at him proudly as if appreciating a luxurious car, shower Ali's little body with kisses while whispering sweet baby-talk in his ear. After a few minutes, he would hand him to the *ayah* to put him back in the cot. He never left before admonishing the poor woman to drape the mosquito net over it and to tuck it securely under the mattress.

Karin hated the patronising way he spoke to her, someone who was clearly experienced with babies and trying her best to come up to the differing expectations in this family.

With time, Karin reasserted her authority; at first she stole more secret moments than scheduled to spend with her child before laying a firm claim to his entire care. Eventually she alone fed and bathed him, changed his cloth nappies, tickled his little toes, sang to him for hours; she told him stories about his grand-parents far away and to delighted squeals, she prodded the musical mobile, they had sent, into turning above his bed, throwing rainbow patterns on the ceiling and tinkling Mozart's *Guten Abend, gute Nacht.*

This change of rules proved very unpopular with the *ayah* and the women in the family who withdrew sulkily and reported back to Raj.

Karin was oblivious of the storm she had aroused and unrepentant when Raj confronted her:

'He is my son.' She snapped. 'I want to decide what happens to him. I want to care for him. I want to decide how to bring him up. He has got his mother, why should he be looked after by a stranger…'

Her voice was filled with passion, ready for a fight:

'And what else is there for me to do anyway; let me at least be a good mother!' she added spitefully. 'And why don't you ever play with him properly? You only nibble at him as if he was a piece of cake,' she continued to rant.

'I am not a child; I am his father,' he answered truculently.

'Does that mean you will never play football or hide and seek or any games with him?' Raj was taken aback by the menace in her voice.

'He'll have plenty of friends his own age to play with,' he defended himself..

'But I play with him and I'm not his age.' Raj fidgeted and wanted to be gone, sensing that he would not win this battle. This new stubborn, disobedient, rebellious woman was different from the malleable girl he had married. It disconcerted and discomforted him. Could it be excused with the havoc motherhood plays with hormones?

In the following months, the dry burning heat of spring, the stiflingly hot and clammy summer months and the monsoon bursts of June, July and August passed by outside as if they had nothing to do with Karin's life, leaving her cocooned in her own little world.

When not tending to Ali, she had plenty of time to muse why her relationship with Raj had become one of disagreements and alienation. Gone was the common platform of fighting for the same things, of building up their family and of sharing each other's cultures.

What was worse was that Raj did not seem interested in her anymore, never mind her needs, thoughts and increasing isolation. He did not understand that she felt a personal loneliness amidst the crowds and that she was longing for closeness to him more than anybody else. She was the one who had agreed to live in a foreign country; now she needed his support to stay integrated. He always seemed to be in a rush to leave the house, found excuses to miss family dinners and hardly talked to her in private. There had been a time when his face had lit up when he had seen her, but now he looked past her.

She suspected that he found her irritating and combative, better left to her own devices. Ali seemed to be the only reason for him to ever return home. What was it that had been different in the months of their courtship and the early days of their

223

marriage? Karin was convinced that it was the concept of privacy. It didn't exist here and nobody seemed to miss it. During those early days, they had had time to themselves, space to feel close, to share and do things together, to talk to each other, to sort out any problems they might have had without constantly fearing to be overheard or even interrupted by family or servants milling around their bedroom door. If they could recover their privacy, she convinced herself, they could recover their cherished intimacy, pleasure in each other and the willingness to bridge any obstacles to their harmony.

'When are we going to get our own place?' Karin tried her hardest to sound reasonable and friendly.

'What brought that on?' Raj had not expected this new angle of tactic and was suspicious of her motives.

'I would like us to have more of a family life, just the three of us,' she looked at him pleadingly. 'You are hardly ever at home anymore. And even then we are rarely on our own. We need to be together more... as we used to be...' she added in a whisper.

'Don't you have everything you need here? You couldn't cope looking after a big house and the baby.'

'Why not? At one time, I managed a high-powered job and a household!' she reminded him.

'That was different,' but even he had to admit to himself that he didn't really know why.

'The family will be devastated. They will think that you don't like them.'

'Don't be silly, Raj. They will surely understand that a young family needs their privacy.'

'Why should they? They don't need it. And by the way, it is much safer for you and Ali to be surrounded by people who love you, while I am away at work.'

'Ah, you mean, your conscience is clear; you don't ever have to hurry back to us. But I tell you how it feels: It feels as if you have dumped me with the women, like in a harem... like a suitcase full of stuff abandoned in a locker,' she could have added: 'like an appendage to your ego, like a porcelain figurine which is only taken out of its display cabinet on the odd occasion,' but she ran out of steam and simply ended with: 'That's how it feels!'

'That is totally unfair,' he shouted, every word accusing her of ingratitude. 'My sisters would be horrified if they heard you.'

Karin tried to salvage her last shred of calm and courage to direct the discussion back to its original purpose.

'Raj, just imagine, having our own house, our own garden. Your family could visit us any time. It would make such a difference!' She spoke with great feeling; she was so sure that privacy was what they needed to recapture their happiness.

He looked as if he couldn't wait to flee.

'I'll think about it,' he mumbled, already turning towards the door, but she knew that he would rather discuss it with his relatives than with her. His decision and her future lay in their hands.

A few weeks later he announced proudly that he had bought a plot in the countryside with a little house for holidays and as an investment for retirement. He didn't mention that it was next door to his eldest sister's country retreat.

❧ ❧ ❧

Ali grew quickly into a lively toddler, spoilt by his aunties, cousins and the servants. They loved the honey-coloured tint of his skin, much lighter than their own; they fell for his smiles and dimples and his natural trust in people. The milestones of first tooth, first step and first word were celebrated with exuberance and acknowledged with pride by his father. The boy's parents had settled into an unspoken truce and Karin had given in to resignation, making it her priority to provide an unperturbed environment for her child.

She sent piles of pictures to her parents whose pleas to bring Ali over grew more urgent with every letter. She began to make plans without consulting Raj but enlisting her favourite niece's help, grateful for the girl's understanding and cooperation. They worked out a strategy how to wear down Raj's stubborn refusal and sabotage his defence. How could he deny this visit to his wife and son?

But just when they were sure that their plans would be acceptable, Karin discovered that she was pregnant again.

Chapter Twenty-Four

☙❧

When we two first met
  My heart rang out in music…
      Rabrindranath Tagore

Ali has gone to see some friends after Karin has reassured him that she does not need his constant protection. She has asked for Farook to drive her to the hospital and the hotel receptionist arranged it for her.

Karin is well known to the staff now, and well-respected, too, since Ali has joined her. It is still a society where single women are a puzzle, especially one who seems to have one foot in the West and the other in the East. They sense that she is a lady with memories and they know that trying to revive memories is not a good idea; they are always disappointing.

Farook is punctual as usual and drives her straight to the hospital.

'I think Memsahib gone now,' he dares to say in his broken English.

She smiles: 'I would not have left without saying good-bye, Farook. No, I changed my flight home; I haven't quite finished yet what I set out to do.'

'I wait here,' he promises and helps her out of the passenger door.

She gives Raj's name at the hospital reception and admits that she can't remember where to find his room in the maze of corridors. One of the porters is summoned and given instructions. He rushes Karin along landings until he points to a door and turns to leave immediately.

Karin knocks. The door opens almost instantaneously, but a big, white woman in a nurse's uniform squeezes through the gap and bids her to stay outside.

'Mrs. Khan?' she asks. Karin nods.

'We have an emergency,' she says matter-of-factly with a heavy American accent.

'Would you mind waiting in the family lounge?' This is more of an order than a question.

Karin is taken back the way she came. Just a few doors along, they turn off left into a secluded waiting area with plush seats.

'I shall call you when we have finished,' the American nurse promises and rushes off.

Karin settles down on a rattan chair; she likes the pattern of the cushions: little pink rose buds cupped by tiny green leaves on a cream cotton canvas. There are some old women's magazines on a low table, mainly American, a few Bengali, but Karin can't summon up any interest. She is restless and fearful.

She hopes that someone will tell Raj that she has kept her promise and that she is here to see him. Instinctively, she feels that something has been left unsaid yesterday, something he has wanted to convey to her, when they were interrupted by Ali's and Priti's return. She can't imagine what it might be but it seemed important enough to him to summon her again.

She knows that he is seriously ill but she hopes that he will rally, that her visit will give him inner peace and encouragement to carry on. How can she leave tomorrow without a proper good-bye?

She has to wait a good hour before the nurse returns.

'I am so sorry,' she says in a more relaxed tone. 'I am Sister Gloria,' she extends her hand to shake Karin's.

'Mr. Khan had a relapse, but he is ready for you now. '

'He is very tired. Please, keep your visit as short as possible. He needs to sleep,' Sister Gloria says while she takes Karin back along the clinically white walls. She then almost pushes her into the room:

'Mr. Khan, your wife is here.'

There is no time to explain the mistake although the incorrectness, the un-deservedness of the title, grates as Karin accepts it silently.

Karin steps closer to the bed and hears the door close softly behind her. Raj is propped up, his pale face sunken into eiderdown pillows whose whiteness surrounds his head like a nasty halo.

He tries to smile, but even smiling is an effort now.

'Come here, Mita; don't be afraid.'

She takes his hand which lies limply on the bed cover, and returns a smile diluted by sorrow. They look at each other wordlessly, each knowing that they are both sorry that his life is slipping away, sorry about missed opportunities, sorry about lost years and the hurt they have inflicted upon each other. There is nothing to be said or done now.

'I have something to give you,' he perks up a little and tries to guide her search with a nod towards his bedside table. She sees her little elephant standing under a vase of white lilies. She has always hated lilies with their cloying scent and pretend-purity; to her they are flowers for the grave, symbols of a dying summer.

'Drawer,' rasps his voice.

She opens it and sees a little package wrapped in pink tissue paper.

'Take it out,' Raj urges her breathlessly and adds faintly: 'Open...!'

Karin unwraps the delicate paper and finds a little red box with a gold-coloured clasp and lettering giving the name of a Dhaka shop. The clasp springs open easily. When the lid lifts, she doesn't know at first what she is looking at, but when she picks up the silver bracelet, little bells tinkle. She looks at him. Not only has he remembered, he concedes to an innocent wish she had harboured as his young wife. In spite the delay of years, she is touched.

'Put them on,' His body is still, but his eyes sparkle in excitement. She fastens the bands around her ankles and stamps her feet – at first hesitantly, then with more force. The bells jump up and down and ring in unison. She imitates dancing, gliding around the room, stamping her feet in a developing rhythm. For a moment, she is that young woman again, carefree, in love and besotted by her new surroundings.

Raj smiles indulgently at her childish pleasure and closes his eyes.

'It's very sweet of you,' she sits down on the edge of his bed. 'Thank you!'

He is nearly asleep but as she bends over him to plant a soft kiss on his sweaty forehead, she hears him mumble: 'Long overdue...'

She gets up. 'Good-bye, Raj,' she murmurs into his ear. 'I shall see you tomorrow before my flight.'

She is not sure whether he can hear her. She takes a piece of paper from a pad on his bedside table, writes a short thank-you note and slips it under the little elephant, before leaving the room on tiptoes.

Chapter Twenty-Five

ᘓᔓᔔᘐ

Life of my life, I shall ever try…
Rabrindranath Tagore

Raj was not amused when he heard that Karin expected their second child. She had been excited all day, decorating their cool bedroom with lotus, hibiscus and bakul flowers. She had told cook to prepare her husband's favourite lamb curry with tomatoes and lentils, and had rehearsed her little speech to him. As it happened so often, her relatives forestalled her, not out of spite, but thoughtless exuberance. As soon as he entered, Karin saw that Raj was in a bad mood.

'Is it true?' He looked at her with his beautiful eyes.

She was a little taken aback that her news had obviously leaked out, and she was disconcerted at the lack of a smile.

He took her silence for an affirmation:

'It is far too early. Ali is not even a year old.'

She was fumbling for words: 'It will be good for the two of them to be close in age.'

She was astonished that the husband who came from a family of eight children minded that she was having a second baby.

'I am thinking of your health.' He was sure of the validity of his argument.

'As long as I feel fine – and I do – and the doctor is happy, there is no need to worry.'

Her streak of stubbornness, rarely reaching the light of day, came to the fore. She really couldn't understand why he fussed while she was blissfully happy. There was no good reason to object, because they were neither strapped for cash nor short of assistance with relatives and servants constantly milling around. Karin was hurt and hugely disappointed. She was willing to give him the benefit of the doubt considering it was a surprise to both of them, but inside, a section of her heart shattered into small pieces.

One afternoon, Raj turned up unexpectedly early from work. She watched him as he stood around looking sheepish before picking up the courage to ask her to sit down for a chat. The chair legs screeched on the stone floor as they were pulled in position. Once seated opposite each other, Karin leant suspiciously into the back of her chair, while Raj hunched over the dining table, his arms resting on the top and his fists folded as if in prayer. He came out with his suggestion in a dangerously quiet, seductive voice. Every word ended with an icy tone, hard and shiny like steel. Karin could not believe what she was hearing; it felt as if swords were piercing her body, and cold drafts of despair began floating menacingly between her and her husband.

When he had finished, he paused and looked at her with hope in his eyes.

'You are not serious!' she gasped. 'You are not suggesting that I have an abortion and combine it with a visit to my parents as if nothing had happened?'

He averted his eyes and stared at his clasped fists on the table. When she remained silent, he peered up and was met by her hostile gaze. She got up without another word, her knees trembling. She felt sick, sick with revulsion. This couldn't be the man she had married, the man she had given up her life and family for! As she walked towards the curtained exit of the room, hardly aware of what she was doing, just knowing that she had to flee, he followed her, grasped first one, then both her wrists and hissed into her face:

'If you don't do it… I will not have you disobey me.' As she tried to free herself, his grip tightened:

'You are hurting me!' she stuttered in disbelief and fear.

'It's your fault! I'll hurt you a lot more…' At that moment, the curtain was pushed back and Lakshmi's husband Amir looked at both of them, eyes wide with astonishment and disapproval. Karin fled, holding back her tears until she had reached the relative privacy of her bedroom. She crawled underneath the mosquito net and threw herself onto the bed. Lying in foetal position she rocked herself to deaden the sounds of her sobs. She did not want the entire household alarmed to their row and have everyone standing around her bed with words of consolation and advice.

She must have fallen asleep, when she heard her name whispered: 'Can I come in?'

It was Amir, the soft-hearted, wise and generous brother-in-law who had been her kind host for so many months. So far he had kept in the background, occupied with his business and faithful adherence to five prayers a day.

'I have spoken to your husband,' he began calmly. 'He won't quite tell me what it is about but I can guess. I told him that in my house, we treat our women well and that it mustn't happen again.'

'Thank you, Amir,' Karin whispered.

'Now, dry your tears, go down to have some tea with Lakshmi and Priti and then they will take you shopping! And tonight, you will both try to make up!'

His benign half-smile indicated that he understood marital mishaps but that 'to make up' was an order, which he had quite possibly issued to Raj as well.

Raj remained bad tempered and grumpy for weeks, but they had grudgingly declared another truce. He was cross that he had no power over his wife's body. He was determined to make her see sense, but realised eventually that there was nothing he could do against her will. It irked him that Karin's parents wrote glowing letters of congratulations and suggestions for baby names. His sisters shushed him out of the room whenever he began his lament, pointing out that he knew very little about women's matters and that he could not help reacting like a man. This was their territory and they were delighted.

His brothers were no help either; they just shrugged their shoulders, grinned and suggested he leave it to the women folk;

they had suffered the same fate many times and had learnt to give in gracefully.

Below the forced civility, there grumbled a power struggle like the rumblings before an earthquake; it was banished for the moment to the depths of their consciences. They had to observe their host's ruling and had to put on a brave façade whenever they left their bedroom.

The continued tensions between the couple did not go unnoticed and the family directed hints of disapproval at their brother. To Karin's surprise, they shared her opinion that he spent far too much time away from his young family, took too little interest in his child's life and carried on to neglect his wife.

'I don't know what's wrong with him,' Karin overheard whispers, 'he has a young, pretty, intelligent wife who gave him already one adorable son, and he dares to treat her like that.'

'And she makes such an effort to fit in,' said another.

'Yes, in some ways she is more Bengali than we are,' agreed someone else. 'She tries so hard.'

Karin was pleasantly surprised that they were on her side and gratified to hear that it was not the difference between their cultures she failed to bridge but that her husband was, even in Bengali eyes, badly behaved.

She still didn't know what to do about it and kept quiet for the sake of peace.

At times, Raj turned up unexpectedly early from work and played listlessly and unenthusiastically with Ali, as if it was beneath him, as if his job was finished with simply fathering him.

'I can't bear to see them like that,' Priti said to her mother. 'They fought so hard to be with each other, and now look at them!'

'Maybe we should intervene a little.' They organised a sequence of family outings and did not allow anyone to escape; there was a picnic which was – to the children's delight – interrupted by a heavy pre-monsoon downpour.

Soon afterwards, they invited everyone to their favourite Chinese restaurant in town, which had to close to the public for the afternoon to accommodate them all. Even the old man, the head of the family, Karin's father-in-law, came along – to Babul's dismay, who still hadn't told him that he was a smoker. Holding a cigarette behind his back, he seated himself at the other end of the table, hoping that, in the general mayhem, father wouldn't notice that smoke was curling up into the air further down the row of his large brood.

On another occasion, the men took Raj to an international cricket tournament in Dhaka's stadium, England against Bangladesh. The women hoped it would give the brothers ample time to have a heart to heart chat and to instil some sense into their errant sibling.

The men returned exhilarated after a dramatic game in which the hosts had acquitted themselves better than expected and had only narrowly lost. The brothers were so inspired that they decided to meet up daily, including their sons, to play cricket and to recapture the excitement of those three days. Raj soon lost interest; physical exertion wasn't for him, and his son was still too young to make father's participation obligatory.

They had enormous trouble recruiting Raj for the next outing.: they wanted him to accompany the women as a chaperone on a shopping expedition. Karin was not known to be a keen shopper, but she was grateful for the diversion and thought it might make a nice change for Ali to go out with father and mother. As usual they went to New Market and strolled between rickety stands and solid wooden shops, laden with household wares, shoes, draperies, saris and, at the far end, with fruit and vegetables. Karin had no intention of buying anything for herself, but maybe some clothes or shoes for her son.

She didn't have to make an effort in selecting anything, because no sooner did she show interest in something, her *bhabis* took over, debating the item vociferously before haggling down the price and buying it for her. They settled down for refreshments under an improvised pergola of a tearoom, but soon she was pulled away to be dragged up wooden steps and pushed into a temple of cloth.

'Raj, you stay in the teashop and watch the little ones,' they ordered their brother. Sullenly, he gave in, as this was clearly the better of the two options.

The owner of the sari shop rushed towards them, greeting the distinguished group with reverence and greedy courtesy. Rolls of fabric were taken from the glass show-cases behind the counters, the silks, chiffons and brocades shaken to fly for a moment through the air like exotic birds and then spread over the cutting tables. Their beauty found great approval with the ladies who showed their appreciation with 'oohs' and 'aaahs' and broad smiles.

One by one, they succumbed to temptation, chose a new sari and held still for their measurements to be taken for the blouses and satin petticoats.

'Come on, you choose one,' their lust of purchasing stilled, they now descended on Karin.

She could see Raj standing outside; he must have got bored baby-sitting in the tearoom and peered in their direction with impatience, occasionally talking down to his off-spring who clung on to his father's hand. It was a pity that her husband could not enter into the spirit of things.

'That's his problem! It's rare enough that I have a bit of fun,' Karin thought, a touch of mutinous courage rearing its head. She nodded and her *bhabis* were delighted to take charge. Balls of cloth, just rolled up and stashed away, were taken out of the glass cupboards again and spread out in front of her. Karin felt a frisson of recklessness and childish pleasure. She indulged in admiring the various patterns and embroideries, letting her fingers glide over the smooth silks and finally chose a bottle-green sari with pastel-coloured flowers, bordered by gold threat embroidery.

'I'll ask Raj what he thinks,' and before they could stop her she had rushed out to fetch him. He entered reluctantly, while his sisters retreated one by one filing out of the shop.

'You don't need another sari,' was his comment before they had even reached what she wanted to show him.

She pointed to it: 'But look. It's so lovely; the colour of the Bangladeshi flag.' Nothing made an impression.

'Do what you like,' he spat out scornfully and turned to leave.

'I am so sorry,' Karin stuttered apologetically to the shop's owner and hurried out after her husband.

The *bhabis* looked at the two of them with clenched teeth and displeasure, clearly disappointed with this turn of events.

It was obvious: Raj had still not forgiven his young wife that she had gone ahead with the pregnancy.

'Why don't we spend some time in our house in Sonargaon?'
Karin suggested to Raj.

'Do you really think I will get leave? I only started the job six months ago. You go if you like.'

However, it was not as simple as that. She needed someone to take her, someone to stay with her and various servants, according to her relatives, who did not quite understand her need for privacy however much she tried to explain. They finally agreed to let her go with the chauffeur, Lakshmi's cook, one of the servant girls who was known to be particularly reliable and little Ali.

These turned out to be the most idyllic weeks for a long time. The house was hardly habitable, but with energetic sweeping, polishing and furniture sent on request from Dhaka, Karin turned it into a modest but comfortable country retreat. Once the accommodation was sorted out, she continued in the garden. It was a struggle against watery corners as much as dusty soil. None of the flower seeds her mother had sent germinated in the baking sun. Cook helped her plant a few fruit trees, but otherwise she learnt to be happy to leave the garden to do its own thing.

She found peace and balance in taking Ali to the local market or for walks along the edges of paddy fields or simply to play with him in the garden during the cool early morning hours or after dusk. During lazy afternoons, she contemplated her life, future and the child she was carrying and found contentment.

The peace did not hold for long. Soon members of the family descended to give her company and cheer her up and finally, to take her back to Dhaka.

The baby girl was born in August. She had a heart-shaped face, a hint of Raj's wide nose, almond-shaped eyes of a yet undefined bluish-green colour and jet black straggly wisps of hair. She was a serious baby who seemed to study whoever looked into her cot rather than beam at everyone as her brother had done. From birth, she had a lithe little body, far taller than any of the babies ever born into the family, like a sapling willow. In spite of this, she was unusually heavy for a Bengali child.

The first time, Karin had lifted one of her new-born nieces, she had nearly dropped her with surprise, because she was light like a cloud of cotton wool and soft and bendy like play-dough.

Jasmine was different, a wiry, determined little thing without charm and smiles. She learnt to walk and talk much sooner than her brother had done and insisted on using the grown-ups' toilet as soon as she could waddle, ignoring the brightly coloured potty lovingly selected by her father – one of the few times he had shown an interest in his off-spring – as if it were an insult to her intelligence.

Karin smirked in secret admiration and could well imagine the battles in years ahead between father and daughter. In a way, Karin was in awe of this bright little girl of hers and hoped that the name Jasmine would add some much needed fragrance and femininity to her to cover up the already evident zeal and competitiveness.

Karin was more relaxed with her second born, not so much because of her acquired experience, but because baby Jasmine didn't tolerate fuss. Karin took to having long cuddling sessions with Ali when his sister wasn't looking. He had become clingy and demanded his mother's affection more than ever.

Whenever Karin tried to hug Jasmine, she earned herself a look as if the little girl was evaluating what the point and benefit of hugs would be. There was already an innate logic behind her actions and a determination to see things through.

Raj was more delighted with his daughter than Karin had hoped for and seemed to have forgiven his wife for having her against his will. Karin was pleased that she had stood her ground and was prepared, for the sake of family harmony, to forget the past.

She knew that something had broken inside her when he had mentioned abortion instead of sweeping her up in his arms and thanking her that she was going to give him another child. But she was prepared to put this sad episode aside.

At times, Raj seemed a little disappointed that Jasmine was not as attractive a child as her brother; but he spent the occasional hour with her or took her out on family visits, sunning himself in the reflected glory of her intelligence, until he realised that he would get no closer to her than anybody else and that she decidedly rejected his attempts at smothering her with kisses. The novelty wore off and soon Raj was again hardly at home anymore.

Karin was left to spend her days with the women and children, who frequently entertained themselves mocking the foibles of their husbands once they knew that they were safely out of the way.

Karin had nothing to add; Raj's short-comings were too private and sad that she wanted them discussed; there was nothing light-hearted and humorous about him that she could contribute.

'Oh, Raj *bhai*,' Karin heard through the mist of her own thoughts, twiddling a corner of her sari. Priti was imitating someone's theatrical exclamations. The other women began to giggle, pulling their *achols* over their mouths, sneaking looks in Karin's direction.

'I am feeling so unwell…' Priti continued in a ridiculously wimpish voice, flinging the back of her hand dramatically against her forehead, as if feeling for fever.

'I might die soon…' another sister-in-law quipped. 'You are the only one who can save me, Raj *bhai*,' added another, cupping her hand over her mouth when she saw Karin's confused glance at her.

By now, they cried with laughter, holding their bellies, hitting the table with their palms in merriment. The imitation must have been spot on. The laughter was so infectious that Karin couldn't help but chuckle along, although she had no idea whom they were talking about.

'Don't you mind that he is always visiting her?' It was Priti who addressed this question to her auntie; everyone hung on Karin's lips awaiting the answer with baited breath.

'Who are you talking about?' Karin was honestly baffled.

There followed an embarrassed silence, but not for long. They lost interest. Hilarity resumed and moved on to another victim, leaving the question hanging in the air. Priti avoided her auntie's looks realising that she had no idea what her question had been about.

'Never mind,' she said, stroking Karin's hand absent-mindedly.

Suddenly someone stood in the doorway of the dining room like a menacing shadow. The speaker, who had just been in full flow mocking her husband, began to cough violently. Fortunately, it wasn't her husband but Karin's who had appeared from nowhere.

'Lucky he didn't come five minutes earlier,' Priti mumbled.

Karin got up to join Raj, wondering; they had – on purpose or not – sown a seed of suspicion and confused her. Her *bhabis* might be frivolous and mischievous, but there had been an underlying tone of seriousness among all the joking which gnawed at Karin's conviction that it might have been a harmless jibe.

Karin was painfully aware that her relationship with Raj had cooled, that they had rows and disagreements, however muffled, to observe Amir's request; she had often wondered whether it was necessary that Raj spent so much time away from his young family and she had always managed to reassure herself that he was busy at work and preferred the company of men as is usual in Muslim societies. There were sometimes good moments which had usually to do with the children, but as a couple they had never recovered the loving intimacy she had so enjoyed, which had swept her off her feet, away from everything she had ever known.

Karin's belief in Raj's loyalty had so far been rock-solid and unquestionable. It was the one thing she held on to; it gave her hope that things would improve with time. However many quarrels they had, she trusted him and was quite determined not to overturn that trust because of gossip.

Deep down, however, she decided to be more vigilant; a chink of mistrust had entered the bubble of her safe world.

Chapter Twenty-Six

CRXO

The night deepens and the dying flame flickers…
                                    Rabrindranath Tagore

Karin is glad that she has brought her green *sari*.

For her second visit to the hospital she had again chosen western style clothing. Intuitively, she wanted to underline that she was not a Bengali wife any longer, obedient, submissive and seeking approval.

She was out to re-assert herself as a different person, self-confident, emotionally balanced and independent, risen from the ashes of a broken marriage and broken dreams. She has raised two children single-handedly, has held down a responsible job and earned her own keep for years. Why shouldn't she be her own woman and proud of what she has become?

However, she doubts that Raj has noticed anything different about her. Appearance and clothes become unimportant when one is consumed by illness.

Karin shivers at the thought of her next assignment: The visit to the family. She has no idea what kind of reception she will get. She doesn't entirely trust Priti's enthusiastic description of how thrilled they will be to see her. Some might be, if she is lucky.

241

'Better get on with the sari otherwise I won't be going at all,' she marshals her thoughts, pushing the more unpleasant possibilities to the back of her mind. She takes off her white cotton trousers and short-sleeved blouse and puts on the green satin petticoat which nearly reaches the floor. She slips into the green silk blouse which ends somewhere above her waist. She has to contort her body to button it up at the back. She can't manage the little pearl-shaped, jade-green top-button; maybe she will be able to hide it with the width of the sari or with some luck, Ali will pop in and do it up for her. The puff-sleeves are surely out of fashion and a little quaint, but she has always loved this outfit. It was one of the first gestures to re-assert her independence against her husband's so-called 'unshakable better judgement'.

Next she unfolds the five metre long train of green silk, which, when neatly folded into a square, has not taken up much space in her suitcase.

She struggles to find the plain end of the sari without dropping everything else on the floor. When the top end is tucked into the waistband of her petticoat, she sighs with relief – she has made a start. Now very carefully, she winds the precious silk around her body to form a skirt and when reaching her navel, she quickly tucks it in again. After the second layer, Karin weaves plaits of silk between the fingers of her right hand, gathers them to overlap at the top and tugs them into the petticoat waistband, too. She rummages around her wash bag for a safety pin which will secure the bunch of pleats unfolding down her leg like a flirty fan. It takes her a while to force the needle through the pile of silk and the petticoat's satin for the two to hold on to each other.

She looks down at herself and decides that it is probably nowhere near as beautiful as it could be, but that it would have to do. She is simply out of practice, and a second attempt would not necessarily assure a better result. After that, it is just another twist around her waist and a swish across her shoulder, which should then display the most elaborate part of the sari, the *achol*. Hers is not any different from the rest of the cloth, simply a repetition of the delicate pastel water-colour flowers edged by gold embroidery on dark green background.

She would have liked to do it justice and sighs.

She shouldn't have worried. An hour before Farook is due to take her to the family reunion, Priti turns up unannounced.

With a lot of head-shaking, she tugs, pulls and pins her auntie's sari into place until she is satisfied.

'Didn't you bring another one?' the young woman scolds the older one and tut-tuts in mock despair.

'I love this one the most.'

Priti remembers immediately why. Fierce rows are not often fought in public in her society.

'You know, auntie, you don't look much different from when you were here last.'

It sounds like a genuine compliment, but Karin knows how many years lie in-between.

'Don't be silly,' she retorts a little more sharply than she had intended, colouring nevertheless like a beetroot. 'Look at you!' They haven't heard Ali enter the room, smiling at his mother with admiration.

'Did you have a nice morning?' Karin quickly changes the subject.

'You can say that. I met some friends, and...' he pauses to choose the words carefully, 'I also enquired about,' he pauses again before saying haltingly as if trying out their effect with caution, '...charity work.'

Karin doesn't give her reaction away. She stops looking at her image in the wardrobe mirror and turns her full attention to Ali.

'And?' she asks.

'It looks promising,' he grins triumphantly, but he won't disclose more than that.

In any case, it is time for them to move. A few sprays of perfume on her neck, elbows and hair, and they are out of the door.

The exclusive suburb of Dhanmondi hasn't changed much. As they rattle along in Farook's car and look out at the passing widening avenues and ever larger and more beautiful residences, surrounded by luscious gardens, Karin recaptures the feeling that had overcome her when she had visited Dhanmondi for the first time.

To the young woman it had been like a cultivated oasis on the edge of the slums, totally separated and untouched by the dust and chaos of millions of people living by roadsides only a mile away.

'What happened to your mother's huge old house by the Burigonga?' Karin asks.

'*Ayah* sold it shortly after Dad died. She couldn't bear to live there anymore…. Dhanmondi is much safer and the new house is more manageable,' Priti explains.

'Amir died rather young. He seemed perfectly healthy when I knew him.'

'We think he never told us when he wasn't feeling well. We were so totally unprepared when he collapsed with a heart attack. At one stage, I thought mother would die from grief, too.'

'They were very devoted.' Karin remembers the short, wiry man with great affection. He had been deeply but unobtrusively religious, praying five times a day, observing the Koran's teachings and going to the mosque every Friday, living modestly and giving regularly to charity. A wealthy man by then he was the epitome of modesty, sincerity and a never ending love, patience and generosity for his large clan.

As a young man, he had come with five hundred saved-up Rupees from his village to the capital and, with intelligence, honest hard work and a talent to manage people with kindness, had built up various lucrative businesses, a textile factory, a river cargo shipping and a property development company. In spite of having done so well, he put his success down to the Grace of Allah.

He had been the only man in the family who had openly spoken to Karin about feelings, emotions and his courtship of Lakshmi when she had only been fourteen years of age, his voice overflowing with love and pride. He had kept his word to her father that he would look after his young wife and protect her from all unpleasantness of life. To Karin, he had been a tower of strength and a true sounding board when she had been torn by self-doubt and agonising choices.

They have arrived.

'Look at this lovely garden,' Karin exclaims. The profusion of greens and colourful blooms is delightful; a riot of roses, chrysanthemums and flowering shrubs welcome them in orderly beds with neatly trimmed edges. They walk up to the house, heady scents following them along the path where blooms stand like a guard of honour and nod their welcome in the gentle breeze.

At the far end of the path stands a motherly figure, arms folded. Karin's heart sinks and terror sweeps over her. She begins to tremble and only stops when Priti squeezes her hand in sympathy. As they get closer, Karin makes out a head of grey hair bunched up in a bun, thick glasses and a sari in muted silvery grey satin with purple embroideries.

'*As Salaam aleikum, Bhabi!*' says the figure still standing there motionless.

Karin is disconcerted and at a loss what to reply. At last she simply offers a smile and the only words that come into her head: '*Waleikum as salaam*, Lakshmi!'

She has no idea whether calling her by her name is appropriate or not and fears for the worst. However, faux-pas or not, it seems to break the ice. A huge, sparkling smile spreads over Lakshmi's face and suddenly the hostess moves at lightening speed. She enfolds Karin into a soft bear-hug and squashes the years of separation into nothing. Then she grabs Karin's arm by the elbow and declares:

'Well, come on in then; everybody is waiting.' They enter a wide and high-ceilinged vestibule, from which a sweeping staircase rises up to the first floor. All walls are kept in pristine white and only a sideboard with an attached umbrella-stand on the left; a few modern pictures break up the whiteness. White wood-panelled doors lead off into various directions, one of them double doors. This is the one Lakshmi opens and pushes her guest through.

Karin feels like a reluctant child which is shoved to perform in front of relatives. At first, there is a moment of complete silence until one from the group of women gets up from her settee and comes towards Karin with outstretched hands. Karin remembers vaguely her oldest sister-in-law Hasina. An unbelievable din of chatter and delighted cries fills the air as everybody follows Hasina's example. Karin is hugged and squeezed, kissed on both cheeks and shaken by the hand. One old lady in a white sari – Karin has no idea who she is – stops the foreign *bhabi* before she can make the first movement to pay respectfully her *salaam*. She grabs both of her hands, keeps hold of them and shakes them incessantly as if she would never let them go.

Priti murmurs familiar and unfamiliar names into Karin's ear which become a blur of faces and sounds. She doesn't want to disappoint her ex-relatives by not recognising them and failing to put faces, names and memories together. She hopes that a friendly smile will cover up for her ignorance.

At last, everybody takes a seat again; the servants are called to provide tea, cakes and sweets and a different kind of clatter starts up. For the first time, Karin gets an idea how many women have gathered: They must nearly all be there – Raj's three sisters and about thirty of their and their brothers' daughters who in turn have brought along the new generation. The thought that they all came to see her is overwhelming, although, Karin suspects, there is a strong element of curiosity involved, an eagerness not wanting to miss such a unique event. 'Still no men,' Karin thinks by herself. 'Some things change quicker than others.'

For a moment, she pictures the brand-new, ultra-modern shopping centre in the middle of Dhaka where, according to Ali, one can sit and sip a cappuccino or shop in western designer stores; or the peculiar sight of rickshaw *wallahs* with a mobile phone clamped to their ears, which still brings a smile to her face.

Privately, however, in the intimate circle of families, the man is still the head of the household to whom the women, however educated and emancipated, defer. The measures of moral rectitude, decency and society's expectations of traditional behaviour where the women know their place and are, or at least pretend they are, content with it, seem to be still the norm.

As she looks around the room and observes some teenage girls in jeans and tight T-shirts she can imagine the struggle and family rifts between the old and the young generations. After all, a great number of Bangladeshis have meanwhile studied, worked or visited abroad and are able to make comparisons, absorb new ideas and bring them home.

They hear shouting and heavy boots outside the double doors which are suddenly thrown open. A young man dressed in a white *kurta* and prayer cap with a sparse fluff of black beard and moustache, covering up an otherwise handsome face, strides in. He looks furious and determined, scrutinising the gaggle of chattering women as if to seek out somebody in particular. His glance comes to rest on Karin and, after a moment's hesitation and recognition, a fierce light switches on behind his eyes and his eyebrows wrinkle above his nose in distaste. His mouth sets in bitter disapproval before it opens and spits out: 'What is she doing here?' He continues to jab the air with an arrow finger in Karin's direction, shouting: 'You should be ashamed of yourself, coming here, after all you have done!'

246

Lakshmi jumps up quickly, as do her daughters, and together they hustle him back out among urgent whispers. Everyone can hear his excited, high-pitched voice before the double doors are closed. Priti seats herself next to Karin.

'Who was that?' Karin asks in a hoarse whisper.

'Never mind that,' Priti tries to fob her off, but when she sees her auntie's pleading look she adds unwillingly: 'Reena's grandson.'

'There it is again, the emotional blackmail of bringing shame on the family,' Karin thinks but only nods in recognition of the name.

'I am sorry,' Karin mouths and lowers her head.

'It's not your fault,' Priti says with spirit and adds: 'He is a student and got in with a rather fanatical crowd at university. Somehow he found out what happened in the past. No one knows how, but then we are never good at keeping secrets.' Priti shrugs her shoulders wistfully. 'Goodness knows which version he got hold of from his grandmother; probably distorted beyond recognition over the years.'

'What happened to her afterwards?'

'She was ostracised by our family. We knew that uncle still went there frequently, but we ignored it. Then she married again. It wasn't a happy marriage by all accounts.'

The room goes quiet in anticipation of an explanation when the three women return, but when they only smile mysteriously as if nothing had happened, everyone continues to chat and laugh animatedly.

There is Hasina with her three daughters and four grand-daughters. Mumtaz must have come all the way from Sylhet with her daughter Suriya and two grand-daughters. Farah from Chittagong still has the cheeky, throaty laughter which deepens the dimples in her cheeks.

'I remember your impersonations,' Karin says and they both burst out laughing. They know who used to be the butt of their jokes.

Nasma is now living in the capital, her young family's England odyssey long forgotten. Her husband has worked for many years in Dhaka's main hospital as a lung specialist, and Kitty, the adorable three year old at Karin's wedding, has grown into a smart, elegant but reticent woman who formally introduces her two teenage sons.

Lakshmi now claps her hands and calls everyone to the dining room table decorated with *shapla* blooms where a feast awaits them. Priti and Laksmi sit on either side of their guest. After dinner, people dwindle away, their chauffeurs waiting outside with cars to take them home. Karin as the guest of honour is only allowed to leave last. She is weighed down with little gift-wrapped packages, pieces of fine paper or bits torn off from somewhere, on which addresses have been written in ornate letters or scribbled in haste, so that she can stay in contact. Most of all, she has been showered with good wishes, expressions of joy to see her again and requests to promise that she would return… 'preferably during my life time' to give it dramatic urgency.

Karin has always loved her sisters-in-law and had been assured that in return, they had regarded her with sneaking admiration for her courage and had appreciated that she respected their choice of not rocking the boat.

She embraces Lakshmi, thanks her for her kindness and invites her to visit. Neither of them can be sure whether that will happen.

When Karin reaches the hotel lobby, the receptionist hands her a note with a stony face.

Chapter Twenty-Seven

᱒᱒

Early in the day it was whispered…
Rabrindranath Tagore

'Where are you going?' Karin asked Raj with as much innocence as she could muster.

He was suspicious. 'Out!' he flung into the room.

'It's the weekend. Couldn't we do something as a family?'

'I promised to visit Reena and the children.'

There was that name again! As far as Karin knew, Reena was the wife of a distant cousin, who had died in the Independence War. Not much news had seeped out how he had died, but the family considered him a hero. Karin had seen the woman a couple of times at family gatherings and had found her – with her hooked nose and bad skin, but beautifully thick, black hair down to her waist - moderately pretty, not particularly smart with a tendency to self-pity.

Of course, it was a tragedy that she had lost her husband at such a young age, leaving her with three children under the age of ten, but the women in the family rallied around until they were made to feel unwelcome. Reena had her own ideas by whom she wanted to be looked after. One of those chosen ones was Raj who took this duty seriously. How often Raj visited the widow,

Karin didn't know. She hated keeping a tally of her husband's whereabouts, but she assumed that he would frequently pop in after work to see that everybody in that family was alright. She hadn't realised that he was using spare time at weekends to pay visits, too. Karin had put Reena to the back of her mind after first meeting her, because she had been confronted by stiffness and unwillingness to engage. She had put it down to grief and tried to be understanding. Looking back and with the rumours buzzing in her ears, Karin suspected, that there had been more to the awkwardness between the three of them than she had imagined.

When the visits had first begun, Raj had taken his wife and some of his sisters to Reena's flat which was a dark, cave-like ground-floor warren of corridors and rooms in an old-fashioned army brick-building. Although they had announced their visit, the hostess was lying in bed, fully dressed in a sari the colour of saffron which underlined the pallor of her heavily made-up skin. Shahana, Raj's second eldest sister-in-law, had enquired what it was that was ailing her and, hardly waiting for an answer, added sarcastically that she really liked her new eye shadow. Karin had found it quite sickening the way Raj fussed and worried over Reena. She had never known him to behave with her like that.

On another visit, Reena had made her three children line-up at the dining room door, each carrying a favourite dish for uncle who sat at the head of an old, oblong dining table as if he were the master of the house. Once each dish had been put before him, he thanked the child profusely, padded it on the head or held its lower jaw between thumb and fingers, sliding them gently to the tip of the chin and then kissing his own finger tips as a declaration of affection. The children were quite familiar with this drill, but being children, they seemed glad to rush back to their games once their duty was done.

Karin, who had declined politely to eat a big meal in the middle of the afternoon, had found the scene contrived and, if she was honest, nauseating. As this was still during her adjusting and settling-in stage, she had assumed that this was the norm in Bengali society. Since she had overheard her sisters-in-law ridiculing Reena's sisterly attachment to Raj, Karin began to doubt whether her husband's behaviour towards the widow was indeed nothing out of the ordinary.

She decided to find out for herself.

'Can I come along?' she carried on, as if it was nothing much of importance. She saw the shock in his face

'Why?' he asked aghast.

'Just to get out of the house, to spend some time with you and I haven't seen Reena for ages,' each a good enough reason, she thought.

'What about the children?' He clearly tried to fob her off.

'*Ayah* will look after them. We won't be staying that long anyway, will we?' she smiled at him amiably.

'I was going to help her with her finances, bank statements, bills. It's going to be very boring.' He was putting up a fight.

'That's fine. You go through her papers and she and I can catch up on news.

He looked extremely uncomfortable but couldn't think of any more obstacles to throw into the way of her coming along.

As it happened, the ensuing visit to Reena was brief. It began with an enthusiastic welcome until Reena discovered Karin behind Raj's back. The rest of the time was laced with artificial courtesies and the same stiff atmosphere between them that Karin remembered from earlier meetings. She had obviously spoiled whatever they had planned, paperwork or not, their afternoon like a splendid firework hissing and spluttering, preparing to get off the ground before succumbing to damp air and rain showers.

Karin was asked to make herself comfortable in a wicker arm chair while Reena professed to show Raj the paperwork which needed sorting out. Karin could hear them whispering in the room next door; it sounded a little heated with the occasional shrill sound which was immediately suppressed. Karin thought that, to be fair, it could be her imagination playing tricks.

Finally, Reena joined her and they conducted a stilted conversation filled with false pleasantries and feigned interest in each others' families. Karin was glad when Raj returned after a short while.

'Everything seems in order,' he said briskly, 'but I will have to go into detail some other time.' Karin couldn't see the point of having come in the first place if he didn't conclude the business, but she kept quiet and was relieved when they left. For a while, Raj did not mention visits to Reena. Karin was still not certain what to read into their relationship and was torn between suspicion and trust in her husband's loyalty; the whole thing might indeed be innocent; was she begrudging a little attention to a woman who had lost everything?

Reena was a relative by marriage, and given the lack of privacy in Bengali society, they were surely not tempted to have an affair, which was bound to be discovered. Maybe it was a harmless flirtation to lift the widow's spirits? Karin did not want to be mean. She was willing to give her husband the benefit of the doubt and didn't object when he resumed his dutiful visits, but abstained from accompanying him.

'Can I ask you a question?' Karin was lingering by Amir's desk where he was reading the *Financial Express*.

She wanted to be diplomatic but needed to address the nagging doubt swirling around in her mind. She wanted to hang on to her dream of 'love conquers everything', but Raj's indifference hurt…

She had thought that from the outset, they had agreed to respect each other, each other's background and that, from that position, they would share and enjoy each others' cultures. One of her bug-bears was the constant struggle to learn Bengali; as a linguist, it frustrated her and she had bought herself three different *Teach Yourself Bengali* books. Unfortunately, the print was so poor that, considering it was a different script altogether, she had no chance of learning the language by herself. Whenever she asked Raj to help her, expecting him to be delighted that she was willing to make an effort, he was either too busy or not in the mood. Twice he sat next to her, but lost patience rather quickly.

'Why do you want to learn Bengali?' he asked in an exasperated tone. 'Everyone speaks English anyway.'

With that the matter was, in his opinion, settled. No one else seemed particularly interested in teaching her their mother tongue; after a while she stopped trying. There were times of normality and pleasure amongst the many days of boredom. One event created joyful anticipation and a divine evening of music. The principal of Dhaka University had invited the Khan family and around a hundred selected guests to his private residence to attend a concert of Ravi Shankar. Observing the elaborate preparations of her sisters-in-law, their difficulties in deciding which saris to wear and which jewellery to parade, Karin had the distinct feeling that it was an occasion as much to be seen as to savour the music.

Karin took some care in choosing, too, and wrapped herself in her nicest sari, a pink creation with black stylised flower-borders. It wasn't silk, but tulle stiffened by the laundry woman's starch making it look like a puffy cloud around her body and crackle with every step. Karin thought with longing of the elegant green sari with the pastel flowers and gold stitching she hadn't been allowed to buy; she had really loved that sari; in her mind it had become a symbol of some kind – maybe freedom, she thought, freedom for the new country – and herself.

The concert began at six in the evening, much earlier than concerts would start in Europe. It took a while until every guest was seated in the half-circle of chairs around a dais at the far end of the enormous drawing room. As soon as the revered musician appeared, a hush fell over the crowd and without any introduction the master began to play his sitar, accompanied by two *tabla* drummers. Karin was riveted by the melodiously whining and lamenting sound of the instrument; it lulled her into a dream, the best of the exotic dreams which had brought her to Bangladesh. The sitar represented all the sounds of her new world and anew, she vowed that she would get involved and try to make a difference. She would study her new country's literature, music, art, traditions, customs, and she would have another go at learning the language. There was so much for her to find out and her waning interests were invigorated by the evening.

The concert went on until midnight with only a brief break half-way through. It was exhausting for musicians and listeners alike but in equal measure exhilarating. In the reality of the days to follow, it was far more difficult to realise her new ambitions. It was not deemed suitable for her to go to college un-chaperoned and no one seemed available or willing to accompany her. She asked for home tuition but that seemed equally difficult to organise, why, she could not say. It was as if every solution she had found was doomed to stumble towards more obstacles.

'Why would you want to study again? You have a degree already!' It was beyond her husband's comprehension why she had the urge to do more than being a wife and mother. Her restlessness was becoming uncomfortable and embarrassing.

Finally, Lakshmi agreed to join her in some singing lessons and rudimentary yoga exercises and meditation. She had a lovely voice and learnt the high twirls of sounds with ease, while Karin's throat simply couldn't produce the strangled heights of eastern tunes. However, there was one song she loved; it was closer than any other to a western melody and the lyrics were romantic and sweet; this she sang with gusto and feeling: *Oliro kota shuno bokhul ache...*

Yoga became Karin's obsession. Although Lakshmi, averse to physical exertion, gave it up almost immediately, the two women kept this secret so that Karin could continue to practise and learn with the guru. She took to repeating the exercises whenever the children were taking a nap or were playing under the watchful eye of their devoted *ayah*. Most days, she could hardly wait to slip over the border into her parallel universe of peace and serenity.

Raj hadn't paid attention the first time she had mentioned yoga, so she never told him about it later. It was her very private, innocent pleasure which gave her inner tranquillity.

※　※　※

'...can I talk to you, please?' she begged Amir again.

'Come into my office,' he said; he sensed that the matter to be discussed could be a delicate one and deserved privacy. Once the only door in the house was shut behind them, Amir took a seat behind his massive, wooden desk and gestured that she should sit opposite him like an employee.

'Amir, do you think it is all my fault?' she looked him straight into the eyes, her voice full of doubt and misery. She didn't have to explain that she was talking about her marriage.

He didn't flinch, but stared thoughtfully at the leather top of his desk in front of him. She could almost see how furiously his brain worked to find a diplomatic but truthful answer without taking sides. After a long pause he found the words: 'It is not your fault, Karin. You try so hard and we all love you...' Amir wetted his lips with his tongue to continue: 'Your husband is

254

basically a good man; he has qualities I appreciate, but I admit that he has a few faults I have always disliked, even disapproved of, and I hoped that by marrying you, he would correct them.'

Karin was eager to hear more detail, but Amir's speech came to a disappointingly quick end: 'Frankly, every marriage goes through rough patches from time to time. You just have to work at it together.'

She felt let down by this non-committal advice and none the wiser about what really bothered her: 'Do you think he is having an affair?'

Now she had really embarrassed him. He shook his head sadly; still patient and understanding, he leant forward and said to her as kindly as possible: 'I wouldn't know, Karin. It is for my brother-in-law to answer this question. You have to ask him.'

Of course, she didn't. She wasn't going to risk the end of her dream.

Her life meandered through the pleasurable duties of a mother, giving her children undivided attention. As the concept of sending children to nursery school did not exist, she began to teach them the alphabet. They drew a page for each letter and painted various examples of German words beginning with that letter. She taught them German nursery rhymes and asked the *ayah* to do the same in Bengali. They sang songs in both languages and recited simple times tables. They were bright children and Karin was sad that her parents could take no part in their upbringing. Occasionally, she felt homesick but scolded herself that this life had been her choice and that she had every reason to be content.

She wrote elaborate letters home, read the books her mother kept sending and practised yoga at least twice a day. Once a week the entire clan went to the movies, and the various branches of the family paid each other regular visits which were filled with food and gossip. It wasn't enough. Karin felt restless, with energy to spare and brain power to be used; she wanted to do something useful with her life and she was convinced that she could easily accommodate another activity without neglecting her children. She was therefore, overjoyed when Padma, the wife of one of Raj's cousins, invited her to join her one morning in voluntary work she did regularly for Unicef. It was as if a light had been switched on in Karin's monotonous life. First they visited the children's hospital where the organisation sponsored treatment of sick children from poor families. Afterwards, they went to Padma's office to supervise some admin-work. Karin was surprised how many different strands of voluntary work were available.

'I saw a school in Chittagong,' she told Padma. 'I didn't know that millions of children don't go to school because their parents can't afford the fees.'

Padma looked at her encouragingly..

'Why doesn't the State provide free education?'

'You can choose between any amount of excuses; I prefer these: The Government is bankrupt, not bothered or corrupt,' was the sarcastic answer.

'Even the money donated by international charities disappears. Our American sponsors try to bring it over, but it doesn't always work.'

'I would like to start a school for children who can't pay fees,' Karin blurted out. 'Do you think it could be done?'

'I should think so,' Padma looked at Karin as if to gage whether she was serious or not.

'I could help you,' she offered, a sceptical smile playing around her lips. 'it is important to know the right people; you need to get some international sponsors behind you.'

A wave of missionary zeal welled up in Karin. The more she thought about it and listened to Padma, the more she was convinced that this was what she should do.

'Make a plan, a business plan; think about premises, location, staffing, representations to the Education Ministry, your target group, materials, furnishings, books, blackboards and so on.'

It sounded like hard work, but Karin was ready and eager to commit. During her studies and her brief career in Germany, she had been industrious and efficient; she could apply those qualities to her new project. She needed one to feel that she was useful, that she was making a difference to her new country.. With this mission, she had found something to give her life a sense of fulfilment and meaning. In her mind, there was no point in living in a third world country unless one was prepared to help to improve things. Suddenly she could clearly see her path into the future.

She intended to broach the subject with Raj carefully and diplomatically, so that he would have no reason to reject it out of hand. She waited a few days for a convenient moment. Once again, she first confided in Amir, who readily agreed to let her have one of his smaller office buildings in the centre of Dhaka, which had been unoccupied for a while awaiting refurbishment.

'I won't make any money,' Karin warned him.

'I shall get my reward in heaven,' he laughed; he was so pleased to see her happy and full of renewed energy. In secret, he admired Western women who generally had a lot more get-up-and-go than their Bengali sisters. Even his own wife who was entirely free to do what she wanted, was adamant that the role of wife and mother was quite enough for her; any activity outside the home turned usually out to be strenuous and altogether too much.

'I just have to get it okayed by Raj,' Karin ended the conversation, breathless with excitement.

'Good luck!'. Amir's smile did not give away what he thought of her chances.

❀ ❀ ❀

She could have guessed. Raj was dead-set against any sort of career which would take her away from home, whether professional or charitable, profitable or not.

'In our family women don't work! How often do I have to tell you that?' He was exasperated by her constant attempts at breaking the rules.

'It's not work like it was in Germany. It's something to do with my life, to fill my days and to do some good,' she fought for her dream.

'When will you ever understand that your place is at home, with your children; they should be enough for you. I cannot for the life of me understand why you need a mission.'

'Padma works for Unicef,' Karin changed tactic.

'That's her husband's business,' and she could hear strong disapproval of said husband in Raj's voice.

All the time while they were arguing, Raj hadn't looked her in the eye. Now she made a step towards him, touched his arm and looked him straight in the face:

'I have always worked. It is so hard to do nothing of importance

257

or value. Please, Raj, let me do this. I promise, I won't neglect the family!' she pleaded, tears in her voice.

'I shall go crazy just wasting my time when I have a good brain and lots of energy to give.'

Hope flickered when she saw that he was a little moved, his adam's apple gliding up and down from swallowing hard and his eyes lowered to the floor.

'I shall discuss it with my brothers,' he conceded without committing himself.

She never found out if he did; he never reported any out-come back to her, and a few feeble attempts to bring the subject up again were brushed aside and stifled by abrupt departures. Bitterness grew within her; she felt abandoned and frightened because her husband had turned into someone she didn't know, someone, whose thinking she didn't understand anymore and who didn't understand her. Their old closeness and affinity seemed to have been replaced by mistrust and constant irritation. Whilst he had been proud of her talents before, he now resented her meek bursts to create a tiny niche of independence. It wasn't interest in her or in what she was doing; it was simply to protect his and the family's honour and reputation. Far from commiserating when she rattled the golden cage, he resented her; sometimes she thought she saw hatred glimmer in his eyes.

'Where was the charming, thoughtful, handsome man she had fallen in love with, who had swept her off her feet with his unexpectedly good sense of humour, good manners, protectiveness and irresistible charm?' she thought, confused and fearful that the foundations of the future, she had been willing to build, were crumbling before her eyes.

'I am going to New Market,' Priti sounded mischievous. 'We could get your green sari. Uncle won't probably even notice.'

Karin was fearful of yet another scene, but also mutinous considering that she had given in to Raj on every front.

They went back to the Sari Emporium and bought the green one with the rainbow-coloured flowers and golden stitching. Karin was measured up for a blouse and a petticoat; the following day, they picked up the bundle wrapped in brown paper. They had a wonderful time winding it round Karin's slender frame and complementing it with her wedding gold necklace and long filigree earrings. Swirling around in front of the mirror to Priti's exclamations of approval, Karin saw suddenly Raj's thunderous face behind her.

'Did you buy that?' He had recognised it.

'It's pretty, isn't it?' Karin tried to sound light-hearted, although she was afraid of his temper

'Why do you keep defying me?'

She just stood there paralysed and still like a stone statue; all pleasure in her new acquisition evaporated.

'You will take it back tomorrow,' Raj insisted.

'We won't get the money back because the blouse and petticoat won't fit anyone else,' Priti butted in trying to help.

'This has nothing to do with you,' he turned on her, hissing in a dangerously low voice. Priti retreated with an apologetic shrug and regret written all over her face.

'You will bring shame on me and my family!' The words flew through the air like swords. Karin searched her husband's face with sadness and incomprehension.

'Take it off!'

He made a move towards her as if to tear the sari off her body, but he went for the jewellery, his wedding gift, her dowry, the insurance for a Bengali wife should her husband die or should the marriage fail.

He nearly strangled her, removing the necklace, demanding she add the earrings as well. As she didn't want her ear lobes ripped, she complied. A commotion developed outside the room. Among others, Karin could hear her father-in-law's voice shouting his son's name. Raj turned and ran out, jewellery in hand. Karin never saw her dowry again, but she hid the green sari in Priti's room.

Chapter Twenty-Eight

Peace, my heart,
Let time for the parting be sweet…
Rabrindranath Tagore

The news is bad. Karin can see it in the face of the receptionist. She takes the hotel's elaborately letter-headed compliment slip gently out of his hand, thanks him and turns round to read it, his concerned look burning into her neck. The message is from Priti:

Auntie, uncle has died this evening. Got call from hospital just after you left. Funeral tomorrow 11 am. Shall pick you and Ali up at 10.

This is a shock in spite of the advance warning. Karin doesn't know what to feel. Sadness, yes, but with some distance; she hadn't been close to Raj for years, and even when she had thought of him in the past, it was with recriminations and disappointment; she had stopped being his adoring wife ages ago.

She could think of one reason to be sad: that they were not given more time together to re-visit the past, to explain further, to regret together. They could have been company for each other in a civilised manner, knowing that all was forgiven, that they had left the hurt behind; two people in the autumn of their lives having risen above the past, just being good friends.

A sneaky suspicion infiltrates her mind and spreads doubt that she would have entirely enjoyed this experience, fearing that he would eventually have reverted to his true self. She folds the compliment slip and takes the lift to her room.

For a long time, she sits on her bed, motionless, not getting ready for bed. In the swirl of her emotions, one feeling wins and rises to the surface: relief that Raj does not have to suffer any longer, and moments later, relief also at the chapter of her story closing. She is free! No more subtle ties to her old life, no more emotional roller-coasters!

With a sigh, she takes the telephone receiver and asks the reception to put her through to Ali's mobile phone.

'Hi, Mum.'

'Darling, Abbu has died.'

'I knew he had not long to go… You'd better postpone your flight until after the funeral.'

'Priti will pick us up at ten.'

'Yes, to make sure your sari is okay,' he says half-jokingly.

'That won't be necessary,' Karin says because at that moment she has decided to begin her new, detached life by wearing western clothing for Raj's funeral.

The airline turns out to be kind and postpones her return flight free of charge for another three days – 'due to circumstances,' as they remark with feeling.

Karin also rings Jasmine and leaves a message on her answer machine. Her daughter won't be able to make it from England to her father's funeral tomorrow, but at least she could be with them in spirit. 'You do realise,' Priti says anxiously when she arrives the following morning, 'that you will be with the women, and we are not allowed to be at the graveside.'

'Why ever not?' Karin has never been to an Islamic funeral and is taken aback, but then she realises that this is the world she will soon leave behind; it won't do any harm to be adaptable one more, one last time.

Raj's body is lying in a small courtyard, in the hospital grounds, wrapped in a *kafan*, white sheets, sparkling with cleanliness and purity in the bright late morning sun. Washing the body with scented water and shrouding it, is usually performed by members of the family. If she was still married to him, it would with certainty have been her task.

An Imam positions himself in front of the deceased, facing away from the worshippers; only his moving lips indicate that he is reciting silently the *salat-l-janazah*, the funeral prayers. Karin is amazed at the stillness and dignity with which the ceremony is held and at the total absence of wailing, thrashing about and prostrations of grief, which are so often shown on television news programmes in the West. She can only see the odd tear rolling down the cheek of one female relative or another, or hear someone discreetly blowing their nose.

'Now is the time to say good-bye,' Priti squeezes her aunt's arm. 'Only the men will take him to his grave for burial.'

Black cars wait outside the hospital. The crowd of mourners halves as the women climb into the cars at the front to be driven to Laksmi's place, where the family will receive condolences. Raj's brothers, other male relatives, Ali among them, friends and old colleagues accompany the body to the cemetery in a cavalcade of their own.

'Where will he be buried?' Karin asks.

'In the cemetery, next to grand-father. It will only be a shallow grave, very simple, no flowers or headstone. He wanted a burial according to the Koran.' In the car, Karin mentions the absence of wailing..

'The Koran actually forbids wailing and excessive crying. Allah is the One who gives life and takes it away at a time appointed by Him. It is not for us to question His wisdom,' Priti explains quietly.

This is the Islam Karin likes, simple, god-fearing, practical and kind.

'Will you come with us?' Priti asks and, when Karin shakes her head, gives the driver the address of the hotel.

'I am afraid, I shall have to leave you,' Priti says regretfully, 'but I'll give you a call tonight.' Karin spends the rest of the afternoon lying on her hotel bed, reminiscing, thinking about Raj and how things have turned out.

She is asleep, when Ali knocks on the door.

'Let's have dinner together,' he suggests.

They go downstairs to the dining hall. Over another series of her favourite curries, he asks:

'When will you fly home?'

'Day after tomorrow.'

'Great! How do you feel about coming with me tomorrow?'

'Where to?'

'I shall have to drive out to The Children's Village for a job interview. I can show you where Martha and I will be living and working if they will have us.'

Karin sends a little thank you towards heaven, that her son will be able to make a difference.

Chapter Twenty-Nine

CREACD

Clouds heap upon clouds
And it darkens...
Rabrindranath Tagore

Bangladesh was shaken out of its dreamy lull and searing heat. It was all over the news and the topic of every conversation: A cyclone was heading for the Bay of Bengal. The people of Bangladesh could have been forgiven for ignoring the warning. After all, cyclones were an annual occurrence and the resulting floods usually affected only rural areas. The town dwellers just had to put up with a few stormy days during which they rarely left their houses. However, this cyclone was supposed to be particularly fierce and was compared in advance with the one in 1971 which had killed one million people. The disaster had been featured in western news and collections of money, blankets and tents had been sent from Europe and the USA to assuage any feelings of guilt and genuine compassion.

Karin remembered that the Western media had been critical: How could this happen time and time again in the same country without anyone having thought of any precautions? To Western minds it was incomprehensible why people would want to move back to islands and coast strips of land which were at sea level, not giving anyone a chance to escape higher tides. What people in the rest of the world didn't know was that these people had nowhere else to go; they didn't have the money, knowledge or initiative to re-locate: This was the place where they and their families had lived for generations and it was all they knew.

Maybe re-education by the well-heeled and well-educated might have made a difference, but they were no more interested than they would be in any other news item; they considered these episodes as irritations to their cosy lives and shielded behind the argument that everything happened according to 'Allah's Will.'

The worrying aspect this time was, that, if the cyclone was stronger than usual, the rains could flood the silted up riverbeds and water would spread throughout the city. Karin had heard through the family grapevine that the Government had plans to dredge the rivers some time in the future, but that would take years considering the number of rivers and lack of priority in Government planning. Donations from western organisations for this purpose had long been allocated by ministers to more deserving projects.

Karin shuddered at the thought that she would now find out for herself, although she took heart from the calm preparations her family undertook, like a well-rehearsed military operation. The servants were rushing about, following instructions from their master and mistress, securing the window shutters with iron bars and locking gates and doors. Amir called everyone for a head count to make sure nobody was missing. Then he gave orders to their cook to set about providing an elaborate meal. Having moved his utensils and family to the western style kitchen on the first floor, it was a noisy and cluttered affair.

Food was always good to divert attention and anxiety.

'Have you rung Raj yet?' Amir asked Karin.

She shook her head.

'Tell him to come home immediately,' he ordered shaking his head.

She rang Raj's office, but there was no answer. Maybe he was on his way home already.

As the water-laden skies darkened and the winds howled and screeched, the family sat down by candle light on rattan settees and floor cushions. They were well prepared for the unavoidable loss of electricity and hours of boredom. The children were given board games, while the adults chatted or read newspapers by candle light. Karin tried to concentrate on a novel, her mother had sent her recently, but all the while she wondered where Raj had got to. The cyclone would be raging for hours and no one in their right mind would remain outdoors. She could only hope that he had taken shelter with other relatives. Amir and Lakshmi urged her to ring various numbers, but no one had seen him.

As the evening progressed and the rains were battering the house like a hail of drumsticks, the winds began to drown out conversations as if the end of the world was near. The more frightened the children became, the more cheerfully the adults reassured them that it would all be over soon.

Distraction came in the form of more food: Everyone was ushered into the dining room where cook had prepared a feast of culinary family favourites. Cheers and laughter, chattering and munching helped to banish the onset of fear.

Raj still hadn't come home and Karin noticed a few sideways glances from her *bhabis* to monitor her reaction.

After dinner, the children were put to bed with extra long stories, songs and assurances that the storm would be over by the morning if they only went to sleep quickly.

No one seemed to worry about the servants and their children who simply gathered their sleeping mats and put them on the floor in the kitchen. The roof top where they usually slept, was, they reported, sodden and slippery like an ice rink already.

Having succeeded in singing Ali and Jasmine to sleep, Karin returned to the sitting room, where she only found Amir, reading the paper. Everyone else had gone to bed, too.

'Do you think Raj will be alright?' she asked him anxiously.

'He knows what to do,' was the curt reply before he added with distaste: 'He'll be safe somewhere!'

'We won't be flooded, will we?' she whispered fearfully.

'No, of course not, Karin! Our bedrooms are on the fourth floor. Even if the ground floor floods, we have removed everything that is important.'

She stood miserably in the room, unable even to shrug her shoulders.

'Go to bed, Karin. Tomorrow will be another day. He'll be back, you'll see!'

Without another word, she left the room.

Once she had checked the regular breathing of her sleeping

children, she climbed stiffly under her mosquito net and pulled the blanket over her ears to block out the squalls of ferocious howling, unleashed rains and river waters rearing up against the storm. The world was in the grip of an angry giant who was shaking it with all his might. The turmoil outside was equalled by the turmoil in her mind

After a restless night, Karin got up, weary, rubbing her stiff joints. The storm had subsided a little, but when she opened the window shutters, strong winds were still sweeping around the verandas like the tail of a cat in flight. The air was grey with humidity and dust. The usually lazy waters of the Burigonga river rolled, wild and brown like whipped up hot chocolate. Its bed had widened and waves were battering at the walls of the house. There were none of the usual hammering or bustling noises coming from ships or boats; everyone seemed to have taken shelter on shore. There was one lonely fishing boat bopping and battling forlornly on the rough waters having been torn from its moorings.

Karin, holding on to the balustrade, fought her way along the veranda towards the front of the house, gusts tearing at her nightgown and hair. The road below was near empty bar the debris from houses and trees which had been strewn around by the storm.

A few human figures were bending over the chaos, trying to salvage something usable. The asphalt glistened menacingly, black and wet, as if angry with the rubbish deposited on it. Clammy dust and claggy soil clung to it like sand on a beach after high tide. The sky was still sobbing with rain drops the size of bullets, drenching everything and everybody, saturating the already soggy town. The grey, leaden horizon was bereft of birds and there was an eerie quietness in the air, where usually shrieks of monkeys, screeches of crows, trilling of song birds and a multitude of human activity would resound. Karin, buffered by the wind in her back, returned to the bedroom to wake the children. At breakfast, she met the family again, but nobody mentioned Raj's absence.

'The worst seems to be over,' someone proclaimed.

Nobody thought of considering the effects of the cyclone on the rural population – hundreds or even thousands might have died.

'We got away lightly,' someone else said. Electricity was still disrupted, but nobody minded that during day time. A dreary morning merged into a dreary day. The children could not be allowed out and were understandably irritable for being cooped up again. The grown-ups hunted for forgotten board games; it didn't take long before the youngsters got boisterous and scuffles broke out. Finally, everyone was told to retreat for a nap; there really was nothing else to do.

Would you like to come to my room?' Priti offered to Karin.

'Cook's children can play with Ali and Jasmine.'

Karin nodded, explained to the children where she would be and slid behind Priti through the door curtain.

'Did you manage to sleep a little?'

'So, so,' was Karin's lacklustre response.

'I really don't know where uncle's got to…'

Karin kept quiet with her suspicions. It had been a mistake to seek Priti's company. She was too tired and dispirited to discuss her worries.

'I better go and catch up on some sleep; the children will be fine, won't they?'

'Of course, they will. Ayah is there to keep an eye on them.'

When Karin awoke from her disturbed doze, it was getting dark. She had forgotten to close the window shutters and a strong breeze made the curtains flutter into the room. She poured cold water from a jug into a porcelain basin, splashed it in her face, tidied her hair, straightened her red sari embroidered with orange swirls and headed for the sitting room.

As she approached she could hear raised voices, one of them was definitely her husband's.

'It's none of your business,' she heard him defend himself angrily.

'It is my business if you leave me to look after your wife and children,' said the other voice sternly.

'She was safe, wasn't she?'

'Yes, no thanks to you! This is your family; they are your responsibility! Where the hell have you been anyway?' The other voice sounded threatening.

'I was held up and took shelter. You didn't expect me to walk through a cyclone,' it sounded like the lame excuse it was.

'It had been forecast and was expected by the entire country.' Karin recognised Amir's voice.

'If you had left your office at lunchtime, you would have easily made it home... Where were you?' Amir persisted.

Raj obviously refused an answer.

'With her?' A guilty silence spread like a poisonous cloud.

'I don't believe you! After all these years of sponging off the family and refusing every match your loving sisters came up with, you finally find yourself a nice wife, who really tries hard to fit in, you have two lovely children and all you can think of is to start your affair again!' Amir was incandescent with rage; Karin had never heard him like that. There were two pieces of information which were news to Karin: Raj had had an affair with Reena before he had married her and before her husband had died a martyr's death; and secondly, the family had been delighted about his match with a western girl because they had hoped that his scandalous behaviour would stop. They had hoped that the young European wife would not take kindly to any such nonsense and would snuff it out. She, Karin, had failed on all accounts. At that moment, Raj, having turned on his heels, stormed out of the room, nearly brought the door curtain down, and crashed into Karin. He slung the full force of his wrath at her: 'Spying, are you? Standing behind curtains? Colluding against me? How low can you sink?'

She had wanted to say something soothing, but the words got stuck in her mouth and she could only shake her head in horror and lower her gaze to the floor. This wasn't the man, whom she had first known. He had developed into a monster who resented her presence, considered her as an obstacle to his freedom to do as he pleased. In every aspect, she was in his way. He pushed her aside and disappeared into the bedroom. She followed him, desperately sad. She waited a little by the entrance, trying to compose herself.

He was busy undressing, preparing to have a shower.

'Raj, I wasn't spying,' she said simply.

He mumbled something, she couldn't catch.

'I missed you last night. I was worried about you, and the children were asking for you.'

No answer.

270

'Were you with Ree…?'

Before she could say the name, Raj cut across, shouting: 'You do not mention her name.' He came up to Karin, his naked chest protruding towards her menacingly, his eyes glinting with malice staring straight into her face. 'She is an angel; you will never be like her; so don't you ever talk about her or mention her name!'

Karin was in complete shock, standing frozen to the ground, unable to move a muscle. Her heart had stopped beating, her mouth had gone dry, and tears were burning in her eyes.

She had come to salvage affection; he had trampled it to smithereens. It was unbearably sad that he hated her, but what hurt even more was that he showed no consideration for their children.

Rage rose up in her and still holding on to her dignity, she told him in a dangerously controlled voice

'I am your wife. She isn't. Your duty is to protect me and our children, not her. Have you got no heart and no shame? Your entire family knows about this…'

The turmoil of the last days took its toll; she began to sob but continued under her tears: 'You brought me to this country, but I am not allowed to have my own home, I am not allowed to have a job or do anything meaningful, you dump me with the women, take no interest in me or the children and expect me to accept all that, while you go your own way. I would not have married you if I had known, and I certainly would not have agreed to move here…'

Something stung her left cheek. Raj had slapped her with full force across the face.

'Stop it, you two, stop it!' Amir yelled and caught Karin by the elbow. Before she became aware of anything, she was pulled out of the room and handed over to Lakshmi and Priti who had come running. As she was dragged away, she heard Amir's stern rebuke: 'In our family, we do n o t beat our wives. I repeat: we do not…' The rest trailed away out of earshot.

Made to sit in a wicker chair, Karin sobbed uncontrollably, her hopes and dreams dissolving with her tears.

271

She was told off as sternly as Raj. The lecture she received reminded her of her duties as a wife and mother, as that of a guest in their house and as a member of a distinguished family which had a reputation to uphold.

She would have liked to argue that she had suggested, even begged for a home of her own; that she had been the one who was sensitive to the possibility that they might overstay their welcome. In the end, she didn't bother, trapped between good manners, gratitude for the family's support and the feeble acceptance that this was the life she had chosen.

❀ ❀ ❀

Raj stayed away even more, and in spite of feeling abandoned and cheated, she was glad that they had no opportunity to quarrel. Deep down, she had become fearful of his fierce temper and emotional cruelty. The least she could aim for now, was to protect her children from witnessing any of it.

She rarely went out and hid indoors instead, because her eyes were often red-rimmed from crying and her usually smooth face blotchy and dry like parchment.

She confided in Priti: 'Maybe it would help matters if I went home for a while? I haven't seen my parents for years.'

Their letters had dwindled to a steady but thin trickle, sensing that their only daughter and grand-children were lost to them in a world they didn't know or understand. The relationship between parents and daughter had become loose like a limp elastic band.

'You mean, absence makes the heart grow fonder? You could try it.' Priti did her best to cheer her up with girlie talk.

'Priti, I am beyond all that. I just need peace and quiet and a bit of sympathy from my own family.' She lowered her head dejectedly.

'I need to find a way to carry on. I can't bring up the children in such an atmosphere.'

'I think it's a smart idea; a visit to your parents is quite natural and doesn't look suspicious to the family,' Priti said with forced cheerfulness. Even in tragedy, it was still important how things looked. Priti hated seeing her beloved, exotic auntie so unhappy and would do anything to help turn things round.

'Uncle really needs his head examined,' she thought

272

disrespectfully, but even the rebelliousness of youth had to admit that in a Muslim society men had always the decisive word.

Over the next few weeks, Karin pleaded at every opportunity with Raj to give his permission that she could visit her parents; she cajoled, begged, painted the advantages in tempting colours and sulked. Finally, she thought he had relented – to her surprise he smiled at her and said: 'maybe...'

Just as she turned round to impart the good news to the children, who stood in the door frame, Raj's face went dark as if triggered by a switch and the mask of joviality was replaced in an instant by a mask of hatred. He smacked her across the face in front of the children and yelled:

'You will not visit your parents! I forbid it! Or, if you insist, you can go but you leave the children here!' at which point he stormed towards Jasmine and Ali, held each by the hand on either side and screamed: 'Go and leave us alone!'

Hearing the children crying in fear, her inner confidence, composure and resistance broke like thin glass. She knew that she couldn't bear to leave the children behind; it was out of the question. The only alternative was to submit and concede defeat.

Chapter Thirty

CR80

O you shaggy-headed banyan tree…
To be the wind and blow through your rustling branches,
To be your shadow and lengthen with the day…
Rabrindranath Tagore

On the morning after the funeral, Karin is up early and ready like a little excited girl on Christmas morning. She meets Ali for an early breakfast of modest tea and buttered toast. Farook's arrival is announced on the dot at seven-thirty as arranged by the headwaiter. Mother and son quickly swallow the last morsels, wipe their mouths with the starched white serviettes and hurry out to the car.

Karin feels happy and free; this is how she had wanted to live when she was the young wife of a Bengali man: busy with useful projects, helpful to those less fortunate than her – there were millions of them!

'What other purpose is there for Westerners to live in a poor country?' had always been her argument; work would never have dried up and life would have been satisfying and fulfilling. She had intended to introduce her children at a young age to giving charity freely, to learn from an early age how to lighten other people's suffering.

But it wasn't to be; she hadn't been in the right position to realise her ideals; she had been bound by family ties and social restrictions, and she had only been brave enough to rattle the chains, not break them.

She is so happy that her son has inherited her idealistic leanings and combines them with more determination than she had ever mustered. He will soon be leading the life she had always coveted. Karin is thrilled and grateful to whichever God has planted that seed in her son's heart.

'It's not far; only about forty miles,' Ali reassures her, as she wipes the first beads of sweat from her forehead.

'It's lovely driving through the countryside,' she squeezes his hand and smiles at him. 'Tell me about the charity you are going to work for.'

He laughs the shy and embarrassed laugh of a teenager who has been complimented on his first girlfriend.

'Well, it's a self-contained village, an orphanage of six hundred children, boys and girls, from babies to adolescents. It was founded by an English lady but is now run by a Mr. Abdullah.'

'So what's your job going to be?'

'They are looking for English teachers who can double up as housemasters. Basically, we shall live there and devote ourselves to the children entirely; it's perfect for Martha and I.' Ali adds with feeling.

'How wonderful it must be to have found your soul mate!' she whispers into her lap and Ali puts his arm around her shoulders. Strange that her son has become the person who understands her like no one else has ever done.

Once they have left Dhaka behind, it doesn't take Farook long to steer the car along the straight road. They drive for miles alongside paddy and jute fields interspersed with villages which are shaded by clusters of coconut palms, banana, mango and lime trees. There are also the obligatory rivers to cross, but the three of them wait patiently for the ferries like everyone else.

Karin and Ali are lulled into a pleasant, lazy silence by the creeping late morning heat, the steady whirring of the car engine, the crunching of the tyres over the uneven road and the warm breeze from the open windows fluttering around their faces. They ignore most vendors at the roadside and only stop once to accept a cup of lukewarm, milky tea which they receive and pay for through the window.

They approach a huddle of farm buildings. Chickens are running all over the place and Farook does his best not to run those over which have strayed into the road. Fields boast healthy crops of different vegetables; carrots, onions, cabbages, cauliflowers, leeks are the ones Karin can spot from the car.

The country lane turns into a freshly tarmac-ed drive; a colourful wooden sign directs them to The Children's Village. They drive through a black wrought-iron gate which has figures of children marching in single file soldered on top of its arch. There are a few children, adolescents and adults milling around. Everyone stands still and watches them drive by with curiosity and a welcoming smile.

The road ends in a cobbled square, shaded by a huge tree in its middle and surrounded by sturdy bungalow-type buildings. Farook stays by the car, grateful for a rest and the shade, while Ali and Karin head for the bungalow closest to them. It has a sign over the entrance indicating that this is the administration block and presumably the reception.

'I am Ali Khan, I am applying for the post of English teacher,' her son introduces himself to a beautiful young Bengali woman whose smile could melt icebergs. The pattern of her sari reminds Karin of an old Laura Ashley wallpaper called 'nutmeg'.

'Welcome, Ali! I am Sara the dogsbody,' she laughs without shyness.

'I have to sign the contract and...' he nods in Karin's direction and waves for her to come closer, 'to show my mother where I shall be working and playing.' Sara extends her hand to the guest; it feels soft, delicate and gentle.

'I hope you will approve,' she says simply with that ravishing smile.

'Let me call Cora to take my place here, then I shall be your guide.'

She waves to a little boy who has been skipping under the tree and now approaches with alacrity. He obviously likes being an important messenger. He is dispatched to the headmaster's office to announce the visitors; after that he is asked to fetch Cora to stand in at reception.

'I shall catch up with you soon,' Ali promises before following the little boy at a leisurely pace.

For a moment, the two women watch how his back disappears in the door frame, they then turn and stroll across the square, underneath the cooling crown of the tree in the middle.

'What sort of tree is this?' Karin asks pointing to its big trunk.
'It's a banyan tree, a kind of fig.'
'I love how the branches bow to the ground.'
'That's why we had to cobble the square. The branches would root if they came in contact with soil. Banyans were actually Indian traders. The tree was named after a famous specimen which grew in Bandar Abbas on the Persian Gulf. Banyans, who used to trade in its shade, built a pagoda there.'

They have reached another row of bungalows. 'These are the carpentry workshops,' Sara explains proudly.

Young men in check shirts and light grey trousers are sawing, planing and carving wood on long work benches.

'They can also learn auto-mechanics in the villages outside, and agriculture.' She gestures towards a gap between the buildings where small figures of people can be seen tending a field in the far distance.

'We grow a lot of food ourselves, even the rice we eat. The rest we get from the fishermen and farmers outside the compound.'
'These chaps do all our maintenance work,' Sara says proudly, 'they really do earn their keep!'

Karin is dragged to the next building. When they enter it looks like a sea of blue. All the young girls working here are dressed in light blue kaftans over white trousers and adorned with white feathery scarves around their shoulders. When the two women enter, the girls' chattering, giggling and the clinking of their bangles around busy wrists stop, and they watch the visitors, grinning shyly as if caught in a slightly risqué act. Sara nods at them, a sign for them to continue with their work. Then she explains to Karin:

'They are our senior girls. They are taught weaving, embroidery, tailoring and dyeing fabric, so they will be able to support themselves in the future and contribute to the family budget once they are married.'

As they come back out into the blazing sunshine, Karin sees bamboo racks on which freshly dyed ribbons of cloth are drying, their bold colours emphasized by the bright light. She is impressed to learn that all the children's uniforms are woven and tailored in these workshops.

Next they visit the paper manufacturing group. Huge barrels of water and milky mush stand outside the huts beside which girls are sieving a soggy brown substance through wire-mesh frames.

'Why are you producing paper?' Karin asks.

'For greeting cards which we sell through our founder in England. The girls decorate them with wheat straw.'

Even Sara can't help laughing, realising that she has just pitched her speech like a tourist guide or a sales women.

Karin laughs with her and takes her arm.

'There is also a manual printing press, but I won't bore you with the details,' she mentions a little embarrassed now.

'Have you got younger children here, too?' Karin asks..

'We are coming to them now.' Sara is soon back in her element.

They sneak up to the school building and stand quietly in the doorway of a class room, but within seconds, about thirty pairs of big, brown eyes fix the intruders with curiosity and gratitude for the interruption.

It's a class of little girls, all dressed in short blue dresses, some wearing black trousers underneath the swinging skirts. Their feet are clad like everyone else's in sandals, whose two strips of brown leather are held between toes. Their teacher blends in well and could be taken for a pupil herself.

Some of the girls look older than others and have yellow or pink scarves wrapped around their shoulders or head: 'We put classes together by ability not age.'

The wooden desks are dark brown with age and the bare stone walls are brightened up occasionally by the colourful display of children's work. A fan swivelling from side to side on the teacher's table whirls around the stifling air which must make the first two rows of desks particularly popular.

'It's a pity you missed assembly this morning. Everyone lines up at eight o'clock on the assembly green. The headmaster wishes children and staff a 'good morning'; then the PE teacher takes over and everyone does a bit of light gymnastics; after that the headmaster gives a talk, a sort of 'thought for the day', and lastly, we sing the national anthem: *Amar Shonar Bangla*, My Golden Bengal

'Which subjects do the children study?'

'Literacy, numeracy, hygiene, spoken English and, if they wish, computers. That's till they are fourteen. They have to pass exams every year, and if they don't pass they will have to repeat the whole year.'

'When they are fourteen, they can either choose to learn a skill here or go to college in the nearby town. Many would like to study further but they are reluctant to leave. They find it unsettling and are a bit frightened. That's where Ali and Martha come in; they will teach English and any other subject they know about up to A-levels. Anyone who passes A-levels will have a chance to go to university in Dhaka, where we have just purchased a residential home for our students.'

'Where do the children sleep?'

'The boys occupy one house and are supervised by their housemaster who is also their PE teacher. The girls live here,' she points to the block they have just passed. 'They have each a bunk-bed and a trunk for their personal possessions; schoolwork, which is overseen by their housemother, is done in the home work room.'

They enter a room full of cots and women in saris fussing over babies and toddlers. Karin feels an illogical urge to adopt each and every child.

Sara notices and laughs: 'Shame they won't stay that cute.'

As they come out of the baby house, Karin notices the tip of a little dome peeping from behind a dense hedge of overgrown shrubs: 'Is this a mosque?' she guesses.

'Yes, we got that for free from the Ministry of Education.' Her laugh is a little sarcastic, from which Karin concludes that not many other donations had been forthcoming when the Children's Village was built.

'This is a remarkable place! What wonderful work you are all doing!'

Sara glows with pride.

'I shall introduce you now to Dr. Chowdhury. He was one of our first orphans to grow up here after the centre opened. He came back two years ago and is now our doctor.'

They approach the little clinic which boasts five sick-rooms with four beds in each. A cheerful, bespectacled young man shakes Karin's hand and tells her a little about his childhood in the Children's Village and how grateful he is that they have given him a chance when nobody else did.'.

'The last years of my medical studies, I lived in England with the founder of The Children's Village. She was like a mother to me. When I got my doctorate, she and her husband gave a big party. They are constantly fundraising for us...' He pauses for a moment before ending, as if this is self-understood: 'Now I am here to give something back to them and to the place which saved my life.'

'We have also a national cricket player among our old boys,' Sara pipes up. He sometimes comes back − but...' she turns to Karin, 'that's not half as useful as being a doctor.'

They are all laughing when three young women in nurses' uniforms join them:

'Well, here are some more useful people, Shazia, Safda and Sufi, our three 'Ss'. They studied nursing at Dhaka Hospital and have returned to become my very able assistants.'

As Karin looks around the clinic appreciatively, she is amazed how everything is gleaming with cleanliness.

They see Ali coming towards them, accompanied by an older man in a formal suit.

'Dr. Shamsur Abdullah − my mother, Mrs. Karin Khan.'

'Let's have lunch,' the headmaster suggests jovially after the formal introduction and handshakes.

'I hope you don't mind eating with the children,' and warns: 'it will be a bit noisy. We do feed them in two sittings, but they are still a big crowd.'

They enter a hall the entire width and length of a bungalow brimming with chatter, laughter and clattering. The children, all young boys, sit at trestle tables, large, white bowls with blue rims in front of them. At the back of the hall, in a separate room, Karin spots huge wood-burning stoves carved out of stone, with two holes on the side for stoking and pushing in wood and one on top for the pot. Karin has never seen such big cookery ware: blackened, deep tin pots the size of wine barrels and wide bowls with handles for the enormous quantities of rice, like huge paella pans or woks. It looks a hot place to work in.

Now the children begin to line up at the canteen counter, orderly, in single file.

'No pushing allowed! They know they will go back to the end of the queue if they push,' says the headmaster.

The party of visitors and staff seat themselves at the end of one of the tables and are given forks and knives.

A huge pot is carried from the kitchen to the canteen by two ladies holding the handles on either side. A wonderful smell of curry wafts through the room. The first children hold out their bowls and the cooks ladle rice and curry into them. The children return to their seats and begin to eat greedily with their hands.

'Meat and fish days are particularly popular,' Sara explains; 'today it's chicken curry.'

More pots are lugged onto the canteen by ladies with hot faces and strands of hair having escaped from their twisted *benis*.

As the first, urgent hunger of the children is stilled, their chattering between mouthfuls gets louder. The cooks look relieved as their main task comes to an end. They look forward to escaping the hot kitchen and having a few hours' rest before beginning with the preparations for dinner time. Meanwhile, Ali and Dr. Abdullah are in deep conversation and Karin overhears a glowing report that the English cricket team had visited two years ago.

'There are photographs of the event in the reception. It was such an inspiration for our boys! They went quite crazy and are still boasting about how each met the most famous cricket player in the world; how they had spoken to them and even given them practice tips.'

The headmaster is obviously out to impress his new recruit. Karin acknowledges happily that the two have already struck up an easy relationship.

'Are the children ever taken into town?' Karin asks Sara, but the headmaster cuts in before she can answer:

'No, not really. We make our own entertainment. Twice a week, the dining room doubles up as a cinema when we wheel in a television and show a Bengali film… We celebrate all the festivals… We have traditional dance performances; the girls love those because they are allowed to dress and make up and to wear ankle bracelets with bells… Sometimes we invite singers or speakers… The boys organise tournaments for cricket or badminton or football… and we organise big celebrations twice a year, when our founder visits from England.

The children begin to file out of the dining room and the adults follow slowly.

Farook has waited patiently all this time by the car. Now Karin and Ali join him and, as they drive away, they are waved off by staff and children. Along the drive back to the gates, they pass groups of boys imitating their cricket heroes; others crouching in the shade of a tree over their favourite board game *Carom*; gaggles of little girls skipping or playing hide and seek; and senior girls sitting in the grass, leaning languidly on their elbows, reading or chatting to each other.

'What a happy place,' Karin thinks as she looks back towards the gate framed by a bright blue sky and the intense green of palm trees.

'Have you accepted?' she asks hopefully.

'Of course,' Ali replies as if it was self-understood.

She squeezes her son's arm and says: 'Lucky boy!'

Chapter Thirty-One

☙❧

The trumpet lies in the dust...
Rabrindranath Tagore

Raj kept very close to Karin for a couple of weeks as if to check on her. He taunted her with remarks that she could invite her parents or that they could all go to Europe the following year. By this stage, she didn't believe in any of it any more and she certainly did not want to invite her parents into an atmosphere of tension and unhappiness.

Priti having guessed that her auntie's plans had come to nothing, never touched on the subject again. 'If you really loved me,' Raj said several times portraying himself as the injured party, 'you wouldn't make such a fuss.' Karin was tired of the emotional blackmail; she felt battered and bruised, tossed around as if riding waves in a stormy sea. She had lost the will to fight and had just enough strength to see to her children. Her love had been shattered into a thousand pieces and she thought she would never recover from it.

She went quietly about her daily tasks trying to escape his cruelty. She retreated even from the family, found excuses to avoid outings and spent a lot of the time in their room which had become her room. She played with the children, read and re-read her favourite books and wrote letters home hoping that her despair did not reverberate in her words.

She weighed up various scenarios of escape, but, as she was never allowed to go out without a chaperone, she had no chance of plotting and preparing anything. What she needed was an ally who had more freedom to go around. As she was surrounded by family, the prospect was hopeless.

It didn't help either that every telephone call to or from the house was directed via Amir's office downstairs. There was no chance of making a furtive phone call to her parents or to the Embassy. She was trapped and powerless.

'Can I go for a while to Sonargaon?' she suggested meekly but of course, permission was refused.

Help arrived unexpectedly in the form of her niece.

'You have always been so good to me, auntie. I am just so sorry that Uncle is making you so unhappy!'

They both smiled wryly. Priti's wedding would take place within six weeks. It would be an arranged marriage, but thanks to Karin, Priti knew her future husband reasonably well. Karin had provided an alibi on several occasions, so that the young couple could meet in secret and have proper conversations. As it happened, Priti's parents had chosen well and the bride was looking forward to the union with excitement and confidence. It was ironical, that her favourite auntie's love match was in tatters.

'What do you want me to do?'

Karin could hardly believe that she had found a conspirator. The timing was ideal because the entire family would be wrapped up in elaborate preparations for the wedding. A shopping trip to India was planned to make sure that the bride would wear the most precious red and gold wedding sari. All the jewellery would be provided by Dhaka's Elephant Road stores, but there was no harm in browsing in Delhi shops as well.

No one noticed in the general mayhem and excitement that Karin secretly prepared her exit. The first call was not to her parents. There was no point in upsetting them over this distance; more importantly she did not want Raj alerted by anything unusual.

Priti rang the German Embassy on Karin's behalf. It took a few attempts before she got hold of staff and some vital advice.

The next step was to smuggle Karin's and the children's passports to their offices, have them verified and photocopied. Karin had seen Raj checking on them. It was vital that they remained in their place; their absence would arouse his suspicion.

Two weeks passed without any contact while Priti had gone to India with a huge entourage including her mother, several aunts, her best friend and personal servants to ensure comfort at every step of the journey. Karin had declined to go along.

It was difficult for Priti to fit in another visit to the Embassy on her return and to get hold of money for flight tickets. Everyone around her fussed and didn't leave her a moment alone but finally, one evening she gave the thumbs-up to Karin as they walked into the dining room together.

'Best that I keep them,' she whispered. 'Next Thursday, one o'clock.'

'I am taking the children to see Reena!' said Raj unexpectedly on Monday morning.

Those few words put the fear of God into Karin. It could mean that Raj took charge of them and possibly moved them in with his mistress.

'Please, don't!' she pleaded. 'I promised to take them to the zoo today,' was the first excuse that came into her head.

'You can visit the zoo at the end of the week,' he determined and there was nothing she could do without giving away her anxiety.

'When will they be back?' she asked meekly and near tears.

'Maybe tonight… Maybe at the end of the week? Maybe not at all? Who knows…' he taunted her with a sarcastic, victorious laugh.

The children were not returned to Karin on the Monday evening nor on Tuesday. Frantic with worry and panic-stricken, Karin confided in Priti, who was absolutely appalled at how her charming uncle had turned into an ogre.

'This is too big for us,' she concluded, 'I am going to tell Dad!'

Karin had no idea what had gone on, but the same evening, Amir turned up at her bedroom door with little Ali and Jasmine, cheerfully telling them to be good children and to go to bed immediately.

According to Priti, Amir had marched up to Reena's house while Raj was at work, had demanded to see the children, simply taken them by their little hands and marched out with them. Reena, who had at first been reluctant to even let him in, did not dare to disobey a senior male relative.

Sometime in the evening, Karin heard raised voices, suspecting one of them to be that of her husband, but he did not come to her room. She checked that the children were fast asleep before she went out to the sitting room.

Approaching footsteps belonged to Abdul, Raj's servant carrying his master's fine leather briefcase. It meant that Raj wasn't far behind. The curtain in the door frame was pushed aside. In the past, her husband's face would light up when he would see her and his eyes would sparkle with pleasure. It was a long time ago since that had happened. Now he totally ignored his wife looking around aimlessly as if searching for the newspaper. He found it on the chest of drawers.

'Good day?' he mumbled without looking up, scanning the headlines already.

Karin could not understand where the sudden interest sprang from; nowadays it confused her when he was trying to be nice. She wondered whether Amir had ordered him to be at least civil.

'Yes, thank you,' was all she could bring herself to say.

'Any plans for tomorrow?' It was a rhetorical question; he wasn't really interested.

Why these sudden, courteous enquiries? Did he suspect anything? Her heart thumped.

'Not really,' she swallowed hard and rubbed her sweaty palms.

'I might be going to the bazaar,' she said in a whisper.

He hadn't expected her to say more. He looked up in surprise, scanning her face and she hoped fervently that she hadn't blushed or that the nervous wringing of her hands would betray her anxiety. The cynical smile at the corners of his mouth confirmed that he enjoyed having subjugated her; he liked his wife being submissive and insecure.

He directed his attention already back to the newspaper. 'With Priti I expect?'

'Yes,' she croaked before she turned and fled out of the room.

Priti had ordered the rickshaw for the last possible moment on Thursday. Apart from a large handbag, in which she had hidden the children's most favourite teddy bears, Karin could not take anything with her. She didn't care; nothing meant anything any more. She fled for her and her children's lives. If they were discovered, she would loose them and even the relatives who had been sympathetic so far, would shun her.

Disgracing the family by running away was unforgivable and would make her an outcast; her life would not be worth living. Without looking back, she left Amir and Lakshmi's house, pretending to the children that they were going to the zoo. She stared blankly at the places that had become familiar to her, the markets, the mosques, the shopping streets, the parks, the crowds and noise of millions of people, the heat and the blue sky. She could only think of the aircraft waiting for them as if pulled by a bungee rope towards the airport.

At the airport, the Embassy official channelled them through controls, showing the copied paperwork. As Karin had no luggage, she could board straight away. The children were utterly confused and she tried to divert their attention with the promise that they would visit the zoo near grandma's and grandpa's. They had no idea who these people were, but were quite willing to accept the fact that they had to fly to them first.

'Daddy will come later,' she said, hating herself for lying to them, but she needn't have worried because they hadn't seen much of him anyway and this was not something that seemed to worry them.

The pilot greeted her personally as the little group boarded and moments later, the doors were shut. Waiting on the runway seemed to take forever, and Karin had visions that Raj would use his influence to stop the plane before take-off.

It didn't happen.

As they hurtled along the runway and rose into the air, Karin looked down on the sea of houses and shacks, huddling together, only the mosque's roofs glinting in the sun. Minutes later the sprawl of Dhaka was replaced by green paddy fields divided up by rivers like bloodvessels or the threads of a spider's web. She sighed with relief and sadness.

She rummaged around her handbag for the teddy bears at the bottom and found a note, folded several times into a tiny square. She unfolded it carefully not to tear it. It read:

My dearest Auntie,

What a pity that you won't be at my wedding, but knowing that you are safe and happy will be my consolation. Don't forget us!

All my love

Priti

P.S. I pushed the green sari to the bottom of your bag.

Karin smiled through her tears and drew the children close to her.

Chapter Thirty-Two

ℭℬℭ

My bonds are cut
My debts are paid...
Rabrindranath Tagore

Karin looks around the light, airy room, cotton curtains fluttering by the window frame like lace butterflies. It is now free of any trace of her, except for her battered suitcase and bulky handbag filled with small souvenirs and personal gifts. They both stand side by side on the floor by the door, ready to be carried away.

Karin hands in the key at reception, leaves an envelope from the hotel's own stationery with tips for the staff. She hands it to the hotel manager, thanks everyone for their excellent care and walks out behind the porter, who has taken charge of her modest luggage, into the blazing sunshine.

Farook is already waiting with his trusty Ambassador and smiles broadly. He stows the cases into the boot and holds the door open for her to climb in for the last time. Then they sit and wait until Ali races out of the hotel, breathless, to join his mother.

'Sorry about that,' he laughs. 'I was on the phone to Martha.'

'He sounds so happy,' thinks Karin with relief. 'An easy-going relationship is what he was looking for after all.'

291

Ali throws himself on the back seat beside his mother. 'We finalised our plans. It's all settled!' he continues excitedly. '…and I am sure you will approve, because…' he paused to savour the suspense, '…I proposed to her!'

'We can't really work in the Children's Village being boyfriend and girlfriend,' he adds with a delighted grin.

'Congratulations,' Karin hugs her son in the cramped confines of the car, takes his face between both her hands and kisses him on the nose.

'That's my boy,' she says like a mum to a school boy. He is please with her reaction.

'…and,' he continues – he has another surprise in store: 'we shall get married in London and spend our honeymoon travelling around the country. Martha has never been to England and there is so much I want to show her.'

'How wonderful,' Karin exclaims. 'I shall finally meet your Martha.'

'…and then of course, we shall fly to Bangladesh to start work,' he concludes.

Karin smiles proudly at him. 'Did you hear that, Farook? Next time you will see my son, he will be a married man and he and his wife will be working with the orphans we saw yesterday.'

Farook nods respectfully as if he had always known that he was in charge of very important people.

'You let hotel know when you come, Sir,' he says, 'and I drive you again,' he says full of pride, already accepting the sweet burden of responsibility..

*   *   *

The airport is crowded as usual, but Priti has brought a gaggle of women and her own husband in army uniform, who is determined to sort out formalities with minimum delay. Karin accepts the privileged treatment one more time. There wouldn't be any of that ever again, so she might as well enjoy it.

The good-byes are chaotic, but she manages to hug everyone and Priti promises to visit her auntie soon in London. Karin does not doubt that she will.

'You can time it so that it coincides with my wedding… It's only going to be a small affair…'

The rest of his words are drowned out by the eruption of

tumultuous shrieks and cries. Bengali women liked nothing better than a wedding. Everybody has to get married sometime, particularly such a good-looking boy.

'Your wife will be most welcome, when you return with her,' says Lakshmi with the dignity of the most senior person of the family present.

More hugs, then Karin has to go on board.

'I'll call you as soon as the dates are fixed,' Ali shouts after her. She turns round and waves to him, then to everybody else like an ageing film star departing into oblivion. Everybody waves back furiously, their faces getting smaller, only their big eyes like shiny black buttons and wide, laughing mouths remain discernible.

Ali will leave tomorrow for America. Tonight he will be fed and pampered by his aunties as only they can. Karin smiles to herself imagining him trying to fight them off.

As she climbs the gangway she hears a familiar voice:

'Hello again!' It's Serena, the young mother with little Omar, who had sat next to her on the airplane from London.

The boy was supposed to stay behind with uncles and aunts in Sylhet and Karin begins to wonder what has happened; obviously there has been a change of plan.

He is holding firmly on to mummy's hand.

'Hallo, Omar,' she bends down to the little chap. 'Did you have a nice holiday?'

He nods, grabbing his mother's sari with his other little fist, almost disappearing in its folds.

'How did it go?' Karin straightens up and looks at Serena. She can't detect the same anxiety and worry in her face which she had displayed on the way here.

'I couldn't do it,' the young mother says simply. 'I couldn't leave him behind.' Serena sighs, not in despair but with relief and resignation.

'He was so bewildered. All these new people. A totally different life. It wouldn't be fair,' she concludes.

As they settle into their seats for the long flight – they manage to swap with two other passengers to sit together.

Three weeks ago, she had led an unbelievably spinsterish life, drawing happiness from the occasional telephone call from her children and from memories. It was ticking along in isolation, peaceful, yes, but boring and useless.

The visit to Bangladesh has changed her outlook: Strange, that the life she had once fled from, the golden cage, has now freed her soul and opened doors to a new future and purpose. As little Omar snuggles in his seat and falls asleep, the women chat about their visit, their respective families, Ali's impending marriage and move to Bangladesh.

At last, the conversation fizzles out and they snuggle into their seats to get comfortable for sleep.

'I wish I could help that lovely young woman,' Karin thinks. 'Help a little with the emancipation of Bengali women,' a sneaky thought creeps in. Pity they lived too far from London.

Before Karin dozes off she wonders how Jasmine was doing and tries to guess what it was her daughter had wanted to tell her before her hurried departure.

Karin has become estranged from her modest and tidy flat. The imprisoned stale air makes her gasp and throw open the windows. Only a little dust has settled on her desk and chest of drawers. The rooms look tiny, cheerless and drained of colour. Bangladesh was the glamorous parakeet to the drab little dunnock of her flat. It used to be her sanctuary, her refuge from life's ups and downs, securing stability and defence from the world; now it exudes an atmosphere of estrangement and betrayal about her going away.

Karin, aware now that the world is waiting outside for her, decides to ignore it and see it as the launch pad into her new life. The shrill ring from the hall telephone interrupts the stifling stillness.

'I must change the ring tone,' she promises herself; this one makes her jump every time it sounds as if any call was unwelcome.

'Hallo?' she says briskly into the mouth piece.

'Oh you are back – good!' It is Jasmine. Even she sounds less harassed and more cheerful. 'I got an e-mail from Ali. Isn't it great, he is getting married in London!'

'It might have to be Manchester…' Karin blurts out taking great delight in the mystery she has thrown into the conversation.

'Go on!' urges Jasmine prepared for another shock from her newly adventurous, unpredictable mother.

'What would you think, if I moved to Manchester?' Karin is taken aback by the unheard sound of: 'Yipee!!!' from her daughter.

They both burst into giggles and Karin feels tons of emotional ice blocks between them melt away.

'I was going to come down and tell you in person.' Karin can feel through the telephone wire that Jasmine is eager to be rid of her news, '…but I might as well tell you now: I am pregnant.'

Karin is stunned. Her daughter in the arms of a man, feeling tenderness and making love?

'Who is the lucky father?' she enquires tentatively.

'He is not important. We have broken up; actually, he doesn't even know and I want to keep it that way.'

In moments like these, Karin feels that there was something to be said for arranged marriages leading to an orderly family life with two parents for the children. This new world with its new morals is alien to her, and she can't help fearing that the modern young women make a rod for their own back. However, it is not for her to judge nor disapprove.

'Why don't you want to marry him?' she asks instead.

'Mum, he is Indian!'

Whatever she means with this and all the unspoken words she could have said make them laugh.

'There are nice Indian men, I am sure!' Karin prompts but gets no answer.

No, submission was not Jasmine's thing, Karin could see that.

'Congratulations, darling.' Karin puts as much warmth and sincerity into her words as she can muster.

'So you see, you moving to Manchester will be perfect. I can't afford to give up work, so I am counting on you!'

'It's a bit of an assumption,' flits through Karin's mind, but only for a second. The thought is quickly replaced by the pleasure of being needed, being dragged out of this drab little place, her dreary, uneventful life, the time warp which she had created and in which she had hidden herself away.

Jasmine burst into her thoughts: 'You know, when I rang you before your trip, I was actually debating whether to have an abortion or not.'

'Oh no!' Karin gasps. 'I am so sorry! I didn't even give you the chance to discuss it.'

'You couldn't have made the decision for me. In a way it was better that you were not involved,' Jasmine dismisses her mother's anguish. She pauses and then simply adds: 'I am so pleased I kept my baby. Just imagine: a little boy or girl…'

Karin had never known Jasmine to wax lyrical about anything, displaying her soft, feminine side and pure affection. This little creature has obviously brought already more contentment and happiness into her daughter's life than all the big career moves and salaries could have done.

'Come down next weekend,' Karin suggests, 'and we can make plans.'

'I will – and I can help you putting your flat on the market as well.' The practical Jasmine is never far away.

When Karin puts the telephone receiver back, she imagines Raj's reaction to such news – he wouldn't approve of Jasmine being a single mother.

'May his soul rest in ignorance and peace.'

Karin smiles thinking of her new life. She takes the receiver again and dials a Manchester number: 'Serena?' she burst out breathless with excitement. 'Serena, I am moving to Manchester. My daughter is expecting. Do enrol in your course, I am definitely coming!'

※ ※ ※

Karin unpacks her battered little suitcase. Something tinkles: it's Raj's ankle bracelet. At the bottom lies the green sari, dazzling with rainbow colours and gold threads. She will hand it on to Martha, her new daughter-in-law.

THE END